To Joe + Bobbi —
More Willie
Mitchell.
Mike
2-1-11

At Random

By
Michael Henry

At Random

Copyright © 2010 by Michael Henry

Cover Art and Formatting by Laura Shinn

ISBN: 1456308009
EAN-13: 9781456308001

At Random is a work of fiction. City and town locations are used in a fictitious manner for purposes of this work. All characters are works of fiction and any names or characteristics similar to any person past, present or future are coincidental.

Other books available by this author:
Three Bad Years

Dedication:

For Gayle

Acknowledgments

Many thanks to my wife, Gayle, for her encouraging me to write, and for listening. *Gracias* to my son William Henry, for his research and development of the character Adolfo Zegarra Gálvan aka *El Moro*, for his insight into Adolfo's early years, and for his creativity. Thanks as well to sons Joseph and Stephen for their help and support.

Thanks to publishing pros Robert Vaughan for his time and encouragement and Greg Tobin for his superb editing and moral support. Many thanks to agent Bob Diforio for his wisdom and efforts for me.

Thanks to Jim Wilson, longtime friend and counselor; to Pete Adams and David Fite for their unflagging encouragement; to Marlene Mendoza Henry *para ayuda con Español;* to Ken Stubbs and Fred Emrick for medical matters; to Ronnie Harper for legal aid; to a multitude of patient readers for their time, comments, and for suspending disbelief: Bob Dowd, Betty Paradise, Ann Paradise, Joe and Bobbie Smith, golfers Bobby Ray Flurry and Tow Meason; John McCullough, Chuck Thomas, Diane Freniere; Bill and Davilyn Furlow; Babs Zimmerman.

Finally, thanks to readers out there for your interest in Willie Mitchell Banks and his life in Sunshine, Mississippi.

Blurb

Narco-terrorist Adolfo Zegarra Gálvan a.k.a., *El Moro*, kills a deputy sheriff in Yaloquena County, Mississippi, and District Attorney Willie Mitchell Banks seeks the death penalty.

The U.S. Justice Department battles Willie Mitchell to take control of the case to get information about *El Cartel de Campeche* from Zegarra, but Willie Mitchell refuses to turn over the defendant to the feds—he wants capital punishment for the murder of his friend.

In the midst of the jurisdictional battle, the powerful drug cartel fights to free Zegarra, but so does another ultraviolent, shadowy group driven by a hatred of America and its culture—a group willing to kill as many Mississippians as necessary to prevent Willie Mitchell's trial of Zegarra—a group dedicated to bringing the criminal justice system to a halt in Mississippi and the entire United States.

There's a serious question whether Willie Mitchell can win the murder case against Zegarra—and whether the D.A. will survive the devastating attack on the legal system.

To view more of Michael Henry's work, visit:
http://michaelhenryauthor.com

Chapter One

El Moro drove his 2003 Maxima slowly along the shell road that ran in a northeasterly direction from Terrebonne Parish into Lafourche Parish. He was looking for the unmarked turnoff onto an abandoned levee north of Larose. He had made this trip many, many times. But this time was more important than any of the others. It would be his most successful. It would be his last.

He squinted, searching for the landmark.

At last he saw it, the rusted corpse of a refrigerator, upside down in the ditch, dumped there years before by one of the countless hurricane tidal surges that periodically inundated the marsh. Even before Katrina, hurricanes interfered with his business.

El Moro turned east just past the refrigerator, driving up the ramp and onto the levee. Branches from marsh willows and Chinese tallows scraped the side of the Maxima. The grass atop the levee was too high, concealing the travel lane. He strained in the dim light to see where he was going.

In another ten minutes it would be too dark to travel safely on the levee. But, no matter how dangerous driving on the levee in the dark, he was not about to turn on his headlights.

He saw a flash, on and quickly off, a half-mile ahead. El Moro drove toward it. On his left in the disappearing light he saw eerie skeletons of live oaks with dead white branches reaching toward the sky like bony fingers. The oaks had been poisoned by salt water intrusion from hurricanes and canals dredged by oil companies to accommodate access to the oil and gas production units that littered the marsh.

The landing area ahead had been in use for the last year. The previous drop zone was further south. It had gradually disappeared under water as the Gulf of Mexico crept farther north, devouring the alluvial fan created by the Mississippi River eons before.

El Moro maneuvered down the shell-covered ramp near the end of the levee and stopped in the darkness near a pickup truck. He turned his parking lights on and off. The truck parking lights flashed twice. El Moro exited his car at the same time as the driver of the pickup. They shook hands.

"El Moro," the truck driver said.

"*Buenas tardes, Esteban.*"

Both men were born in *El Estado de Tamaulipas* on the east coast of Mexico, and both were in the employ of *El Cártel de Campeche.* They looked nothing alike.

The thirty-eight-year-old El Moro had hazel eyes and Caucasian features, light brown hair and fair skin. Esteban was dark and ten years older, with black hair and a Mayan forehead sloping on the same plane as his large nose. Esteban was six inches shorter than El Moro, who stood at five-ten.

"On time?" El Moro asked.

"*Sí . Diez minutos.*"

Esteban lit a cigarette and looked at his watch. He rapped his knuckles on the hood of the truck. Two small men jumped out of the truck bed and scampered off into the darkness.

In the distance, El Moro heard the drone of a plane engine. Esteban cocked his head and listened for a moment, then hit the talk button three times on the walkie-talkie in his right hand. He held it to his lips.

"*Ya.*"

Portable lights marking the outline of a grassy landing strip flashed on. A minute later, the landing lights on a twin-engine plane came on and a Beechcraft touched down.

"*Está bueno,*" Esteban said into his radio, and his men turned off the runway lights. The plane taxied slowly towards them, bouncing on the uneven surface. Esteban gestured to the pilot, who immediately darkened his lights and cut the engines.

As he had done so many times before, El Moro drove the Maxima close to the plane and popped the trunk. One of Esteban's little men opened the rear cargo door and tossed bread loaf-sized, shrink-wrapped packages to his co-worker, who packed them neatly into El Moro's trunk.

Within minutes the transfer was complete.

El Moro waved. "I'll be back after midnight."

Getting from the landing area to U.S. 90 was the most difficult part of the drive to New Orleans. Once he turned onto Highway 90, it was a short drive to the antiquated, rust-rimmed Huey P. Long Bridge to cross the Mississippi, then another forty minutes to the deserted warehouse jutting into the river on the Tchoupitoulas Street wharf.

Exchanging the cocaine packets for the five million in one-hundred-dollar bills took fifteen minutes. El Moro pulled out of the warehouse after midnight, but instead of turning left to head west on Tchoupitoulas Street, he turned right toward downtown.

Passing under the towering arches of the Crescent City Connection, the twin bridges crossing the Mississippi from downtown to Algiers on the west bank, he turned west onto the ramp for Interstate 10 and followed the signs to Baton Rouge.

6

He crossed the western edge of Lake Ponchartrain and left I-10 for I-55 at LaPlace, then headed due north, past Lake Maurepas and Ponchatoula, finally exiting Tangipahoa Parish at the Mississippi line.

Pushing steadily north a few miles over the speed limit, El Moro thought about Esteban, who would be looking at his watch about now, wondering where El Moro was with the money. The Beechcraft pilot would have already warmed up his engines, ready to take off on his return trip over the Gulf of Mexico.

"*Lo siento, muchachos,*" El Moro said out loud. He mentally calculated the rest of the trip, figuring he would be in Jackson by four-fifteen or so, then Memphis around seven-thirty to deliver the money on schedule.

If he didn't run into any problems along the way.

Chapter Two

God I hate that bitch, Carl Lippmann thought to himself as he glanced over at the goofy white rookie cop driving him around Jackson at four in the morning. It was his second wife, D'Rosia, he was hating. He called her "Dee." He did not hate his driver, JPD patrol officer Hubert Holland. Like Carl's late dog Paco, Hubert was way too dumb to hate.

Should have never run around on Alice, Carl muttered as he considered the circumstances under which his first wife got the restraining order putting him out of the house and ultimately taking everything he had, including a substantial part of his Mississippi Public Employee Retirement System benefit. He had to hand it to old Alice, she had done her homework. Got a decent private eye who documented with photographs and surveillance records all three of Carl's simultaneous dalliances.

"Did you say something?" Hubert Holland asked.

"Nothing. Don't ever get divorced."

"I ain't married."

"Could you and I agree that someday you might get married?"

"I hope to."

"Okay. If you do, then remember that I highly recommend that you stay with your wife. Don't cheat on her. It's not worth it."

"If I ain't married, I cain't hardly step out on a wife I ain't got."

Hubert, at twenty-seven, was fresh out of the academy. Raised up around Pontotoc. Skinny and at least six-five, Carl figured, but never asked because he was sure Hubert would not know. Hubert didn't know much. Sucker had the biggest Adam's apple Carl had ever seen, and it jumped up and down when Hubert did that obnoxious thing he called "scratching his throat" making some kind of strange sound with his mouth closed.

Carl was eleven months from finishing his thirty years with JPD. His second "ex," Dee, had filed so many complaints with the department, Carl had to call in favors and throw himself on the mercy of his supervisors. Dee ratted him out on some things that could have cost him his pension, so Carl jumped at the deal the brass offered: accept a demotion and pay cut and end his career in a squad car.

His retirement would be figured on his best three years, so his sergeant's pay would be the multiplier. Alice took everything, but she was smart—or ruthless—enough to protect

8

the pension. After all, Carl thought, it was in her best interest because she got part of it. He never could get the concept through Dee's thick skull...

He had to admit, though, Dee was hot. She was really something.

"You want to stop at the doughnut shop?" Hubert asked. "They'll be real fresh right now."

"Damn, boy, you just had a double-meat hamburger three hours ago. And onion rings."

"You don't have to get nothing."

"Whatever. Do what you want."

"You could get some coffee. They got good coffee. Real hot."

"Okay."

Hubert pulled into the doughnut shop. Theirs was the only vehicle in the parking spaces in front, and the two cops were the only customers. Hubert ordered a half-dozen glazed and a medium coffee. Carl got a small.

Hubert stuffed the first doughnut into his mouth while standing outside the black and white.

"Why don't you put the whole damn thing in your mouth at once?"

"Humpf?" Hubert said, unable to chew and listen at the same time.

"Never mind. Let's go."

Hubert sat behind the wheel and stuffed another entire doughnut into his big mouth. He placed the box with the remaining four on his lap. Carl blew on his coffee and wrapped a second napkin around the bottom of the paper cup.

"Too hot to drink," the veteran cop said. He blew on it again.

Hubert made a loud sucking sound taking in his coffee. His gargantuan Adam's apple ratcheted up a couple of inches then back down to accommodate the sip. Carl stared at him.

"Man, you got a lot of shit happening when you drink coffee and inhale doughnuts."

"What do you mean?"

"I mean—" Carl started, then thought better of it. If he explained, it would just lead to another inane conversation with Hubert. Better keep it simple.

"Let's get up on the interstate."

"Ten-four."

Carl rolled his eyes in the darkness. Eleven months with this Cro-Magnon. At least when Carl talked to his late dog Paco, the Chihuahua had enough sense to keep quiet and not make stupid responses. He got Paco after Taco Bell ran those commercials with the Chihuahua that Carl thought was the coolest dog he had ever seen. *"Yo quiero Taco Bell."*

Too bad Paco turned out to be dumb as dirt. Just like Hubert. Except cute.

Eleven months couldn't end too soon. He was moving from Jackson to his mama's old home place in the Delta just north of Yazoo City. She and her two sisters had inherited their part of the forty acres from Carl's grandmother, who owned the forty with her seven brothers and sisters, all of whom had passed on. The way Carl figured it, he owned about a half-acre interest in the forty, just like all his cousins, some of whom had also died. He couldn't be sure of his percentage because there had been no estate opened for his grandmother, his seven great uncles and aunts, his mother and her sisters, and his dead first and second cousins. "Heir property" was what everyone called it, and since no one was living in the shotgun house on the place, he was moving in.

A guy on the force going to law school at night told Carl he had just as much right to use it as any of his cousins. Carl decided he would do just that. The half of his monthly pension he had left after Alice and the bitch Dee got theirs was enough to live on in the Delta.

Hubert wolfed down a third doughnut and raised the steaming coffee cup to his mouth as he reached the top of the on ramp. The cup slipped, and Hubert tried to catch it as the patrol car entered the northbound traffic lanes of Interstate 55.

Hubert was not only dumb—he was spectacularly uncoordinated. His attempt to catch the cup wasn't even close and one hundred eighty degree Fahrenheit coffee spilled all over Hubert. Looking down in shock at the mess he had made of his new uniform, Hubert sped across the three northbound lanes at a forty-five degree angle.

"Shit!" Carl yelled as Hubert T-boned a 2003 Nissan Maxima in the left northbound lane driven by thirty-eight year old Adolfo Zegarra Galván, known to his associates as "El Moro."

On impact, the El Moro's trunk popped open. The one hundred, ten pounds of hundred-dollar bills stacked in cardboard boxes in the Maxima's trunk exploded into a violent snow storm of United States currency. Bills floated and fluttered around the two vehicles. Steam and smoke rose from the police cruiser, and its windshield, shattered, but in once piece, rested on the crunched hood.

The front of the cruiser was wedged into the passenger side of the Maxima; the driver's side was crushed against the concrete rail along the interstate.

10

A refreshing pre-dawn breeze scattered the money over the cars and across the concrete. The bills were an odd gray under the orange interstate lights.

"Owww," Hubert moaned, rubbing his forehead. He pawed at the C-notes stuck to the blood on his face.

Carl opened his eyes. There were hundred-dollar bills all over him. He grabbed up two hands full of cash. "The bitch Dee ain't getting any of this." Carl blinked and tried to clear his head.

"Huh?" Hubert's Adam's apple bobbed up and down. "That coffee *was* too hot."

Carl tossed the bills he held onto the floor, reached over and pulled a one-hundred dollar bill off Hubert's bloody ear. Disappointed, he realized he wasn't in heaven after all, because he knew his heaven most certainly did not include Hubert.

Chapter Three

El Moro came to a couple of minutes after Hubert smashed the Maxima against the concrete rail. He raised his head slowly and opened his eyes. His left temple hurt. He touched it and the pain blinded him. He vomited.

He wiped his mouth and nose with his sleeve, doing his best to keep still. He reached down and released the seat belt. He touched his left temple, gentler this time. A sizable, bloody knot grew there, and he turned his head slightly to look at the door post where he must have hit his skull when the patrol car struck him. His driver's-side window was gone.

He never saw what hit him until he turned his head gingerly to the right and saw two cops, the driver a skinny gringo with a bloody face papered with hundred-dollar bills, and a short, dark-skinned old cop in the passenger seat holding a wad of cash in both hands. They were no more than six feet from him. Since they had no windshield, he saw them clearly. They moved as slowly as El Moro.

He realized none of his doors would open and his only way out was through the hole where his window used to be. He moved to extend his legs toward the cops and rest his back against the driver's side door. The pain in his head almost caused him to pass out. He took a deep breath and stuck his arms through the window and pulled himself up to sit on the door frame. Behind him he saw a thirty-foot drop to the frontage road below. On Interstate 55, he watched his five million dollars swirl and tumble across the concrete.

"*Chingada,*" he cursed.

The cops stirred and El Moro decided he had to forget about the money and get away. The money was expendable, but he was not. However, his Maxima wasn't going anywhere. He needed alternative transportation.

He saw several northbound vehicles stopped on the interstate just south of the dancing hundred-dollar bills. Grimacing in anticipation of the pain in his temple, El Moro ducked back into the Maxima and grabbed his H&K USP .45 caliber, then carefully climbed through the window and across the concrete rail to the road surface.

The tall cop spotted him and said something to the short black cop. El Moro held his forty-five behind him and half-jogged toward the dozen cars stopped on the interstate behind the wreck. He watched a young white guy exit a red Chevrolet Malibu and leave the door open.

The kid whooped as he picked up hundred-dollar bills and stuffed them into his pockets—and didn't notice El Moro ease into the Chevy. El Moro turned the Malibu around and headed southbound in the northbound lanes.

It was no trouble to dodge the few oncoming cars on I-55 in the pre-dawn darkness. He drove the wrong way down the first ramp he saw to get off the interstate. On the surface streets, El Moro drove northwest, searching for highway signs. He had studied Mississippi state and county roads in case he ever encountered a problem. He definitely had a problem now.

His left eye closed involuntarily in response to a stabbing pain in his temple. He pulled over, opened his door and threw up, then leaned back against the Chevy's headrest until the nausea passed. When he opened his eyes, he saw a street sign that said Woodrow Wilson and followed it until he ran up on a black and white sign for U.S. 49.

After heading north on U.S. 49 for forty-five minutes, El Moro noticed the eastern sky getting lighter. He drove west on Mississippi 410 before he reached Yazoo City then north on Mississippi 19, leaving the hills of central Mississippi for the Delta. El Moro had been through the area before, driving north from Baton Rouge on U.S. 61 to aid recruitment in Memphis. In the early morning light, he watched egrets fly from their cypress aeries in the stump-studded swamps on either side of the road. Without a hill or elevation in sight, he passed mile after mile of row crops and fallow, flat fields.

The Delta was too open for comfort. Even on the county roads there were few trees and El Moro could see another vehicle coming for miles. He knew they could see him as well—he was vulnerable. He passed a green road sign that read, YALOQUENA COUNTY.

As he mouthed Yaloquena in an attempt to pronounce the strange word, he touched his left temple. The knot was even bigger, now covered with dried, crusty blood that flaked off onto his shoulder when he softly massaged the knot.

"*Unh*," he groaned when his finger probed too hard. He felt the nausea returning. Slowing down on the side of the road, he lowered his window to heave once more, but a stomach spasm caused his head to lurch to the side. El Moro's knot scored a direct hit on the sturdy Chevrolet door post. It seemed he saw a bolt of lightning in the car, then all went black.

Chapter Four

Willie Mitchell Banks ran across the highway sweating bullets and singing along with Don Henley, summoning as many words to "Boys of Summer" as he could remember. He loved the black and white video—an eight or nine-year old boy with a fifties-style hairdo playing a set of drums like Phil Collins. He wished he had some musical talent, that he could play some musical instrument—any instrument. But he didn't, he couldn't, and that was that.

He could still jog decently, though, at fifty-four, and could play his iPod. "I got that going for me," he said out loud, sounding as stupid as he could. He entered the final half-mile of his four-mile run.

Sheriff Lee Jones had cautioned Willie Mitchell about running by himself on the same routes. Lee said predictability put the D.A. in jeopardy from bad guys who might want to harm him. Willie Mitchell never gave it a second thought. He had run the streets in Sunshine and the roads in Yaloquena County all his adult life and was not going to stop now.

Bad guys who may want to harm me.

He started thinking about his only recent controversial case. Nobody was around from that fiasco who might want to harm him. The case involved the prosecution of McKinley Owens, the yardman of Mary Margaret Anderson, with whom Willie Mitchell had carried on an affair in the third year of his wife Susan's sabbatical from their marriage. The sordid romance was a singular and uncharacteristic episode in Willie Mitchell's life.

McKinley had come out smelling like a rose, Willie Mitchell thought as he ran, considering McKinley had committed murder. He was currently in Parchman Farm, serving a fifteen year sentence on one count of manslaughter. Willie Mitchell was okay with the amount of time Judge Zelda Williams gave McKinley.

The asshole Little Al needed killing.

Willie Mitchell grew angry thinking about what Mary Margaret did. But he could not stay mad very long.

"She made her bed," the old folks said.

His anger dissipated when he thought about Mary Margaret in his bed, in his home, in his life—an alien, secret presence filling the void left by Susan's unexpected departure. He remembered the day he first ran into Mary Margaret in the Jitney Mart and she had started up the conversation. It was so nice to talk to a pretty woman again. She seemed so unhappy, so undeserving of the life of oppression she endured under Little Al's thumb.

She wasn't the only one unhappy.

Willie Mitchell was depressed and lonely that same day in the store, standing there in the cereal aisle with a box of Grape Nuts in one hand and Total Raisin Bran in the other, comparing the calories and vitamin content. Mary Margaret seemed a refined Southern lady, conservative in her white blouse and khaki skirt, making small talk and asking about Jake and Scott. What a ravenous femme fatale with an insatiable appetite for all manner of sexual gratification she turned out to be. A guilty excitement coursed through his body at the thought of her naked body, her pheremone-rich aura that made him weak at their first physical encounter.

Enough of that, dammit. What you did was monumentally stupid and almost ruined your life.

He began to run faster, shaking his head to cast off the memory. He loved Susan and would remain faithful to her no matter what. Except for Mary Margaret, Willie Mitchell had never broken his marital vows. He swore he never would again.

It was just as hot this morning as it was a month ago. August and September in the Mississippi Delta were interchangeable—hot and humid mornings and evenings, blistering sun in the middle of the day. Willie Mitchell ran through Sunshine and passed his house, which was looking much better since Susan had finally come home. She paid attention to details around the house and in the yard that Willie Mitchell barely noticed. But her positive impact on their home and surroundings was at the end of a very long list of reasons why he was so glad his wife had come back to him.

He turned off the street into Jimmy Gray's driveway and tapped lightly on the banker's carport door. He stretched on the concrete while he waited. The three-hundred-five-pound Jimmy Gray, Willie Mitchell's best friend for life, walked out the door and joined the district attorney.

"Where'd you get those?" Willie Mitchell stared at Jimmy's bright red silky athletic shorts that hung below his knees. "You look like an NBA power forward."

"Starting at forward, at five-eleven, three-oh-five. Let's give it up for Jumpin' Jimmy Gray." He simulated a turnaround jump shot. "Martha got 'em in Jackson. And she customized this T-shirt. *Tres* cool, huh?"

He turned his back to Willie Mitchell and pointed with both index fingers over his shoulders. WIDE LOAD was printed across the gray shirt covering his broad back in bright red letters. "You think I should put a safety flag back there?"

"Nah. I think they'll see you okay."

They walked down the driveway and into the street.

"How was your run?"

"Okay. It feels really good when I quit."

"I haven't lost any weight yet."

"This is only our second day to walk."

"But I really worked up a sweat yesterday."

"You only walked two blocks."

"I'm just saying. This exercising is hard."

"Let's do ten minutes today," Willie Mitchell said, setting his timer.

Within three minutes, Jimmy was breathing hard. They turned right at the first intersection. A white pickup truck passed. The driver, an older man with white hair, waved.

"You heard Sheila left him," Jimmy panted.

"Ethel told me at the office."

"Seems like if they were going to split they'd have done it long time ago, not wait until now."

"Ethel said Sheila told her that she'd been miserable the last thirty of the thirty-five years they'd been married, and she was going to try to be happy for whatever time she had left."

"Don't that beat all." Jimmy exhaled with considerable force. "How much longer?"

"Six minutes."

""We're walking a lot faster than yesterday."

"Nope. Same pace."

"Maybe I ought to walk every other day."

"When you get in better shape."

"How long will that take?"

"I figure twelve to fifteen."

"Months?"

"Years."

Jimmy grimaced. "You smell that?"

"What?"

"My thighs starting to smolder."

"Did you use the Vaseline like I told you?"

"Yeah," Jimmy said. "But I didn't cover enough territory down there. There's a lot of skin in play and the coefficient of friction is off the charts. You've heard of spontaneous human combustion?"

Willie Mitchell laughed and sniffed. "Smells like bacon."

"Canadian bacon, which is really ham, if you ask me. And how come they call it Canadian? I've had it in England. How much longer?"

Willie Mitchell checked his running watch. "Not much longer. Just do the best you can."

"That's all a mule can do," Jimmy said.

They laughed together, because, "That's all a mule can do," was a phrase Willie Mitchell's father, Monroe Banks, uttered every time his wife encouraged young Willie Mitchell to do the best he could.

Willie Mitchell thought of the hundreds of times he and his late parents were at the breakfast table in the kitchen. He would tell his mother, Katherine, about an essay or an algebra problem at school, or about problems on the basketball or baseball team. She was always sweet and encouraging, telling him to just do the best he could.

"That's all a mule can do," Monroe Banks added every time.

Usually the words emanated from somewhere behind an open newspaper, giving the homespun adage an ethereal, disembodied tone, which Willie Mitchell considered an apt metaphor for the relationship he had with his father. His mother Katherine was fully engaged, his father Monroe, a banker, though a constant presence in his life, was distant, quiet. Willie Mitchell knew his father was a good businessman, a successful banker who made a lot of money by small town standards with Jimmy Gray's father in the bank they started. But he always considered Monroe Banks to be a passive sort, and was shocked when he found out the previous year Monroe Banks had been on the White Citizens Council for Yaloquena County.

How could he have kept that from me? Why didn't I know?

"Yo," Jimmy Gray said, huffing and sweating. "Come back to earth, asshole. I'm dying here."

"We're almost through."

"Come on, you son of a bitch. I'm working my ass off here and you're off in Willie Land thinking about God knows what you think about when you zone out like that. How much longer?"

"Time," Willie Mitchell said.

Jimmy stopped dead in his tracks. Unable to find a place to sit, Jimmy walked toward an ancient live oak in the yard of a low slung, ranch-style brick-veneer house. He turned and backed up until his rump hit the tree, then spread his huge legs to give himself a wide base of support. He leaned forward and inspected the red abrasions between his legs.

17

"Is it just me or does it look like my thighs are glowing?"

"Relax. They start smoking I'll get the hose and wet 'em down."

"It's not my fault that I have my mother's thighs."

"From the size of those things, it looks like you got hers and yours."

"Funny. Real funny you skinny little shit head."

Willie Mitchell said, "You know who lives in this house?"

"Nope. Not now, since the Carsons moved out."

Sweat flowed from every pore. Jimmy's loud breathing became less urgent. Willie Mitchell stood next to him and saw a curtain open in the house. He waved at the thirty-something woman, pointed at Jimmy, and simulated panting. The woman waved and laughed, then closed the curtain.

"This is Brandy McCain's house," Willie Mitchell said.

"The woman with the short blond hair that works the counter in the post office?"

"Yep. She was one of those Andrews girls from Greenville."

"Oh, yeah. They were all good-looking. Brandy looks pretty good even in those crappy government uniforms. She's married to Skeeter McCain's boy?"

"She was. I don't know if she still is." Willie Mitchell tapped the rough bark of the live oak. "You make a habit of trespassing like this, pressing your fat ass against trees you don't own?"

"I got to rest somewhere I can get up. I sit on that concrete curb over there and you'd have to call Bad Man José to pick me up with his wrecker. Or get a fork lift from the Jitney Mart."

Willie Mitchell took Jimmy's extended hand and pulled the big banker away from the tree.

"This is a bait and switch," Jimmy said, feigning anger. "We finished the ten minutes and I've still got a ways to go to get home."

"I'll go get my truck if you don't think you can make it. I don't want you to do anything you don't want to."

Willie Mitchell paused and stared. He became serious. "Look at me."

Jimmy Gray did.

"It's entirely up to you."

"Gene Hackman as film producer Harry Zimm in *Get Shorty*."

"Who'd he say it to?"

"The actor who used to be a cop. Give me a minute."

"Dennis Farina."

"Aw, Goddammit. I would have gotten that."

"What's the name of the character he played?"

"Bones. From Miami. He took over Momo's operation after Momo had the heart attack."

"Ray Barboni."

"Yeah, but they called him Bones."

"You owe me fifty cents."

"Bull shit. I should get credit for Bones."

"One for three. Quarter per miss."

Jimmy Gray began to traipse toward home. "Let's go, asshole. Slower this time."

Chapter Five

El Moro had been eight when his mother died. Like any other day, Adolfo Zegarra Galván, as he was known then, came home from the refinery after he searched for hours to pick up pieces of metal they might sell for a peso to the scrap metal man who pushed his cart by their shanty once a week. They lived in Madero, an impoverished port town south of Tampico.

"Mama, I found some copper today," he said with pride. She wasn't in the front room, so he rushed into the back room where they slept and saw her face down on the floor, a rickety table turned over on her back. There wasn't much blood under her head, but her dress was torn.

"Mama?" he said. He moved the table and kneeled down next to her body. He pushed on her but she didn't move. *"Mama?"* He tried to turn her over but couldn't. Adolfo rested his head on her back. She was cold, not like normal. He tried to be completely still so he could hear her breathe and feel her moving. Nothing.

He walked around the bed and picked up the cover from the floor and put it over his mother. Adolfo sat down cross-legged on the floor next to her and cried for a long time.

For two weeks he kept her covered. Adolfo went to the refinery every day as usual and found enough scrap to make a few pesos to buy tortillas to go with the beans his mother had put away in the corner of the front room where she cooked. He knew where she had hidden a few pesos in a hole in the dirt in the front room. When he ran out of the beans he used her savings to buy more.

On a day when he found no metal in the refinery after two hours of searching, he walked to the port. He loved the big ships. He and his mother had taken many walks by the port to watch the big tankers come and go. He thought about those walks as he watched the ships alone this day.

He remembered the tall white man who used to visit their shanty now and then a long time ago. The man had blond hair, fair skin, and blue eyes. His mother called him "Vikingo" and talked about him like a God. The man brought money and food when he came, and his mother always asked Adolfo to go hunt for metal. He was happy to leave them alone because Vikingo made his mother so happy. Adolfo never spoke to Vikingo, but Vikingo would nod and smile at Adolfo before the boy left on his metal search.

He often stayed gone for hours, and when he returned, it did not matter to his mother whether he had found any iron or copper. His mother was always singing and laughing to herself for days after the visits.

He remembered the last visit of Vikingo. Instead of singing when he returned to their shanty, his mother had been crying. When Adolfo moved her hand from her eye, he saw that it was swollen and starting to bruise.

"Why did Vikingo hit you?" he asked.

"It was my fault, little one," his mother said. "And he will not be coming back to Madero ever again. He must stay in America from now on."

Adolfo could not understand how any man could strike someone so innocent and sweet as his mother. When Vikingo left for good, Adolfo did not miss him, but his mother did. She was sadder than ever from that day forward. It seemed to Adolfo that Vikingo had knocked the happiness from his mother the day he left.

When he returned to the shanty from his lonely visit to the port, the only home he ever knew was on fire. He ran to the house but it was too hot and smoky to go in. Adolfo screamed at the neighbors who gathered to watch it burn. He knew one of them had set it on fire because he heard them talking one day about the bad odors coming from the shanty. They never liked Adolfo or his mother. The neighborhood children made fun of his light eyes and skin. So did the grownups. His mother would sit on their dirt floor with him on her lap and rock him back and forth, singing old songs and smoothing his hair until Adolfo stopped crying. She told him he would grow up strong and tall and handsome like Vikingo, and would tower over the little brown men and women that mocked him. He could hardly wait for that day to come.

A month after his mother died, he sat on the end of an old wooden pier near the mouth of the Pánuco River. He was hungry and tired. It was getting harder to find metal scraps at the refinery, and the bigger boys would knock him down and steal the pieces he did find. Since the fire, Adolfo had been living in an old, rusty tank at the edge of the refinery yard. He thought the air he breathed at night was not clean, but he had nowhere else to go. The people in the neighborhood threw things at him and chased him away when he came back to the charred remains of the shanty.

From the pier he often watched the men get off the big tankers. He examined each sailor, constantly looking for Vikingo, hoping that maybe he could go to America with him. He had done this many, many times since his mother died. He swung his feet over the water. The wind picked up and the waves splashed against the crooked wooden pier.

The sky had grown darker, and he smelled the rain coming from the gulf. In the distance he watched a slow moving tanker enter the mouth of the Pánuco. Behind the tanker a jagged streak of lightning brightened the sky for a moment.

Then came the thunder that he could feel in his empty belly. When the thunder quieted, a deep, loud bellow came from the tanker. He felt it in his stomach, too.

Adolfo liked it when a storm blew ashore. He would have liked it better if his stomach were not so empty.

"Oye. Oye. Gringo."

Adolfo turned quickly when he heard it and caught a glimpse of the big boys from the neighborhood who tormented him all his life, getting worse since his mother died. He turned back to the storm, hoping they would go away.

"Gringo. Gringo."

Adolfo recognized the voice. It belonged to Carlos, the leader of the teenagers and the biggest. The eight-year-old turned to see how many others were with Carlos.

He would never know, because a rock hit him on the left side of his forehead and knocked him off the pier into the churning salty water of the Pánuco. Adolfo's limp body sank to the bottom of the river. He remembered later floating peacefully below the turmoil of the surface and thinking:

This must be how it is when you die, and this peace must be what Mama feels all the time now...

When he opened his eyes he didn't know where he was or what had happened. Then he remembered. He stayed calm, paddling from the bottom to the surface. When he broke through he took a deep breath, grateful to see the pier through the rain and the dirty, salty foam. Carlos and the other teenagers were gone.

He swam to the shore and climbed back up on the pier. Adolfo walked to the end and sat again. He quietly sang a song his mother used to sing to him, rocking him in her arms on the dirt floor. The song made him feel better. He saw a new kind of tanker he had never seen, and watched it pass him on the pier, leaving the port of Madero on its way to the Gulf of Mexico. He saw through the rain and wind an American flag on the back of the tanker, and wondered if he would ever be able to find Vikingo.

Swinging his legs on the edge of the pier, Adolfo rubbed the knot where the rock had hit him and closed his eyes...

~ * ~

When he tried to open his eyes, El Moro was in the Malibu in a ditch in Yaloquena County, gently rubbing the aching knot on the side of his head. It was the door post of the Malibu, not a rock, that knocked him out this time.

The early morning sun was bright and hot. After a glimpse at the blinding light, he closed his eyes, and started to dream again.

"You okay?" he thought he heard someone say, but he wasn't sure.

There was a tapping on his window. Each tap echoed through El Moro's skull.

"Hey, buddy," the voice said louder. "You okay?"

Chapter Six

A different voice, this one amplified electronically, pierced El Moro's skull like a blade, much worse than the earlier tapping on his window. He started to raise his right hand to shield his eyes before he opened them, but stopped when he realized he was holding his forty-five. He opened his eyes enough to sense that the sun was so bright it hurt. After a moment, he opened them wider.

He moved forward slightly from the head restraint and the pain in his temple returned, causing him to wonder if his skull were fractured.

"Step out of the car," the electronic voice said.

El Moro boosted himself higher in his seat and turned gingerly to look outside his window, toward the voice. He saw several police cars with blue and red strobes flashing. Through his windshield, he saw two directly in front of him, blocking the road. In the rear view mirror he saw two more patrol cars. On the other side of the ditch, on his passenger side, El Moro saw a huge pickup truck with oversized tires and a law enforcement logo on the door. Around the truck, several shotgun and rifle barrels were aimed directly at him. Black armor-clad, helmeted police officers stood next to the cruisers in front of him, ready to kill him with assault rifles.

There was nowhere for El Moro to go, nothing he could do. He did not want to die on this lonely road; he had too much left to accomplish.

He gently placed his forty-five on the passenger seat, pulled his door handle, raised both hands and slowly opened his door with his left leg. When the door swung open, El Moro saw a black man in a police uniform on his back on the pavement next to the Malibu. He noticed the top of the black man's head was gone and brain matter and blood covered the road around his dead body.

It was then El Moro vaguely remembered the black man opening his door and asking him if he was okay. El Moro's memory was hazy, but he was pretty sure he had responded instinctively to the polite inquiry by blowing the top of the man's head completely off.

"Get out of the car with your hands up," the electronic voice commanded.

He stood next to the dead officer with hands raised high. A dozen cops stepped slowly toward him with guns pointed, ready to kill. The first officer to touch him grabbed his left arm and jerked it behind his back, simultaneously pushing him to the front of the Malibu face down against the hood. He didn't know how many cops were grabbing him, but he didn't resist.

Each movement the police initiated sent a current of pain through El Moro's head and spine. It would be fine with him if they let him rest his face on the hood for a while. It was cool to the touch, and it soothed the pain.

They jerked him up and turned him around. El Moro tried his best to stand straight, but he tilted forward in spite of all the hands on him. For the first time since he heard the amplified voice, he forced himself to concentrate. The cops surrounding him on every side were awash in the pulsating blue and red lights.

Two men parted the crowd of uniforms and stood before him. El Moro overcame the pain and stood straight. His head pounded as he studied the men. One was a muscular black man wearing a beige Stetson, thick-chested and dark-skinned, seven or eight years older than El Moro. His uniform was different, and he did not have a gun. El Moro knew the man had to be the sheriff, and from the look in the man's eyes, the sheriff wanted to kill him.

The other was a young white man in a business suit, about thirty or so. El Moro guessed he would be considered nice-looking, with dark hair and an athletic build. His right hand rested on his hip near a holstered automatic pistol. El Moro was not sure what the white man's role was, perhaps a detective. He appeared just as angry as the sheriff.

"You have the right to remain silent," the young man said. "Anything you say can be used against you. You have the right to an attorney, and if you cannot afford one, one will be appointed for you. Do you understand these rights?"

El Moro nodded.

The sheriff moved closer. "You have murdered deputy sheriff Travis Ware, one of the finest men in this county, and my friend," the sheriff said, "and I will make sure you regret it. Do you understand *me*?"

El Moro nodded again.

"Speak, you bastard," the sheriff said.

"Yes, sir," El Moro said quietly, a Mona Lisa smile on his lips.

The sheriff drew back and punched El Moro in the face as hard as he could. The young white man grabbed the sheriff's strong right arm as the sheriff prepared to hit El Moro again.

The sheriff's men moved quickly to help the young man subdue their boss. They were silent, and appeared to El Moro to be stunned by the sheriff's assault on him.

"Go see if you can find Willie Mitchell now," the sheriff said to the young man in the suit. "We'll secure the scene until the state crime lab people show. I'm bringing this... piece of crap to the courthouse."

"Okay," the young man said to the sheriff. "If you're—"

"Sorry. It won't happen again. He'll be in a holding cell under heavy guard."

~ * ~

Assistant District Attorney Walton Donaldson was Willie Mitchell's right-hand man. He had grown up an hour from Sunshine. Willie Mitchell recruited him out of Ole Miss Law School and put him in the courtroom right away. In four years as an attorney, Walton had tried more jury trials than any of his peers from Ole Miss law. Willie Mitchell said that he was an excellent trial lawyer, mature in his approach to juries and witnesses.

The one black mark on Walton's record with Willie Mitchell was a by-product of the Mary Margaret Anderson mess that had entangled Willie Mitchell and the entire office when Susan Banks took her three-year "leave of absence" from her husband.

Walton had tried unsuccessfully to stop an angry mob heading toward Little Al Anderson's house. Fortunately, when Walton reached for his pistol in his boot, McKinley Owens kneed him in the nose, knocking Walton out cold.

Willie Mitchell asked him the next day if he'd "planned on shooting every one of the rioters, or just picking off a few?"

Willie Mitchell made him stop carrying his gun for a while. Walton thought long and hard about the incident's potential impact on his wife Gayle and their twin sons. It was a sobering experience. He matured a lot that night in front of the Anderson mansion. From that point on, he channeled his aggression into the courtroom, saving it for lying defendants and obstreperous witnesses.

Walton slid his Ford Sport Trac pickup to a stop in fat banker Jimmy Gray's driveway.

"Where's the fire, hoss?" Jimmy asked.

"Come on, Willie Mitchell," Walton said. "Some guy murdered Travis Ware on Highway 19. I just came from there. Lee's got him in custody."

"The murder happened in Yaloquena?"

"A mile inside the county line."

"Damn," Willie Mitchell said. "What happened?"

"All I know is he blew the top of Travis's head off. He was passed out in his car when we got there to arrest him."

"Aw, man," Jimmy Gray said. "Travis was a good guy."

26

Willie Mitchell moved quickly into the passenger seat. "Let's go."

In less than two minutes Walton pulled into the reserved parking area for deputies on duty not thirty feet from the side door of the courthouse. The two men walked quickly inside and stopped at the dispatcher's window.

"Where are they, Bessie?" Willie Mitchell asked.

Bessie Jackson had been crying. She dabbed her big brown eyes with a Kleenex. The light brown skin around her eyes had reddened from wiping. Willie Mitchell stuck his hand through the opening in the sliding Plexiglass window and patted Bessie on the shoulder.

"Sorry," Willie Mitchell said. He knew Bessie had known Travis Ware all her life. So had he.

"They're a block away," she said as a burst of static and jumbled voices filled her small office adjacent to the vestibule. She turned a knob and responded. "Ten-four," she said.

Still in his jogging attire, Willie Mitchell walked out the side door with Walton to wait on the concrete parking area. Within seconds, the sheriff's car pulled in and parked, followed by a half-dozen other units that scattered and stopped close as they could to the side door. Some parked on the grass near the fountain that the jail trusties worked on at least once a week to keep water trickling out the mouth of a fish the smiling, bronze cherub held high in the fountain's center.

Sheriff Lee Jones opened his car's back door and pulled out a handcuffed and shackled El Moro. Lee grabbed the back of his arm and led him toward the side door past Willie Mitchell. Lee said nothing; just shook his head at the D.A. Other than a quick glance at the older gringo in a wet shirt, jogging shorts and shoes standing next to the young man in the business suit who read him his rights, El Moro kept his eyes on the concrete.

Two deputies jumped in front of Lee and El Moro and held open the door. A dozen officers hustled in behind them.

"What happened to his jaw?" Willie Mitchell asked Walton.

"Lee punched the crap out of him. Standing right next to me. Knocked him out for a minute."

Willie Mitchell pursed his lips, shook his head, and grunted. "Come on," he said. "Let's make sure this bastard's safe."

The grim deputies that crowded the vestibule made way for Willie Mitchell and Walton. No one said anything, but Willie Mitchell could feel the tension. He knew every one of the deputies wanted to kill the man who took easygoing Travis Ware away from them. Willie Mitchell understood the feeling, but he had to check on Lee and make sure nothing else happened to the defendant.

Willie Mitchell and Walton walked between the deputies lining the narrow hallway and stopped at the door of the holding cell where the sheriff stood. Willie Mitchell peered through the thick, reinforced glass window in the door and saw the suspect seated, shackled to the table.

"You okay?" Willie Mitchell asked Lee Jones.

"Yeah. Sorry I lost it back there. Hope it doesn't cause too much of a problem for us."

"Did he say anything?"

"Not a word," Lee said. "I've been with him since the arrest."

"Shouldn't be too big a problem, then. You got to promise me you got that out of your system. Your men, too."

"You got my word, Willie Mitchell. I'll protect this no good murdering asshole from harm long as he's in my custody."

"You must be skipping the gym," Willie Mitchell said. "A punch from the Lee I know should have broken his jaw."

"Ain't got what I used to have."

Walton stared through the window. "Is he white?"

"Looks like it to me," Lee said.

"He have any ID on him?" Willie Mitchell asked.

"We're going through his wallet. He's got a Louisiana driver's license that looks real. It's him in the picture and it has his name as Ronald Duhon, but the name and Social Security number come back fake. We're running a trace on his gun. Vehicle comes back registered to a James Nixon in Ridgeland. We're trying to contact him now."

"Hey, Sheriff," a deputy called out. "Bessie's got something on the Malibu."

Lee, Willie Mitchell, and Walton walked through the crowded hallway and stopped at Bessie's window.

"The car was jacked on I-55 in Jackson about four-thirty this morning," Bessie said, reading from her computer. "Big wreck involving JPD patrol unit and a car with a trunk full of money."

"Get the chief in Jackson on the phone for me," Lee said.

Lee walked back to the holding cell, the prosecutors behind him. He opened the door. "We found out where you got the car," he said.

"I want a lawyer," El Moro said loud enough for the prosecutors and the deputies in the hall to hear.

"That's that," Willie Mitchell said. "We cannot question him until he has an attorney present."

28

"It doesn't matter," Walton said. "We've got him dead to rights. We don't need a confession."

Lee gestured to an intense, young black deputy with a military bearing, flat stomach, and shaved head. "Sammy, take him upstairs and put him in the cell we just put the new locks on. Clear the cells around him. I want you in one and Big Boy in the other. Don't say a word to him. Just watch him. Check in with me every thirty minutes."

"Yes, sir," the deputy said.

Sheriff Jones called out to the others. "I want one of you every twenty feet between here and the elevator. Sammy's going to walk him from here to the elevator with Big Boy and Frankie and we're putting him upstairs in a cell for now. Sammy and Big Boy are staying up there with him until we work out shifts to relieve them. I don't want anything happening to him. Is that clear?"

The grim deputies spread out between the holding cell and the elevator. Sammy walked into the cell and unlocked the shackles from the table and led El Moro out. Deputy Frankie Ellis walked in front of them, and Big Boy behind, all the way to the elevator, which was open and waiting for them.

Upstairs on the top floor of the ancient courthouse, Sammy led El Moro out of the elevator and into the cell the jailer had prepared. El Moro stood calmly and held out his hands for the handcuff removal. Sammy shook his head. "Not yet. Not until the sheriff says."

El Moro sat down on the bunk. He lay down gently on his right side facing the wall. He first prayed that his head would stop throbbing, then started on his usual devotions. Within seconds, he fell fast asleep.

Chapter Seven

After his mother was killed, Adolfo lived like an animal on the streets of Madero. He slept in doorways covered in cardboard when he could find it, and became adept at eating out of trash cans, discarding the garbage that was obviously rotted and toxic.

One day an older boy, José, saw Adolfo searching a can for food.

"You a gringo?" José asked.

"No," Adolfo said. He was afraid. Older boys who called him "gringo" always tried to hurt him bad.

José shrugged. "You want to come with me?"

Adolfo wasn't sure, but he was tired of being alone and scared all the time. José gestured for him to follow.

They walked the dirty streets for a while. José ducked into an alley and led Adolfo through a narrow doorway covered with a thin cloth. They stood in a sunlit courtyard. It was like heaven to Adolfo. José led him to a bench built around a big tree in the middle of the courtyard and told him to sit and wait. José ran through another door and after a minute, walked out with a lady behind him. She wore a white cotton dress with red and green and yellow border around the neck. She seemed old to Adolfo, but beautiful, too. She held his chin in her hand and gently wiped the dirt from his face with a wet cloth.

"*Como te llamas, niño?*" she asked.

Her touch was so soft and her voice so sweet, Adolfo began to cry. His mother had a touch as soft and a voice as sweet. He had not thought of her in a long time. The nice lady took him in her arms and hugged him tightly, and Adolfo cried harder. He had made himself stop thinking about his mother, because it hurt him so. He missed her so much.

"Adolfo," he said. The lady wiped his eyes.

She gestured for him to sit on the bench. The lady reached into a pocket in her dress and pulled out an orange. She held it out to Adolfo. The lady wanted him to take it.

He bit into the orange and peeled it quickly and watched the lady walk back to the door. By the time he finished devouring the orange, the lady was back and held out a flour tortilla filled with chicken and salsa. Adolfo's eyes grew wide and he took it from the lady and ate it. It was the best thing he had eaten since his mother had died.

The lady smiled at him and patted him on the cheek. She sat next to him and José until Adolfo was through, then she took him by the hand and led him inside.

Thirty minutes later, Adolfo walked out into the courtyard in white cotton pants and shirt that were so clean they smelled better than the ocean. They weren't new, but they were the best clothes Adolfo had ever worn. And he was clean. Before she gave him the clothes to wear, the lady filled a washtub with hot water and left him alone to scrub himself with the soap and rag she gave him. When he stepped out of the tub, the bath water was almost black. His skin tingled. It was the first bath he had in fresh water since the neighbors burned his house with his dead mama in it.

José clapped Adolfo on the back and gestured for him to follow, then ran out of the courtyard into the streets. José spent the rest of the day showing Adolfo the secret hideouts around the city José and his buddies used, and introduced Adolfo to a lot of boys his age, all of whom looked up to José.

That night about midnight, in a room off the courtyard where the sweet lady lived, José shook Adolfo awake. The lady had put up a small hammock for Adolfo, and he slept off the ground for the first time in longer than he could remember. He was scared when he saw José, but José calmed him down and told him to follow him.

They joined three other boys on the street and walked for many, many blocks to the port, where Adolfo learned from José and the others how to rob drunken American sailors after they left their *putas* and walked back toward their ships. Sometimes they walked all the way to the wharfs in Tampico. For the first few months, Adolfo thought it was fun to rob the sailors, like a game.

After a while, seeing the drunk sailors and the way they treated the *prostitutas* was no longer fun for Adolfo. Sometimes it made him angry, and sometimes he tried to hurt the men.

One night in Tampico, he and José hid and waited for a sailor to walk by. They saw a tall one stumbling along a dimly lit street and began to follow him and the woman with him. The woman moved away from the sailor but he pulled her back. She struggled to leave and the sailor tried to slap her. He missed and fell down in the street.

José and Adolfo charged at the couple and chased the *puta* away. She cursed them over her shoulder because she had not gotten paid. They turned the sailor over. He was so drunk he couldn't get up.

Then José picked up a piece of iron from the street and hit the sailor in the head. Adolfo stared down at the blond American as José removed everything from the sailor's pockets. José stood up to leave and gestured for Adolfo to follow him.

31

Adolfo stood there staring down at the blond gringo. He glanced at José, then picked up the piece of iron and beat the sailor in the head, slamming the iron bar over and over until the gringo's skull was crushed and he stopped breathing. José grabbed Adolfo and shook him. He dropped the iron and ran away with his friend.

The two boys kept running all the way back to the sweet lady's home. She was cooking breakfast in the kitchen off the courtyard. Adolfo watched José walk into the kitchen and give the lady all the money they had taken off the sailor. She fed them a big breakfast of *tortillas, frijoles, y huevos con tomate y queso*. Adolfo ate until he thought his stomach would burst.

He crawled into his hammock and slept until supper, dreaming about his mother in their old shanty, rocking him in her arms while she sang old songs and smoothed his hair over and over.

Life around the courtyard was good for Adolfo but in the second year there, he and José began to hang out at a park controlled by the *Contreras* gang. José and Adolfo played soccer and kept to themselves. One day in the middle of a match, Adolfo stopped on the field and stared at a boy across the park. He left the field and walked to where five *Contreras* gangsters leaned against an old Dodge.

Adolfo walked up to the young *pandillero* he thought was in charge and spoke to him. The *pandillero* laughed and patted Adolfo on the head, said something to the others and they all laughed. Adolfo got close to the *pandillero* and spoke quietly to him.

The *pandillero* smiled at Adolfo, pulled up his shirt and gave Adolfo the rusted six-shooter he had stuck in his pants. The *pandillero* crossed his arms, leaned against the old car, and watched Adolfo walk across the field.

Adolfo hid the gun in his shirt. He walked toward the boy who was laughing with another guy. When he got close, Adolfo called out.

"*Carlos.*"

The boy grinned. "*Gringo,*" he said.

Adolfo never forgot Carlos, the boy in Adolfo's old neighborhood who tormented him after Adolfo's mama died. The boy that threw the rock that knocked Adolfo off the pier and almost drowned him. The boy who thought it so funny to make fun of Adolfo and his Mama.

Adolfo drew the gun from under his shirt and shot Carlos in the stomach. The other boy ran, and Carlos fell to the ground.

Adolfo walked closer and held the gun to Carlos's forehead. He shot Carlos again, this time between his wide-open eyes.

Adolfo walked calmly back across the field and gave the gun back to the *Contreras pandillero*. The *pandilleros* drove Adolfo in the old Dodge to the home of Ernesto Contreras. Adolfo waited in the back yard for a while. The *pandillero* who loaned him the gun walked out with a grown man, not too old, who extended his hand to Adolfo and asked if he wanted to join their organization. Adolfo said yes. Ernesto signaled to some teens who walked out of the house and encircled Adolfo.

They beat him for a while, then picked Adolfo up off the ground and congratulated him. They took turns wiping the blood from Adolfo's face and head.

That night, Adolfo was drunk when they tattooed the three-dot *Mi Vida Loca* between his thumb and forefinger. They cheered when he stood, took the oath, and showed them the tattoo. Then they gave him a bottle of Tequila and a thirteen-year-old prostitute. Adolfo was ten years old, and now a sworn member of the *Contreras* gang.

Chapter Eight

At five-forty-five, little more than an hour after the JPD cruiser piloted by gangly Hubert Holland slammed into El Moro's Maxima on I-55, Jake Banks, twenty-six, almost a year into his job as assistant United States attorney in Jackson, felt a slight twinge in his right wrist when he slammed an uppercut into the heavy bag. He knew he should have wrapped it better before he started his workout. Jake had been pummeling the big bag with his bright red gloves for fifteen minutes, and was about to take a break anyway.

It took persistence and jawboning to get the apartment manager to let him hang the big bag in the community workout room. There was plenty of room, but the bag had to be suspended from a structural beam in the ceiling, and the manager had to get the owners' okay. Jake knew he irritated the manager by staying on him about it, but he kept at it and finally wore him down. Two weeks after Jake hung the heavy bag, he started working on the manager for permission to hang his speed bag.

Twenty minutes on the speed bag starting at five a.m. A short break, and fifteen minutes on the heavy bag. Jake was sweating bullets. Iron Maiden blared from his music box, amping Jake, driving his rhythm. Everyone else hated the music and treated Jake like a throwback, so he had to finish his boxing while he was alone. Most mornings at six, a handful of other apartment residents straggled in to use the treadmill or Stairmaster. Seconds after he stopped to re-wrap his right wrist, Jake saw his iPhone light up on the floor close to the bag. He always put the phone where he could see it, because he could hear nothing over the blaring, head-banging music.

Jake picked up the phone. *Unknown caller.* He turned off the music and punched the answer button. A puddle of sweat ran from his right index finger onto the phone. "Hello."

"You told me to call you with anything special, Jake."

"Yes, sir, Agent Milton. What do you have?"

"I told you to call me George."

"Sorry. George."

It was George Milton, Supervising Special Agent in the Jackson FBI office. Jake felt an adrenaline rush—he knew it was something big.

Jake walked into the men's locker room, slipped out of his silk boxing shorts and walked into the shower.

He was built like his father—lean and hard. His muscles were well-defined from the training he had put himself through

34

since he moved to Jackson after law school at Ole Miss. He ran five miles three days during the week and once on the weekend. Free weights every other day. Boxing at the gym for an hour on the mornings he did not run. He restricted his eating during the week, too. Not much fat, a lot of protein, enough good carbs to keep his energy level up. He eased off on the weekends with a few beers and pizza. Even so, Jake was in the best shape of his young life, and planned on getting stronger.

"Got a heads up from JPD about a collision on Interstate 55 near the Medical Center exit. Drug money runner collided with JPD unit and there's hundred-dollar bills all over the place."

"Where'd the money come from?"

"The trunk. It's a lot of money. JPD's got a crew picking it up now. They say it's millions."

"I'm headed that way soon as I clean up. You going to be there?"

"Not me," George said. "Got a rookie going, fresh out of Quantico."

"What's his name?"

"Kitty. The bad guy is long gone. Took a rubbernecker's car and drove off to who knows where. There's a statewide bulletin out with a description of the car and license. Late model Malibu."

Jake knew George Milton wouldn't be at the scene. George was marking time, just taking up space, waiting to retire after almost thirty years in government service. Jake's boss said it would take a bomb scare to get George out of the FBI office in the federal building on Capitol Street. But Jake liked George and the war stories he told at Bubba's Sports Bar about the old days, the eighties, before everything in the bureau went online and electronic.

Jake had turned down offers from the best civil firms in Jackson to take the assistant U.S. attorney position. He wanted to try cases right away, like Walton Donaldson was doing in Sunshine. He itched to prosecute bad guys—send them away. The fact that his father, Willie Mitchell Banks, was well-respected and perceived to be the best prosecutor in Mississippi by every member of the state and federal bar in Mississippi, and was good friends with Governor Jim Bob Bailey and knew most of the Congressional delegation, did not hurt Jake's job prospects with the Justice Department. Jake thought it was a real credit to Willie Mitchell that his sordid involvement with Mary Margaret Anderson did not diminish him in the eyes of the lawyers and politicians in the state. Anyone aware of the facts knew that Willie Mitchell was guilty of nothing but bad judgment resulting from loneliness.

Jake still did not know the full story of why Willie Mitchell and his mother Susan had separated for three years. Jake and Scott, the youngest son, a junior at Ole Miss, did their best to get them back together. Jake didn't know if they did any good, he was just glad his mother Susan had come back home. They sure seemed happy these days, enjoying the condo in Oxford and the beach house on Perdido Key Susan had bought when they were living apart.

Jake stopped at the on ramp where JPD had blocked off access to the interstate. They were re-routing traffic on I-55 two exits south of the collision. Jake showed his Justice Department badge and slowly drove his 2010 Toyota 4Runner up the ramp. His mother gave him the 4Runner as a law school graduation gift.

The Haynesville Shale natural gas wells on her one hundred acres of pine timber land in DeSoto Parish, Louisiana was gushing money her way every month. Chesapeake Oil transferred the payments electronically to Susan's bank account. Jake did not know exactly how much the payments were, but when he thanked Susan for the generous gift of the 4Runner, she said her monthly royalty from Chesapeake was enough to buy lots of 4Runners, even with natural gas at five dollars. Now it was at seven, headed to ten, according to the Wall Street Journal article he read the previous day. He wondered what his mother was going to do with all that money.

Jake stopped at the top of the ramp and laughed. There were jail inmates in green-striped outfits and cops in uniform hustling and chasing bills all over the three lanes and shoulders of I-55. Some of the inmates had pickup tools they used for highway trash detail, grabbing the bills and stuffing them into black plastic trash bags.

Jake drove the 4Runner slowly toward what appeared to be the central collection point for the money near a Maxima that was impaled on the passenger side by a JPD black and white patrol car. He stopped about two hundred feet away, stepped onto the concrete, and adjusted the Sig Sauer P229 forty caliber in the black leather holster he wore under his suit coat, behind him on his strong side, above his right cheek.

Looking at it in the mirror whenever he passed one, Jake knew there was a detectible bulge at times, but he wasn't concerned about it. He knew at least one other assistant U.S. attorney in the Jackson office who carried. There was no policy in the office, written or otherwise, that said he couldn't. And he was sure his boss, U.S. Attorney Leopold Whitman, wouldn't know the difference between an automatic and a revolver, much less detect Jake's Sig.

Mississippi had granted him a concealed carry license when he was in law school. During his third year, when Willie Mitchell's trouble with Mary Margaret Anderson surfaced, Jake started carrying a smaller automatic, a nine millimeter Baby Glock, with him at all times. Just in case. Since he came on with the U.S. attorney's office, Jake felt he needed the enhanced stopping power of the Sig. Jake liked the feel of the Sig Sauer better, and read online that SEAL teams used it.

On I-55, he saw crime scene specialists had the area around the vehicles taped off. Several worked the wreck, taking measurements and examining the interior of the Maxima and the police cruiser.

Jake held up his badge for the JPD officer in charge. "Jake Banks with the U.S. attorney's office."

"You got an FBI agent around here somewhere," the policeman said to Jake.

"Kitty?"

"Yeah," the officer grinned. "*Kitty.*"

"We might want you to secure the vehicles for a more thorough check in the lab."

The officer gritted his teeth. "Already taken care of that. They're just checking for weapons and drugs in the Maxima, then we'll secure it and haul it to the State Police lab. That's where *Miss Kitty* told us they wanted it held."

"Okay."

"Going to be a big fight over this cash. Local district attorney's going to want to forfeit the car and the cash to his office if there's any traces of dope in the car, which the crime scene guys already say there is. You feds are going to want it too."

"Be a nice feather in our office's cap," Jake said, looking around. "Where's the driver of the car that was taken?"

"He left. We got all his information, said we'd call him when we locate the vehicle. *Miss Kitty's* got all the details on the car."

"Thanks," Jake said and walked away, thinking Kitty must have pissed off the JPD officer. He walked north until he saw a young woman in a navy blue suit coat and matching slacks writing on a small notepad. Her suit coat opened when she turned toward him and he saw a matte finish automatic holstered on her side.

"Kitty?" he said when he got close.

"Let me finish this. Be right with you."

Jake waited a minute or two until she folded her notebook cover over and stuck it in her coat pocket. She walked to him and extended her hand.

"S.A. Kitty Douglas," she said.

"Jake Banks, assistant U.S. attorney," he said. "Welcome to Jackson. You sure started off with a big case."

"Yeah."

"You say something to that cop over there?"

"Not really. He offered to show me around Jackson. Wanted to know where I was living. My phone number, too."

"Maybe he was just being nice."

"I know when someone is being nice."

Jake really couldn't blame the cop. Kitty was good-looking. Tall with broad, strong shoulders. Long brunette hair she wore straight, and beautiful olive skin. Jake couldn't remember seeing skin more beautiful. Dark eyes, flawless white teeth, and a perfect nose. But she didn't seem quite feminine. Maybe it was the automatic holstered on her side. Maybe it was because Jake had spent the previous seven years on the campus of Ole Miss among the prettiest, most feminine women in the United States.

The green-striped inmates and JPD officers huddled around the collection point and turned in their bags and grabbers. Jake saw no more bills anywhere.

"What about the money that blew off the interstate?"

"No way to retrieve it," Kitty said.

"Maybe we could announce it was part of the second stimulus."

He grinned, but Kitty didn't. "You know. From the government."

"I got it. I just didn't think it was funny."

Jake paused. *Smart ass.*

"Who's keeping the money?"

"We agreed with JPD that we'll store it in the state police lab until jurisdictional and forfeiture issues are settled. They're already talking to the D.A. about splitting it between JPD and us."

"What's next?" he asked.

"I've got to check with Agent Milton. Is there some reason why the U.S. attorney's office needs to know?"

Jake had heard enough of her mouth. He walked away without saying anything, drove the 4Runner down the ramp to the federal building. He was there in a few minutes, parked and bounded up the stairs to the U.S. attorney's office. He swiped his government identity card and the main entry door clicked.

He punched in the code and opened the door after looking directly into the lens of the camera above the door.

"*It's me,*" he mumbled.

Jake walked through the empty reception area down the vacant hall to his office. He was the only one there.

"Hey, George," Jake said after he dialed the FBI supervising agent. "I just got back from the interstate. Y'all got anything yet on the driver."

"You got a TV in your office?"

"Yeah."

"Turn on Channel 12."

Jake grabbed his remote and turned on the thirteen-inch Sanyo on his ugly, government issued credenza to Channel 12. There was a TV helicopter overhead shot of a car in a ditch on a rural road surrounded by police vehicles.

"You see it?" George asked.

"Yeah. Where is that?"

"Your dad's jurisdiction."

"Yaloquena?"

"You bet. That's where our millionaire landed."

Jake read a "Breaking News" crawl across the bottom of the screen: *Driver in Crash on I-55 with Millions in Trunk Arrested and Charged with Murder in Shooting Death of Yaloquena Deputy Sheriff Travis Ware.*

"Holy shit," Jake said.

"Exactly."

Chapter Nine

El Moro awoke with a start. His head seemed better. It still hurt, but the throbbing was muted. He turned over carefully in his bed and rested a moment on his back. In the cell across the narrow walkway sat a young black deputy with a shaved head and military bearing. And in the cell next to El Moro's was a large black deputy, tall and fat.

El Moro sat up slowly. He swung his feet around to rest on the floor. The fat deputy stared at El Moro, mad-dogging him. El Moro was not impressed by the hard look the fat man was trying to pull off. The fat man was not mean. After years of dealing with murderers and gangsters, El Moro could tell immediately who was dangerous. It was an indispensable skill. It kept him alive.

El Moro's light eyes were hard, cold. They met the fat deputy's. Big Boy could not handle it and broke off after only a moment of engaging El Moro. Nervous, the fat deputy stood and turned, moving away from the steel bars his cell shared with the prisoner's.

The jail elevator opened. El Moro watched the sheriff and the gringo in the exercise clothing walk out of the elevator down the narrow hall. They stopped at El Moro's cell. El Moro stood up slowly until he was at eye level with his captors.

"My name is Willie Mitchell Banks. I am the district attorney for this county, Yaloquena. I think you've already met Sheriff Lee Jones."

El Moro was glad the cell bars were between them.

"You got the Malibu in Jackson after crashing into a cop car," Willie Mitchell Banks said.

"You must be a big time drug dealer," Lee said. "All that money. You want to tell us who you are so we can make you famous? Media from Jackson starting to show up outside now. You could be a big man on the news. Maybe CNN and Fox News will pick it and take it national."

"I want a lawyer. Please."

Lee Jones and Willie Mitchell said nothing else. El Moro watched them walk back toward the elevator. He heard the elevator door close. El Moro sat down on his bunk and gingerly lay back on the thin mattress. He joined his hands behind his head and closed his eyes.

~ * ~

Seven hours after El Moro stood him up in the landing area in the marsh in Lafourche Parish, Esteban's cell phone rang. He watched the number come up. He did not recognize it, but he dreaded answering.

"*Bueno?*" he said, expecting an explosion.

"Do you know anything?" the voice said.

Esteban breathed a sigh of relief. It was Rique Bustamante, *El Cártel de Campeche's* man in Beaumont. Esteban spent years working air and sea imports with Rique as far west as Galveston Bay and the Houston ship channel eastward to Port Arthur. He was happier now working the Louisiana marshes because there were fewer civilians and law enforcement in the marshes between Lake Charles and Plaquemines Parish than in *Tejas.*

Rique was up the chain of command from Esteban, but understood the pitfalls that crop up with delivery and transfers more than the big boss in Veracruz. The big boss only cared about getting the job done. He dealt harshly with those that couldn't.

"I know he made the exchange. Other than that, *nada.*"

"Well, I do," Rique said. "In Jackson, Mississippi, at about four-fifteen this morning, El Moro had a collision with a police car on the interstate, and everything he picked up in New Orleans is now in the possession of the authorities there."

"What was he doing up there?"

"What do you think he was doing up there?"

"*No sé.*"

"Big Boss wants to know."

Esteban was quiet.

"Is he now in Jackson in jail?"

"No. He's in a small town in north Mississippi called Sunshine. They say he murdered a *policía* up there."

"Why?"

"There are many questions," Rique said. "The man wants answers. Did he decide to go off on his own for his own purposes? Or did someone take him and force him to do these things? Because he is so valuable to the organization, the big man does not want to take a chance. He wants an answer from El Moro's own lips."

"Yes," Esteban said. "El Moro knows a lot."

"You have nothing to add?"

"No. Sorry."

"Do you still work with the pilot from Lafayette? The Frenchman?"

"Yes. But he lives now in Opelousas, north of Lafayette."

"Is his number the same?"

"Yes."

41

"I will talk to you later."

~ * ~

In his bunk, El Moro's mind drifted. He slept.

He was twelve and riding in the back of a rusted, red Chevrolet pickup truck through the streets of Tampico, admiring the beautiful buildings with red and pink bougainvillea winding through their black wrought iron balconies. His long blond hair blew in the wind. Riding in the back of the pickup made him feel important.

Look at me. I'm a big shot delivering to Homero Bernal. I even have a driver who takes me to Villa Bernal.

Adolfo was a reliable producer for the *Contreras* gang, and had made several deliveries of money to Señor Bernal. But life was far from glamorous. Adolfo made enough money to buy food and beer, and at *Contreras* parties the girls were free, but he still lived on the streets, sleeping where he could, crashing at members' *casas* for a night or two, but constantly on the move. He had killed twice since the bully Carlos, but the two victims after Carlos he did not know. He was told to kill them, given a gun and bullets, and picked the time and place on his own.

There were lots of boys his age in the Tampico gangs, and when one was murdered, it was no big deal to anyone, including Adolfo. Police looked the other way. His bosses paid them off. Adolfo was not afraid of dying at the hands of the cops or being thrown in jail. It was the other gangs that made his life dangerous.

Once another gangster his age tried to kill him. But the assassin was clumsy and missed with the screwdriver he thrust at Adolfo's neck. Adolfo ran away, his neck cut and bleeding, but nothing serious.

Adolfo jumped out the back of the red Chevy before it came to a complete stop in front of Villa Bernal, about five miles west of Tampico, in the country near the marshes. Señor Bernal's man, Luis, stood outside the iron gate entrance in the light yellow stucco wall that surrounded the *villa.*

As usual, a small, rectangular machine gun hung from a shoulder strap at Luis's side. Adolfo brought the bag of money to Luis as he had done many times before, and turned to jump back into the bed of the pickup.

Luis grabbed his arm.

"*Un momento, muchacho,*" Luis said. "Señor Bernal wants to talk to you. Follow me inside."

Adolfo was shocked. Luis dismissed the driver with a wave of his hand and led Adolfo through the iron gate. Adolfo stopped for a moment when the gate closed behind him.

It was the most beautiful home he had ever seen. Red clay tiles on the roof and thick, yellow stucco walls, a wide porch around the house like the *haciendas* in the country Adolfo saw on television in the appliance store windows.

He followed Luis up the steps and onto the shaded porch and felt the cool breeze in the walkway. Luis opened a large wooden door with ornate carvings. Adolfo stared at the door. *This is the way kings live.*

Adolfo walked slowly behind Luis, looking down at the highly polished dark red tiles covering the floor. When Adolfo screwed up the courage to raise his eyes, Luis stood at a large desk, behind which was an older man with jet black hair combed straight back tight upon his head. The man gestured with his index finger for Adolfo to come closer. Luis retreated to the side of the desk.

"Do you know who I am?" the man asked.

"*Sí, señor.*"

"What is my name?"

"Señor Bernal.*"

"Very good. And your name is Adolfo, correct?"

"*Sí, señor.*"

"Your hair is yellow and your skin is white. Your eyes are not brown. What color are they?"

Adolfo shrugged.

"Speak."

"*No sé, Señor Bernal.*"

"Come closer. Look at me."

Adolfo walked forward until his stomach touched the big desk. Señor Bernal studied him for a moment. "Your eyes are hazel, a kind of light green and gray. Where did you get such eyes? Do you know?"

Luis stared at the boy.

"From your father, the American merchant sailor from Mississippi."

"Sí," Adolfo said quietly.

"What did you call him?"

"*Vikingo.*"

Bernal laughed. Adolfo did not know why. "Do you know his name?"

Adolfo shook his head. *Why is he asking me these questions?*

"And *su madre* was a *mestizo*. Her skin was dark. How old were you when she died."

Adolfo shrugged.

"Do you know how she died?"

"Someone killed her."

43

"Do you know who?"

"No."

"Was it *Vikingo*?"

"No."

"How do you know?"

Adolfo did not answer and showed no reaction at all. No tears or sad thoughts.

He felt a slight twinge in his stomach near the place he stored all his thoughts about his mother and their life together in the barrio. It was the size of an avocado seed, a small one, and he kept all those memories locked tight in there, so they did not come out and bother him. Adolfo had not thought much about his mother since he met the sweet lady who fed him the day José brought him to the house in town with the big courtyard.

"Does it bother you to talk about your mother and father?"

"No."

"Do you speak English?"

"*Un poco.* I learn from the sailors near the port."

"I have an organization, a business. Did you know that?"

"*Sí, señor.*"

"Would you be interested in working for me all the time?"

Eyes widening, Adolfo shook his head up and down vigorously.

"I am told you have a quick mind. Is this correct?"

"The older boys tell me that. I know my numbers, and I read things for many of the other boys."

"You will stay here at my house for a while. We will meet once a day for one hour in this room. I will ask you many things. If I decide you are not right for the kind of work I need you to do, you will be free to go. You will take your meals in the kitchen with María and she will give you work to do every day. When María tells you to do something, it will be as if I am telling you. Do you understand?"

"*Sí, señor.*"

Luis walked over and guided Adolfo out of the room.

Three weeks went by quickly. Adolfo and Señor Bernal had many, many conversations about many things. He read aloud in Spanish and in English from different books for Señor Bernal. Adolfo did exactly as María told him every day. He worked in the garden or the kitchen, and sometimes helped her take in clothes drying in the sun on the line hidden behind the villa.

María was a wonderful cook and Adolfo had never eaten such delicious food. He ate fruits and nuts he had never seen before. His bed was so clean and comfortable that he looked forward every night to climbing under the soft covers and going to sleep. One day Luis got Adolfo from the kitchen and took him to Bernal. He stood before the great man at the desk.

"Adolfo, I have enjoyed our time together these past weeks."

"So have I, Señor Bernal. I thank you."

"I have a plan for you. I am confident that you can do this and will be successful and help our organization very much. But it is a long-term plan. Do you know what that means?"

"It will take a long time."

"Yes. You came into this world different. You look like a gringo, with your light skin and hair, but you have been raised Mexican. If you can learn to speak English as well as a gringo, so others do not know you are Mexican, do you realize how valuable you would be to my company across the border, *en Los Estados Unidos*?"

The thought of being in *El Norte*, in the big cities he saw on television, excited him. "Yes, sir."

"Are you willing to do whatever it takes to do this job I have for you? No matter how long?"

"*Sí,* Señor Bernal. I can do it for you."

"Luis will arrange for you to travel north, across the border. You will live with a woman I know in a town called McAllen, Texas. Your job is to learn perfect English, learn to speak like a gringo with no accent. Do you understand?"

"*Sí, señor.*"

"Now. If you fail to obey this lady or cause trouble for her, if you do not learn perfect English in three years, you will have failed me and I will deal harshly with you. If you run away, no matter where, I will find you and you will be sorry."

"I will be good. I can learn English. I can do all this for you."

"If you do, I will make you rich. One day you can have a house just like this, or bigger. You will be a powerful soldier in my army."

"I am ready."

Chapter Ten

Willie Mitchell walked past Ethel Morris, his white-haired sixty-one-year old gatekeeper who had been with him since he was first elected district attorney for Yaloquena County twenty-five years earlier. He glanced out the window of his second-story office and, as always, firemen were shooting hoops behind Sunshine's main fire station. Ethel walked in with her notepad.

He removed his suit coat, draped it over the edge of his desk, and sat down. He had worked in his running stuff all morning, showered and changed at home then had lunch with Susan. She knew Travis Ware, and was sick about his unnecessary death. Willie Mitchell told her what he knew over a sandwich. She made the best homemade chicken salad.

Ethel Morris had been busy.

"I set up a press conference for two o'clock."

He glanced at his Casio with the big numbers. "Who?"

"All the Jackson stations. Greenville. Greenwood. The print reporters from Jackson, Memphis, and local."

"I talked to all those people this morning."

"They want more. They want video for tonight's news, and the print reporters want to be here because the TV people are."

"Did you talk to Judge Williams about notifying the grand jurors?"

"She signed an order getting the clerk to issue subpoenas."

"We're lucky we already have a grand jury empaneled."

Ethel moved back to allow Assistant District Attorney Walton Donaldson and Sheriff Lee Jones into the office. Willie Mitchell gestured and she walked out.

"The clerk got the grand jury subpoenas to us just now. We'll get them all served this afternoon and tomorrow," Sheriff Jones said.

"Next Wednesday's pretty soon to be presenting this guy's case to the grand jury," Walton said. "We don't even know his name."

"We will by then."

"Still, it just happened today."

Willie Mitchell stood up. "Why wait? We've got enough to indict him on capital murder right now. Coroner said there was no bullet or fragments in what was left of Travis's skull, so there's no forensic work to wait for. The forty-five had just been fired, right Lee?"

"I smelled it myself."

"We've got the tape of Travis calling in the Malibu in the ditch, saying there was one man in the car, maybe asleep or hurt, and he was going to check it out, see if the man needed help. There's no evidence anyone else was in the car."

"We had the jail doctor check him out in the cell," the sheriff said. "Doc said he may have a concussion."

"Nothing better than bed rest for a concussion," the D.A. said. "He'll get plenty of that upstairs. What about his jaw?"

"Doc said nothing was broken," Lee said. "Just bruised. Sorry."

"It's okay, Lee. What's done is done. We'll deal with it down the road if it comes up. People will understand.

"Walton, I want you to spend the rest of the day helping Lee contact any agency we can to get this guy identified. Give Jake a call in Jackson to see if he can get the FBI and Justice to search their drug courier database. Send him the picture. See if they can do a facial identification scan like they do on TV. And send the prints again. They didn't get an IAFIS hit this morning but just ask them to double-check."

"Okay," Walton said. He and Lee headed out.

"Hold on," Willie Mitchell said. "You deserve a better answer to your question, Walton." They stopped.

"We're moving on this right now, getting the bastard indicted for capital murder and I'm announcing in about an hour," he glanced at his watch, "at two o'clock, that we're seeking the death penalty for the murder of Travis."

Walton and Lee waited.

"I want to get ahead of the feds on this."

"What do you mean?" Lee Jones asked.

"I mean, with the amount of money this guy was carrying, he's high up and privy to a lot of information the feds are going to want, and they'll initiate prosecution and try to get that money forfeited to them soon as they can. They will want this guy in a secure federal lockup, not in a ninety-year-old courthouse in an antiquated, third-floor jail that this county has been able to keep in operation only by going along with a consent decree issued by the federal judge in Oxford."

"You think they'd really try to do all that?" Walton asked.

"You hide and watch."

"Wednesday grand jury session is sounding better all the time," Walton said. "We need to get the needle for this guy."

"I'm not letting the feds take him," Sheriff Jones said.

"Then you guys help me move this thing forward as fast as we can. We've got the advantage of being a lot more nimble than the feds. Fed leviathan takes a while to get cranked up. Faster we get this guy indicted and headed to trial, the better our chances of keeping him in the state system."

47

Walton and the sheriff left. Willie Mitchell's cell phone vibrated in his front pocket. He checked the number.

"Jake," Willie Mitchell said. "I guess you heard."

"I saw it on Channel 12. Who's the guy?"

"We don't know yet. Had a fake Louisiana driver's license. Walton's going to call you in a few minutes to see if you can help us with identifying him."

"We'll get right on it."

"No hits on IAFIS."

"He's not in the system?"

"Apparently not."

"Is he Hispanic?"

"I'm not sure. He looks white, but something's not right."

"What do you mean?"

"I don't know. Just something about his demeanor. How much money was he carrying?"

"Don't know the total yet, but it's several million. Maybe as much as four or five."

Willie Mitchell whistled.

"Have you talked to Travis's family?" Jake asked.

"No. Lee's been to see his wife. Your boss okay with helping us get the ID?"

"I haven't talked to him yet, but I'm sure. He's on the coast today. I sent him a text and asked him to call me. I'll call George Milton about it when Walton gets the stuff to me."

"Okay. I'm moving on this right away. Bringing him to grand jury next Wednesday on capital murder."

"That's fast, even for you, Daddy."

"Yeah, well. I don't want you feds interfering with my case. I've got a press conference at two. We're seeking the death penalty."

"I knew you would. I don't think Mr. Whitman is going to interfere with your going forward first. We may need him for a hearing on the forfeiture proceedings down here, but a murder of a deputy has to take precedence over a drug courier bust, no matter how big."

"I hope that's right. Can't ever be sure when the federal government is involved. When are you coming home?"

"I don't know right now. I was going up for the Tennessee game and stop by the house on the way back, but now that this has come up I don't know."

"Come see us when you can."

"Talk to you later," Jake said and hung up.

~ * ~

48

Willie Mitchell parked in the detached garage next to his home on a corner lot in the center of the downtown Sunshine residential area. The house was built in 1910, old for the Delta, and had four two-story white columns in front. He had inherited the house from his folks, along with roomfuls of English antiques his parents and grandparents accumulated during their lives. The antiques he and Susan bought together were now in the Oxford condo, where they landed during the three-year hiatus in their marriage.

The separation had ended last year when Susan came home.

Willie Mitchell was happier in their marriage than ever, and he hoped Susan was. She said so, and to him, she seemed to be. "So far," Susan would say when he asked if she were happy. "Forever," was her answer when he asked her if she loved him. "Love me," was what she said when he asked her what he needed to do to make her happy.

She was tall and lithe. She kept her hair blonde, covering the gray, and was the best dressed, most tasteful woman in Sunshine. The most arcane of southern protocols were second nature to her, but she was the least stuck-up beautiful woman Willie Mitchell had ever known. She loved the Southern traditions and styles, but did not care if strangers, or her friends, felt the same.

He kissed her, lit the grill outside, and went upstairs to change. Twenty minutes later, he sat with Susan at the solid pine kitchen table. It was full of wormholes and uneven places, but it had been in their kitchen during their entire married life.

"I took a pound cake by Frances' this afternoon," Susan said.

"How's she doing?"

He took a bite of the salmon he had brought in from the grill five minutes earlier.

"She's in shock. Like you'd expect."

"I hate it for her and the kids. Travis loved his family."

"You did really well in the press conference. I saw it at five."

He took a bite of salad. "Good thing about being district attorney in a small town. The press all look like they're nineteen or twenty years old. Right out of college and they don't know much."

"You were handsome on TV."

He smiled. "That's the most important thing. I talked to Jake."

"What's he up to?"

"He went to the scene on the interstate, watched them pick up all those hundred dollar bills. Their office will handle the forfeiture of the drug money and any drug charges in Jackson."

"Maybe you'll get to work with him on this case."

He finished his salmon and took his plate to the sink. "I've had better days."

"I know," she said. "I hate for you to have to try another big murder case. I don't guess Walton could do it."

"He can help, but this is my case all the way to death row. I owe it to Travis and Frances."

He stood by the sink while she rinsed the plates and put them in the dishwasher. He grabbed an insulated plastic glass with tennis rackets crossed on each side and filled it with ice from his favorite kitchen appliance, the ice maker under the cabinet. He took a sip of water and admired Susan's figure. He wasn't sure how he had convinced her to marry him almost thirty years before, but he was glad she went along with the plan.

He had met her when he was in law school at Ole Miss. Saw her in The Grove before the Alabama game his second year. She had a date with an undergraduate who was so drunk he could barely stand up, much less communicate. Susan was with a half-dozen other Tri Deltas in their sorority tent, including a girl from Sunshine Willie Mitchell knew. He asked the Sunshine coed to introduce him to Susan. He talked to her for a long time in The Grove that afternoon.

The game was well into the first quarter, but he decided talking to the beautiful senior from Louisiana was more fun than sitting in the stadium watching the game. Susan's date was carried from the tent by some of his Kappa Alpha buddies. At the end of the first half, with Ole Miss down by seven, Willie Mitchell and Susan were the only ones in the Tri Delta tent. They sat in lawn chairs and talked.

She seemed more mature than her sorority sisters. Time flew. When the other Tri Deltas and their dates returned after Ole Miss's come from behind win, Willie Mitchell was surprised the game was over so soon. He and Susan partied and laughed with everyone in the tent. He asked if he could call her for a date. She said "sure" and he called her the next day.

From that point forward, he never dated another girl. Willie Mitchell knew he wanted to marry her the first time he talked to her in The Grove in the Tri Delta tent. They were pinned at the end of the year, and a year later they married at her family home in Mansfield, a small town in DeSoto Parish in the northwest part of Louisiana. The same parish where the four natural gas wells on her one hundred acres of pine timber land were producing several million cubic feet per hour of a *smorgasbord* of methane, ethane, propane, and butane.

Willie Mitchell put his ice water down on the old pine table, smiled and took Susan in his arms. He hugged her tightly, kissed her on the lips and lingered. "Going up to put on my PJ's."

"Need any help?" she asked.

He smiled. "That is so thoughtful of you."

"I'm a thoughtful girl," she said. "I'll be up in a minute."

He walked out of the kitchen and up the stairs. He undressed slowly and waited. His heart rate quickened slightly when he heard her walking up the stairs in the center of the old house.

"Tomorrow's got to be better," she said at the top of the stairs then walked in their bedroom. Willie Mitchell stood by the bed naked.

"I couldn't find my PJ's."

"Well," she said and walked into his open arms. "Would you like me to find them for you?"

"Not yet." He pulled her close.

"It feels like you're glad to see me."

"Susan Woodfork, you are as beautiful today as you were when I met you in The Grove before the Alabama game." They kissed slowly. He unbuttoned her blouse and kissed her harder and deeper. She stepped out of her skirt and shed the rest of her clothing.

"I'm already thinking that everything is better," he said. "Thanks to you."

"I love you more than you can possibly know," Susan said.

Chapter Eleven

Lionel Gautreaux stood just five-two on his tiptoes. He possessed a helmet of black hair cut close and square above his forehead, hair so thick and wiry that category three hurricane force winds would not budge it. He was stocky and proud to be called a coonass, a term synonymous with Cajun, but not nearly as polite.

Gautreaux could land a helicopter on a drilling rig in the gulf no matter the conditions and was reputed to be the best chopper pilot on the Louisiana gulf coast. He made substantial money at his job flying to and from the rigs—but could not make ends meet because of a ferocious gambling addiction.

The same qualities that made him fearless as a pilot made him a daredevil on the craps tables. Unlike most coonasses, he didn't drink alcohol, smoke or go to Mass. He did drink vast quantities of strong chicory coffee, which never made his hand quiver on the stick or holding the dice.

Lionel supplemented his pay by flying low-altitude missions for *El Cártel de Campeche*. It was dangerous work and certainly illegal, but they paid in cash, which converted easily into chips at the Indian casinos in Marksville and Kinder, his preferred venues.

Lionel shared his cash with Bernie Batson, head of maintenance at the Loh Brothers helicopter fleet hangar outside Opelousas in St. Landry Parish. The Lohs owned huge tracts of pine timber in central Louisiana that they patrolled with a fleet of choppers to dust the trees for pine beetles and other insects that bored into pines and killed them.

Bernie was a top-notch mechanic who kept his helicopters in perfect condition. Conveniently, Bernie really liked crystal meth and always needed cash from Lionel. Theirs was a match made in heaven.

Bernie had some last-minute maintenance on the helicopter Lionel was using for the mission. It took longer than Bernie estimated, so Lionel was late getting started on the job he undertook for the cartel. It was the highest-paying gig Lionel had ever done for them—two hundred fifty K in cash, a hundred twenty-five in advance, the rest on completion.

It was also the most dangerous. But he didn't have a choice. The Coushattas had their collection goons after him. He needed money in a hurry. They made it clear to Lionel his scalp was in jeopardy if he didn't pay by Friday.

He took off at three-thirty a.m. from Opelousas with his two passengers delivered by Rique Bustamante, his handler for this contract. They were dark, spoke no English or Cajun, and were dressed and equipped like members of a SWAT team. Each carried a black duffel bag. Lionel knew they were some kind of Mexicans, and didn't care what their names were. He just wanted to get there, do the job, and get back to Opelousas before eight.

He flew low and fast on a straight line from Opelousas to Vicksburg, Mississippi, hugging the west bank, the right descending bank of the Mississippi River. The land below him was a marshy wasteland, unpopulated and unsuitable for anything but the willow trees that dominated the landscape. The river was the boundary between Louisiana and Mississippi above Simmesport, and it moved from east to west in a series of compressed S's more than it moved south. He veered westward to avoid the lights of Vicksburg and crossed the river just south of Lake Providence in the Louisiana Delta.

The Mexicans stared straight ahead into the inky darkness. Lionel said nothing to them the entire flight, the only sound the roar of the engine.

"Crap," Lionel said as the eastern sky brightened on his final approach to Sunshine. They didn't have much time.

~ * ~

Everett Long took off at first light in his yellow double-winged Grumman AG-CAT crop duster from the Yaloquena County airport. He banked and headed southwest to Barrett Morgan's cotton fields about ten miles from Sunshine to spray for bugs. Halfway there, he watched a small commercial helicopter approach with no running lights. It was barely above the treetops and blew past him at a high rate of speed on his left flank heading toward Sunshine.

"What the hell?" he said.

Everett had a feeling something was not right about the helicopter. He was a civil defense deputy, and did volunteer flying for the Yaloquena sheriff's office. The Morgan pesticide spraying was his only job of the morning, so Everett turned to follow the chopper. Even though his crop duster turned on a dime, the helicopter was miles ahead of him before he started his pursuit.

~ * ~

Lionel saw the courthouse on the horizon. As in most small towns, it was in the center of the business district and the tallest building in town. It had a flat roof, plenty of landing room, just as Rique Bustamante had said. He also assured Lionel the two Mexicans were demolition experts, and that he would be on the roof for no more than ten minutes before he

53

took off with El Moro. Lionel told Rique that the two Mexicans better be good, because he wasn't hanging around for long. If he hadn't needed the money so damned bad, Lionel never would have taken this high risk job.

His choice was between this and losing his scalp to the Coushatta collection thugs, and he figured even if he got caught, it was better than getting beaten or killed over what he owed the Indians.

Besides, Lionel liked living on the edge. He liked the adrenaline rush he was starting to feel as he slowed on his approach to the roof.

"Get ready," he said to the Mexicans, who grabbed their duffel bags and squatted near the small exit door. One of them gave him the thumbs up, and Lionel used his forefinger to simulate a spinning tire. The Mexican nodded vigorously and pumped his thumb. He understood. Time was of the essence.

Below Lionel, the streets of Sunshine were empty. Maybe the timing of their arrival was good after all. Just enough light to land, but still too early for people to be moving around.

He hovered for a few seconds over the roof then gently landed, the gravel on the flat roof crunching as he set down. Lionel grabbed the door handle and popped it open. The Mexicans hopped onto the roof and scurried to a spot fifty feet from Lionel. They lay their AK-47s on the gravel, opened their duffel bags, pulled out the plastic explosive and began to shape the blast so the force was directed downward to blow a hole in the roof.

~ * ~

Everett saw the helicopter slow down and hover over the courthouse. "Holy shit," he said when he saw the armed SWAT clad men jump out of the chopper and get busy on the roof. He grabbed his cell phone and called his high school classmate, Willie Mitchell Banks.

"Willie Mitchell!" he yelled when the district attorney answered.

"Yeah."

"You up?"

"Yeah. What do you think, I'm talking in my sleep?"

"Listen up. A small commercial helicopter just landed on the roof of the courthouse. Two guys in body armor with automatic rifles are doing something, putting something together."

"What?"

"I don't know. I didn't want to get too close."

"Where are you?"

"Circling downtown, staying low, staying behind the chopper."

"What are you carrying?"

"Temik. Going to kill some bugs at Barrett Morgan's place until I saw this helicopter."

"They're trying to break out the guy we put up there yesterday."

"The guy that killed Travis?"

"Yeah. Got to be. How's that Temik work on humans?"

"Well, it's in the same chemical family as the stuff that killed a bunch of people at Bhopal a few years back. I ain't sure this is as strong a mixture as that, but at the very least it'll make these guys really sick."

"Can you dust 'em with it?"

"You mean drop it on them?"

"Yeah."

"How much?"

"All of it."

Everett thought for a minute. He searched downtown for a suitable approach—so they couldn't see him coming.

"Yep," he said. "I can drop the whole load right on top of them."

"Do it."

"What if it kills them?"

"If you had a gun with you I'd authorize you to shoot at them. Deadly force is okay to stop a jail break. You're a part-time deputy sheriff. You don't have a gun with you, do you?"

"No. You sure you want me to do this?"

"Do it!" Willie Mitchell screamed into the phone. "Do it now."

Everett pocketed his phone and turned sharply, heading away from downtown, then banked and came in low, just above the trees. As he approached the courthouse, he got lower, then at the last minute, pulled straight up and gunned it, just like he had done a million times to avoid trees at the end of a cotton row. He pulled the dusting lever all the way back. "Bombs away," he said.

Everett's entire load of Temik fell on the courthouse roof, dousing the Mexicans as they huddled over their explosives, and soaking their getaway helicopter.

As Everett leveled off and turned around, he could not believe what he saw. Like a giant blender, the helicopter blades caught the Temik and swirled it around, making a poisonous funnel cloud above the roof.

Everett moved closer, low and slow, and watched the two men stumble away from what they were working on and stagger toward the helicopter. They struggled through the small door and closed it behind them. The chopper took off and flew in a southwesterly direction. Everett caught up with them and flew alongside.

He didn't know how the pilot could see. There was a dense cloud of Temik in the helicopter.

"Unless he's got oxygen," Everett muttered.

~ * ~

Lionel's eyes burned like they were on fire. He tried to open them just enough to see, but the Temik cloud was impenetrable. Every few seconds he saw enough to fly, but that wasn't his only problem. His chest closed up and he could no longer breathe. His throat was scorched.

He imagined the Mexicans were even worse, but he didn't care if they died or not. Lionel's throttle hand twitched and went numb. He tried to move the stick but his hand paid no attention to him.

He thought about the time he landed on a rig south of Vermillion Bay in a bad hurricane and flew the drilling crew and roustabouts safely ashore. He remembered the hot streak he was on at Marksville, when dozens of coonasses in the casino gathered around to watch him roll the bones. He remembered the crawfish *etouffee* his mama made for him growing up in Breaux Bridge. Lionel felt the helicopter going down, but he could do nothing about it.

"Hail Mary, full of grace..." were the last words he said, right before his chopper hit the ground and exploded in a ball of flames.

Chapter Twelve

Willie Mitchell walked away from what was left of the helicopter in the parking lot of the abandoned sewing machine factory just south of downtown Sunshine. The odor of the three bodies that were burned to a crisp lingered in his nose—not much different from an overcooked steak on the grill. He'd smelled a lot worse.

The parking lot was concrete, a tribute to the way things used to be constructed. It was cracked and buckled in places, but still usable. Now every parking lot in the Delta was asphalt. He bent down to pull up a young sycamore tree growing between the concrete in the rotted expansion joints. It did not come up easily. Though only a foot high, the sycamore clung to life tenaciously. Willie Mitchell had to use both hands to pull it up and toss it away.

The coroner used a separate body bag for each of the three dead men, though their remains would have fit easily into just one. Identification was going to be a problem, but Willie Mitchell was not worried about that. He was worried about keeping their mystery man in the county's ancient third-floor jail. Travis Ware's murderer was important to someone in addition to Willie Mitchell and Sheriff Lee Jones—someone with a lot of money to waste on a spectacular and high-risk escape attempt, someone who employed men not afraid to die.

Willie Mitchell joined three-hundred-five-pound banker Jimmy Gray and crop duster Everett Long at the edge of the parking lot near the highway. Everett stood with his hands stuck in his jean pockets.

"I'd say that Temik got the job done," Willie Mitchell said.

"Wouldn't that be a great ad on the farm news?" Jimmy said. "Temik—kills bugs in your field, and brings down helicopters, too."

"It's strong stuff," Everett said. "Sorry those fellows had to die."

"I'm not," Jimmy said. "Bastard drug dealers deserve it."

"I read up on it when I landed at the airport. Temik's an aldicarb, whatever that is. It kills nematodes, thrips, and spider mites by shutting down their neurological and respiratory systems."

"What about humans?" Jimmy asked.

"Aldicarb poisoning short circuits the central nervous system and if they survive that it attacks the gastrointestinal system. Lots of the Bhopal victims had terminal diarrhea.

57

Doctors couldn't stop it and they dehydrated and eventually died."

"These fellows didn't live long enough to get the shits," Jimmy said. "They died of an acute impact with the ground."

"I'm just glad you spotted the helicopter when you did," Willie Mitchell said to Everett. "If you hadn't been suspicious and checked on what they were doing, they would have broken him out."

"I knew something was wrong," Everett said. "Flying that low at that speed with no lights at all. They were sneaking in for a reason, and it had to be something illegal."

Willie Mitchell extended his right hand to Everett and patted him on the shoulder with the other. "You saved the day for us, Everett, and I appreciate what you did."

Everett smiled. "Well, if you guys don't need me any more, I got to reload and get that Morgan cotton dusted before the wind picks up."

"Thanks again," Willie Mitchell said to Everett as he left. "Send me a bill for the pesticide." The district attorney turned to the fat banker. "We dodged a bullet."

"Big time," Jimmy said. "What are the odds of Everett being there at the right time?"

"Astronomical."

"I'm glad Lee brought in the state crime scene people."

"He knows his office doesn't have the capability to handle anything like this. A man's got to know his limitations."

"Eastwood," Jimmy said. "In *Dirty Harry*."

"Wrong."

"That's right, that's right—it was the sequel, *Magnum Force*."

"Correct. What actor did he say it about?"

"Mark Twain."

"Nope."

"You know, the guy that did the Mark Twain one-man show."

"Name."

Jimmy shrugged. "I know it. Gimme a second."

"Hal Holbrook."

"Shit. I'd a gotten both those you gimme enough time. You're too quick on the trigger."

"Big talk. Fifty cents you owe me. See you later. I've got to get to the courthouse."

"Bet you the clean up crew's not through. I watched 'em in those HazMat suits for a while power washing the roof and the walls."

"I like the smell of Temik in the morning," Willie Mitchell said.

"Robert Duvall. Call me if you need me to do anything," Jimmy said as Willie Mitchell walked to his truck, a new Ford F-150 with just enough bells and whistles to make it reasonably comfortable to drive on his short road trips to Jackson and Oxford. Anything longer or when Susan was with him, they went in Susan's big silver Lexus.

Before he opened the truck door, Willie Mitchell called out to Jimmy. "Did you walk this morning?"

"No."

"Why not?"

"You didn't come by."

"My fault. I thought the jail break was more important."

"You need to get your priorities straight."

Willie Mitchell aimed his right index finger at Jimmy.

"Look, big boy, you need to make a commitment here—walk every day, whether I walk with you or not. You have got to drop some weight."

Jimmy Gray joined him next to the truck. "There's something you got to understand, Willie Mitchell. You and I ain't alike. You eat like a bird, that oatmeal shit. Me, I got a vociferous appetite."

"Voracious."

"Same thing."

"No, sir. Vociferous means boisterous, insistently loud."

"Exactly. My appetite insists that I eat often and a lot. It demands it, and sometimes in not such a nice way. Sometimes loud. You just don't know the half of what I go through, you with your flat belly and skinny little ass."

"Try to do better."

"I will. I promise. But you better show up tomorrow."

Willie Mitchell cranked the truck and slowly left the parking lot, chuckling. Jimmy Gray was one of the smartest people he knew, an award-winning banker who ran the cleanest, most profitable small bank in the Delta.

Though he came off to strangers as funny and dull-witted as Junior Samples on *Hee Haw*, whom he closely resembled, he had quietly grown the bank's assets from two hundred million to four hundred million since he took over the management from his father. Jimmy and his brother in New Orleans owned a majority stake in Sunshine Bank. Willie Mitchell was the third largest shareholder, inheriting ten thousand shares from Monroe Banks, who operated the bank with Jimmy's father for thirty years, until Jimmy took over.

Even in the Delta's challenging agricultural climate, with farmers frequently filing bankruptcy and losing their land, the bank's loan losses were miniscule, and its capital base strong. Jimmy Gray was close to all his major customers. They made sure they paid Jimmy before any other creditors.

On the drive to his office, Willie Mitchell thought about the odds against Everett spotting the helicopter. The idea that such a random event could come out of nowhere to foil the jail break flew in the face of the need for forethought and planning.

Just like Jimmy and Martha losing their youngest son, Beau, in a hunting accident crossing a fence. His rifle fell and went off, striking him in the torso. He lived for several hours, but eventually bled out. Alone.

Jimmy cried to Willie Mitchell many times in the year after it happened, wanting to know the odds of the gun falling at exactly the right spot to discharge and hit Beau. Jimmy reconstructed the accident with a protractor to determine that the gun had to fire within a five degree arc to hit Beau. And it did. Willie Mitchell's youngest son, Scott, a junior at Ole Miss, was Beau's best friend.

The entire Banks family mourned with the Grays. Susan suspended her sabbatical from their marriage for a week to mourn with Martha and Jimmy. Willie Mitchell tried to get her to stay, but she wouldn't—not then.

He still wasn't sure of the reason for the separation. He knew he was drinking too much at the time and had lost his drive, reaching the age where he looked back and realized he could have accomplished so much more. But Susan told him several weeks after her coming home for good, the separation wasn't just about Willie Mitchell's *malaise*. She had issues of her own—menopause, for one, and the odd physical and mental changes it brought about. There was psychic unsteadiness she said she felt, her two boys all but grown, no real purpose other than being a wife in a small Delta town. The irrational thought that she had lived fifty-two years and had accomplished nothing.

Willie Mitchell knew the feeling. He was better than every lawyer he had faced in his career, but here he was, still district attorney in a small, rural county—he had never left home.

He had tried scores of murder cases and lost only a few. He was not afraid to let the jurors see him angry, or elated, or disappointed. He knew trying to conceal true feelings from a jury was a mistake—you lose their trust. That's what Willie Mitchell believed. If he thought a witness was lying, he let his sarcasm and disbelief hang out there, for everyone in the courtroom to see.

He parked in his reserved space near the courthouse and walked up the steps. The place was deserted because of the Temik. Everyone except essential personnel in the sheriff's office and the jail was gone, told to return tomorrow after the cleanup. Willie Mitchell was sure some of the inmates would sue the county for exposure to a dangerous substance. They sued for everything else.

He called the sheriff and asked him to join him for a brief meeting. Moments later, Lee Jones walked in.

"Ghost town up here," he said.

"It's kind of nice and peaceful," Willie Mitchell said. "I can't hear the phone ring up front, and I'm not answering it anyway."

"We've got a skeleton crew downstairs."

"What about the jail?"

"I've got my regular jailers and another deputy up there around the clock. I've also set up a twenty-four hour watch on the roof. When the clean-up crew and the state police bomb squad finished up there we set up a structure, kind of like a deer stand, and we're operating four-hour shifts, one man per shift with binoculars and an automatic rifle."

"Good to err on the side of too much security."

"I've got detectives running down the helicopter. None of the three men had any identification and there ain't much left of them. Teeth are no good if we don't have anything to compare them with."

"Don't waste much manpower on that. They were sent by whomever our prisoner works for and we're not going to be able to trace it back to them. That's something we can turn over to the feds later on. We need to concentrate on keeping the jail secure going forward, keeping our heads down and our mouths shut, and moving the case to trial as fast as we can. I told the press no more conferences until after grand jury indicts him."

"I'm not talking to the media either. My men will finish serving the grand jurors tomorrow. I know most of the jurors, and I'm following up with a phone call to make sure they show up on Wednesday."

"Tell them it's going to be a short session. Just this one case. Nothing else. And let's play our regular game Saturday," Willie Mitchell said.

"You sure?"

"Good for the brain. All this going on, we'll need a break by the weekend. We need to play"

"Okay."

"You call Edgar and I'll call Jimmy. Usual time."

~ * ~

Willie Mitchell and Jimmy Gray rode in one cart, Lee Jones and Edgar Creed in the other. They teed off at eleven so they could finish by three to avoid the hottest part of the day.

Edgar Creed was short and muscular, totally bald on top, and was a manufacturer's rep, selling chemicals to farmers in the Delta. Edgar was the second-best golfer in the foursome, behind Willie Mitchell, who had a four handicap and who could play just about as well as needed to win a bet or make a difficult shot. Jimmy Gray was decent, but his girth made it a chore to swing the club properly. He had trouble getting around the course and in and out of hazards.

Lucky for Jimmy, Sunshine Country Club had few sand traps.

Lee Jones was the worst, but the most improved. Growing up in the Delta, there was no place for black kids to play golf. He started playing a little in the military. When he became a state policeman, he would play at their meetings on the coast. He knew golf was difficult to learn as an adult, but began playing in earnest when he moved back to Sunshine and was elected sheriff.

Jones was the first black member of the Sunshine Country Club. Willie Mitchell brought him out to play after he was elected sheriff. No one said anything, though many eyebrows were raised. After playing with Lee every Saturday for a month, he proposed Lee for membership at a board meeting. There was some grumbling, but Lee's membership was approved because every board member, to a man, liked and respected Lee Jones.

There was also the recognition that if the club did not increase its dues paying membership, it would continue to deteriorate and become more of a goat ranch than it already was.

With Sunshine's black citizens constituting about seventy-five percent of the population, the board members recognized that if they didn't accept black members, the country club was doomed financially. Since Lee joined the club, two dozen other black families had joined, and so far, there was peaceful coexistence.

The social events were still primarily segregated, but by choice. The black members chose not to attend the functions to which all members were invited, and tended to have informal gatherings of their own. They rented the club for their wedding receptions and anniversary parties, which helped the club's bottom line considerably.

Willie Mitchell noticed lately more and more black members eating Sunday lunch at the club, and it was gratifying to him that the gradual voluntary integration was taking place organically with no directives from anyone, and with no fanfare. Everybody was doing just what they wanted to do. It was not like the new members were strangers. In such a small town, almost all the white members knew the new black members, worked alongside them, and got along in the community. Sunshine and Yaloquena County had come a long way.

"Me and Lee," Willie Mitchell said on the first tee. "Three-dollar Nassau. Dollar scats."

"Let's play a five-dollar Nassau," Edgar said. "I've sold a ton of Temik this week to sheriff's offices all over the Delta."

They all laughed.

"Three dollars," Lee said. "That's all I can risk on a public employee's salary."

"Chicken shit," Jimmy Gray huffed, struggling to bend down to stick a Sunshine Bank tee in the ground. "You never lose with Willie Mitchell as a partner. Why you worried about a five dollar bet?"

"Three dollars," Willie Mitchell said. "Hit the ball."

Jimmy drove his Titleist down the center of the fairway about two hundred and forty yards. Edgar Creed pulled his left, but had a decent lie in the short rough.

Lee teed up and took two practice swings.

"Goddammit, Lee," Jimmy said, "your swing makes Charles Barkley's look as smooth as Freddie Couples'."

Lee laughed. "At least I can see my dick," he said.

"What do I need to see Tiny for?" Jimmy said.

After Lee hit an ugly slice, Willie Mitchell addressed the ball and smoothed it down the middle about two-forty, coming to rest next to Jimmy Gray's Titleist.

"Man, I wish I could swing like that," Lee said.

"Yes, and I can also see my dick," Willie Mitchell said.

He sat in the cart, squeezing in the passenger side next to Jimmy Gray. He elbowed Jimmy to get more room, and they headed off down the concrete path.

The golf cart listed fifteen degrees to the banker's side.

Chapter Thirteen

Willie Mitchell finished his run early so he could get to his office by seven-thirty. He knew from experience the grand jurors would begin showing up at eight-thirty to drink coffee in the small anteroom outside the grand jury room.

He unlocked his door on the second floor and walked through the office. His cell phone vibrated. It was his son Jake checking in.

"You ready?"

"Ready as I'll ever be," Willie Mitchell said.

"How many witnesses are you calling?"

"Just Lee for everything that happened in Yaloquena. I've got him playing Travis's radio call about the Malibu, and then describing the scene when the prisoner was arrested."

"What about the wreck on I-55?"

"I've got the two JPD cops coming, but I'm not sure I'm going to use them. If I were a defense lawyer at the trial I'd argue what happened there is irrelevant. Whoever represents him will move to exclude any testimony about the money as prejudicial, outweighing its relevance to the homicide."

"I agree," Jake said. "It would probably help with the sentencing."

"I'll definitely use it in the sentencing phase. Makes the death penalty a lot more likely if the jurors know he's a drug dealer."

"We still don't have anything on his identity. FBI has used every database they have, but nothing."

"I'm going to indict him as a John Doe. We'll get him ID'd sooner or later, before trial."

"Hope so."

"I've got to get some things done, so I'll talk to you later."

"Daddy. Let me tell you why I called."

"Let's have it."

"There's something going on down here."

"What do you mean?"

"I mean there's guys from agencies in D.C. down here I've never seen before. Mr. Whitman's keeping me out of the loop. Lots of closed door meetings. But I've got a strong feeling it's about your guy."

"They say anything to you?"

"No, but the way they look at me. My gut tells me there's something going on about the guy you got in jail."

"Well, keep me posted, but don't put yourself out on a limb. Don't try to find out something you're not supposed to know."

"I won't. Later."

Willie Mitchell studied his file on Travis's murder. He re-read all the statements from the deputies at the scene and what few forensic reports he had. Ethel showed up at eight and closed his door so he could work in private.

At eight-thirty, Ethel tapped on the door and entered quietly.

"There's a lawyer here that says he's representing the prisoner."

Willie Mitchell raised his eyebrows. "Who is he?"

"He says his name is John Boardman from Houston."

"You're kidding," Willie Mitchell said. "Does he have long hair pulled back in a ponytail?"

"Yes, gray hair. And an Italian suit that must cost as much as I make in two months."

"Johnny 'Ace High' Boardman from Houston, Texas," Willie Mitchell said. "I know you've seen him on CNN. He was their expert commentator on the Fort Polk bomber trial. Show him in."

Ace High bounced in like he owned Willie Mitchell's office. He had a salesman's smile and charisma to spare. High energy. About Willie Mitchell's height and weight, and probably the same age. His hair was thick and long, ninety percent salt, ten percent pepper.

"Johnny Boardman," he said cocking his head and extending his hand. "Houston, Texas."

Willie Mitchell stood and shook hands. "Willie Mitchell Banks. I've seen you on television. Nice to meet you in person."

"Likewise. Checked you out. Hear good things about the way you do your job."

"Thanks. I hear you try a pretty good case yourself."

Ace High laughed. "Thanks. At my level a lot of it is show." He grabbed his ponytail. "Why I keep this horsetail. Part of my *schtick*."

"Have a seat," Willie Mitchell said. "I've got a feeling I know what brings you to Yaloquena County."

"Yep," he said. "I'm enrolling as counsel for Adolfo Zegarra Galván, your guest upstairs."

"At last. We finally know his name."

"Glad to be of service."

"He's certainly an enigma. He's not in any of the national systems. Now that we have his name... "

"You still won't find anything on him. Native of Mexico."

"Doesn't look Hispanic," Willie Mitchell said.

"So I understand."

65

"You haven't met him? So how'd you get hired?
"We're veering into some privileged areas here, Mr. Banks. I'm afraid I can't share any more information with you."

"Willie Mitchell. No problem. Wasn't prying, just curious. I'm glad to finally have his name." He paused a moment. "What do you like to be called?"

"Ace High is fine for print descriptions and television introductions, but a bit much for conversation. Ace is fine, Willie Mitchell."

"I'm presenting his case to the grand jury this morning at nine."

"I see you don't like to waste time. Impressive."

"I don't plan on calling many witnesses."

"No reason you should. I assume you're not planning to ask me if Mr. Zegarra will make himself available."

"Don't need him."

"I agree. I like the way you work, Willie Mitchell."

"And, if I tell you I'm going to do something or not do something, you can count on it."

Ace Boardman paused. "I wish I could say the same. I admire your straightforwardness, but I have to demur on my ability to shoot straight with you. As I am compelled to use my best efforts to have my client acquitted, I plan to use every artifice and subterfuge at my disposal. In that way, Willie Mitchell, my side of this battle is much easier than yours. You're bound by integrity, honesty, and the rules of law and procedure much more than I am. All I have to do is avoid committing a crime in court. Any other scurrilous thing I do or say in the defense of Zegarra I get a pass from the appellate courts. I don't want the truth to emerge from the adversarial arena. As a prosecutor, you risk being sanctioned for misleading the court or the jury. As a zealous advocate for the defense, *it is my job to mislead and obfuscate.*"

"At least you're honest about being a sneaky bastard."

Ace High laughed. "I am not totally without honor, however, as I think you'll come to learn. I'm honorable, but in my own way."

Willie Mitchell stood. "Anything I can do for you right now?"

"I'd like to meet with my client, and I know about the deplorable incident last week on the roof, so I will agree to more stringent security procedures than I would normally accept."

"You cannot take him out of the jail."

"I fully understand."

"You'll have to be searched and can have no physical contact with him. He'll stay in his cell, and we'll put a chair outside for you."

"I don't like talking to clients through bars, Willie Mitchell, but in this case I certainly understand."

"As we move forward and we put some separation between the attempted escape, we can make it more comfortable for you."

"That's all I really care about, my comfort, not his. I know you'll have a man watching me, and that's all right, just no recording or videotaping, and place your man far enough away so that he cannot hear us whisper."

"No problem. While you're making your way down to the first floor to see the sheriff I'll call him and relate all this. His name is Lee Jones."

"Right," Boardman said. "Thank you for your courtesy. I look forward to working with you in this matter."

Ace High bowed slightly and backed away for his first couple of steps, then turned with a flair and marched away.

Ethel appeared in the door.

"You look terrific today, Ethel," Willie Mitchell said. "Why so dressed up?"

"You wanted me to be with you to the noon press conference and I know there will be television cameras there. I wanted to look nice for the evening news."

"When they start rolling, walk up to me and whisper something, anything, that way you'll be sure to be in the picture."

She smiled. "The two Jackson police officers you subpoenaed are here to see you."

"Bring them in."

Willie Mitchell walked to his window. For the first time in recent memory, there were no firemen playing basketball or lifting weights on the concrete behind the station.

Carl Lippmann and Hubert Holland walked in. Willie Mitchell suppressed a grin. A pale white Mutt and a dark black Jeff, the Mutt having the biggest Adam's apple Willie Mitchell had ever seen.

He shook their hands and gestured for them to sit. Carl held up his subpoena. Hubert saw him and quickly did the same. Carl rolled his eyes, put his hand on Hubert's forearm and pushed it down.

"We brought our subpoenas," Carl said.

"Take them to the clerk's office after the grand jury session and the clerk will give you your travel check."

Hubert must have been impressed. Willie Mitchell noticed his Adam's apple moving up and down.

"It is important that you guys came this morning, even though I might not call you to testify. If I do need one of you, who was in the best position to see—"

Hubert pointed to Carl. "Him," he said.

"Hubert's right out of the academy and never has testified in any kind of trial or anything," Carl said, "so I'll be doing the talking if need be. We both saw the same thing."

"Okay, Carl. It's not necessary for the grand jury to know what happened on I-55 with the wreck and the money in order for me to get a capital murder indictment."

"Because the victim was a deputy sheriff doing his duty at the time he was shot," Carl said.

Hubert was even more impressed.

"That's right. But I do want you guys to tell me what happened that morning. Carl, why don't you start?"

Carl began at the donut shop and proceeded to describe to Willie Mitchell the events in great and unnecessary detail. After listening politely for what seemed like forever, Willie Mitchell excused himself to appear before the grand jury to presenting the capital murder case styled "State of Mississippi vs. Adolfo Zegarra Galván."

~ * ~

Willie Mitchell stood at one end of a long conference table in the narrow room across the hall from his suite of offices. The stenciled letters on the door read GRAND JURY ROOM. The room was narrow, with enough room at one end of the table for Willie Mitchell and Walton, and a small credenza behind them on which they put their books and files. At the other end was the empty witness chair.

The fourteen grand jurors sat on either side of the long conference table. There were eight women and six men, most in their fifties or older. Ten of the fourteen were black. Willie Mitchell knew a lot of them before the grand jury term started. Because of the previous sessions with this grand jury, he now knew them all. He knew which ones would ask questions of the witnesses just to hear their own voice.

Through years of practice, he was adept at cutting off questioning without appearing abrasive. There was no court reporter, so Willie Mitchell or Walton administered the oath to the witness. Willie Mitchell did not record the proceedings and rarely took notes. He already knew what the witnesses were going to say. Creating any kind of notes or record of the testimony ran the risk of the defense obtaining them later through the discovery process.

"Ladies and gentlemen," he started, "thanks for being here on such short notice. I know all of you heard about the death of Travis Ware, and that's the only case I'm presenting to you today. I'm going to call just one witness, Sheriff Lee Jones, who will tell you what happened to Travis on Highway 19 just inside the county last week. At the end of the sheriff's testimony, I'll ask you to bring back a true bill against the defendant, Adolfo Zegarra Galván, for capital murder."

An older black woman raised her hand. "Is that the same as first-degree murder? Do we have to vote on the death penalty?"

"On your first question, ma'am, capital murder means the death penalty is a possible sentence. Death or life imprisonment. However, I make the decision, not you grand jurors, on whether to seek the death penalty, and it's up to the trial jury to decide on death or life imprisonment after a sentencing hearing. You just decide if there's probable cause to bind this defendant over for trial on the capital murder charge. After you hear the testimony, I'm sure you will."

He turned to Walton. "Ask the bailiff to call Sheriff Jones to testify." Walton hustled out of the room.

In less than a minute, the sheriff removed his beige Stetson and stood at the end of long table opposite Willie Mitchell.

"Raise your right hand, please, sir."

Chapter Fourteen

Jake Banks parked his 4Runner in the gravel near a sign that read HINDS COUNTY GUN RANGE. He walked toward the shooting range past an old Dodge pickup truck and dark blue Ford Crown Victoria sedan with U.S. government plates. It was five in the afternoon, plenty of daylight left.

Jake scanned the range after he placed his black tote bag on a rickety wooden table under the rusted tin shed behind the gun lanes. There were two people shooting: an older man in jeans, T-shirt, and a Jackson Braves baseball cap at the last lane on the left, and a girl in the second to last lane to the right. She wore dark blue slacks and a gray T-shirt, and had a long, brown ponytail sticking through the hole above the adjustment strap of a dark blue baseball cap.

"Miss Kitty," he grumbled.

He watched her shoot long enough to learn she was an excellent shooter. Her stance was perfect, and though Jake had to squint to see the target in the distance, it appeared she was placing her rounds in a nice, tight grouping. He unzipped his bag, removed his ammunition and a small, blue pistol case and thought about which lane to select for his practice. Kitty shot twice, lowered her weapon briefly, then twice again. He couldn't tell where the four shots hit the target, but he sure admired her shooting style and her looks.

Maybe she was having a bad day on I-55, nervous about being the agent responsible for gathering all those hundred-dollar bills. Maybe she's not really a bitch with a smart mouth. Maybe she'll be nice this time.

"Nothing ventured," he muttered as he walked toward her, eventually stopping at the lane next to her. He noticed the older man leaving in the Dodge truck, leaving Jake and Kitty alone.

It wasn't just her great figure and good looks that struck him. It was the confidence she exuded. There was nothing tentative in the way she handled her weapon, or in the way she held herself.

Kitty shot again, three sets of twos. From his adjacent lane he could see the target torso clearly. All six grouped around the sternum.

Impressive, Jake almost said, but didn't because she couldn't hear him with ear protection on. He didn't want to end up feeling foolish like he did on the interstate. He had talked to and flirted with hundreds of girls. Why was he nervous and second guessing himself? Why was he trying to come up with a plan just to say hello? He didn't know, but did it anyway, deciding to wait until she went back to the shed to reload. That way she'd have her ears off.

Jake aimed his Sig Sauer P229 down range and fired. After he shot six rounds, Kitty walked to the shed. He finished the magazine and headed her way.

"Nice shooting," he said when he reached the shed.

She removed her shooting glasses. "Not really. My gun's screwed up. Everything's shooting to the right."

"That a Glock?"

"Glock 23." She concentrated on loading her magazines.

"I met you on the interstate last week."

"I know who you are. Jake Banks. Assistant U.S. attorney."

She continued to shove forty-caliber rounds into her three magazines with great efficiency.

"You must shoot a lot," he said. "Those double taps you were placing on that target are hard to do."

"I have to qualify with my sidearm this week. That's why I'm out here. I'm a little rusty."

"I'm out here because I like guns and I like to shoot."

She finished loading and started back to her lane.

"Hey. Can I ask you something?"

She turned around.

"Is there something about me that irritates you?"

"No."

"Then why are you so unfriendly? Are you married or engaged or something? I'm just trying to make conversation. We're going to be working together, so we ought to get along."

"I don't think I've been unfriendly. And I don't have a husband or a boyfriend."

"No husband or boyfriend for me either."

Jake watched her respond. "You came close to smiling."

"Look, I'm not from down here," she said. "Everybody's so nosy in the South. I say hello and people are asking me where I'm from and what I do and am I married and other things that are none of their business."

"Where are you from?" Jake asked. He grinned. So did she. "What do you do?" he asked. She almost laughed.

"Down here," Jake went on, "we don't mean anything by these questions. It's just our way of being friendly and getting to know someone. I guess it's nosy, but not in a bad way."

"Seattle."

"Seattle? Shouldn't you be saving trees or dolphins? And what are you doing shooting an evil weapon? Are you recycling your bullets?"

"Actually, it's Tacoma. A little smaller and further south."

71

"I'm familiar with Tacoma, Washington."

"You've been there?"

"No, but I watch *Cops* on cable. It seems like Tacoma is on every other episode."

"I know. I've seen some of our best and brightest citizens showing how stupid they can be. Pitiful. Not everyone out there acts like those idiots you see on that show."

"I'm from Yaloquena County by way of Ole Miss Law School."

"I know. Your father's the district attorney holding our multi-millionaire Maxima driver."

"How'd you know that?"

"George Milton. Who I think is a nice guy for a supervisor. Apparently, down here everyone talks about everybody and everything."

"Pretty much. Everybody knows everyone, too, or at least has a connection. My mother? You let her talk to someone for five minutes and she'll find some person they both know."

"You said you don't have a boyfriend. What about a girlfriend?"

"No."

"Why not?"

"Now who's being nosy? Why don't you have a boyfriend?"

"I had one at Washington State. He didn't think being an FBI agent was all that great. He didn't want me coming down here."

"You broke up?"

"Over a year ago. I majored in accounting in undergraduate and then got a master's in finance."

"How did you end up with the FBI?"

"A recruiter came to campus. They recruited me for my accounting background, encouraged me to be in their forensic accounting section, but after Quantico, I wanted to be in the field. I loved the physicality of the training. It just made me feel so strong."

"Me, I've wanted to prosecute bad guys since I was a little boy. I used to go watch my daddy's trials, the ones he let me come to. It's all I ever wanted to be, but I'm no politician, so the Justice Department was the best shot I had at trying good cases."

They shot three more magazines each. Jake couldn't help trying to outshoot her, and he did.

"Nice shooting, Jake. You're good with that Sig."

"That reminds me, would you like to go get a beer?"

"With you?"

"Sorry, let me be more clear in my question. Would you like to go get a beer *with me*?"

"I would love to," she said. "I think that might be nice." She batted her eyes while pronouncing the "i" in nice like "eye." "Isn't that what one of your Southern girls would say?"

Jake followed Kitty to her office where she dropped off the government sedan. He offered her a ride to the sports bar but she said she would follow him. He waited for Kitty to get in her car, an older model BMW convertible.

They parked at Ollie's, one of Jake's favorite hangouts. He walked to the BMW and opened her door.

"What a fine car. What year is it?"

"1996. It's an E-36. I bought it from the assistant soccer coach at college who was going through a divorce. She took really good care of it. I couldn't afford it but I had to have it. I did some accounting tutoring to make the monthly notes."

"You don't have a problem with the stick shift?"

"You're kidding, right?"

"Never mind. Let's go in."

They grabbed a booth. Jake highly recommended the Amstel Light draft and they ordered two. A minute later he raised his mug to Kitty.

"Welcome to Mississippi."

She tapped his mug with hers. "It's going to take some getting used to. Compared to the West Coast this is a foreign country."

They talked through several more Amstel Lights, and split a hamburger and sweet potato fries. Jake was starting to like her.

Kitty tried to pay for her share but Jake would have none of it. They had three more shooting range dates followed by beer and something to eat at Ollie's, with a couple of jogging dates in between.

Jake suspected that she liked him as well, because one afternoon after work, she let him drive her beloved BMW with the top down around the Ross Barnett reservoir. When he stopped to get into his 4Runner and drive home, he leaned across the stick shift and kissed her. The short kiss turned into a long, passionate one.

"What took you so long?" Kitty asked.

~ * ~

The next morning, Jake walked into his boss's office. Leopold Whitman was the U.S. attorney for the Southern District of Mississippi. Short with a close-trimmed reddish-brown beard with specks of gray and tortoise shell glasses,

Leopold appeared more like a college English professor than a federal prosecutor.

"You asked to see me, Mr. Whitman?"

Leopold smiled. "Yes. It's about your father's prisoner, Zegarra."

"Yes, sir."

"Did you know the deputy who died?"

"I did. Known him since I was ten or eleven. He was a good man, family man. Nice to me, too."

"It's a real tragedy, his death. Have you talked to your father about the case?"

"Not Since Zegarra was indicted. I talked to Dad before he presented to the grand jury."

"Your father got an indictment for capital murder. At the press conference he indicated he was seeking the death penalty."

"It's the only sentence that would be appropriate."

"I agree, if there were no compelling reason to talk to Zegarra."

"About what?"

"Our information, from the bureau and other agencies is that Zegarra has a wealth of knowledge about *El Cártel de Campeche*."

"He was carrying a lot of money."

"We think... No, let me rephrase. We *know* he can give us some major higher ups, if we can make it worth his while to talk to us."

"How would you do that?"

"Well, we would have to work something out with your father. Is he dead set on executing this guy?"

"I assume he is."

"Would you be willing to talk to your father, informally, about letting us bring Zegarra here for our agents to talk to him, see what information he has that might help us break the back of the cartel."

"I'll talk to him if you want me to."

"It's a real risk holding him in that old courthouse jail you have up there. They're lucky the cartel didn't break him out with the helicopter."

"Yes, sir."

"Kindly advise your father we'd like to work with him on this."

Jake got up to leave. Whitman stood behind his desk. "We could get a writ to bring Zegarra here," Leopold said, "but I don't think that's going to be necessary. Surely your father will

74

see the sense in letting us work with Zegarra, prosecute him federally, take the death penalty off the table in the state court to give the man an incentive to talk."

"I'll talk to him today and let you know."

Jake walked to his office. He closed the door and spun around his chair to look out the window.

So that's why I've been kept out of the loop and not included in all those closed-door meetings. Leopold Whitman, the bureaucrat, the U.S. attorney for the Southern District of Mississippi, who has never tried a jury trial in his entire career, is going to need a lot more than a writ if he thinks he's going to get Zegarra out of Yaloquena jail and away from Daddy and Lee Jones.

He put his feet up on the corner of his desk and called Willie Mitchell.

Chapter Fifteen

Susan sat with Ina at the rugged pine kitchen table and dabbed her eyes with a Kleenex. Ina's eyes were watery, but she wasn't crying. Ina never cried, as far as Susan could tell. The moments Ina talked about her personal struggles were rare, but this was one of them. Ina's eyes produced tears, but somehow she fought them off, suppressing them by sheer strength of will so that they never escaped her eyes to run down her dark brown cheeks.

Ina had been twenty-one when Willie Mitchell was born, and by then had already worked for the late Monroe and Katherine Banks for four years. She cleaned the house, cooked, and helped Katherine raise Willie Mitchell, then helped Susan and Willie Mitchell raise Jake and Scott. During the separation, when Susan was elsewhere, Ina continued to work for Willie Mitchell three days a week, after an initial three-month boycott. When Susan came back for good, Ina returned to her five-day-per-week, full-time status. Nothing was ever said by Willie Mitchell or Susan, or Ina, about Ina's status in the house. It was all just understood.

Ina was stern. She rarely smiled, and pleasant words about her children, eleven grandchildren, and thirty-two great-grandchildren, were few and far between. Susan knew Ina had great-great-grandchildren as well, but they were never discussed. Ina never referred to her late husband John, nor did she gossip about people in Sunshine. Neither did Susan. Ina's favorites in the Banks family were Susan and Scott. She tolerated Willie Mitchell and Jake. If she had a favorite child, grandchild, or great grandchild, Susan wasn't aware of it.

Ina talked to Susan about Ina's vast family only when there was a crisis. At the level of Ina's great grandchildren, the problems were legion.

"The child is sixteen," Ina said, her voice both angry and sad, "and just had her second baby. And she don't know who it's for."

Susan felt only sadness. Children having babies was beyond epidemic in the Delta. The children giving birth were uneducated and poor, and their infants had no chance to succeed in the world. The problem overwhelmed Susan, and she saw it in Sunshine every day.

Willie Mitchell walked through the kitchen door. Ina stood up from the worm-damaged pine table and wiped the Corian counter by the sink as if she were just finishing up. Susan remained at the table.

"I'm gonna see to those new sheets upstairs," Ina said on the way out of the kitchen.

"How was your morning?" Susan asked.

Willie Mitchell grabbed an enamel pot from under the cook top and put it on a burner. "Fine," he said and poured Quaker Old-Fashioned Oatmeal, not the nasty one-minute kind, into the pot, eyeballed it, and poured a little more. He held it under the faucet until a quarter-inch of water covered the oats, added a handful of raisins and put the pot on the gas burner. He ate oatmeal for lunch four or five days out of each week to keep his cholesterol level down. Willie Mitchell had championship quality HDL, but his LDL was too high.

"What's the latest on Zegarra?" she asked.

"Had a long talk with Jake on the phone this morning. He said the U.S. attorney wants to question Zegarra in Jackson, and wanted Jake to talk to me about taking the death penalty off the table so they can use Zegarra to go after the cartel he works for."

"Jake thinks you should do that?"

"No. He wants me to put Zegarra to death. Jake and Travis were buddies. Jake's just passing along to me what Leopold Whitman asked him to." Willie Mitchell paused for a moment. "What are you and Ina upset about?"

"One of her great grandaughters just had her second baby. She's sixteen. Doesn't know who the father is, or so she says."

"Man-oh-man," Willie Mitchell said.

"I've been thinking. Maybe that's something I could try to help."

"What?"

"Helping these young girls with their babies, and trying to keep them from having more."

"That would be a good thing if you could."

"Well, I've got all this money from the gas wells. I paid cash for the condo and the beach house, and I've still got tons pouring in."

Susan had bought the Oxford condominium on University Street for just under a million in the last year of their separation. It was almost new, a couple of years old, and only three blocks from the Grove, where they partied before Ole Miss football games in the fall, then another ten minute walk to the stadium. The trial lawyer who bought it from the developer had run into some legal problems of his own. Susan benefited from his need to get as many assets out of his name as he could in as short a time as possible.

She took advantage of another distress sale in the last year when she bought a hundred foot lot and beach house at Perdido Key about a mile inside the Florida line on the western edge of the panhandle. Katrina missed the narrow spit of land running eastward from the beautiful bridge over Perdido Pass at Orange Beach, Alabama to the Intercoastal Canal bridge in Florida, but Ivan did not. Hurricane Ivan had savaged the Alabama beaches at Fort Morgan, Gulf Shores, Orange Beach, and the white beaches of Perdido Key in Alabama and Florida. The older couple who sold Susan the beach house were initially determined to hang on after Ivan, but the value of the lot and house continued to decline with the financial meltdown and real estate devaluation all over the country. When the husband began to experience the early signs of Alzheimer's, they decided to sell.

Susan had kept her eye on their beach house for years, and as soon as they put it on the market, she scooped it up for one point two million. Her hundred feet ran between parallel lines four hundred feet from the highway in the center of the key to the Gulf of Mexico. The house was sturdy enough to survive Ivan, ten feet above ground level, built on a foundation of pilings driven deep into the sand then surrounded by concrete. Susan was delighted with it. Until Travis Ware was murdered, Susan managed to get Willie Mitchell to the beach house a couple of times a month. Now, it seemed it would be a while before they would make another visit.

"Why don't you come up with a plan, go online maybe and find a model to follow for these teenaged girls." Willie Mitchell said.

"I don't want to get any government money."

"I don't think you should, but you might want to set up a foundation as the legal entity, make it a 501(c)(3) organization so that every dollar you give is tax deductible."

"Would you brainstorm it with me? Help me understand the legal part of setting it up?"

He took her hand and kissed it. "Your wish is my command."

"I know you're all tied up with Zegarra now."

"Zegarra's lawyer did something odd this morning," he said.

"What?"

"Ace High filed his first motion, and it was a speedy trial motion."

"Is that unusual?"

"I can't remember a defense attorney filing one in all the murder cases I've tried my entire career. Not one."

"I wonder what he's up to? Can you ask him?"

"I can," Willie Mitchell said. "But he's not like you or me. He wouldn't tell me the truth even if he could."

~ * ~

El Moro sat next to the bars of his cell door and listened to Ace High talk quietly to him. A few minutes into the conference, El Moro's mind began to drift, settling on his first years in the United States and the dream he had the night before. He was in the eighth grade in McAllen, and late for an English test. When he walked into class, everyone stared at him, especially the whites. The teacher gave him his exam questions. He had studied the wrong topics. The fear he felt was much greater than the fear he felt now in the Yaloquena jail.

El Moro went along with whatever the gringo *abogado* whispered as if it mattered. El Moro would not be calling the shots in his own defense, nor would Ace High, so what good was this conference? The lawyer and his ponytail left, and El Moro returned to his bunk, faced the wall and tried to pray and sleep, but his mind took him back to McAllen.

Chapter Sixteen

Adolfo was thirteen when he crossed the border and arrived at the home of Dominica Ayala. The house was old and small, and most unattractive. He knocked on the door and turned to look at the dead grass and potted cacti in the front yard.

"¿Quién es?" the old lady said through the door.

"Adolfo," he said.

She opened the door and pulled him inside. The front room was cluttered, filled with statutes and pictures of *La Virgen de Guadalupe*. A yellow cat and a smaller gray cat ran across the room behind the old lady. The house smelled of the cats and was stuffy, but Adolfo had lived in much worse. He heard a window air-conditioner blowing full blast in the adjoining bedroom. It struggled to stay ahead of the heat and humidity.

She pulled a small wooden chair with a cane bottom into the center of the room. "Sit," she said and took her place on the couch facing him.

"¿Dónde está el dinero?"

Adolfo reached into his backpack and pulled out an envelope. She snatched it and tore it open, quickly counting. *"Bien."*

"Welcome to my home," she said in superb English. "From this day forward in this home, we will speak only English. You will speak only English outside my home as well, and if I ever hear you speaking or reading or watching anything on TV in Spanish, I will report you to the *Señor*. Do you understand?"

"Yes."

"And his name will never be spoken, no matter what. And you are known here as Adolfo Ayala, the grandson of my brother in Tampico. His only daughter, your mother, died and you came to live with me. Do you understand?"

"Yes."

She reached into a pocket in her apron and dramatically unfolded a piece of paper. She held it at arm's length.

"These rules are written in English, and I am going to read them to you one at a time. These are my rules for you." She read them to him slowly, then gave him the paper. "You read these over many times today and ask me questions about them. After today, you know all my rules, so if you break one, I know it is on purpose."

"I will follow the rules," he said.

"They say you are thirteen. Is this true?"

Adolfo made sure he understood her before he answered. "Yes."

"You look much older. Maybe because you are tall, and white."

Adolfo stood quietly, concentrating on her words.

"Starting next Monday your tutor starts. She will come here every day of the week and teach you from nine in the morning until two in the afternoon. Saturday is cleaning day for you and me, and Sunday is Church. I will show you your room."

She led him through the kitchen to a small bedroom with a dirty window. There was a single bed, a wooden desk and chair, and paper and a pencil on the desk. A bare bulb hung from electric wires in the ceiling. She grabbed the string hanging from the bulb. It was brown with age. She turned the bare bulb on, then off. "Only for night-time. Do not waste electricity in the day."

Adolfo sat at the desk and began reading the rules written in English while his recollection of her reciting them was fresh.

"Dinner is at six o'clock," Dominica said and left his room.

The next morning, the big yellow cat scratching the wooden chair in his room woke him. Dominica sat a bowl of cold beans, rice, and a store-bought flour tortilla in front of him and left for work at a local factory. "The tutor will be here at nine."

Adolfo sat on the front steps for a few minutes to watch the neighborhood activity and smoke an unfiltered cigarette. At nine sharp, there was a knock on the door. A young, white woman holding a stack of books appeared surprised when he opened it. She glanced at her notepad and the number over the door.

"Are you the tutor?" Adolfo asked.

She smiled and walked in, relieved. She extended her hand.

"Bethany Clark," she said. "You can call me Beth."

"Adolfo Ayala," he said and shook her hand.

Beth put down her books on the kitchen table and they sat. "This is probably the best place to work for now," she said.

Adolfo smiled. He knew some time in the future he would have sex with Beth. He had many experiences starting at age ten with older girls in Tampico and Madero, and he knew how to flirt. Beth was blonde with glasses, plain but not unattractive. He liked her skin, little makeup. He would study to make his English perfect, and later he would start having sex with her. By then she would want to. Adolfo knew that's how it would go.

"Do you speak any English?"

"Yes," he said.

"Good. Where are you from?"

"Tampico. You?"

"Harlingen. East of here."

He said nothing.

"I moved here for a teaching job and it's been postponed. You know? Postponed?"

"Later," he said.

"Right. Very good. How old are you, Adolfo?"

"You say."

"All right." She studied him for a moment. "Seventeen?"

He grinned. "Very good. And you?"

She laughed and touched his arm. "A lady is not supposed to tell her age, but I'll tell you. Twenty-two. You never went to school in Tampico?"

"No. I can read. Spanish and English."

"Math?"

"I work with money."

"You can make change?"

"Yes."

"All right. Mrs. Ayala told me on the phone that we are to go over subjects from the first grade through seventh, to catch you up so you can go to school here in McAllen and start at grade eight."

"Yes."

"Let's start with your letters."

Adolfo soaked up English and math. He was like a machine, dedicated to fulfilling Bernal's confidence and one day being rich and owning a house as grand as his. Every day after Beth left he fed the cats then did his homework. If he finished his homework before Dominica came home, he read the novels and history books that Beth loaned him.

On Saturdays he worked hard cleaning, and on Sundays he accompanied Dominica to Mass, the only day of the week he left the house and his studies. She told everyone at Mass he was her great nephew from Tampico. People were friendly to him but he could tell no one liked Dominica. He did not care that she was a mean old lady. She did for him exactly what she said she would, gave him a place to live and study with the tutor. He asked for no more.

Adolfo listened to Dominica report his progress when Señor Bernal called. She told the truth. Adolfo was speaking English more like a gringo every day, and he would be ready to start school in the fall.

In the late spring, after many months of hard work, Adolfo reached his grade level and began to get restless. He began his seduction of Beth. It was easy. He knew she liked him, and she was not accustomed to having the attention of boys. The study

82

of his elementary subjects was over, and now they spent much of the five hours talking. One thing led to another, until every day they started with sex, and then did it again before she left. In early June, Adolfo told the old lady Dominica he no longer needed a tutor. Dominica was not sure, but Adolfo told her she could keep the money herself instead of paying the tutor. Dominica considered that for a moment, and agreed it was time. She told Beth.

Beth cried when she talked to Adolfo, and said she wanted to come see him anyway. But he was bored with her. She kept sending him notes and dropping in when Dominica was at work. Adolfo told her he was thirteen, not seventeen, and if she came to the house again, he would call the police and tell them she seduced him. He never heard from her after that.

Adolfo convinced Dominica to let him explore McAllen in the two months before he started school. Dominica was reluctant, but with her work, could not keep an eye on him. She agreed as long as he kept up his English and finished the books on the reading list Beth left.

In the city, Adolfo became accustomed to people staring at him. He spoke to shopkeepers from time to time, telling them in his unaccented English he was a tourist from Houston, in town with his parents. They treated him like a gringo.

Young people in town did not know what to make of Adolfo. He liked being an enigma, a young man not easy to figure out. In learning about the cross-border drug trade from boys his age in town, he realized the wisdom of Señor Bernal in recognizing how valuable Adolfo would be to the cartel, a Mexican made tough on the streets of Tampico who spoke English like a *norteamericano*. It made him feel powerful.

School started. Some of the young people whom he had met in the summer were a grade or two ahead of him. The Mexican teens first called him the white Mexican, then *Blanco*. The white girls paid attention to Adolfo because he was tall and handsome, and he spoke English like them. Once they knew his name, they withdrew, not sure what he was. *Blanco* intrigued the Mexican girls, but the boys saw him as a rival with an unfair advantage. White boys ignored him because he did not fit in. It was fine with Adolfo if they did not like him.

Adolfo did not need any of them. He smoked pot sometimes with the Mexican boys in the *arroyos* south of town between the airport and the Rio Grande.

A group of white boys led by John Kirkpatrick made it their business to make Adolfo miserable. Kirkpatrick was the son of the McAllen fire chief. He was popular with the whites and called Adolfo "vanilla bean" or muttered "half-breed" whenever he saw him. Kirkpatrick was relentless in his degrading comments to Adolfo in the two years Adolfo stayed in school in McAllen. Other white boys with Kirkpatrick followed suit, but Adolfo could not afford to get in any trouble at school. Adolfo knew he would settle up with John Kirkpatrick someday; no need to rush.

In spring of Adolfo's eighth grade year, he left the skating rink with a classmate named José and several other Mexicans to a local park to buy some grass. Adolfo hung back while José negotiated with the dealer Gonzo. Gonzo noticed Adolfo and asked José about him. Gonzo said he wasn't selling his grass "to no gringo," and pushed José. José stood his ground and shook his fist at Gonzo, who pulled a switchblade.

José backed away and gestured for his friends to leave with him. Adolfo told them to wait. He walked over to Gonzo. He spoke to the dealer in the language he learned on the streets of Tampico. Gonzo raised the switchblade and Adolfo grabbed his wrist, then put all his strength into his other fist and rammed it into Gonzo's throat. Gonzo dropped the knife and began choking and coughing. Adolfo moved to Gonzo's stash and picked up a small baggie of grass, tossed two dollars at Gonzo, and walked away.

When he got home, he called Señor Bernal to let him know what happened.

Though Adolfo saw Gonzo several times over the next year, the dealer indicated with body language he respected Adolfo and did not want to bother him. Adolfo knew Señor Bernal must have put out the word, because *machismo* would have forced Gonzo to retaliate.

The ninth grade passed quickly. Adolfo liked his studies, even algebra, and made A's and B's. The Mexicans liked him, but John Kirkpatrick and the whites around him still treated Adolfo badly. Adolfo grew taller and his chest and shoulders grew thicker. By the end of the year, he looked older than many of the white seniors, and all of the Mexicans.

Adolfo had experienced enough school. He was ready to work.

Adolfo asked Dominica to call Señor Bernal to ask if Adolfo could come see him in Tampico after school ended. She made the call and told Adolfo Señor Bernal agreed. He stuffed a duffel bag with the clothes he wanted to take and said goodbye to Dominica.

He gave her his hand to shake, but the old lady grabbed him and pulled him to her, squeezing him tight. "You came to me a boy, but you are leaving a man." She had never hugged him in the almost three years, but now she cried, and Adolfo did not know quite what to make of it. It made him uncomfortable. He patted her on the upper arm and smiled the way he thought she would like.

"I'll be in town off and on from now on. If you like, I can stay here when I am in town. I will have money and will pay you for your room and your food."

She cupped his face in her hands, pulled him to her and kissed him on the forehead.

Adolfo walked out of the little house and never saw Dominica Ayala or her two nasty cats again.

Chapter Seventeen

The Friday run was always the best for Willie Mitchell. Two days until the next run, unless he got restless and decided to run Sunday. This Friday, the iPod was shuffling good songs his way. Lionel Richie's "All Night Long" started just as Willie Mitchell began to pick up the pace for his final half-mile.

He cruised into Jimmy Gray's driveway with energy to spare, and cut off his iPod, ready to walk with his fat friend. Jimmy's enthusiasm for his exercise regimen was waning and Willie Mitchell had to make sure he continued to badger and shame Jimmy into walking at least Monday, Wednesday, and Friday at the end of Willie Mitchell's run. He had to make Jimmy exercise and extend his life—he was his closest friend, and he did not want to lose him.

Jimmy dashed out on his tiptoes, spinning with his right index finger touching the center of his skull and his left arm akimbo. A three hundred five pound ballerina in long red shorts.

Willie Mitchell laughed out loud. "Where's your tutu?"

"Don't mess with my toot toot," Jimmy sang.

"What is a toot toot, anyway?"

"Who sang it?"

"No idea," Willie Mitchell said.

"Rockin' Sidney Simien from Ville Platte, Louisiana on his 1984 zydeco album. You owe me two bits."

Willie Mitchell stared at Jimmy. No way Jimmy knew that.

"I Googled it right before you got here. I knew you'd make some tutu comment."

"Let's go," Willie Mitchell said and started his stop watch.

It took four minutes for Jimmy to start breathing heavily.

"When's your meeting?" Jimmy asked between gasps.

"One o'clock. He's going to look at the jail about twelve-thirty."

"What for?"

"He's got the right. We're still under a consent decree with the Justice Department."

"I thought they supervised that out of Oxford."

"They do, but it's all one federal agency. Any U.S. attorney gets to see our jail if he wants."

"But *why* does he want to look at it?"

"I've got my suspicions, but I don't know. Whatever his reason it's not good. You know what they say. 'I'm from the government and I'm here to help you'."

"Yep. FDIC auditors give me the willies. You know this Whitman guy at all?"

"I've met him a few times, just chit chat stuff. Jake says he's smart as a whip. Kind of an academic."

"Got any common sense? Lot of those federal types don't."

"I don't know. He's never tried a case before a jury his entire career."

"How do you know that?"

"Jake."

"Martha said Jake's bringing a girl with him."

"FBI agent he's been seeing down there."

"Not sure I'd want to date a girl who carries a gun."

"He says she's a crack shot, too."

Jimmy raised his eyebrows.

"Don't say it," Willie Mitchell said. "Don't say any sentence that has the word crack in it. This could be my daughter-in-law."

"Really?"

"No, but you need to practice being nice."

"What for?"

"I don't know. You just do."

"Next Wednesday's the third anniversary."

"I know."

"You available?"

"I told you I'll never miss it. I'll pick you up."

Jimmy Gray's eyes were watery. Willie Mitchell promised Jimmy he'd go every year on the anniversary of Beau's death to the fence where Jimmy's youngest son was crossing when his hunting rifle fell and killed him. Beau was the apple of his father's eye.

Willie Mitchell jogged the few blocks from Jimmy's driveway to his house to clean up and get to the office. Susan sat at the pine table in the kitchen, a mug of coffee in front of her.

"How was your run?" she asked.

"Hot." He kissed her on the cheek and she grimaced.

"I know. I'm headed to the shower."

"Ina cleaned the guest room. It's ready for the FBI agent."

"Good. You give any more thought to the project to help with the teenage pregnancy thing?"

"I've thought about it and gotten some statistics from the county. I'm just not sure I want to tackle it."

"Why not?"

"If I got the project under way, the number of girls I could realistically help... ." She paused. "I just don't think I could make a difference. Do you know what percentage of teenaged girls giving birth in Yaloquena county are unwed mothers?"

"I'm sure it's high."

"Seventy-five percent. I might be able to help maybe one-tenth."

Willie Mitchell whistled. "Man-oh-man," he said and hustled upstairs to shower, dress, and get to the office.

At one o'clock that afternoon, Ethel walked in his office.

"The U.S. attorney is here. So is Jake, and a pretty young lady who says she's with the FBI."

"What about Lee Jones?"

"The sheriff is with them."

"Ask them to come in," Willie Mitchell said, and dragged in two additional chairs from the small conference room just outside his inner sanctum.

Jake stopped at the door and gestured for his boss to precede him. Leopold Whitman walked in wearing a tan poplin suit, his beard neatly trimmed. He shook Willie Mitchell's hand.

"Good to see you again, Willie Mitchell," Whitman said.

"You too, Leopold." Willie Mitchell gestured to Jake. "You getting any work out of Jake down there?"

Leopold Whitman glanced at Jake and turned back to Willie Mitchell with a twisted smile, an awkward attempt at charm. Willie Mitchell picked up impressions better than anyone he knew, except the late Katherine Banks, from whom he inherited his ability. His feelings were always on the money, and he was picking up an unfriendly, sneaky vibe from the U.S. attorney that told him Leopold Whitman was not a man to trust. He was not here to help.

"Jake's doing quite well in our system. Quite well."

Jake inherited the ability too, and was the only other person in the room to pick up on the tension. He stepped forward and half-turned toward Kitty, giving part of his back to his boss. "This is Kitty Douglas, Daddy, the FBI agent I told you and Mom about."

Willie Mitchell extended his hand and Kitty gave him a firm handshake. "Nice to meet you, Kitty," he said. She was prettier than he imagined.

"Let's all have a seat," Willie Mitchell said. "Well, Leopold, what did you think of our state of the art facility upstairs?"

Jake and Sheriff Jones chuckled. Whitman managed another piss-poor smile that just did not work.

"Frankly, I am appalled at what I saw."

There was silence for a moment. The arrogance and condescension in his tone was evident to everyone in the room, not just Willie Mitchell and Jake.

"It's an old facility," Willie Mitchell said. "This is an impoverished county with high unemployment and a disappearing tax base. Mississippi has no funds to offer to build a new facility, nor does your employer," Willie Mitchell taking the opportunity to remind the little prick that he was just an employee of the government, way down on the food chain in Mississippi, the southern state the career bureaucrats in the Justice Department loved to hate the most. "We're in full compliance with the consent decree handed down in Oxford four years ago. There are many old jails in the Delta that are worse than ours. Much worse."

"I understand," Whitman said. "But the situation upstairs is problematic for me. You see, Willie Mitchell, in my position I am responsible for bringing the full weight and force of our government against Mr. Zegarra to force him to provide information to help us break down the powerful cartel for whom he works. He has literally dropped in my lap, and I would be remiss if I did not do everything in my power to extract the knowledge he has of the cartel structure to bring it to its knees and stem the flow of illegal drugs into my jurisdiction."

"We're all in favor of doing that," Willie Mitchell said. "But Zegarra killed one of the best law enforcement officers in this county."

"A good family man, and a good friend of mine," Lee Jones said. He turned in his seat to face the U.S. attorney. "I've sworn an oath that I will be there at Parchman when they inject him with the drug."

"That will not bring your officer back," Whitman said.

"You're right, but it'll sure kill the son of a bitch that murdered him for no good reason," the sheriff said directly to Whitman.

Jake sat up. "Maybe we can work something out with his lawyer to allow the FBI and DEA to question him here—" Jake stopped when his boss Leopold Whitman glared at him.

Which really pissed Willie Mitchell off. He knew Jake was already a better lawyer than the effete, meddlesome shrimp in charge.

"Out of the question," Whitman said. "Zegarra should be in federal custody right now. The security upstairs is abominable. The cartel almost broke him out his first day you had him. Undoubtedly they'll try again and probably succeed."

"We're ready for them," Lee said.

Whitman uttered a dismissive "*humph*" at the idea.

"All right," Willie Mitchell said. "I think we're all after the same thing here."

"I don't think we are," Whitman said. "Have you ever read the supremacy clause of the Constitution?"

"Do you mean the actual words of Article Six, paragraph two, or what the Warren Court claimed it said?" Willie Mitchell said.

The U.S. attorney sat back in his chair.

"There's nothing in the U.S. Constitution," Willie Mitchell said, "even seen through the eyes of the most liberal of Supreme Court justices that allows a federal prosecution to supersede a state court murder prosecution when the state has physical custody of the offender."

"I don't think that's correct," Whitman said.

"Have you read the cases?"

The U.S. attorney did not respond.

"Well, I have. And they say that physical custody of the defendant is paramount in determining which jurisdiction gets to proceed."

"I can get a writ of *habeas corpus ad testificandum*," Whitman said.

"Does not allow you to take custody. Only allows you to take testimony from the defendant in Sheriff Jones's jail. It does not permit you to remove him from here to federal detention."

"We'll see about that."

"Read 'United States of America versus State of Georgia In re Samuel Tolliver.' I don't have the citation in front of me, but it's a Fifth Circuit case exactly on point. The Supreme Court denied writs."

Leopold Whitman rose. His ears were crimson.

"This is unbelievable. I am giving you the opportunity to save your county the expense of a capital murder trial. You're not going to be able to get the death penalty anyway."

Every eye turned to the U.S. attorney.

"We most certainly will," Sheriff Jones said.

Jake started to speak but Willie Mitchell gestured for him to wait.

"What is it you think you know, Mr. Whitman?" Willie Mitchell said. "Why don't you share it with us?"

"I don't think. I know for a fact that Mrs. Frances Ware, the deceased's widow, is opposed to the death penalty on religious and moral grounds."

"And how do you know that?" Sheriff Jones asked.

"Two of our agents interviewed her."

Kitty reacted. Willie Mitchell could tell this was news to her. "DEA agents out of D.C."

Willie Mitchell knew Sheriff Lee Jones well. He could tell from the way Lee stared at the U.S. attorney that he was fuming.

"Whatever happened to comity between the systems?" Willie Mitchell said. "Or at least common courtesy? Your predecessor always let me know when they were going to talk to one of our witnesses."

"She's not a witness."

"She will be testifying at the sentencing hearing."

"She was not a witness to the incident."

"I'm sure you've never handled a sentencing hearing," Willie Mitchell said, "because if you had, you'd know that the widow gets to tell the jury what kind of man her husband was and what he meant to her family and the community. I don't guess you've had any testimony like that in any of the jury trials you've handled in the federal system."

The U.S. attorney's face was now a deeper shade of red than his ears.

"I've never been pregnant, either, Mr. Banks, but my wife has, and I have a good grasp of every step of that process."

Whitman walked toward the door and stopped. "Two things," he said. "First, I would ask you to take into account the widow's feeling about the death penalty and consider offering to take it off the table in your murder prosecution."

"No way," Lee said.

"Let him finish," Willie Mitchell said.

"And allow us to make it part of our negotiations with Zegarra and his attorney to get him to cooperate."

"And second?" Willie Mitchell said.

"Do your part to destroy the cartel and help the federal government stop the flow of illegal drugs across our southern border."

"That it?" Willie Mitchell said. "I can give you my answer now."

Leopold Whitman waited.

"Drugs have been pouring into this country through Mexico and the Gulf of Mexico for at least thirty-five years," Willie Mitchell said. "There's more coming across the border now than ever before. The feds have been making deals with men like Zegarra all that time, and nothing you've done has had any impact whatsoever. I'll talk to Frances Ware, and so will Lee, but no matter what the widow says, we're keeping the death penalty in the case. This ain't the Los Angeles D.A.'s office and

Zegarra ain't O.J. Simpson." Willie Mitchell raised one finger. "You've demonstrated you cannot stop the flow of drugs across the border, but I guarantee you this one thing: I can and will put Adolfo Zegarra Galván to death in Parchman Farm and he'll never kill again. And, Mr. Whitman, after he's dead, he'll never distribute another ounce of cocaine."

"We'll be in touch," the U.S. attorney said. "The U.S. Marshal's Service will be serving you with papers soon. We'll let someone else decide this issue."

He walked out.

Willie Mitchell smiled at Jake's friend. "So, Kitty, is this your first intergovernmental conference on jurisdictional issues?"

Jake exhaled audibly and chuckled.

"Yes, sir," Kitty said. "Are they all like this?"

"Not exactly," Willie Mitchell said and turned to the sheriff, who had yet to smile. "Lee, you better give Rose Jackson's office a call. See if she can talk to us for ten minutes sometime Monday morning."

Chapter Eighteen

Jake told Willie Mitchell he was going to give Kitty a tour of Sunshine and left the courthouse. She had ridden from Jackson with Jake in his 4Runner. Jake was glad he wasn't riding back to Jackson with the U.S. attorney.

What a pompous ass Leopold turned out to be.

"You want to drop our stuff by the house and meet my mother? There's really nothing to tour. After this weekend, you'll have seen everything there is to see around here, whether you intended to or not."

"Sure, but I'd really like to run."

"Now? It's pretty hot."

"We don't have to run far. After that meeting I'd like to work the stress out."

"What did you think of that?"

"Your Dad's cool. Smooth under pressure and smarter than Whitman. You didn't tell me how handsome Willie Mitchell was."

Jake shrugged.

"You see how red in the face Whitman got?" she asked.

"Because he's not used to people standing up to him. Daddy's tried so many murder trials and been under the gun so much it'd take a lot more than Whitman can muster to get to him."

"You don't think Whitman got under his skin a little?"

"Nope. He was just telling Leopold how it's going to be."

Jake pulled the 4Runner into the circular pea gravel drive in front of the house. He grabbed his canvas duffel bag and Kitty's soft leather bag, and walked up the front steps. Kitty stopped at the base of the steps and looked up, following the big white columns to the portico extending from the roof above the second story.

"Some house," she said.

"It's old. My grandparents lived here before us. You sure you want to run? It's a little too warm if you ask me."

"I've got to get the kinks out. And after we run, I want to arm wrestle."

He laughed and winked. "Now I get it. But you've never won."

"There's always a first time."

Jake said quietly, "We can drive out to our duck camp and run on the turn rows a mile and a half out, then back. Three miles is plenty in this heat. We can arm wrestle at the camp."

"You're on," she said.

He knocked on the front door.

"You knock?"

"When I'm by myself I park in the garage and go in the side door, but Mother says when we bring someone home for the first time, always bring them in the front door. She keeps it locked."

"Why the front door?"

"She says that's the way it's supposed to be done."

He shrugged and Susan opened the door. She took Kitty's hand.

"Mom, this is Kitty Douglas."

"Come in," she said, half singing, her voice an octave higher than usual. "It's so nice to meet you, Kitty. I'm so glad Jake brought you home with him this weekend."

"Thank you. It's nice to meet you, Mrs. Banks."

"Please. Call me Susan. I feel old enough as it is."

Susan gave Jake a big hug and stuck her arm through his, walking together into the wide entrance hall and stopping at the base of the stairs. Trailing behind, Kitty glanced in all the rooms on the way.

"I've never been inside a house like this," Kitty said. "And the furniture. Are they all antiques?"

"Most of them Willie Mitchell inherited from his folks. It was all here when we moved in."

"This is nice, Susan."

Susan touched Kitty's arm. "You're even prettier than Jake said you were."

Jake noticed Kitty was uncomfortable.

"Now Jake," Susan said, "I've put Kitty in the guest room upstairs. All the linens are fresh. Ina made sure of that." She turned to Kitty. "Your bathroom adjoins your bedroom, so you don't have to share."

"Great," Kitty said.

"We're going to go for a run out in the country, Mom."

"Okay. Jake tells me you're quite an athlete."

"Not as good as he is."

"Would you like some fruit or iced tea?"

Kitty deferred to Jake. Jake said, "That would be great. We'll go get our stuff on and be right down."

After they snacked on apple and melon slices and mild Edam cheese, then jumped in the 4Runner.

"She's nice," Kitty said. "So gracious."

"Mother's a real Southern lady." He paused. "And when someone tells you that you're pretty, you should say thank you."

94

"Well, I never know what to say."

"Now you do."

Jake drove Kitty to the nine hundred ninety-acre farm Willie Mitchell inherited from his parents and leased to the Hudson brothers for a quarter of the crop. Jake showed her the private cemetery in the corner of the farm where his grandparents and great grandparents on the Banks side were buried.

They drove north from Highway 82 about seven miles and turned off the blacktop onto the dirt road leading to the Banks' duck camp. After a couple of miles, he pulled up to a frame cabin built on piers out over a black water pond dotted with cypress trees. They walked in and Jake turned on the air conditioner.

"Air's kind of stale in here. It won't be exactly cool when we get back, but it will be a little fresher and won't be so hot."

She walked out on the back porch. "This is like Jurassic Park."

Jake stripped off his shirt and tossed it on the sofa. "Let's go."

They took off, Kitty leaping from the front porch and hitting the ground running, skipping the steps. Jake laughed and followed after her, admiring her figure. She wore black spandex shorts and a white jog bra. She had an odd stride, picking up her feet much higher than he did, almost bouncing. Jake ran economically, sliding his feet just above the ground and barely moving his arms. When he sprinted, he pumped his arms to increase speed. On social runs with Kitty, he preserved his strength. When he tired, he energized himself by dropping back and running behind Kitty, his eyes on her perfect backside.

They passed catfish ponds, aerators working overtime in the heat to keep the water oxygenated and prevent a fish kill. Jake stopped and threw a rock at a cormorant swimming in the pond.

"Why'd you do that?" she asked.

"They eat the catfish."

Kitty pointed to a rusted grain silo overgrown with kudzu. Jake signaled to turn around and head back, and he took off with a burst leaving her yards behind. When he slowed, he knew from past experience she would blow past him in a matter of seconds.

They sat on the duck camp porch, catching their breath and sweating. She took off her shoes and rubbed his sweaty bare back. He took off his, leaned over and kissed her. She held his eyes as she took off her top.

"You ready to arm wrestle?" she asked.

95

They walked in and Jake locked the front and back doors.

He pulled a wooden picnic table out into the center of the room and they both stripped. Sitting across the table from each other, naked, they placed their right elbows on the table and gripped hands that were wet with perspiration.

Jake had never encountered a girl with such strength. He was stronger, but it was a struggle to put her down. She used every ounce of power and body English she could muster to counteract his strength, but after a while Jake prevailed, and pulled the back of her glistening forearm gently down until it touched the table.

Like every time before, they kissed across the table. Long, slow kisses—until Jake could stand it no longer. He led her to the bed and they made passionate love, moving together in rhythm. Jake had never encountered such athleticism and stamina. Their ferocious completions together left them dripping, spent.

Jake rolled onto his back and rested the back of his hand on his forehead. Eyes closed, he thought about the two of them. Their physical relationship started in Jackson the evening he kissed her in the BMW. Their first sexual encounter took his breath away. Jake had never been with such a strong-willed, forceful woman. She was beautiful and aggressive; her body sleek, muscular.

Jake had begun to like her—a lot.

Even exercising with Kitty was a trip. He had never before enjoyed working out or running with a woman. She was a great athlete, smart, and funny in an unusual, direct sort of way. Jake hoped she would learn a few Southern female traits during her tour of duty in Jackson. Maybe Susan would rub off on her.

Jake opened his eyes and studied the beaded-pine ceiling. He remembered he was with Willie Mitchell at the used materials yard west of downtown Sunshine when he picked it out for the camp interior. Jake figured he would have been about ten. He thought of all the great duck hunts he and Scott shared with Willie Mitchell at the camp, especially when the winters were dry and their pond was a welcome sight for mallards, teal, and pintails on their yearly flight from Canada to Mexico via the Mississippi flyway. Lots of cold mornings they woke up in the bunk beds with Beau Gray and his older brother Jimmy Jr., and paddled in the darkness from the camp to their duck blind brushed with cypress and willow limbs in the center of the pond. He chuckled remembering the time the big water moccasin was curled up inside the blind and Beau was the first one in.

Jake listened to Kitty breathe, then leaned on his elbow and kissed her on the cheek. "We better get going."

"We can't do this in your house, can we?"

"No way," Jake said.

"Then let's stay here just a little longer," she said, moving her hand from his chest, past his stomach and further down.

"You bring up an excellent point, Special Agent Douglas," he said rolling onto his back again. He closed his eyes as Kitty continued.

~ * ~

Kitty sat at the dining room table, confronted by two spoons, two forks, and something on the table above her plate that was a combination fork and spoon. Susan called it a spork. Only one knife, thank God. The silver flatware was old and heavy, with an ornate B engraved on the handles. The china was beautiful, and fragile. Jake referred to it as their "good china." All the crystal was Waterford. A tumbler with ice water and a crystal wine glass sat northeast of the plate on crystal coasters. Kitty fingered the white tablecloth, which she thought was some sort of thick linen. Susan served a broccoli casserole and broiled chicken with a green salad and fresh fruit.

She hoped Susan did not notice her watching Jake pick up his utensils before she touched hers. "Everything is so delicious," Kitty said. "And the table is so... elegant."

Willie Mitchell raised his wine glass. "Here's to two beautiful girls."

The two couples clinked glasses all around. "I guess it's okay to toast ourselves." Susan raised her glass to Willie Mitchell.

"Now, tell us something about your folks," Susan said.

Kitty was grateful to Jake for warning him on the ride up from Jackson. She had given some thought to how she would answer when Susan asked. Jake reminded Kitty his mother was not being nosy, it's just how Southerners communicate. Kitty decided Jake was right in his advice; there is no substitute for the truth.

"I never knew my father. My mother was from Tacoma and she raised me by herself. She didn't have any other children."

"That must have been hard," Susan said.

"We didn't have any money. She worked in a cannery and I went to public schools then to Washington State on a soccer scholarship."

"Here's to the Huskies and to Title Nine," Willie Mitchell said and raised his glass.

"Cougars," she said.

"It was a full ride," Jake said. "She made all-PAC Ten her junior and senior years. First team."

"Great," Willie Mitchell said. "I'm impressed."

"Do you see your mother much?" Susan asked.

Kitty saw Jake's subtle, encouraging wink. "No." She paused. "She's in an institution. She had kind of a nervous breakdown when I was in college, and I went through the commitment process and got her placed in a state mental facility."

"Can you talk to her?" Susan asked.

"She doesn't know who I am or where she is. The doctors say it's developed into some sort of dementia, extremely early onset, and she won't be getting better."

Susan's eyes filled with tears. She placed her hand on Kitty's. "I'm so sorry."

There were no tears in Kitty's eyes. "It's okay, really. She doesn't suffer. She's just kind of... not there."

Willie Mitchell stood behind Susan's chair. "Let's serve the dessert," he said. Susan pushed away from the table as Willie Mitchell pulled out her chair.

After their slices of buttermilk pie, Jake and Kitty cleared the table and helped scrape the plates and put things away or in the refrigerator. Kitty watched Susan at the sink soaking the silver flatware and the china, then washing each piece by hand. Willie Mitchell dried.

"I don't put these things in the dishwasher," Susan said to Kitty. "I know it's old-fashioned but I don't mind doing them by hand."

Kitty grabbed a towel and began drying. Susan turned to the men. "Let Kitty and me finish up. There's not much left to do."

Willie Mitchell and Jake left the kitchen. The swinging door to the dining room eventually stopped. Kitty concentrated on drying the china carefully. When she put the first plate on the worm-eaten pine table, she turned back and Susan was staring at her with tears streaming down her cheeks.

"I'm so sorry about your mother. And I admire you for all you've accomplished on your own. I know it hasn't been easy."

Susan hugged her tight, and Kitty hugged her back. They separated and Kitty was surprised to feel tears in her own eyes.

Kitty had not cried in years, and wasn't sure why she was crying now. She did not think about her mother that often. Maybe, she figured, that's exactly why she was crying.

In the guest room that night, Kitty lay in the darkness, waiting for sleep. She thought about her mother in the state facility. Kitty had reminded herself over and over that the doctor said she did not suffer, and was not aware of her surroundings. He said Kitty could not take care of her—she had to be in an institution. Before the breakdown, Kitty remembered her mother as acutely aware of their modest circumstances. Her mother hated their poverty and her job, suffering to the point of depression.

Kitty blamed her mother for not doing something about it. Her mother was intelligent, but weak. She was too feminine and deferred to the men that came around the house when Kitty was young. Kitty hated watching her mother act that way, coquettish and subservient. The men would boss her around and she would take it. Kitty wanted her to stand up to them and make them leave, but her mother would not do it.

"Having a strong-willed, real man around is better than not having any man at all," her mother said.

From those childhood days on, Kitty swore she would never be weak like her mother. She vowed to control her own destiny, an attitude that had cost her the boyfriend in Washington State. He said he loved her. She said the same but wasn't sure. He wanted more say so about her life than she was willing to let him have. He hated the idea of the FBI and told her if she took the job he was through with her.

That was all he needed to say to Kitty. She took the job. A month later he tracked her down and called to ask her to come back to marry him. It was then she was positive she never really loved him, because once she took the FBI job and went off to training, she never looked back. She never missed him. Marrying her old boyfriend and becoming a housewife in Pullman, Washington was the last thing on her mind.

Kitty heard a board creak in the hall outside the guest bedroom and hoped it was not Jake. She held her breath and listened.

There were no other sounds from the other side of her door, so she chalked it up to the old house. Jake better not try to sneak in her room. Not that she wasn't interested, but after meeting Susan, Kitty would never do anything that might make Susan look with disfavor on her.

She thought about the first day she met Jake on I-55. She was physically attracted to him immediately, but did not want him to know it. She was hit on every day at Quantico, and had built up her defenses. Kitty was called a dyke more than once by the jarheads she trained with, but that was all right. She knew she swaggered like an athlete and was stronger than most women. She'd rather men think of her as masculine rather than be perceived as a weak, girly woman to be pushed around and taken advantage of like her mother.

She liked Jake and liked making love with him. He was strong and self-confident. Jake was amped up around her, the opposite of her laid-back Washington State boyfriend. Jake's dad was cool. His mom, Kitty wasn't sure about. Susan seemed genuine and intelligent, but she was a housewife, the kind of woman Kitty did not want to become. She knew that was unfair, to judge another woman who grew up at a different time under different circumstances. Susan's tears were real when they talked about Kitty's mother, and her empathy was heartfelt.

Kitty decided to give herself some time to evaluate Susan. Susan did have a good life. Jake had told Kitty his parents separated for three years and got back together a year ago. As she finally drifted off to sleep, she wondered what that was all about.

Chapter Nineteen

Monday morning, Sheriff Jones sat close to Willie Mitchell's desk.

"Wonder how long we're going to be on hold?" Lee asked.

Willie Mitchell shrugged. "Long as it takes. We may be wasting our time, but politics plays a big part in Justice Department prosecution policy, and I don't want us to be the only ones not talking to someone up there in Washington."

Ethel walked in. "She's on line two."

Willie Mitchell punched the phone button and the speaker function. "Good morning, Congresswoman. This is Willie Mitchell Banks in Sunshine. How are you?"

"On the run, as usual," she said. "Is Lee there with you?"

"Right here, Rose," Lee Jones said. "Thanks for talking to us."

"I'm always here for you two. What's going on down there?"

"We've got the U.S. attorney for the Southern District in Jackson making noises like he's going to try to take our prisoner from us, the Zegarra fellow that shot and killed Travis Ware."

"And we plan to try him for capital murder and execute him—without the Justice Department's help," Lee Jones added.

"I know about Deputy Ware's death. I read about it in the papers. My Greenville office manager called me, too. We've reached out to Mrs. Ware."

"That's nice of you, Congresswoman," Willie Mitchell said.

"What can I do to help you?"

"Justice Department seems to think Zegarra's drug operations are more important than Deputy Ware's life, and they're going to be filing something to try to take custody and pre-empt our murder prosecution."

"Nobody in the Delta wants that to happen, Rose."

Willie Mitchell gave Lee a thumbs up for letting the Washington politician hear what her voters are thinking. Rose Jackson was the first black woman elected to represent the Delta in Congress.

"I have a contact at Justice," she said, "who is close to the attorney general. Let me make a call and see what's shaking over there."

"Congresswoman," Willie Mitchell said, "that would be great, and you can tell the Justice Department they can have him after we finish prosecuting him, and the trial will take place in less than sixty days."

"All right," she said. "Anything else?"

"Not today. Thank you, Congresswoman Jackson."

"You're welcome, Mr. D.A. And Lee, you tell that pretty wife of yours hello."

"Will do. Thanks, Rose."

Willie Mitchell disconnected. The sheriff appeared surprised.

"You think Department of Corrections will really let the feds take him after you convict him?"

"Not no, but *hell* no. But no need to clutter up our distinguished Congresswoman's mind with that sort of thing."

Lee left and Willie Mitchell went home to eat his oatmeal. He read the *Wall Street Journal* for fifteen minutes in his easy chair then returned to work.

Walking through the corridor on the first floor of the courthouse, Lee waved him down and handed him a document. "We got a situation."

"This is bull shit," Willie Mitchell said after checking the motion and order. "Who served this?"

"They're in my office."

Willie Mitchell and Lee walked into the sheriff's office. The office was cramped, painfully small. The men sat close.

"This writ is unenforceable," Willie Mitchell blurted, then remembered his manners. "Sorry." He extended his hand. "I'm Willie Mitchell Banks, district attorney. I assume you've met the sheriff."

Both men said yes.

"I'd like to see your identification."

One man leaned over and removed his wallet from his hip; the other, bigger and bulkier, reached inside his sport coat. Willie Mitchell studied their identification. He compared the ID photos with the men before him.

"U.S. Marshal and DEA," he said. "You guys must be expecting trouble out of us."

They smiled. "No, sir," the bigger man from DEA said. "We're just serving the court order. We're not here to make trouble."

"No way," the U.S. marshal said.

"You guys are just doing your jobs. This writ is not worth the paper it's written on and has no legal effect *vis a vis* Zegarra. The U.S. district court does not have the authority to interfere with our custody on the capital murder charge."

"These guys told me they don't want to take him," Lee said.

"Up to us, we'd help you fry the bastard on the murder charge," the bigger man said.

"Okay," Willie Mitchell said, "I'd like for you to step outside and call Mr. Whitman. Tell him this order is illegal and we are not releasing the prisoner. We have a hearing set at ten o'clock in the morning before Judge Zelda Williams, and he needs to be here with any statute or case that gives him the constitutional authority to remove Zegarra, and we'll see what Judge Williams says."

The men left with their writ. "See you tomorrow," DEA said. "Hope you win."

"I didn't know you had already gotten a hearing on this."

"I didn't, but as soon as I can get upstairs and prepare a motion and order, Zelda will set it for us."

"You talk to her?"

"No, but while I'm putting the motion and memorandum together, you're going to let her know what's going on. I saw her car in the parking lot. Tell her I'll be in her office in thirty minutes. Don't let her leave before she signs the order."

Forty-five minutes later Judge Williams signed Willie Mitchell's order setting the hearing for ten the next morning on the federal writ demanding Zegarra's delivery to the custody of the United States.

~ * ~

At ten-fifteen the next day, Ace High Boardman entered the humble Yaloquena courtroom with a flourish. He pointed his female assistant to the first row behind the defense table and stood next to the local attorney he associated for the appearance, Eleanor Bernstein.

Judge Zelda Williams surveyed the courtroom. In her mid-forties now, she had presided over dozens of Willie Mitchell's homicide trials. Judge Williams' skin was medium brown, and she carried herself with great dignity. Willie Mitchell Banks enjoyed practicing in front of Zelda Williams. She was well-versed in the statutes and case law involved in the cases she heard, and she was fair, unlike many of the Delta judges who bent over backward to help the criminal defense lawyers and plaintiff's lawyers because they were the heaviest contributors to the judges' re-election campaigns. Judge Williams was impartial, which was all Willie Mitchell could ask, that the presiding judge make a decision on the law and facts presented, not on some pre-existing prejudice against either side's politics or position.

It didn't hurt that Zelda and Willie Mitchell saw each other every day, and were sincerely fond of each other.

The parties were arrayed around the courtroom at tables configured and placed by Deputy Clerk Eddie Bordelon, a small, bald man with rimless glasses and a residual Cajun accent resulting from his rearing in Acadia Parish, Louisiana. Eddie ran the circuit clerk's office for the elected clerk for Yaloquena

County, Winston Moore, a peacock of a politician who knew little more about the workings of his office and courtroom procedure than the voters who showed up for jury duty. He had black skin and neat, salt and pepper hair, and dressed to the nines for jury selection or important hearings. Clerk Moore sat in the foreman's seat in the jury box, resplendent in a dark suit, white shirt with French cuffs, gold cuff links, and a bright red tie and matching pocket handkerchief.

Leopold Whitman and his first assistant United States attorney, Blake Briggs, sat at a small, temporary table adjacent to Willie Mitchell and Walton Donaldson, who were at the long prosecutor's table in Judge Williams' courtroom. Whitman rubbed his close-trimmed beard and leaned over to Briggs, who looked like the aging fullback he was, crew cut hair and thick-necked. Briggs glanced at Willie Mitchell as Whitman whispered to him.

Seated at the defense table with Zegarra before Ace High showed up was Eleanor Bernstein, a single woman in her early thirties, dark brown skin, well-dressed and attractive. As the Yaloquena public defender, it was rare that she had the chance to defend a criminal who could pay. She butted heads with Walton on a regular basis, and on occasion with Willie Mitchell. Eleanor was a competent lawyer, but so overburdened with her caseload she rarely had the time to give her best effort to defend a charge. But with Ace High paying her to be his second chair, Willie Mitchell anticipated seeing her best work so far.

"Nice of you to join us, Mr. Boardman," Judge Williams said.

Ace High stood immediately. "I am deeply sorry, Your Honor. I was only notified of this emergency hearing by Ms. Bernstein late yesterday, and my Lear was having some minor servicing completed in Dallas yesterday, so my pilots had to fly to Houston this morning to pick me up before flying up here. We would have been here on time but for a slight weather delay in Dallas due to a fast-moving front."

She smiled. "I understand, Mr. Boardman. I do appreciate your being here on such short notice, and thank you for the Dallas weather report. Let's make the record first, shall we. Why don't you start, Mr. District Attorney."

Willie Mitchell introduced himself to Judge Williams' Court for the thousandth time and Walton Donaldson as his assistant district attorney.

Leopold Whitman and Ace High did the same, establishing for the record who they were, who they represented, and naming their assistants for the hearing. Ace High acknowledged that the defendant Adolfo Zegarra Galván was presenting in the courtroom and ready to proceed.

"Now, since your motion has brought us all together this morning, Mr. Banks, why don't you explain to the court why we are here and the basis for your motion to set aside the federal writ as a nullity."

Willie Mitchell set forth the brief history of the arrest and indictment. He cited the federal and Mississippi state cases in favor of the state retaining physical custody. Leopold Whitman argued federal pre-emption and the supremacy clause and cited several cases.

"Those decisions are inapposite, Your Honor," Willie Mitchell said.

"Hold on, Mr. Banks. Let the U.S. attorney have his say."

Whitman continued for another ten minutes.

"And now, Mr. Boardman," the judge said, "does the defendant Mr. Zegarra have a position in this matter?"

"Yes, Your Honor," Ace High said, "I would like to be heard."

"I am not surprised, Mr. Boardman. Proceed."

"I'll be brief, Your Honor. The defense agrees with the state's position on the law. The cases cited by Mr. Banks are controlling, and the issue is not even close."

"That's it?" Judge Williams asked.

"Simple but powerful, Your Honor."

She smiled. Willie Mitchell noticed Whitman's assistant, Blake Briggs, pull a BlackBerry device from his coat pocket and read a text message. Briggs whispered to Whitman, who addressed the court.

"Your Honor, may we have a moment? I apologize and assure the court this will only take a second."

"Do you need a recess?"

"Maybe five minutes, Your Honor."

"Court's in recess for five minutes." She stepped from behind the elevated judge's bench and down three steps to the floor.

Eddie Bordelon and his boss, Circuit Clerk Winston Moore, stood and, as if rehearsed, said "All rise" in perfect harmony. Willie Mitchell watched the self-effacing deputy clerk, who lowered his eyes. Judge Williams raised her eyebrows as she passed Willie Mitchell and walked out the side door to access her chambers.

Willie Mitchell tried but could not recall a single time in the past when the Clerk Moore had directed the gallery and officers of the court to rise when the judge arrived or left. Eddie Bordelon, on the other hand, had done it on just about every

105

day for the three decades he had worked the Yaloquena court system as minute clerk. The circuit clerk left the courtroom. Willie Mitchell sidled over to Eddie Bordelon.

"I believe that's a first," Willie Mitchell said.

"I think it is, Willie Mitchell," Eddie said quietly with downcast eyes. The district attorney knew Eddie could not afford to criticize his boss, so the two men left everything else unsaid.

Willie Mitchell waved to Susan in the gallery. He sat down to study the U.S. attorney's memorandum of law in support of his position.

In a few minutes, Blake Briggs returned and huddled in a corner with Leopold Whitman. Whitman said something quietly to Eddie Bordelon. The minute clerk walked quickly out the side door to the judge's chambers. Within a few moments, Judge Williams was seated behind the bench.

"Mr. Whitman, I'm told you have something to share with the court."

Leopold stood. He adjusted his tortoise shell glasses and cleared his throat. "Your Honor, we feel the case law on the issue before the court is well-settled and overwhelmingly in our favor. However, as a matter of comity to the district attorney, and since the Justice Department is loathe to interrupt the state's prosecution on capital murder, my office is ready to defer to the state prosecution and wait until after the murder trial to take custody. I must stress that in the opinion of the legal scholars in the department we clearly have the right to take custody of Mr. Zegarra. However, if Mr. Banks can give us and the court assurance that the case will be tried in a timely manner... "

"Your Honor, Mr. Boardman has filed a speedy trial motion and since he is present in court today, I would ask the court to set the trial date to assure Mr. Whitman that we will start this trial within the sixty days set forth in the statute."

Ace High stood. "I've got my trial calendar with me Your Honor. I'm available to begin four weeks from yesterday if that date is acceptable to Mr. Banks."

"That's fine with us, Your Honor."

"You sure that's enough time to prepare for a capital murder case, Mr. Boardman?"

"Yes, Your Honor. This is not my first rodeo."

"Very well, gentlemen and lady, I'll have the clerk get the notices out and we will begin jury selection four weeks from yesterday. Defense motions need to be filed within ten days, and decided not later than a full week before the trial. Pre-trial order with witness lists and exhibits to be in final form at the same time."

"No problem, Your Honor," Ace said.

Judge Williams adjourned court and walked through the side door to her chambers. Sheriff Lee Jones walked through the rail gate and buttonholed Willie Mitchell.

"What the hell happened to Whitman?"

"I figure the professor and his aide got a text or an e-mail from Washington telling them to back off until we're through. Your pal Congresswoman Rose Jackson came through for us."

"Ain't democracy great," Lee said with a grin.

Standing behind the defense table, Ace High and Eleanor Bernstein huddled. Zegarra sat with his eyes closed and his head resting on the fingertips of both hands joined together as if in prayer.

Chapter Twenty

Adolfo Zegarra Galván had prayed earlier during the hearing, but was now buried deep in his past as his lawyers conferred.

After Adolfo left Casa Ayala, he returned to Tampico and reported to Señor Bernal. Bernal's long-range plan for Adolfo began with him in the lowest rung of the cocaine distribution chain. Adolfo did as he was told and more, because he shared the great man's vision of Adolfo being a key figure for *El Cártel de Campeche* in the United States. As time passed, Adolfo worked his way up the ladder, learning every aspect of the smuggling trade. Because of his white skin, intelligence, and unaccented fluency in both English and Spanish, Adolfo became a major player in Bernal's effort to move the cartel's smuggling to the Mexican border, away from their accustomed reliance on boats and planes moving the cocaine through the Caribbean waters and airspace. Since U.S. interdiction efforts were focused on trafficking through the Caribbean, the Mexican border was a cheaper and simpler alternative.

Moreover, concentrating delivery into Texas made Bernal more essential to the cartel because of his proximity to the border and his vast experience with crossings into Texas. He already had a legion of experienced men working for him, moving contraband into Texas, and the addition of Adolfo enhanced his network considerably.

Eventually, Adolfo began to move cocaine across the border for the cartel at crossings stretching from Nuevo Laredo to Matamoros. He looked like a gringo, so the border agents gave him a perfunctory once over and waved him through. Once in the U.S., Adolfo passed for just another college-aged gringo to law enforcement.

A couple of years into his smuggling career, Adolfo was stopped by a Texas state trooper on U.S. 281 north of Edinburg but still in Hidalgo county. He had many, many kilos of cocaine stuffed in every conceivable hiding place in his small Honda, but was cool when he gave the trooper his Texas driver's license and registration that listed Casa Ayala as his address in McAllen. The trooper was in his mid-thirties and stout. Adolfo made an educated guess, and started talking about high school football rivalries in McAllen. In short order the trooper pushed his hat back and began regaling Adolfo with stories of his high school football prowess as a tight end in McAllen, how he barely missed out on a scholarship to Texas Tech because of a knee injury in the first game of the high school state playoffs.

"Slow it down, partner," the trooper said to Adolfo when he let him off with a warning. Adolfo's only brushes with the law in his first years with the cartel were speeding tickets, which he promptly paid.

In the early nineties, Adolfo travelled constantly between Tampico, Monterrey, and the border crossings at Matamoros, Reynosa, Ciudad Miguel and Nuevo Laredo and into Texas. He grew to know the streets and highways of San Antonio, Corpus Christi, and Houston, and traveled as far north as Memphis and as far east as Pensacola.

Bernal paid Adolfo just enough to get by, and held out the promise of big money down the road as they both ascended in the cartel hierarchy. Adolfo had enough for girls and beer and to keep him in a reliable Honda, Nissan, or Toyota, and he was happy learning the trade.

Adolfo deviated only once from Señor Bernal's order to keep his life simple and legal when he wasn't transporting for the cartel. Adolfo was traveling through McAllen near Casa Ayala and saw his nemesis from school, the bully John Kirkpatrick, drive past him in an open Jeep in a part of town where few gringos ventured. It had been many years since Kirkpatrick terrorized Adolfo, but Adolfo was glad this day had come. Using the skills he learned in the cartel, he followed Kirkpatrick at a safe distance and watched him stop and talk to a Mexican in the park where Adolfo hung out as a student. Adolfo knew there could only be one thing they were talking about.

After Kirkpatrick roared away in his Jeep, Adolfo approached the Mexican and spoke to him long enough to make him understand Adolfo was well-connected with the cartel's upper level management. After reaching an understanding, the Mexican was amenable to doing anything Adolfo suggested with respect to John Kirkpatrick.

When Kirkpatrick showed up the next day at noon to pick up his heroin, Adolfo stepped from behind a tree and startled Kirkpatrick, who had just given the Mexican a wad of cash.

"*Buenas tardes*," Adolfo said in a low voice. "Do you remember Vanilla Bean?"

Kirkpatrick's eyes grew wide. He stammered and tried to smile. "Of course. Of course. How are you these days?"

Adolfo shrugged.

"Me, I kind of messed around partying too much and didn't graduate from the University of Houston, but I'm planning on completing my degree soon."

"Are you working?"

109

"Yes. My father retired from the fire department started a company to market fire extinguishers to businesses. I'm helping him. And what are you doing around these parts?"

"Nothing." Adolfo paused. "Why do you buy heroin?"

Kirkpatrick laughed. "I just use it occasionally to take the edge off. I'm no junkie. I'm under a lot of stress right now at the business and... this smoothes me out better than prescription meds."

"I see." Adolfo pulled from behind his back a nine millimeter automatic stuck in his belt. Kirkpatrick panicked and bolted for his jeep. Adolfo shot into the ground next to the jeep and Kirkpatrick froze. Adolfo walked up to him slowly and tapped him on the shoulder with the automatic.

"You should not run."

Kirkpatrick began to sweat. He stuttered: "P-p-please."

"Let's take a ride. Just you and me."

Adolfo gestured to the Mexican. The dealer lifted a bicycle from behind the tree and put it in the back of the Jeep. Adolfo gestured with the pistol and Kirkpatrick got behind the wheel and Adolfo in the passenger seat. "Drive. We'll get high together—talk about the old days."

Adolfo kept the gun low and pointed at Kirkpatrick. He directed him to a deserted bluff overlooking the Rio Grande. Adolfo pointed the gun at Kirkpatrick's groin. "You have wet your pants for no reason. I'm not going to shoot you."

Adolfo pulled two new syringes from his pocket. He gave one to Kirkpatrick, whose hands shook so badly he could not liquefy the heroin. Adolfo made him sit on his hands while Adolfo heated the heroin granules for him in a large spoon and filled one syringe.

"You go first," Adolfo said and gave the syringe to Kirkpatrick. Adolfo touched the gun to Kirkpatrick's temple. Kirkpatrick pushed the plunger and the warm liquid entered a prominent vein in his left forearm. Within seconds, Kirkpatrick's eyes rolled and he leaned back in his seat, the needle still in his arm.

Adolfo took a handkerchief from his pocket and wiped down everything in the Jeep he touched, including the syringe, which he left dangling from Kirkpatrick's left arm. Adolfo had never been fingerprinted in his life, but he did not want to take any chances. He heated another spoonful of heroin and used the second syringe to inject it into Kirkpatrick's right arm through a pre-existing track mark. Adolfo removed the needle, put a cap on it, and slipped it into his pocket. He waited for a while until Kirkpatrick was no longer breathing and had no pulse. He lifted the bicycle from the back of the Jeep and pedaled away, whistling quietly a song his mother used to sing to him.

Adolfo continued to hone his knowledge and skills working with the cartel, and Señor Bernal began to pay him commensurate with his abilities. He was making a lot of money, more than he ever imagined. Adolfo let Bernal keep it for him in Tampico. He only asked for enough at a time to live comfortably. After a while, Adolfo realized he enjoyed the work more than the money, the tense moments at the borders, the exchanges deep into the night, living under the radar of the U.S. and Mexican governments, a mystery to all whose paths he crossed.

He ceased thinking about a big house like Villa Bernal and servants. Adolfo kept his head down and worked, learning from his mentor.

In early 1999, Bernal called him to Tampico to his home and talked to Adolfo at length about the business.

"I am about to make a move. No one knows this but you. I want you by my side every moment. I need your language skills, your intelligence, and your cool head. I will be meeting a man tomorrow morning in this room, and I will be doing something in our business that has never been done before. I want you to be part of it from the beginning."

Adolfo stared at the man, the closest he ever had to a father.

"I am honored."

"Be back here tomorrow after *siesta*. I will go over everything with you. You will be amazed."

Adolfo could hardly sleep. He imagined different scenarios where he traveled the world with Señor Bernal and saw things of incredible beauty. When Bernal got tired of the business, he would turn it all over to Adolfo, who would continue to accumulate knowledge and skill to make him the best businessman smuggler in the entire world.

The next morning, Adolfo drove to the Madero docks to watch the big tankers come and go. A lot had happened since he sat on the pier as a child. He drove through the barrio where his Mama died. Everything was different.

At four o'clock, he approached Villa Bernal and saw a dark plume of smoke rising from the house. He stopped two blocks away from the fire. He walked toward the house and stopped when he saw Bernal's housekeeper María sitting against the wall surrounding the estate. He squatted next to her. She was crying.

"What happened, María?"

She shook her head.

111

"Did Señor Bernal meet with the man this morning like he told me yesterday?"

"Yes."

"Who was he?"

"I don't know his name. He spoke English. A *norteamericano*."

"Do you know what they talked about?"

"No. They talk very quiet. Two hours. The man leave."

"Then what?"

"I don't know. It happen fast. This afternoon. Many men with big guns and black uniforms knock down the door and rush into Señor Bernal's office. He was resting on the couch."

"They took him?"

"They kill him on the couch. Then they drag him out and throw him in back of a big truck and drive off fast."

Adolfo patted María and pulled her to him so she could cry into his shoulder. After a while she calmed down.

"You are sure he was dead?"

"Yes." She pointed to the top of her head. "Gone."

"What did the men look like? Were they *federals?*"

"No. Maybe some *federals* outside. The men who break the door and kill Señor Bernal were big, taller than you. Black masks. Big boots."

"*Yanquis?*"

"*Sí.*"

"The safe?"

"They use blowtorch to open and take everything. All the money. Then they tell me to leave, and they blow up the house."

Adolfo cared little about his money they took. He cared a lot for the life they took. Señor Bernal treated him better than anyone. Now he was gone.

~ * ~

Willie Mitchell leaned back in his chair and put his feet on the corner of his desk. The morning hearing had concluded so much better than it might have. He shook his head in disgust at the fact that a phone call from a congresswoman who knew nothing of the merits of the case could determine the result of the hearing. It showed the corruption of power in the nation's capitol. The Justice Department should not even *talk* to a member of Congress about a particular case, much less accede to her request to back off. He felt uncomfortable, somewhat compromised, but still was glad to benefit from the corruption this morning. "Whatever... ," he muttered.

"The governor is on one," Ethel said.

Willie Mitchell sat up. "Hello."

"What's up, Willie Mitchell?"

"All right, Jim Bob. How're you doing?"

"Too much traveling. How's Susan and the boys?"

"Fine. You know Jake's in Jackson."

"I see him around the federal building on occasion. He's a chip off the old block."

"Old blockhead."

"Look. I hate to bring this up, and I don't care what you do about it. I've got a friend I got to knew pretty good in the Republican Governor's Association, he's now a U.S. senator on the Homeland Security Committee."

"Okay."

"He asked me to ask you, and that's all I'm doing here is asking you because I told him I would—"

"Let the feds have our prisoner up here," Willie Mitchell said.

"The one that killed the deputy. How'd you know?"

"We had a hearing on it this morning. Professor Leopold Whitman got a text from Washington and they backed off. Said they'll wait until after we convict him of murder."

"Good. So this is resolved?"

"Yes, sir."

"Okay. I told him I'd call, that's all I'm doing. I hope you string the s.o.b. up."

"I plan on it."

"I'll tell the senator that you and Justice worked it out and you're releasing him after the murder trial."

"Between us, Jim Bob, it won't be up to me after I convict him."

"It'll be DOC?"

"That's right."

"Got it. I can take it from there." He paused and chuckled. "*Professor* Whitman. What do you think of the little guy?"

"I think he'd be a good law school teacher somewhere."

"Yale maybe."

"Or Columbia."

"Good luck to you, Willie Mitchell. Tell Susan hi and you call me if you need anything."

Willie Mitchell put his feet back up on the desk. *Take it easy the rest of the day. Tomorrow, start getting ready for trial.*

Chapter Twenty-One

"There's a gentleman to see you," Ethel said. "Here's his card. He's with the FBI."

Willie Mitchell studied the card. "Bring him in."

"I'm David Dunne," the man said.

Willie Mitchell shook his hand. Strong grip. He figured the man stood six-two or so, weighed in around one-eighty, and was about forty-five years old. Extremely clean cut, an athletic bearing. Willie Mitchell noticed a raised two-inch scar along the man's left jawbone.

"I'm Willie Mitchell Banks."

"Yes, sir, I know. I've read up on you."

"Where did you read up on me?"

"Just the stuff on the Mississippi D.A.'s Association Web site. You know, they have a little picture, and some biographical information. But I also talked to some of the agents who've had dealings with you."

"What kind of grade did they give me?"

"All A's. They all say you're a first rate prosecutor."

"That's good to hear. May I look at your credentials?"

"Sure."

Dunne pulled a thin leather wallet from his suit jacket and spread it on the desk in front of Willie Mitchell, who took a minute to examine it closely and compare the photograph.

"That's you, all right." He gave the wallet back to Dunne. "What can I do for you?"

"Nothing."

"Excellent. We're really good at that around here."

"Not as good as the federal government."

"No question about that."

"Let me tell you what I do and why they've sent me here."

"Who is they?"

"Washington. I am technically an FBI agent, but have none of the duties of a typical agent. I'm sort of an ombudsman for the agency and they send me out to liaise with other federal or state agencies in matters that are of particular interest to the director. I do a good bit of work with Homeland Security."

"You're kind of an FBI utility infielder. You can play anywhere."

"That's right. I report only to the director. I didn't come up through the ordinary ranks, so lots of agents don't even know about me."

"I assume you're here about Zegarra. Why does the FBI have a particular interest in our prosecution of Zegarra for capital murder?"

"The director thinks he has some invaluable information about the Mexican drug smugglers, *El Cártel de Campeche,* that we can use to disrupt their operations. Zegarra trained under a man named Bernal in the nineties. Bernal pioneered cocaine smuggling across the Rio Grande, and we think if we can get him to cooperate with us, we can really make some headway in stopping some of the traffic."

Willie Mitchell let that sit there a minute.

"I'm going to get him the death penalty."

"I hope you do."

"I'm not taking it off the table as a bargaining chip for anyone."

"I don't think you should. Some of the bureaucrats in Justice think that's the only way he'll talk. I say let's get him staring at the needle in Parchman to get his attention, then see what he's willing to do."

"I'm never going to agree..."

"We're not asking you to. I say let's have the murder trial and see what happens then. Getting him the death penalty makes our position stronger. And don't be offended at this, but the director also wants me down here to make sure Zegarra is safe in your jail and isn't going to escape."

"You'll have to talk to Sheriff Jones about that."

"I'm going to."

"Your Justice Department is weak on prosecutions."

"If you mean they're a bunch of bureaucratic pussies, I couldn't agree more. How'd you like dealing with Leopold Whitman?"

"Pussy is not a strong enough term for him. We refer to him around here as the professor."

Dunne laughed.

"My son works for him, so I have to tread lightly."

"I know. I hear from the Jackson office Jake's a first-rate young lawyer."

"Thanks. So, where are you staying?"

"One of your lovely local motels. The Travel Light."

"It's probably the best."

"It's all right. All I need is cable television, wi-fi, and air conditioning, and it's got all three. Got decent pillows, too."

"You know we have a hearing at two this afternoon."

"That's why I timed my arrival to get in yesterday afternoon. I'll be here through the trial."

"Today's the last round of hearings. We've resolved everything except the motion to change venue."

"You think she'll grant it?"

"I doubt it. Zelda usually waits until she sees how *voir dire* goes. The people in this county want it tried here. In my experience, change of venue always benefits the defense. Makes the facts more sterile, detached from the nitty-gritty of the real people and lives involved."

"Is it okay if I sit in the courtroom for the hearing?"

"Sure. It's open to the public. Get there early if you want a seat up front."

"Be my first chance to see Zegarra in person."

"He looks like an ordinary guy. Real calm. Not Hispanic-looking." Willie Mitchell stood. "Welcome to Sunshine, David. Hope you don't get too bored in our little town."

"I think I'll like it just fine." Dunne smiled and extended his hand, stroked the scar on his left jaw, and walked out.

At two in the afternoon, Judge Zelda Williams followed clerk Eddie Bordelon into the courtroom. Everyone stood, including Willie Mitchell and Assistant District Attorney Walton Donaldson, and Zegarra and his counsel, Ace High and Eleanor Bernstein.

"Afternoon gentlemen," the judge said, "and lady." She smiled at Eleanor. "I believe all motions have been satisfied or resolved—except the motion to suppress and the motion we have before us this afternoon, for change of venue. Is that correct?"

Ace High and Willie Mitchell stood again. "Yes, Judge Williams," they said in rough unison.

"On the motion to suppress all evidence of the defendant's automobile accident on I-55 and the money and forensic data seized at that scene, and all evidence of the defendant's alleged history as a drug courier, I will continue to research and study that issue and determine if the probative value outweighs the prejudicial effect."

Both Willie Mitchell and Ace High said, "Yes, Your Honor."

"And we are all set for jury selection to begin next Monday, are we not, gentlemen?"

All the lawyers said they were.

Judge Williams held up a document. "Now, Mr. Boardman, I've read your motion to change venue with all its attachments, including the report of Adam Drysdale, your public opinion expert who conducted the poll of Yaloquena County voters. His conclusions and supporting data are in his written report, and

I've read the cases you cite in support of the motion. Is there really any need for testimony?"

"Your Honor," Ace High said, "I have Mr. Drysdale here today and ready to take the stand."

Willie Mitchell rose. "Judge Williams, the state stipulates that Mr. Drysdale is qualified as an expert in his field. I've seen Mr. Drysdale testify in at least two other cases where he's been accepted as an expert, so there's no need to go over his qualifications."

"Given the stipulation, the court accepts Mr. Drysdale as an expert in the field of public opinion."

"And, Judge, I have no objection to the defense entering the entire Drysdale report and attachments into the record solely for the purposes of the change of venue motion."

"Let it be entered as defense one," she said.

Willie Mitchell sat, and Ace High spoke. "Your Honor, Mr. Drysdale is here today from Baton Rouge and I would like to put him on the stand and question him briefly on his conclusion in his report that my client's alleged offense is so notorious in this county through television and newspaper coverage, and even through word of mouth, that he cannot receive a fair trial here."

Willie Mitchell stood again. "The defense is not entitled to jurors who have not heard of the case, only to jurors who have not made up their mind."

"And Mr. Drysdale will testify that many of the citizens in this county have already made up their mind as to my client's guilt."

"Okay, gentlemen," Judge Williams said. "The court will hear Mr. Drysdale's testimony before ruling. Call him to the stand, Mr. Boardman."

Willie Mitchell whispered to Walton, then turned to survey the courtroom while the rotund Adam Drysdale waddled to the stand. Willie Mitchell glanced at David Dunne, then Frances, Travis Ware's widow.

After an hour of direct testimony and cross-examination, Judge Williams ruled like she always did in venue motions.

"Gentlemen, you both make good points and the law on venue is well-settled that it is within my discretion to hold this ruling in abeyance until we hear the testimony in *voir dire* of the prospective jurors. Mr. Drysdale's report is thorough, but it is still somewhat speculative in that it requires the court to extrapolate the opinions of the citizens he polled to the prospective jurors, and I'm not willing to do that. I want to hear it from the horse's mouth, so to speak. Mr. Boardman, since you cited two cases in which I ruled the same way, my decision should not have come as a surprise."

"No, Your Honor. It's not unexpected, but we are making a record here, so the appellate judges who review the court's ruling down the road will have the benefit of all the evidence on this point."

"Anything else?" Judge Williams asked. No one said anything. "All right, I'll see you gentlemen and Ms. Bernstein next Monday and we'll start picking our jury."

Zegarra stood with everyone else when Judge Williams returned to her chambers. His eyes lifeless, he stared out the window as Ace High and Eleanor Bernstein huddled and whispered to each other a few feet from him. He yawned and shuffled off with a deputy on each side to return his cell.

~ * ~

Elbert Dowd and his wife Libby sat across from Willie Mitchell. They were late sixties, both retired; Elbert from Mississippi Wildlife and Fisheries and Libby from the public school system. Willie Mitchell knew both of them well, especially Elbert, who testified for him many times as a wildlife agent ticketing hunters and fishermen for game violations. Elbert was solid, Libby jittery.

"Libby here's nervous as a cat in a room full of rocking chairs about being on this jury, Willie Mitchell."

"I'm scared of those drug people. They're always cutting people's heads off."

"That's along the border with Mexico, Libby," Willie Mitchell said. "We'll have lots of security to make sure you're safe. If I thought there was some danger to you, I would ask Judge Williams to excuse you, but right now, nobody is getting any kind of excuse from jury duty."

"I told her they probably wouldn't take her on the jury anyway."

"Elbert's right. With his law enforcement background and being a witness for me so many times, they'll probably excuse you."

"I hope so."

"And think about this, Libby. From all the registered voters in the county, your name was picked at random along with about two hundred other names. So, you had about a one in forty chance of getting picked to be in the pool."

"But I got picked."

"Bad luck, but all's not lost for you. We'll probably have to question no more than seventy or so of the two-fifty, so the odds are three to one in your favor that you will *not* be questioned by the lawyers. Since you got picked in the county-wide selection, the law of averages is now in your favor. And even if your name is pulled out of the box to be questioned, the defense will try to excuse you for cause because of Elbert. In my opinion, they will probably succeed. I don't believe Judge Williams will let you serve. She will not want to take the chance of getting reversed on appeal on a jury selection issue."

Elbert put his hand on Libby's shoulder. "Because I was a witness for Willie Mitchell so many times." He paused. "And I'll be there with you every day in the courtroom. I won't let nothing happen to you."

"Okay," she said, her voice shaking. "If both of you think it's all right. I just get so nervous around so many people."

Willie Mitchell walked the couple out into the reception area. Elbert pumped his hand and Libby gave him a delicate handshake. Willie Mitchell could feel her hand trembling.

"There's nothing to worry about. See you Monday."

"We'll be here," Elbert said and hung back as Libby left. He said quietly to Willie Mitchell, "She's nervous about everything these days."

Chapter Twenty-Two

Without his sponsor, Adolfo became just another soldier in the cartel. Shortly after Señor Bernal's assassination, Adolfo was summoned to Veracruz to be cross-examined by two men in a seedy motel room on the edge of town. He told them the truth, that Bernal had been his mentor, sent him to McAllen to school, and taught him the ropes in the smuggling trade. He said he went to Villa Bernal the day Señor Bernal was killed to find out the details on the big move that Bernal had planned but the gringo feds killed him before they met.

Adolfo was certain the men already knew these facts about him, so there was no need to lie. He would have if he had thought it would help, but he knew lying would get him killed for sure.

"Do you know what Señor Bernal's plan was?" he asked the men.

The men said no, but Adolfo could tell they did.

"Who allowed the DEA special forces in Tampico to kill him? It had to be our government involved with the United States."

They shrugged. "Who cares?" one of them said. "He's dead."

"You still work for *El Cártel de Campeche*," the other said. "We own you."

"Yes. It is all I know."

"Do you have anything else to ask?"

"No. I would like to get back to work as soon as possible."

They gave him the name and address of a man in Reynosa. "He is your boss now."

Adolfo drove the same day and reported in. That night he took a load across the border into Corpus Christi and spent the night with a Mexican woman he knew. She was thin but pretty. She asked him to get high with her after they had sex. Adolfo did not care one way or the other, and since she wanted him to, he smoked heroin with her.

The woman's home was a safe house for Bernal couriers, and the next morning, he asked her about the assassination.

"I do not know anything about it," she said.

Adolfo suspected she knew more than she let on, but did not push it. He had to assume everything he said or did would be reported.

Adolfo was sure the cartel was in on the gringo federal agents' murder of Bernal, but there was nothing he could do about it. The cartel had no loyalty to Bernal, and would have killed Adolfo in a heartbeat if he gave them any reason to suspect his loyalty. Now he would take his time, but someday he would pay them all back.

Occasionally Adolfo tiptoed around the issue when he was high with other drug runners. He was careful to seem nonchalant about it and concealed his hatred for the United States government and the cartel bosses who killed Bernal. Hiding his feelings was easy, because the people around him knew Adolfo as a man who cared about nothing.

For three years Adolfo drove back and forth across the Rio Grande. He never triggered any behavioral profiles the border agents used. He was calm and friendly, entirely appropriate, as if he had not a care in the world. He actually didn't, except for the eventual need to avenge Señor Bernal's murder.

His drug use increased. When others smoked grass or did cocaine, crystal meth, or the native brown heroin, he joined them if they asked. When he was not smuggling, he had nothing to do, so he partied with his associates and their women. Women desired Adolfo because he was good-looking and white. He accommodated them. If they told him they wanted to have sex with him, he would.

One night, Adolfo did too much Mexican heroin and woke up naked in a ditch in Reynosa when the local *policía* stopped their car on the street. They took him in and beat him at the station, calling him a *"gringo desnudo"* and talking about him as if he could not understand a word of Spanish. Adolfo played the dumb gringo and did not mind the beating. But when one of the cops took him in a back room, locked the door, and tried to rape him, Adolfo knocked him to the floor and kicked him to death, stomping his heel into the cop's temple over and over until the skull crushed and flattened, the sides coming together like a perch.

Adolfo's cartel associates arrived at the station just in time to keep the other cops from killing him. The son of one of the cartel's senior officers, who came up with the idea at the party to undress the passed out Adolfo and put him in the ditch, spread some money around the station, enough to save Adolfo's life, but not enough to keep him out of prison.

The cartel and the *policía* agreed on three years. Adolfo went along because he had no choice. Like a jellyfish pushed by the ocean current, Adolfo had no say in the matter of the next three years of his life. The jokester promised Adolfo that his smuggling job was safe when he finished the three-year sentence, and the jokester's father would provide enough money for Adolfo's reasonable comfort in *El Centro de Readaptacion Social de Reynosa*, the prison not far from where Adolfo spent the night naked in the ditch, and referred to locally as Cereso Reynosa. There was a hint from the jokester that his father might pay enough to get Adolfo out early, but he was not counting on it.

Adolfo had never spent a night in jail, much less high-security prison, but he listened to stories other smugglers told at parties, and everything they said turned out to be true.

His first few days were spent watching his back and figuring out exactly who the guards were. Most lived at the prison during the week and few guards wore uniforms. The guards stayed at the gate or on top of the walls, and only occasionally walked through the prisoner living areas. When they did, they wore their own clothes and remained almost indistinguishable from the inmates. Adolfo learned to recognize every guard, though it did him little good because inside the walls, the prisoners were on their own.

Guards did nothing to interfere with their daily lives. For the tiny sum the guards were paid by the government, they were unwilling to break up fights or rapes. Adolfo likened the guards to men working at the zoo. They made sure the animals did not escape, but it was survival of the fittest inside, every animal for himself.

Nothing was provided to Adolfo by the prison. He was responsible for his own clothes, soap, and food. He had no one on the outside to provide for him, so without the jokester's father's monthly stipend, life would have been difficult in Cereso Reynosa.

Pedro Esperanza, the guard responsible for delivery of his money, and Adolfo found each other. The first delivery, he began to count the money with Pedro standing there, but stopped halfway through. He gave the wad of pesos back to Pedro.

"I know how much money my superiors send me each month. They told me the exact amount. These bills do not appear to add up to that amount. However, I did not finish counting. So, I am not sure. I am willing to pay you a reasonable fee for your services, a *mordida* of ten percent."

Adolfo turned his back on Pedro. "I will turn around when you say, and I will then count the money you give me. If it is not ninety percent of what my superiors provide for me, I will not say anything to you, but I will pass the word along to my managers and your youngest child will be killed."

Adolfo waited. He heard the rustling of money.

"*Ya,*" Pedro said.

Adolfo faced Pedro. He was sweating and his hands shook when he gave Adolfo the money. Adolfo took his time counting. He was calm. Pedro's perspiration intensified. Adolfo finished. Pedro nodded vigorously and pointed to the money.

"*Es todo,*" he said.

Adolfo walked off. The first Monday of each month, Pedro gave him the same amount.

Under the protective umbrella of *El Cártel de Campeche*, Adolfo's days inside were not as dangerous as the typical inmate's. He witnessed many knifings and murders and felt no more for the victims than he did for the rats some of the inmates trapped and cooked. His main problem was boredom. After his life on the road for the cartel, staying in one place, looking at the same walls, he felt his mind was calcifying. At times, the harsh midday sun seemed to cut into his dormant brain.

There was one prisoner he noticed, different from the rest. His skin was a dark copper, not brown or gold like the Mexicans. He heard someone call him El Moro. One day he approached the dark copper man while he knelt with his eyes closed and his hands raised face level, palms inward. His lips moved discreetly.

Adolfo watched the man for a long time. He did not know at the time that the dark copper man would teach Adolfo things that would open his eyes to the truth. The wisdom the man taught him would make Adolfo understand the only thing that was important in this world.

Chapter Twenty-Three

Sheriff Lee Jones, Jake, and Kitty sat together in the middle of the first row behind the prosecutor's table. David Dunne introduced himself to Jake and Kitty, and sat next to the sheriff, the long bench looking like a church pew without the kneeler. Hearing something strange, the four of them turned simultaneously to the right to check out JPD officers Carl Lippmann and Hubert Holland in their patrol uniforms at the end of the row. Carl jerked his head twice toward Hubert, who was making that same odd noise he called "scratching his throat," his massive Adam's apple moving up and down. Carl elbowed Hubert in the side.

"Where's the widow?" Kitty asked Jake.

"Daddy asked her not to be here for *voir dire*, to wait until the first day of testimony. You ever met Agent Dunne before?"

"No. But I don't know anybody in upper management at Quantico who wasn't one of my instructors."

The courtroom was packed. Prospective jurors filled every seat and lined the walls.

"That's Eleanor Bernstein," Jake said to Kitty, moving his head slightly toward the defense table, "the county public defender I was telling you about."

"Nice suit on Ace High," Kitty said.

Jake turned when he felt a tap on his shoulder.

"Morning, Mr. Dowd," he whispered to Elbert and his wife. "Mrs. Dowd." Libby smiled with lips quivering slightly. Elbert winked at Jake.

The little Cajun Eddie Bordelon walked in following his boss. Circuit Clerk Winston Moore, decked out in a metallic royal blue tie and pocket handkerchief, called out for everyone to rise, pronouncing each syllable slowly and distinctly.

Judge Williams walked in with dignity and took the bench.

"You may be seated," the circuit clerk said. "No smoking, spitting, or talking in the courtroom."

"Thank you, Mr. Moore," the judge said. "Deputy Clerk Bordelon will now call the roll."

"Thank God," Jake whispered to Kitty. "We'd have been here all day if Winston Moore had read the names."

Jake was surprised that only a handful of the prospective jurors were absent. When the names of the absentees were called again, Judge Williams issued an order that, "The circuit clerk and sheriff determine why those absent did not appear, and report findings to the court at a later date."

She added, "Bench warrants will be issued in due course for those who did not appear for jury duty, after which they will be required to show cause why they should not be held in contempt of court and face either a fine or jail time."

Jake smiled at his father when Willie Mitchell turned and winked. He advised Jake earlier to pay attention to the admonition and its effect on the prospective jurors. Jake sensed relief in those who did show up; they did their duty and would not face the wrath of the court, no fine, no jail time. Willie Mitchell told Jake that the truth was as follows: the clerk and sheriff *never* investigate the absences, *never* report to Judge Williams, and she *never* asked them about it again. It was a kind of *kabuki* theater for the benefit of the jury prospects that did their duty and appeared in court to be questioned.

Jake discreetly edged his fingertips under Kitty's behind. She cut him a glance that caused him to remove them immediately.

Judge Williams recited the general requirements that jurors had to be over eighteen and not convicted of a felony for which they had not been pardoned. They had to be literate in the English language and not under an order of incompetence. She asked if any had medical conditions or special hardships that rendered them unable to serve, and a dozen prospects walked nervously toward the bench and lined up single file before the judge.

In turn, each one whispered to the Judge Williams to explain his or her particular situation. She listened politely and whispered questions to each, then dismissed seven and directed five to return to their seats and wait to be questioned by the lawyers.

The first twelve jury prospects whose names were drawn randomly from the clerk's box took seats in the jury box. Judge Williams told them that it was a capital murder indictment and that if selected, the jury would be sequestered for the duration of the trial. The jurors cut their eyes at each other and squirmed. Willie Mitchell approached the podium in front of the jury.

Judge Williams explained to the jurors that each side would make a brief opening address dealing with the issues to be raised in *voir dire*, and that the comments were not an opening statement, which would not take place until twelve jurors and two alternates were seated.

Willie Mitchell thanked the judge and introduced himself to the jurors. He explained the procedures in a capital murder case, that the trial was bifurcated, a guilt phase then a sentencing phase.

"Now, do any of you twelve prospective jurors have moral or religious beliefs that would prevent you from imposing the death penalty against Adolfo Zegarra no matter what evidence I present and no matter what the law is? If so, please raise your hand."

Four black and two white jurors raised their hands. Willie Mitchell questioned them in order, starting with an older black woman. He studied the jury seating chart he had before him.

"You are Mrs. Boydstun?"

She nodded.

"You'll have to speak, Mrs. Boydstun, so the recording equipment and the court reporter can record your answers."

"Yes," she said in a loud voice, and giggled when she realized how loudly she had spoken. The packed courtroom tittered with her.

"Do you have an opinion about the death penalty, Mrs. Boydstun?"

"I don't think it's right."

"How do you mean?"

"I don't think the government should kill somebody.

"Under any circumstances?"

"No."

"Even though the law says that in certain, limited cases a jury can consider putting the defendant to death if they find him guilty and find certain aggravating circumstances surrounding the crime and the defendant?"

"Only God should be able to take a life."

"So, if you were selected to serve on the jury, there is no evidence that I presenting that would enable you to vote for the death penalty?"

"That's right. I believe it would be a sin. I would never vote to cause somebody's death."

Willie Mitchell turned to Judge Williams, who looked toward the defense table. "Cross, Mr. Boardman?" Ace High shook his head "no."

"Mrs. Boydstun," the judge said, "you are excused with the thanks of the court."

"I can leave?"

"Yes, ma'am."

Jake Banks watched Mrs. Boydstun leave the jury box clutching her purse and walking out through the center aisle. All eyes were on her. Jake knew that if anyone in the crowded courtroom wanted to get off the case, Mrs. Boydstun had just given them a roadmap. It was the same in every capital case.

The judge released the other five after they had been questioned about the death penalty by Willie Mitchell and Ace High to determine if there was any wiggle room in their refusal to impose the death penalty. Six more names were selected to replace those excused. After Willie Mitchell questioned another nine prospective jurors, he had his first death-qualified panel, twelve people who could administer capital punishment if the evidence called for it. He asked them a few other general questions as a group, then sat down.

"Now, ladies and gentlemen," Judge Williams said to the twelve, Mr. Boardman will make a brief statement about his case solely for the purpose of jury selection, and ask some general questions of the twelve of you. After he finishes his general questions, then Mr. Banks and Mr. Boardman will question each of you individually to ask you about your background and other matters that are particular to each of you.

Ace High took the podium.

"Morning, ladies and gentlemen. As we say in Houston, 'Hi y'all doin' this mornin'?"

The twelve prospects chuckled. Willie Mitchell and Walton smiled with the jurors. Jake thought of Willie Mitchell's comments about humor in the courtroom. "Like laughter in church," his daddy used to tell Jake when he was a kid. "It doesn't take much to provoke it." He warned Jake that in a major case, the prosecutor has to be serious and go along with humor only when it's organic—when not going along would make him look a stiff-necked prick. Just be yourself, he told Jake. "Just like putting a golf ball," he said. "It's all about touch."

"Now," Ace High said, "this is a serious case, ladies and gentlemen. And all twelve of you have said you can impose the death penalty if you think it's appropriate." Big smile. "I'm going to surprise some of you right now and tell you I, too, am in favor of the death penalty. That's right, in favor of it, *but only if it's appropriate in a particular case.*"

Ace High got quiet. "And ladies and gentlemen, it's not appropriate in this case."

He took a deep breath, stared at the ceiling for a moment, and exhaled slowly. He raised one finger. "I'm going to surprise you again." He waited for thirty seconds, looking at each juror, then walked over to the defense table and stood behind Zegarra,

127

his hands on his client's shoulders. "My client shot and killed Travis Ware."

There was a collective, subdued gasp in the courtroom. Ace High walked slowly back to the podium.

"That's right. He killed Travis." He paused for several more seconds. "But he did not intend to."

Willie Mitchell stood. "Your Honor, I object to counsel going beyond the bounds of the *voir dire* opening, beyond the scope of what the court limited us to in chambers."

Ace High feigned surprise. "I certainly did not mean to, Your Honor, but in order to see if these jurors can give my client a fair trial I need to know if they can listen to all the facts, not just the fact of the death of Travis Ware, but what condition my client was in at the time."

Judge Williams thought for a moment. "I'm going to allow this, Mr. Banks, but admonish Mr. Boardman limit his recitation of the facts to the minimum he hopes to prove at trial, and save the rest for his opening statement after jury selection."

"Thank you, Your Honor." Ace High smiled as if the judge had given him a big victory. "When I get to question each of you individually, I will go into this in more detail, but as a question to *all* of you... ." He opened his arms widely as if to gather all twelve to him. "Is there any among you that would order Adolfo to be killed by the state even if I prove to you that due to a concussion and skull fracture he wasn't in his right mind at the time Travis woke him up and surprised the dickens out of him on the side of that road causing Adolfo to act out of instinct without thinking?"

Jake knew Ace High said it fast as he could to get it out of his mouth before the prosecutor objected.

"Your Honor," Willie Mitchell interjected. "The defense has not entered a plea of not guilty by reason of insanity, and I would ask the court to instruct the prospective jurors that the defendant's sanity is not at issue in this trial."

"But his state of mind most certainly is," Ace High said.

"Mr. Boardman," Judge Williams said, "let's you and Mr. Banks approach the bench."

She held her hand over the microphone on the bench and whispered to the two lawyers who stood inches from her.

"He's got guts," Jake whispered to Kitty. "It's smart. If he tried to deny Zegarra killed Travis, he would lose credibility with the jurors. So, he admits it and gets it out of the way early so he can get them to focus on Zegarra, not on Travis. He's trying to take the murder out of play, get them to concentrate on what he feels is the unfairness of the death penalty in these circumstances."

Both lawyers left the bench. Ace High returned to the podium.

"Now, where were we?" he asked with a broad grin, taking the time to look from juror to juror.

Chapter Twenty-Four

Judge Williams recessed for lunch at noon. The prospective jurors who filled the courtroom waited patiently to leave through the back door. The lawyers and the twelve prospects in the jury box being questioned left via the side door inside the courtroom rail along with Jake, Kitty, Lee Jones, and David Dunne, because their front row was closer to the side door than the back.

Downstairs, the first floor of the courthouse was packed. Most people exited the double glass and steel doors that opened on the rear of the courthouse near the parking lot next to the bayou. They walked down the concrete steps leading to the ground level, the older jury prospects holding onto the iron railing down the center of the stairs.

Agent David Dunne turned toward the sheriff's office on the first floor, while Jake and Kitty stepped through the double doors out onto the concrete landing above the steps, waiting for the crowd in front of them to descend the stairs and walk the short distance to their cars in the parking lot. He noticed the old wildlife and fisheries agent Elbert Dowd below him on the second to last concrete step fall into the person in front of him. Jake thought the old man tripped, and hoped he wasn't hurt. Jake saw two others fall against Ace High. When blood splattered on everyone behind them and the people shrieked, Jake knew no one had tripped. They had been shot.

"Get down!" he screamed, but no one did. They froze in place or scattered in every direction, some falling. He knelt behind the iron railing with his gun drawn, and so did Kitty. The railing gave him little cover, but kneeling made him a smaller target.

Jake had heard no shots but decided they had to have come from the parking lot. He gestured for the two armed deputies posted at the back door for trial security to follow him and Kitty with guns drawn to the parking lot.

Running low with his Sig Sauer ready, Jake directed Kitty and the deputies to spread out among the cars. "Check each one," he said.

But the only people they encountered in the parking lot were jury prospects huddled on the concrete next to their own vehicles, scared for their lives.

Jake told the deputies to keep watching the cars for any activity. He yelled at the people squatting or sitting on the concrete behind their cars to stay down. He and Kitty ran back to the courthouse steps.

Deputies tended to the wounded, but crouching to maintain a low profile made their aid attempts awkward at best. Standing next to David Dunne inside, watching Jake and Kitty, Sheriff Jones knocked on the thick glass door and gestured. Kitty and Jake ran up the stairs and through the doors to join them.

"Ambulances are on the way," the sheriff said. "State police, and Med-Evac helicopters, too."

"The shooter's not in the parking lot, unless he's hiding in the trunk of a car," Jake said, still holding his gun. He noticed Agent Dunne staring at him.

Kitty holstered her Glock before she came in the building.

"I don't think he was in the parking lot," Willie Mitchell said when he joined them at the door. "I believe the shots came from across the bayou or from the roof of one of those buildings." He pointed to two old buildings on the south bank of the bayou.

"I've got men headed to Cypress Street right now," Lee said.

Bessie Jackson, the sheriff's dispatcher, called out from the door on the first floor leading into the sheriff's office. "Sheriff Jones."

He walked over and talked to her, then returned.

"Sammy Roberts called in from Cypress Street. One of the neighbors said there was a mini-van backed into the driveway of the old Dillon place. She saw it when she came back from the store at noon. It's gone now. Didn't know what kind it was. Said it was gray or light blue."

"That house has been empty since Mrs. Dillon died," Willie Mitchell said. "Got a 'For Sale' sign in the yard."

Sheriff Jones walked out the door. Jake, Kitty, Willie Mitchell and Agent Dunne followed and stood behind him on the landing atop the concrete steps.

"Listen up, everyone," Jones yelled. "We think the shooter has left the area, but we're not sure. We have to assume the danger to you is not over. Until we get a better handle on things, just stay right where you are. Medical help is on the way. You folks in the parking lot, don't get in your vehicles. We have to recheck every one of them before you can leave. This is a crime scene now, so don't touch or remove anything."

Jake followed the others down the steps. Hubert Holland, the tall JPD officer, cradled his partner Carl Lippmann's head on the walkway ten feet from the steps. The front of Carl's uniform shirt was black with blood. Tears rolled down Hubert's cheeks. "He's dead," he cried. "He was my best friend."

Libby Dowd sobbed and rocked back and forth over the corpse of her husband Elbert. Part of the retired wildlife agent's face was gone.

Jake saw three other prospective jurors in awkward positions on the stairs and the sidewalk. They appeared dead to Jake. He noticed blood puddling on the concrete stairs, dripping slowly, meandering at a leisurely pace down to the lower steps.

Willie Mitchell sidestepped the dead and wounded and turned to go into the bushes next to the steps. Jake and Kitty followed. They saw Ace High on the ground, his back against the brick courthouse wall, the left sleeve of his expensive Italian suit soaked in blood. "Where are you hit?" Willie Mitchell asked him.

"Just my arm. It only grazed it, far as I can tell. But it sure is bleeding. And it hurts like hell."

Willie Mitchell took off his belt and fashioned a tourniquet to stop the bleeding. "Go get an EMT," he told Jake.

David Dunne watched Jake run around the courthouse toward the street. In a few minutes, Jake returned with two EMTs. As they ran toward Willie Mitchell and Ace High, David Dunne whistled. Jake pointed the EMTs toward Ace High and Willie Mitchell, then turned and hustled over to Dunne, who was a hundred feet from the carnage.

Dunne silently grabbed Jake's right arm at the elbow and dug his thumb deep into the joint. Jake's hand went numb, and in the same motion, Dunne caught Jake's forty caliber automatic as Jake's hand involuntarily released it.

Jake grimaced and grabbed his right elbow. "What the hell's wrong with you? That hurts like hell."

"I'm tired of watching you run around waving that pistol. You're posing the only danger now. The shooters who did this are in the wind."

Jake looked at Dunne like he was crazy. Dunne gave Jake his weapon. "Holster it."

Jake shook his right arm and stuck the Sig in his holster. He glared at Dunne. "What is your problem?"

"You're a lawyer, an assistant U.S. attorney. What are you doing carrying a gun?"

"We don't have a policy against it in the district. It's left up to each assistant. I've got a concealed carry permit from the state."

"You talk to the professor about your pistol?"

"No."

"Does he know you carry?"

"I'm not sure."

"I can tell you he doesn't, because if he did, he'd tell you to keep it at home. Why haven't you talked to him about it?"

"Hasn't come up," Jake said.

"You haven't talked to him about it because you know you shouldn't be doing it. Did Judge Williams or your dad know you had your gun in the courtroom?"

Jake shrugged. He watched the EMTs render aid. He hoped no one saw Dunne disarm him so easily.

"Where did you get your firearm training?"

"I've been around guns all my life," Jake said. "Been hunting with shotguns and rifles since I was six, took all the youth courses the Wildlife and Fisheries sponsored. I spend a lot of time at the shooting range. I'm probably a better shot than you."

"You ever shot at someone? A real person?"

"No."

"You ever had tactical training with your weapon and practiced close-quarters combat? What about the twenty-one foot drill?"

"What?"

"You're facing a man with a knife twenty-one feet away and you've got your gun holstered. When the trainer yells, you get the drop on him or he stabs you. Nine times out of ten the man with the knife wins."

"He wouldn't beat me. I'm quick out of the holster."

"You ever try to draw with someone trying to kill you? Or try to re-load when your adrenaline is racing through you and your hands shake like you've got some kind of palsy?"

"What's your point, Agent Dunne?"

"My point is, you have no business doing what you did today, ordering those deputies and the girl into that parking lot. It's a miracle they didn't shoot someone. Kitty's got more firearms training than you do. She should have been giving the orders out there. Those deputies have probably never shot their weapons on duty. They're so fucking out of shape they'd be too winded to shoot accurately even if they could have identified a bad guy."

"And where were you during all this?"

"Inside. Where you and Kitty and the deputies should have been. Why would you want to give the snipers more targets, especially law enforcement targets? You need recon information before you go hauling ass into the line of fire. It's a good thing the shooters left long before you showed your ass in that parking lot, or you'd have been dead as a hammer."

Jake started to walk off, but Dunne grabbed his arm and pulled Jake close to him.

"Listen, Jake, I'm on your side. I like your dad, and I like you. But you've got to give up this cowboy shit until you get

133

some real training. Go to Quantico. They'd love a guy like you. But if you're going to be a lawyer, be a lawyer, and leave the gun-fighting to someone who knows what the fuck they're doing."

Jake jerked his arm away. "If you're through, I'm going to see if I can help someone."

~ * ~

At six that afternoon, Willie Mitchell left the crime scene to the specialists from Jackson and drove toward the Banks family cemetery in the corner of the nine hundred ninety acres of row crop land he inherited from his parents. He had told Ace High how to get there after the Houston lawyer told Willie Mitchell he wanted to talk to him by himself somewhere outdoors, where they could see a long way.

He parked next to Ace High's rented Lincoln MKX and walked to the graves. Ace High sat on the ground, his back against one of the headstones.

"Pardon me if I don't get up, Willie Mitchell."

"Keep your seat. How's your arm?" Willie Mitchell pointed to Ace High's bandaged left arm in a sling.

"Could have been a lot worse. I could have been dead." He paused. "Doctor said it took about a half inch gulley of meat on the outside of my bicep. He cleaned it out and bandaged it. Don't know why he gave me this sling. What's the final count?"

"The Jackson cop, Carl Lippmann, is dead. So is Elbert Dowd, a guy I've know for a long time."

"That's the old man there to escort his wife?"

"That's him. Two prospective jurors are dead, one man, one woman. Five others wounded. One or two of those might not make it through the night."

"Never seen anything like this," Ace High said. "I withdrew from representing Zegarra about an hour ago. I called Judge Williams and told her I was flying back to Houston tonight."

"I wish you wouldn't do that so soon."

"It's done. I have to tell you something, and I don't want you to think I've lost my mind or that I'm a hopeless paranoid, just humor me."

"What?"

Ace High picked up a boxy electronic device resting next to the headstone. It had a metal wand extending out about six inches. "Before I tell you I have to see if you're wired."

"I'm not."

"I know you're not, but this is for my own peace of mind. So I can sleep at night. Okay? If I don't do it, I'll lie awake at night worrying that I trusted you but you wore some kind of device, or somebody a half-mile away recorded me with a directional dish, or a laser, or God knows what."

Willie Mitchell kneeled and extended his arms. Ace High ran the wand all over Willie Mitchell, then put the box down and frisked him with his good right hand, patting him down as best he could from his uncomfortable sitting position. Ace High leaned back against the headstone, worn out from the effort, and gestured for Willie Mitchell to sit next to him. Ace High picked up a legal pad from the ground and covered his mouth with it.

"You and I never had this conversation. If you ever quote me, I'll call you a liar. I think I can trust you. Can you promise me you will never tell anyone that I told you what I'm about to say? I don't care if you act on the information. You just can't say I told you anything. If you can't promise me, I can't say a word. We clear?"

"You have my word."

"You're a smart guy. So you know who hired me?"

"The people that Zegarra works for. A drug cartel."

"They're not just people or just any cartel. It's *El Cártel de Campeche*, the worst of the worst as far as ruthless drug cartels go."

"That's what the feds said."

"Well, it's true." Ace High spoke in a quiet voice, and continued to cover his mouth with the legal pad. "I've got a number of cases for them in Houston, Corpus, Dallas, and other parts of Texas. Cases with a lot more drugs and money at stake than what Zegarra lost on I-55."

"I don't understand how you can work for them."

"I've got my own personal demons. Let's leave it at that. My particular needs make me do a lot of things I don't want to, but we don't have time to go into my problems right now. The helicopter on the courthouse roof shit, that was the cartel. When I found out what they did, I told them how stupid it was. Just plain stupid."

"How do you communicate with them?"

"I've never met any of the cartel members. Never talked to 'em. Every dealing I have with them, and I mean everything, is through an attorney in Houston. I've known him a long time. He's the one that pays me through his trust account, hires me to handle the cases. He tells me he doesn't deal directly with the cartel, that everything comes to him through an attorney at a silk-stocking, big-building law firm in Monterrey, a city of about four million in northern Mexico."

"I know where Monterrey is. So why—?"

"Hold on. I'm telling you all this because I want you to know the shooting today, all these dead and wounded people on the back steps of the courthouse, the cartel had nothing to do with it."

"How can you be sure?"

"I'm telling you, Goddammit, I know for a fact."

Willie Mitchell said nothing.

"I talked to the lawyer in Houston, my liaison, and he tells me the lawyer in Monterrey says the people he works for are mad as hell about this. They don't want the heat this is going to bring. They'd rather have Zegarra dead than be involved in something like this. They're bloodthirsty bastards who would cut off the heads of their own mothers and toss a croaker sack full of their bloody heads into a church house. But take my word for it, Willie Mitchell, they did not have shit to do with this cluster fuck on the steps of the courthouse today."

Willie Mitchell remained quiet.

"I'll tell you something else that corroborates what I just said. *I* almost died on those steps today. Four inches over and I'm a dead son of a bitch. I'm knee deep in three big federal drug prosecutions for the cartel right now in Texas. Been delaying those trials for the last year. After I finished up this trial here, the federal judges over there told me I was going to have to fish or cut bait on the Texas cases. All three involve a lot of money and potentially have big consequences for the cartel structure. Part of my job is to keep my clients happy in the slammer so they don't flip on the people paying my bills."

"You've got a conflict."

"Hell yes, I've got a conflict. And I've got to resolve it soon. But nobody can do it but me, and the big boys who run the cartel are not going to take the chance of their favorite Texas lawyer getting killed or injured so bad he can't pull their collective Mexican nuts out of the fire. They need me over there in Texas a whole lot more than here in Mississippi. And they'd kill Zegarra themselves before they'd let something happen to old Ace High."

"You have any idea who would do something like this?"

"No idea. But that Zegarra is one ice-cold son of a bitch. Half the time I think he doesn't listen to anything I tell him. Like his mind is a thousand miles away."

"Maybe he doesn't understand you, the language... ."

"Bull fuckin' shit. The son of a bitch speaks better English than I do. No Mexican accent at all. Sounds kind of like Johnny Carson. He's supposed to be born in Mexico, but I ain't sure I believe it."

"He doesn't look Mexican," Willie Mitchell said.

"No shit. White as you and me. But according to my people, he is for sure Mexican, born around Tampico. Now, you better get loaded for bear because the feds are going to make a grab for this case. My orders were to keep it in state court, away from the feds. As of now, my people don't give a shit what happens to Zegarra. They're not paying for his defense any more. They just want as far away from him as possible."

Ace High leaned closer to Willie Mitchell. "Let me tell you something else. This is all good advice and it's free. You ought to think about allowing the feds to take over the prosecution. You would be a lot better off. Safer, too."

"Might be," Willie Mitchell said. "I'll sure take that into consideration."

Chapter Twenty-Five

The town of Sunshine and Yaloquena County, Mississippi had never experienced an international media assault like the one that began the afternoon the jurors were slaughtered. Satellite trucks from Mississippi, Louisiana, and Tennessee began arriving at four o'clock and continued to pile up around the courthouse throughout the evening. Every motel room in town was taken or reserved by six p.m., and the fast food restaurants that lined the highway were packed.

Willie Mitchell stood at the window in his office. Outside, daylight was disappearing. He could not believe what had happened.

First time in the history of jury selection in the United States of America there's a mass murder of prospective jurors, and it happens in my case, on my watch. Man-oh-man. What a legacy.

That afternoon Sheriff Jones and his deputies had created a buffer around the courthouse with crime scene tape to keep the media out and let the forensic specialists do their work. Willie Mitchell suggested to Lee they cordon off only the back steps of the courthouse and the driveway across the bayou where the mini-van had been parked. That's where the evidence would be found. But Lee made the decision to establish a gigantic perimeter. Willie Mitchell figured it wouldn't hurt anything, merely waste some time. But that was all right. It gave Lee and the deputies something to do to keep their minds off what had happened.

Willie Mitchell turned from the window. FBI agent David Dunne sat quietly next to Jimmy Gray, who barely fit between the arms of the oak chair. Assistant D.A. Walton Donaldson leaned against the wall behind them. It was a somber scene.

"Go home to your family, Walton. Get some rest. I'm going to need you to be sharp as a tack tomorrow, the next day and the next, until things settle down. The feds are going to be coming back to take the case from us. We've got to be on our toes."

"See you tomorrow, guys." Walton walked out.

Jake and Kitty were called back to Jackson immediately when they phoned their supervisors after the shooting. Jake told his father that "the professor," Leopold Whitman, instructed all federal personnel of any kind to stay away from the scene. "Let the judge, the D.A., and the sheriff and all the state agencies wallow in the mess they made by keeping the case in that nineteenth century hell hole up there," was what Jake's boss actually told him. Jake kept that to himself.

David Dunne told Willie Mitchell he didn't report to Whitman, and did not give a damn what the professor said. He was staying. Earlier, Dunne had taken Willie Mitchell aside and told him about his heated "discussion" with Jake about his gun.

"He's a good kid," Dunne said. "I don't want to see him do something with that gun that will have a long-lasting impact on his life and his career."

"Thanks," Willie Mitchell told him. "I should have been more aware of the situation. I've had the same problem with Walton carrying his pistols. There was an incident last year when he pulled his weapon to try to stop a riot and arson, but thank God he wasn't able to use it. I had a long talk with him. He's got a bright future, a beautiful wife and twin boys. He's a top-notch attorney, getting better by the day. I know he's more mature about brandishing a firearm these days. That incident was a wake-up call for Walton."

"When my testosterone level was at Walton's or Jake's, I had a tendency to overreact. You probably did, too."

Willie Mitchell smiled. "So lower testosterone is a good thing? That's what you're telling me?"

Dunne chuckled. "Sometimes."

Willie Mitchell's was the only office on the second floor with any activity. Judge Williams and all the court personnel cleared out of the courthouse immediately after the shootings, along with the clerks' offices, voter registration, board of supervisors, and everyone else who worked in the building. Willie Mitchell sent his staff home, too, until further notice. Only Mitchell, Dunne, and Jimmy Gray, and a few sheriff's deputies and inmates upstairs remained in the building.

The D.A. answered his cell. "Thanks," he said after listening.

"Who was that?" Dunne asked.

"Lee. There's no word yet on the mini-van. It just disappeared."

"What's next?" Jimmy Gray asked.

"Good question."

~ * ~

At nine-thirty that night David Dunne knocked on Willie Mitchell's door. He had called earlier. Willie Mitchell led him through the entrance hall into the kitchen and introduced him to Susan. She visited with them a while, then told Willie Mitchell she was going upstairs to read.

"How's she taking it?" David asked after she went upstairs.

139

"How is anyone? We're all in a state of shock." He opened the cabinet above the sink. "You want some water or Coke or something?"

"You got anything stronger?"

"Got it all."

"Just some blended whiskey over ice."

Willie Mitchell opened another cabinet and retrieved a squatty bottle of Crown Royal swaddled in a purple cloth bag. "I haven't had any of this in a long time. I think I'll join you."

He filled both glasses from the ice maker under the cabinet and poured the glasses two-thirds of the way to the top with the Crown Royal. "Let's go to the parlor."

Willie Mitchell sat in a wing-backed stuffed chair and gestured to David Dunne to take a seat on the Duncan Phyfe sofa. Willie Mitchell thought it was an original but Susan swore was a nineteen-twenties reproduction. Willie Mitchell rattled his ice and took a sip.

"I got to where I was drinking too much when Susan was gone. But not this. Vodka. Vodka with anything."

David took a sip. "Mmm. Tastes good."

"You married?" Willie Mitchell asked him.

"Nope."

"Ever been?"

"Never stayed in one place long enough."

"It's good to have a wife, David. Take my word for it. Susan's the best thing I ever did. I don't know how I ever talked her into marrying me. I'm really glad she came home."

"Y'all had some trouble?"

"Yep. She took a sabbatical, I call it. Three years. Came back a little over a year ago." He took a drink.

"You worked everything out?"

"Apparently. Where are you from"

"All over. My father was military."

"You followed in his footsteps?"

"Sure did. West Point."

"Then Army Rangers."

"How'd you know?"

"You look like a special forces guy. Where'd you get that scar?"

"IED shrapnel in Baghdad. Lucky it didn't take my head off."

"Where else did you serve?"

"Everywhere. Afghanistan. Pakistan, unofficially. Indonesia for a while. Somalia."

"Mogadishu?"

140

"Early, before it got out of hand. Other than Lagos it's the worse place I've ever been in my life."

Willie Mitchell took a sip of his drink. "Interesting stuff. I've spent all my professional career right here in the Delta."

"You're doing important work. Just a different kind of battle."

"A lot safer than your venues. Until today."

"Nobody could anticipate anything like that. It even surprised me, and I'm supposed to plan for the worst case scenario in every assignment."

"How long have you been with the FBI?"

"A few years. I worked operations alongside them when I was with the army. It was a natural segue."

"So you're mainly involved with national security?"

"That's right."

"Can you tell me now why you're really here?"

David sipped his drink. "That's why I came over tonight. Adolfo Zegarra Galván is no run-of-the-mill drug smuggler. You need to know what you're up against if you're dead set on keeping this case."

"I'm listening."

David Dunne gave his glass to Willie Mitchell Banks. "Freshen this up for me, if you don't mind, and I'll tell you about Zegarra. If you have time."

"I think I have time," Willie Mitchell said and went into the kitchen.

~ * ~

In his apartment in Jackson, Jake was glued to the television, watching reports of the day's shooting on Fox, CNN, and the mainstream networks, the ones Willie Mitchell referred to as the BCs and the BSs. He smashed his right fist into his left palm. "Dammit. I need to be up there with Willie Mitchell."

"The professor says no," Kitty said, next to him on the couch. "What could you do if you were?"

"I don't know. More than I can do here."

"You just want to be in the middle of the action."

"You don't know me well enough to say that."

"Yes, I do. We've spent a lot of time together the last few weeks. You seemed comfortable with that gun in your hand today, running back and forth to the parking lot, itching for something to happen."

"That asshole Dunne didn't think so."

"Well, there's some truth to what he said. Not sure he should have been so forceful with you. You men, it's always physical."

141

He jumped up from the couch. "I hate just sitting here. I ought to be up there helping Dad." He paced in front of the television. "I need to go run five miles or something."

"It's too dark."

"We could run around the reservoir. It's lighted enough."

"It is not. It's pitch black dark in most places. You'll trip over something and break your ankle, then you'll be laid up a month or two."

"I've got to do something."

"Let's Indian wrestle."

He laughed. "You mean arm wrestling?"

"No. Indian wrestling. With your legs."

"Never heard of it," Jake said.

"There's lots of Indians in the Northwest. I'll show you."

Kitty dragged the coffee table out of the way and lay on the carpeted floor on her back. "Now, you lie down on your back next to me, hip to hip, but your head is down there."

Jake lay down like she said.

"Now, we lock arms at the elbow. Raise your leg."

"Which leg?"

"The one next to mine. Straight up in the air three times. On the third time, we lock legs and try to flip each other over. Whoever stays on his or her back wins the match."

"I've never done this before. Let's do a practice before we start."

"All right."

They raised their legs once, twice, and locked them when Kitty said "three." Jake flipped her over easily.

"I get it," he said. "This is fun."

"Okay," she said. "Now these are for real."

Kitty counted one, two, and on three, whipped her leg inside Jake's and flipped him over like a pancake. She laughed out loud. Jake was dumbfounded.

"You cheated," he said.

"Did not. Speed and agility is just as important as strength."

"Let's go again."

She counted—and on three, flipped him sideways. Jake got back on his back in the ready position. "Again. This time I count."

She flipped him again, but it was not as easy as before. They did it a dozen more times, and Jake started to win every time as he figured out the timing, leg speed, and angles of engagement. They sat on the carpet, breathing hard, perspiring. She kissed him on the lips.

"Now," she said. "Let's do it with our clothes off."

Ninety minutes later, after making a date for a rematch the next day, they fell asleep in each other's arms, exhausted.

Chapter Twenty-Six

Adolfo found El Moro intelligent and interesting. He spent most days with him, at first because he had nothing else to do to pass the time in the prison. The man prayed five times a day, which seemed excessive to Adolfo, but as with most things people did, it made no difference to Adolfo.

El Moro told Adolfo he was born in Matamoros but both his parents were from Morocco. They moved from Rabat to Matamoros at the request of their employer, who owned a textile mill producing cotton garments in Rabat. The owner acquired a textile mill in Matamoros that was in bad financial condition and asked El Moro's father to move to Mexico to help get the mill up and running. As a child growing up in Matamoros, other kids made fun of his dark copper skin and began calling him El Moro, "the Moor," and the nickname stuck.

Adolfo told El Moro he was surprised none of the prisoners messed with him. "It's like they're afraid of you," Adolfo said.

"They are. They think I am possessed by the devil."

"Do you have a demon in you?"

"Not one that I am aware of. I believe in Allah, and his prophet Muhammad. I read the Quran every day. The prisoners hear my words and they are frightened."

"You are a Muslim."

"Yes. *Musulman* they say here."

"Have you always been?"

"Yes. My parents were devout and taught me from an early age."

"Are they still alive?"

"No. They were killed in a riot at the mill. The Mexican Christians revolted against the Muslims from Morocco who gave them jobs. The owner closed the mill a year later, and it still sits empty to this day. Another Christian victory."

"Stupid."

"Yes. Are you white?"

"My father was."

"And your mother?"

"She was *mestizo* from Madero, near Tampico. He was a sailor."

"He gave her money?"

"When he was in port."

"Did he mistreat her?"

"Yes."

"White men always mistreat women who are not white. They treat them like animals."

"She seemed to like him."

"She was poor, I am sure. He gave her a little bit of money, which was more than she had. It was nothing to him, as was she."

"Maybe."

"Did he mistreat you?"

"No. He paid little attention to me."

"Where was he from?"

"A port city in a state called Mississippi."

"I know this state. It was built on the back of African slaves."

El Moro asked Adolfo: "What do you believe in?"

Adolfo thought for a moment. "Nothing."

"What do you live for?"

Adolfo shrugged.

"Would you like to learn the truth?"

"About what?"

"About everything."

"And you know what the truth is? Because you read from that book you clutch all day?"

"Let me ask you this one thing. Do you know about the crusades?"

"In the Middle Ages? Yes. Christians from Europe invaded the Middle East. Muslim countries."

"Do you know why?"

"Why are any wars fought? Greed, land, gold."

"In part. But the Christians wanted to kill all Muslims if they did not convert. Just as the Catholics did to Sephardic Jews in Spain. Convert or die in the Inquisition."

Adolfo noticed that some of the other inmates in the central yard were watching Adolfo and El Moro talk.

"So?" Adolfo asked.

"Now, the reverse is true. We are going to tell the Christians in the United States that they must convert or die. Our numbers in Europe are growing. In fifty years Europe will be a Muslim continent. Our Muslim brothers there are having many children and the infidel whites do not reproduce enough to even replace themselves. We will not have to fire a weapon or fly planes into buildings in Europe to bring about this change. It is the will of Allah, and He is infinitely wise."

"You and I will be dead then."

"I will be with Allah and watch it all from heaven. You can be with us also if you like."

"I don't think so. But you are welcome to believe what you want. It makes no difference to me what a man thinks or does."

"How can you live believing in nothing? What is the purpose of your life?"

Adolfo walked off.

"The Great Satan in the north. How has he treated you?"

That night, Adolfo lay awake on his bunk thinking about El Moro and what he said. Adolfo remembered going to Mass with mean old Dominica Ayala in McAllen and listening to the priest. Adolfo was careful to make the sign of the cross when he was supposed to, but mostly he daydreamed about working for Señor Bernal.

Adolfo thought about Vikingo striking his sweet mother. He thought about how John Kirkpatrick and his friends treated him, and how he enjoyed watching Kirkpatrick take his last breaths in his Jeep. He remembered the black smoke rising from the ruins of Villa Bernal, and how the great man's head was blown off by the United States soldiers who invaded his beautiful home. Adolfo decided he would talk to El Moro again tomorrow. He drifted off to sleep.

Adolfo spent every day listening to El Moro for the next three months. Early on, El Moro had Adolfo read the Quran aloud and they discussed the meaning of the passages. El Moro came to know most of them by heart. For the first time in his life, Adolfo began to believe.

El Moro started and ended each day's lesson with the same quote from his Holy Quran: *Kill the unbelievers wherever you find them. But if they repent and accept Islam, then leave their way free.*

The words became his mantra. At night, Adolfo said them over and over until he fell asleep. Each morning, the words were the first thing on his mind. After a while, these words from the Holy Quran made his insides burn with desire, a desire to kill the unbelievers.

~ * ~

With six months to go on his three-year sentence, Adolfo started to think about life on the outside. All he had ever known was drug running, but his conversion to Islam made him look at things in a vastly different way. For the first time, he believed in something larger than himself—the divine words of the Prophet Muhammad and the wisdom of Allah.

El Moro enabled Adolfo to understand why he was put on this earth with white skin, why he was sent to learn perfect English in McAllen, why he had the ability to smuggle drugs better than anyone he knew, and why Adolfo had to kill the sodomite policeman and be brought to Cereso Reynosa. It was the divine will of Allah that he learn the Word of God at the feet of El Moro, and become a weapon in Allah's army to convert or kill all *norteamericanos*. His Muslim brothers had already ignited the war at the World Trade Center in New York, and he was joining the fight. If it were not already crystal clear to Adolfo which path Allah had chosen for him, Allah went one step further.

One day as Adolfo and El Moro sat on the ground near the prison entrance, the gate opened and two guards shoved a bearded black man into the dirt inside. The man was thin and as black as the blackest obsidian Adolfo had seen in the public markets of Tampico. His name was Torrance Shields.

Adolfo was the only inmate who spoke English well enough to understand the deluge of patois that gushed forth from the lips of Torrance Shields. Adolfo approached him the first day and offered to teach him what he needed to know in Cereso Reynosa to survive. Torrance brushed Adolfo aside with a guttural "get lost, white boy." But in a few days, hunger and fear took over, and Torrance approached Adolfo as he sat with El Moro.

"Hey, my man," Torrance said. "I'm sorry I was a little upset the other day. Bummed out being thrown into this place."

Adolfo shrugged. "It's okay."

"How long is your sentence?" El Moro asked.

"I had enough cash on me to bribe the judge down to a year, but not enough to let me go."

"One year. This way, the judge saves face," El Moro said.

"Exactly what kind of dude are you?" Torrance asked El Moro.

"A Moor. A Moroccan Muslim born in Mexico."

"No shit. *Assalaamu alaykum*, brother."

"Are you a believer?" El Moro asked.

"You ain't just whistling Dixie."

"And you?" Torrance said to Adolfo. "You from the U.S.?"

"His father was," El Moro said. "Took advantage of his Mexican mother."

"So, what does that make you?" Torrance asked.

"Nothing," Adolfo said.

"How you speak such good English? You don't sound like no Mexican."

"I went to school in Texas."

"What charges did they bring against you, Torrance Shields?" El Moro asked the black man.

"Trying to set up a little drug-running operation. I came down here to find a supplier for weed and smack. Didn't work out too good."

147

"Do you speak any Spanish?" Adolfo asked.

"Not a lick. Just thought I could talk slow and real loud." He laughed and slapped his knee.

"Do you use drugs?" El Moro asked.

"No, sir. Been clean since I converted."

"Then why are you trying to smuggle them?"

"Raise some money to kill a bunch of white mother fuckers in the good old U.S. of A."

"Allah be praised," Adolfo said.

~ * ~

Two months before his release, Adolfo woke up late one morning. He walked outside to find El Moro. In the central yard, he saw a couple of dozen prisoners milling around something on the ground. He made his way slowly to the center of the crowd. On the ground, his head bashed in and brain matter oozing from his skull, was El Moro. Adolfo knelt beside him and felt his neck for a pulse. The body was already cold. Adolfo picked up El Moro's Quran lying in the dirt next to his body.

Adolfo walked inside and woke up Torrance. The two walked out to the yard, each grabbed a foot, and dragged El Moro to the prison gate. Adolfo thought of the times he watched teams of horses drag the dead bulls from the small bullfighting arena in Tampico.

"Can you bury him today?" Adolfo called out to the guards on top of the gate. "We will help dig the grave."

One guard grabbed another. They opened the gate and dragged El Moro out of the prison. Adolfo and Torrance offered to follow, but the guards said no. "You stay inside," they said.

"Today," Adolfo said. "It must be done today."

The guards said they understood. Adolfo turned to Torrance.

"From this day forward, I am El Moro."

"And you can call me Hassan Malik, my brother."

Chapter Twenty-Seven

"The United States Department of Justice is exercising its jurisdictional authority in the prosecution of Adolfo Zegarra Galván, and I am today announcing his indictment by the federal grand jury sitting in Jackson for violations of Title Eighteen and Twenty-one of the United States Code, including the provisions prohibiting murder during a drug trafficking crime, murder in connection with a racketeering offense, and murder of a local law enforcement officer in connection with a continuing criminal enterprise. These homicide charges carry the death penalty as a possible sentence, and I am announcing today that my office will seek to put to death Adolfo Zegarra Galván for the murder of Yaloquena County Deputy Sheriff Travis Ware."

Jake stood next to Assistant U.S. Attorney Blake Briggs and behind their boss, the professor, Leopold Whitman, as he made the announcement at the press conference he convened. S.A. Kitty Douglas worked security for the event and stood against the back wall. Whitman said he would take a few questions.

A reporter from the Jackson CBS affiliate asked the U.S. attorney if the federal charges were a reaction to the juror killings in Sunshine.

"In part," Whitman said. "We attempted to take custody of the prisoner shortly after his arrest, but met with substantial opposition from the local district attorney and to a lesser extent the local sheriff, who insisted on keeping the defendant in their primitive facility no matter the risk it posed to their constituents."

"Are you saying," the reporter continued, "that the five deaths that occurred on the steps of the Yaloquena courthouse were a direct result of the district attorney's decision?"

"If one made a fair examination of the facts, I believe it might lead one to draw that conclusion."

"Why do you think Mr. Banks made such a decision?"

"My experience with the local authorities is that often times their decisions are driven by local political expediency and ego, to some extent."

There was a buzz in the audience. Several reporters left.

"Are you saying Mr. Banks' ego and political ambitions caused the death of these people in Sunshine?"

"I am saying that these are factors that drive such decisions on occasion. Not always. As I suggested earlier, you'll have to look at the salient facts in this particular case and draw your own conclusions."

Jake felt his face and ears redden. He left the room and picked up speed as he approached his office, slammed the door behind him, grabbed his cell and called Willie Mitchell.

"You're not going to believe what the son of a bitch Whitman just said," Jake told his father.

"I saw it all. Channel Twelve carried it live. The phone's ringing off the hook wanting a response from me."

"What are you going to say?"

"Not sure yet. Probably nothing. Zegarra came into my county and murdered Travis, a friend of mine and yours, for no reason. Whitman can say whatever he wants, but trying Zegarra for murder here and seeking the death penalty is what I consider my job and duty to be. It's why I'm elected to this position. I'm sorry as hell those people got killed, but I can't for the life of me see what that has to do with my decision to prosecute Zegarra. If I back off, then the bastards achieve exactly what they intended to do, disrupt my prosecution of Zegarra. I cannot let that happen."

"Why don't you say that?"

"I might. I'm not sure yet."

"Well, I'm sure. I'm handing in my resignation. I cannot work for the arrogant, pretentious bastard one day longer."

"Don't do that, Jake. You don't work for him. You work for the Justice Department. Don't let him chase you off."

"I don't care."

"Just hold on and cool off. You told me you don't have much contact with Whitman day to day."

"I don't. Blake Briggs gives me my assignments and supervises my work."

"Do something for me, Jake."

"What?"

"Don't resign. Don't do anything. Just go on about your business as if this never happened."

Jake was silent for a moment. "All right. But you know he's coming to get Zegarra."

"I'll be ready. I'm preparing a motion right now."

~ * ~

"I've not heard from anyone else, Your Honor," Eleanor Bernstein told Judge Zelda Williams in response to the question whether any other attorney had contacted her since Ace High Boardman's withdrawal from the case the previous week. Zegarra sat at the defense table, a blank expression on his face, seemingly oblivious to the nature of the hearing before Judge Williams.

"Congratulations on your elevation to first chair, Ms. Bernstein," the judge said. "Mr. Banks?"

"Thank you, Your Honor. When I began to prepare for this hearing, I realized the previous motion that I filed, with its supporting memorandum, sets forth the applicable law giving the state courts jurisdiction in a murder prosecution in which the defendant is in the custody of the state. At the last hearing, Your Honor did not issue a ruling because the U.S. attorney withdrew the claim in open court, conceding, I believe, the strength of our legal authority."

"I see from the record that you served notice of this hearing today on the Justice Department through personal service on the U.S. attorney, Mr. Whitman at his office in Jackson."

"Yes, Your Honor. Sheriff Lee Jones personally served him with the show cause order setting this hearing for this date and time."

Lee Jones sat behind the rail on the first bench. He nodded to the judge to confirm what Willie Mitchell said.

"Have you spoken to Mr. Whitman?"

"I called his office twice yesterday, Your Honor, but he has not returned my call yet."

"Ms. Bernstein, your former first chair, Mr. Boardman, stated at the last hearing that he agreed with Mr. Banks' memorandum citing appropriate legal authority vested primary jurisdiction in the state."

"Yes, Your Honor," Ms. Bernstein said.

"Did you then, and do you now agree with what Mr. Boardman stated to the court?"

The defense attorney glanced at Willie Mitchell for a moment, then whispered something to Zegarra. Willie Mitchell recognized the look. Eleanor had done no independent research on the question of state versus federal jurisdiction and did not have her own legal opinion on the issue. Zegarra listened as Eleanor whispered to him, but he said nothing in response.

Willie Mitchell studied Zegarra. His casual demeanor seemed a lot more sinister in light of what David Dunne shared with the D.A. at his house over drinks.

"I have nothing to present to the court this morning that would deviate from the opinion stated by Mr. Boardman at the previous hearing, Your Honor," Eleanor said. "I would, however, like to reserve the right to submit a memorandum on the issue at a later date."

Judge Williams furrowed her brow at Eleanor. "Feel free to do so at any time, Ms. Bernstein." Willie Mitchell was encouraged that the judge recognized Eleanor's non-answer for what it was. "I'm ready to rule," the judge said.

The back door of the courtroom flew open and Leopold Whitman strode in followed by his stocky first assistant, Blake Briggs, and a half-dozen federal agents in dark blue suits. The U.S. attorney walked through the swinging rail gate and let it go in time to hit Briggs in the knee. Briggs recovered quickly and caught up with his boss.

"Mr. Whitman," Judge Williams said. "You are late."

"I cannot be late for a hearing that has no jurisdiction over me or the defendant, Zegarra. I'm here to serve a writ of *habeas corpus* on District Attorney Banks and Sheriff Jones." Whitman made a sweeping gesture to Briggs, who served Willie Mitchell and Lee Jones with papers.

While Willie Mitchell studied the document, Judge Williams banged her gavel three times.

"Mr. Whitman," she said. "This is my courtroom and I am conducting this hearing. You will not come into my courtroom making demands. You will observe proper protocol or I will hold you in contempt and direct the sheriff to take *you* into custody and place you upstairs with Mr. Zegarra as the county's guest until you learn some manners. Do you understand?"

The professor bristled but held his tongue. Blake Briggs backed up a step, leaving Whitman out front.

"Bring me the writ, Mr. Banks."

Willie Mitchell walked between the lawyer tables and gave her the document that Briggs had served on him.

Willie Mitchell waited for Judge Williams to finish reading. "If I may be heard, Your Honor?"

"Go ahead, Mr. Banks."

"This is an order in a case entitled 'United States versus Adolfo Zegarra Galván' and appears to be an *ex parte* order obtained by the U.S. attorney's office without naming me or the sheriff as a party to the action. So, initially, I would submit to the court that I cannot be bound by an order in a matter to which I have not been made a party."

"It is signed by federal judge Herman Stanwyk in Jackson, Your Honor," Whitman said. "It is well-settled that a federal court order takes precedence over a state court proceeding."

"Where?" the judge asked.

"Excuse me?" Whitman said.

"Where does it say such a thing? You have not provided this court with any statute or jurisprudence that says precisely when a federal court order takes precedence over a state court order in these circumstances."

152

Whitman cut a smug glance at Briggs, who wanted nothing to do with it. "Federal court, Your Honor, the supremacy clause."

"What about the Tenth Amendment to the United States Constitution and these U.S. Supreme Court cases cited by Mr. Banks that appear to be on point? Where is your authority, Mr. Whitman?"

"Here is my authority," Whitman said, shaking his writ at Judge Williams. "An order signed by Judge Stanwyk ordering you people to give me custody of Zegarra. Now."

"And these men behind you in the dark suits, Mr. Whitman, are they going to handcuff me along with Mr. Banks and Sheriff Jones if I rule in favor of Mr. Banks' motion? Are they going to strong-arm these elected officials if they don't do what you say?"

Willie Mitchell saw Briggs take another half-step back. The men in the dark suits looked uncomfortable.

"Your Honor," Willie Mitchell said. "I move to re-set this case for trial in this court two weeks from this coming Monday."

"Ms. Bernstein?"

"Mr. Banks pre-cleared the date with me, Your Honor. We're ready to go on that date."

Whitman stomped his right foot.

"Mr. Whitman," Judge Williams said. "Either have your henchmen draw down on us right now or leave my courtroom. I've never seen such infantile behavior from an officer of the court. Any court."

Whitman stormed out the center aisle, followed at a discreet distance by Blake Briggs and the six feds in dark suits.

"Thank you, Your Honor," Willie Mitchell said.

"Don't thank me, Mr. Banks. I'm just ruling the way I believe the legal authorities you cite require me to. I'm following precedent. If it were up to me, I'd let this cup pass to another judge, in another jurisdiction. Since you are going forward with the case against this defendant in my court come hell or high water, I would ask you to do me one thing."

"What's that, Your Honor?"

"Let's get this over with as soon as possible so the people in this community can get some sleep for a change."

"Will do, Your Honor."

Zegarra yawned.

~ * ~

That night, Susan sat in the kitchen at the worm-eaten pine table. She watched Willie Mitchell peel a grapefruit. He had such nice hands. She noticed them the first day she met him in The Grove.

153

"Thanks again for going with me to Elbert Dowd's memorial service," he said.

"He was a nice old man. I was surprised he was cremated. Country people around here aren't usually in favor of it."

"Elbert was pretty practical minded. Probably didn't see the use in taking up real estate to bury his body." Willie Mitchell said: "What a senseless crime. All those innocent people murdered. Who could do something like that?"

She watched him point the remote. The evening news came up on the small television on the kitchen counter. He switched back and forth between a Jackson channel and the Greenville channel airing portions of Whitman's press conference announcing his indictments, the interview with Willie Mitchell outside the Yaloquena courthouse after the hearing before Judge Williams, and an interview in Whitman's office where he rebutted the D.A.

Usually his jumping between stations and surfing drove her crazy, but tonight she did not mind. He needed to watch all the coverage. So did she. She was proud of how well he handled himself with television reporters. He made it look easy. Susan knew it was not.

He hit the mute button.

"You appear a lot more reasonable than Whitman. He's kind of over the top."

"They should never appoint a U.S. attorney who hasn't tried cases in the trenches."

"Why would they give the job to someone like him?"

"U.S. attorneys are all political appointments. Every one of them, all over the country. They have legions of young lawyers on staff fighting for the trial work."

"Like Jake."

She watched Willie Mitchell concentrate on peeling with his lovely hands the Louisiana-raised grapefruit before him on the pine table. She knew from experience the yellow rind came off easily, but the white underbelly, the tenacious, fibrous material between the rind and the pink fruit, was a challenge. After several minutes of deliberate peeling, he stuck his finger where the navel used to be and spread the pieces. Willie Mitchell separated one section, made sure it was free from the white albedo, and held it out for Susan. She opened her mouth like a bird and captured the whole thing.

She held her hand over her mouth and giggled. "Juicy."

Willie Mitchell hopped up and tore a paper towel from its roll and gave it to her. She held it to her mouth. He kissed her on the cheek.

He sat down and held up another section. "Ready?"

She shook her head, and he ate it himself, snatching her paper towel and dabbing his own mouth. He was so special to her. She wondered what mental state she was in when she almost threw it all away. It was something she had never told him.

Before she had begun her three-year leave of absence, she had come all too close to a man in Oxford. Willie Mitchell was not himself. The boys were gone. He was listless and chronically depressed about his career and the dismal future of the small town in which he lived practically his whole life. She was much the same. There were a lot of days when he told Susan he had wasted his abilities, especially when he was in the vodka, which was often.

She knew she was no prize at the time, either. The change of life had hit her hard, and she suffered on a daily basis the same kind of *malaise* he described. The big difference was Willie Mitchell continued to work and produce. Maybe not at one hundred percent. Susan, on the other hand, spent many mornings in bed, unable or unwilling to get up, miserable at the prospect of facing the day. Scared, too. She wasn't sure of what.

It was no surprise that their physical relationship became non-existent.

She found refuge those dark days in her sorority alumni association in Oxford, working to keep the sorority financially sound and the massive house, where scores of coeds lived and ate their meals, in good repair. She spent more and more time in Oxford, and hours drinking coffee, then cocktails, with an Ole Miss Panhellenic administrator, a guy she knew from her time as an undergraduate. He was a hard-partying frat boy in those days.

His entire working life had been at the university, using his social contacts to climb up the bureaucratic ladder until he had the perfect job: excellent salary and retirement and nothing of importance to do other than entertain the wealthiest donors to the school. Divorced, living from payday to payday, he went out of his way to flirt with Susan. She loved the attention. But one day, he actually made a pass at her. It brought her to her senses.

Looking back, she was glad he came on to her to make her realize how foolish she was being. He was nothing of substance, glib and smooth, a mile wide and half an inch deep. It was a wake-up call, however. Before she could be a contributing partner in a marriage, she had to get a grip on herself, mentally and spiritually. It took longer than she had expected, and a lot of counseling. She did not blame Willie Mitchell for the Mary Margaret Anderson affair. Three years is a long time to be alone. Susan felt lucky that Willie Mitchell wanted her home. Their year together since her return had been all she had hoped.

"I'll be glad when you're through with this case," she said.

"You and me both."

They sat in silence for a moment.

"I'm not going to do the teen pregnancy thing."

"Okay."

"I do wish I could find something that would give me some kind of purpose. Not necessarily a job. I'd like to make a difference somehow."

Willie Mitchell stopped fiddling with the grapefruit. "You are a wonderful wife and a terrific mother. You raised two great kids. When it comes down to it, all we can really accomplish on this earth that has a lasting impact is to raise healthy, well-educated children. Everything else fades away."

"I know that. I'm grateful for them every day. And for you, too. But a lot of women raise successful kids *and* contribute to society in their work or some cause. Here I am, middle-aged, and I've never had a career or accomplished one thing at all."

"What about me? I've been in this county practically all my life. I'm a small town district attorney nearing retirement age and what have I done? Anyone with a modicum of ability can do this job."

"Not like you do it."

"Maybe, but in the long run, what difference does it really make? I think about it a lot. I could have done so much more with my education and my ability. I could have had a successful civil litigation practice with a big firm in Jackson, or New Orleans, or Memphis. Could have made a lot more money, handled cases all over the country. Or maybe I should have moved up the political ladder, go from D.A. to state senator maybe, then, who knows, take a shot at a statewide race, maybe governor some day. But here I sit."

"You don't like politicians."

"I know. I would have been a lousy legislator. Who wants to compromise and make deals all the time. Something's either right or wrong. Besides, I don't like asking people for money, and I hate it when people ask for special treatment."

"You don't really think you would have been happier if you had done a civil practice or run for something else, do you?"

Willie Mitchell walked around the table and washed the grapefruit off his hands at the sink, then turned and took

Susan's hand. He bent to kiss it, and pulled her to her feet and into his arms. They held each other tightly for a while.

"No. I wouldn't. I think I was destined to do just what I'm doing, because here I am." He squeezed her tight. "I'm glad you are here," he said. "I love you more than anything else in the world."

"And this is where I belong, even if I've never done a thing."

They kissed. "At least we've accomplished nothing together," he said, making her laugh.

"Breaking News" crawled across the bottom of the screen and caught Willie Mitchell's eye. He picked up the remote.

"Looks like Mississippi has started another trend," the black female anchor said to the older white male anchor with a white pompadour as impressive as a Pentecostal preacher's. "And this one's more deadly than our number one ranking in obesity and out of wedlock births. Get this, Harry. A woman serving on a jury in Corpus Christi, Texas, was gunned down this afternoon next to her car in the courthouse parking lot in broad daylight after the court had adjourned for the day. We'll have details after the break."

"Uh-oh," Susan said.

Chapter Twenty-Eight

The fact that the woman juror in Corpus Christi had been killed by her estranged husband in violation of a restraining order against him was buried in the third paragraph of the Associated Press story. The second paragraph referred to the killing of the prospective jurors in Yaloquena County. In the fourth paragraph, the reporters who wrote the piece disclosed that the husband in Corpus was being treated for mental health issues after a three-year battle over child custody and community property with the ex-wife he killed in the courthouse parking lot.

"In other words," Willie Mitchell told fat banker Jimmy Gray on their ten-minute morning walk, "the only thing linking this to our murders on the courthouse steps was the location the ex-husband chose to kill her."

"If he'd killed her in her church parking lot, it wouldn't have gotten any coverage outside of Texas," Jimmy said. "Ain't that some shit? I don't believe anything I read any more."

"The story has made the rounds. My phone's been ringing off the hook at the office. Everybody wants off Zegarra jury duty."

"What are you telling them?"

"That I can't excuse them, only the judge can."

"What's she telling them?"

"She's not talking. Her secretary Mona is screening all the calls, and unless someone's got tuberculosis or a spouse on their deathbed, no one is getting excused."

"Is that old biddy Mona Cartwright still working for the judge?"

"Yep."

"Mona's tough as a boot. She won't take any shit. You ought to make sure Mona tells them about all the security y'all got this time."

"She is. Mona says it doesn't make any difference what she tells them about security, they're all scared to death."

"Did the guy in Corpus kill himself after he killed his wife?"

"Yep. Right there next to her body in the parking lot."

"Good. At least he had the courtesy to take himself out. Save those people over there in Texas the trouble and expense of trying him and sending him to the pen."

"Sounds like he would have had a shot at insanity."

"You get down to it, partner, everyone does," Jimmy Gray said.

"Some more than others."

Willie Mitchell left Jimmy in his driveway and jogged back home. There were two men in suits, one with a buzz cut, the other's bumpy skull totally shaved, in a navy blue Mercury Grand Marquis with U.S. government plates waiting for him in the pea graveled circular drive in front of his home. The men exited the Mercury when they saw him.

"I've been expecting you guys," Willie Mitchell said. "What are you serving me with now?"

"Another writ, Mr. Banks," Buzz Cut said and gave Willie Mitchell the paperwork. He read it over quickly.

"This hearing in Jackson is set for next Friday. They must know I start Zegarra's murder trial the following Monday here in Sunshine."

"Yes, sir," Slick Head said.

"You guys want me to call the sheriff so you can serve him?"

"We already got him," Buzz Cut said.

Willie Mitchell stared at the men, trying to recognize them. "Were you guys with the professor when he showed up last week in Judge Williams court?"

Buzz Cut snickered. "The professor," he said.

"Yes, sir," Slick Head said. "We were there behind the rail."

"What did you guys think of all that?"

"Fubar," Buzz Cut said.

"Snafu," Slick Head added.

"All right, guys. Thanks. Give my regards to the professor."

Buzz Cut and Slick Head laughed and drove off.

~ * ~

At two that afternoon, Eleanor Bernstein walked into Willie Mitchell's office accompanied by a sharply dressed black man in his mid- to late fifties. He wore his hair in a close-cut afro, and stylish black rectangular glasses. Even if Willie Mitchell had not had so many cases in which Jerome King was directly or tangentially involved, the D.A. would have recognized him from his billboards all over the state and his full-page ad on the back cover of the Jackson and Greenville telephone books.

"The Honorable Jerome King," Willie Mitchell said with a smile.

"The Honorable Willie Mitchell Banks," Jerome said, extending his hand. "It's a pleasure to see you again."

"Don't tell me you're here on Zegarra."

"Yessirreee Bob, and Ms. Bernstein has kindly agreed to stay on in the same role she had with Mr. Boardman."

"I thought you were going to say you were representing Hubert Holland and the estate of Carl Lippmann in a claim against Zegarra for the wreck on the interstate."

159

"With tort reform raising its ugly head all over the place, my firm is branching out into criminal law, which continues to be a high-growth sector in our fair state."

"He's got five lawyers doing criminal law full-time in his Jackson office," Eleanor said.

"And growing. I'd like for Ms Bernstein to join the firm but she says she likes being a sole practitioner up here in the Delta."

"How many personal injury lawyers now?"

"Twenty—and I don't know how many paralegals. Lots of fender benders. The paralegals and secretaries do all the work. They settle most of them with the adjusters over the phone before any lawyers get involved."

"The class actions may dry up, but there's always going to be car wrecks," Willie Mitchell said. "I'm sure you still do very well, Jerome."

"Life is sweet, Willie Mitchell. Eleanor tells me we're going to trial."

"A week from Monday we start picking a jury. Boardman filed a speedy trial motion."

"Say no more. I'll be ready to go. Ms. Bernstein has everything in good order, I'm glad to say."

"Who hired you?" Willie Mitchell asked.

"You know that's privileged, Willie Mitchell."

"I won't tell anyone."

Jerome winked at Eleanor. "Neither will we."

Chapter Twenty-Nine

In the few remaining months of his sentence, El Moro spent his days talking to Hassan Malik, the former Torrance Shields. The first week after the murder of Adolfo's mentor, Malik occasionally slipped and called him Adolfo, but El Moro corrected him. As El Moro's fervor for Islam grew, assuming the mantle of his mentor seemed natural, and Malik never called him Adolfo again. El Moro questioned Malik about his life and his conversion in Memphis, and Malik was glad to tell his story in colorful detail to pass the time.

Torrance Shields had grown up in North Memphis, in the Frayser neighborhood, which he told El Moro was a tough, dangerous place. He barely knew his parents, both of whom succumbed to the crack epidemic of the eighties. He was raised by his mother's sister, a good woman he said, but once it was clear Torrance could not prosper in school, he spent as little time in his aunt's home as possible.

"Looking back," Torrance said, "I had some kind of learning problem with my brain I guess, because I never could get into the letters and numbers all that good. My aunty eventually gave up on me going to school and just let me come and go as I pleased. I was a skinny little nigger, mean as a snake, and from the time I was ten I was running with a bunch of kids, and we were kind of understudies to the Moto Men, a violent-ass gang of street thugs in Memphis, a branch of a gang headquartered in Detroit. We'd do whatever the Motos told us to do. Never gave it another thought. We was juvies, and we'd do some shit for the Motos 'cause they said we couldn't get no hard time, just 'juvie time.'

"When I was eighteen I did an armed robbery of a liquor store with and older dude. He had the gun and I only drove the getaway car so my lawyer plea-bargained it down to a simple robbery and I got five years in the state pen. Had to do two before I got paroled out to a halfway house in North Memphis. That's where I met my buddy Ahmad Akbar and he introduced me to the man, Hakim Abdullah Al Rashad. He's the dude turned my life around."

"Tell me about Al Rashad," El Moro said.

"Some of this shit about Al Rashad I know for a fact, but lot of it I got from Akbar, my main man in Memphis. He's the one drove me to the border so I could walk across to try to make some connections, but I fucked it up."

El Moro held his Quran. "Al Rashad."

"He's a genius, first of all. You got to know that. He grew up somewhere in California and he's got these Rasta-looking dreads, I mean some nasty looking shit on his head. He's the top dog of the whole thing, you know, the HNIC."

El Moro did not know the acronym.

"You know, Head Nigger in Charge. Man, you sure don't know much." Malik went on about Al Rashad, but the information he provided was so vague and conflicting that El Moro decided he would go to Memphis and meet these men himself, Akbar and Al Rashad, to find out about them and their plans for America. Malik bragged about Al Rashad's plan for jihad in the United States and the ultimate conversion of all the infidels to Islam.

"You ever read the Quran?" El Moro asked, holding out the book.

"Not yet, but I been meanin' to."

~ * ~

When El Moro walked out of Cereso Reynosa in the first week of July 2005, he was a different man, with a different name. For the first time in his life, he had a set of beliefs that gave him a purpose, and a plan. No more alcohol or heroin or women for El Moro—he would live an ascetic life as described in the Quran for holy men. Money, clothes, and material goods had never really mattered to him after Señor Bernal's death, but now he eschewed them as part of the American dream he had learned to hate.

El Moro's plan required money to implement, so he reported first to his cartel boss and began making money the only way he knew how, smuggling drugs across the Rio Grande.

Moving cocaine into the United States was different than it was before nine-eleven, and in some ways easier for El Moro, with Homeland Security's emphasis on bombs, weapons, and Middle Eastern men. He fit none of the Homeland Security border profiles, and the guards gave him little trouble.

His cartel associates had no problem calling him by his new name. They did not give a shit what he called himself as long as he did the job.

El Moro told the cartel he wanted to work as many trips as they could give him. Since he was the best smuggler *El Cártel de Campeche* had, they kept him on the road, and had him drive farther and farther into the United States to deliver, sometimes to pickup and deliver. With his white skin and flawless English, he made new connections and deals in the United States for the cartel that no one else at his level could do.

Malik told El Moro in prison where he could find Ahmad Akbar in Memphis, and Akbar could introduce him to Al Rashad. Malik would join them in Memphis when he got out of Mexico.

El Moro stayed busy for the cartel, picking up loads of cocaine from their planes landing in the Louisiana marshes and delivering them all over the South, hoarding the money he made. Hurricane Katrina had interfered with his deliveries in the New Orleans area for a while, but El Moro realized the disaster made the area ripe for recruiting angry, dangerous black men to the cause.

It was time to meet Al Rashad.

El Moro drove to Memphis a month after Katrina and introduced himself to Malik's buddy Ahmad Akbar, *nee* Bratherton Daniels, who lived in Memphis exactly where Malik said he did. El Moro overcame Akbar's skepticism with the wealth of detail he provided about Malik and Cereso Reynosa. El Moro wanted a meeting with Al Rashad, but Akbar cautioned El Moro to be patient. He had to know much more about Moro before he introduced him to Al Rashad.

El Moro told Akbar his history, from the barrio and the docks of Madero and Tampico, working for Señor Bernal and his education in McAllen, his smuggling days before and after Bernal's murder by the U.S. agents in his home, his time in prison and conversion to Islam.

Akbar listened, then shared his life story. He was not jet-black like Malik, but a dark shade of brown with a full beard and a substantial afro. He was a big man, about six-two, and strong. He was born in Marks, Mississippi, a farming community in the Delta, to a thirteen-year-old named Virginia Daniels. Virginia's mother took the infant a couple of hours north to Memphis for the child's grandmother to rear in the Orange Mound section of South Memphis, not far from the Mississippi state line.

Bratherton's grandmother had more to do than look after him, and he began his criminal career running with the bad boys in the neighborhood. He affiliated with the C-Note Killers, a large, Cincinnati-based gang that invaded Memphis in the seventies. At fourteen, his brothers in the gang carved a large C on his left arm with a box cutter. When the bloody C healed, the keloid tissue that scarred over the wound made the C protrude prominently. His grandmother saw it, but never asked Bratherton about it.

At seventeen he was arrested for burglary, his second felony offense. The Memphis judge took an interest in young

163

Bratherton at the suggestion of his appointed attorney, and Bratherton was given the choice of enlisting in the army or going to prison.

Bratherton chose the military option, and was stationed at Fort Riley, Kansas with the First Infantry Division as a cavalry scout. He was good with a rifle, and the Army trained him to be a sharpshooter. He killed a lot of Iraqis at long range in Desert Storm, a fact he now regretted immensely. Instead of killing his Muslim brothers, he should have been killing the white devils who ordered him to shoot.

Breaking the jaw of a superior officer earned him a dishonorable discharge and a brief stateside stint in Fort Leavenworth prison. When he got out, he hitchhiked west to California, where he strong-armed a sidewalk vendor out of his cash box then passed out a block away leaning against a dumpster in a convenience store parking lot.

His intoxication at the time of the robbery was not considered much of a defense by his court appointed attorney, who pleaded him out to a lesser felony and three years in the custody of California Department of Corrections at Chino. Out on work release after eighteen months, he was befriended by a strange-looking black man named Hakim Abdullah Al Rashad.

"What was Al Rashad doing in California?" El Moro asked.

"That's where he was from. He grew up in North Inglewood."

"And how long before you converted?"

"It took a while. At first I thought the man was crazy. On parole, I had to be careful hanging out with him because he was a con, too. I knew nothing about Islam. I knew a little about Malcolm X from the movie, you know, with Denzel Washington, but I never met a real Muslim until Al Rashad."

"What can you tell me about Al Rashad?" El Moro asked.

"His folks weren't poor, more like middle class, I guess. His Christian slave name was Calvin Ketchums, and his folks were Baptists. His daddy left home when Calvin was in junior high, but Calvin went on and finished high school and moved to Oakland. He got a job in a big hotel and would pick up things from the people from time to time, you know, a wallet or a watch. One day Calvin was going through this rich white dude's suitcase when the man walked in the room. Calvin took off and ran down the hall, knocking this Mexican maid over. She hit her head and died. Dead from just that bump. Calvin didn't even mean to hurt nobody.

"Calvin felt bad about it and got sent up to San Quentin where he ran into this fellow Ronald Johnson, who started the African Identity Movement, AIM. You ever hear of him?"

El Moro said he hadn't.

"Anyway, Calvin learned a lot from Johnson about white America and the black man's struggles from slavery on up to today. He learned about Karl Marx. You know who that is?"

"Yes. The communist."

"Al Rashad says Marxist. Says there's a difference. So then Calvin came across some other brothers in San Quentin who taught him about Islam, and he learned all he could about it his last two years in the pen. He got out and legally changed his name to Hakim Abdullah Al Rashad and started teaching and preaching all over California. Al Rashad made his way to Mecca, and met with some of the men who put together nine-eleven. Don't ask him about that, by the way.

"Anyway, he gets back from Mecca and he starts another outfit called California Afro-Americans for Allah, he called it C triple A for short, and they got into all kinds of shit out there. He built three mosques in California and started recruiting brothers in prison and on parole, giving them something to believe in, like me. This is when I met up with him. C triple A started getting radical, like buying and selling guns, anything to raise money, you know. One of Al Rashad's members got carried away and killed two white tourists. Then the cops claimed C triple A was trying to blow up some baseball park in San Francisco, so Al Rashad, being the smart man he is, figured he had to get out of California, let the heat die down. We were tight by then, and I took him to Memphis and he stayed underground a while until things chilled. He liked Memphis and started organizing, still keeping a low profile. I brought Malik to him."

"Can you tell me Al Rashad's ultimate goal?"

"Jihad against the white Christian establishment in America, man. Get some payback against the fuckin' infidels for what they done in the Middle Ages and to us black men the last two hundred years in the United States. Do anything to fuck 'em up and kill 'em and bring down the evil system. And I mean anything."

"Can I meet him now?"

"Tomorrow. You be here at noon and I'll take you. You try anything funny, or it turn out you ain't who you say you are, and I'm gon' kill you myself. Okay?"

"No problem."

The next day, the meeting with Al Rashad went better than El Moro expected. Once he got past the long, brown dreads and the thick facial hair that left only a small amount of Al Rashad's light brown skin visible, he was impressed with the fire that burned behind the man's black eyes. Al Rashad's black, flowing robe and the round black hat, his immense salt-and-pepper beard and ominous dark circles under his eyes, reminded El Moro of photographs of Ayatollah Khomeini he had seen in old magazine articles in prison about the overthrow of the Shah in Iran.

El Moro spoke to him about the chaos in New Orleans, the brothers shooting at the rescue helicopters and widespread destruction of police cars. He asked Al Rashad to send Akbar with him to New Orleans to recruit followers to the cause, to begin a cell.

"These brothers in New Orleans already hate the white man and feel they have nothing to lose. It will not take much to convince these men of the virtue of Islam and the holiness of our cause," he told Al Rashad.

"I agree with this outreach to New Orleans," Al Rashad said. "After all, it is called the Crescent City."

In the following four years, El Moro delivered to Al Rashad personally or by FedEx a large portion of the cash the cartel paid him after each transaction. He kept enough for food and gasoline, and to keep his vehicles in good condition. He stayed on the road constantly and expanded his repertoire of services to the cartel, making him more valuable to the organization with every trip, building the cartel's confidence in his devotion to their business.

At the same time, the money he provided to Al Rashad was the lifeblood of Al Rashad's Memphis-based group, Africans for Islam. Al Rashad considered El Moro his most valuable follower, and used the regular payments to grow the organization, arm and train the new AFI members in cities all over the United States.

In time, Al Rashad came to believe it was time for AFI to begin its reign of terror. El Moro agreed, and asked Al Rashad to wait for one final funding coup, a big score El Moro promised would put AFI over the top in funding. El Moro said after this final pay day, he would quit smuggling for the cartel and work full time in the cause.

El Moro told Al Rashad: "It's time to start killing thousands at malls and sports events, soft targets we can reach easily. With our network of cells in cities all over the United States, it will be easy to achieve widespread terror and eventually the downfall of the Great Satan."

El Moro was headed north to Memphis in the process of delivering the big score to Al Rashad, five million dollars, in the early morning hours when Hubert Holland spilled his coffee and ran into El Moro's Maxima in Jackson, Mississippi, sending the trunk load of hundred-dollar bills earmarked for Al Rashad dancing and swirling in the wind on Interstate 55.

Later that day, Al Rashad learned from the news report on the Memphis NBC affiliate of the accident in Jackson and the impoundment of his five million dollars, the arrest of El Moro for killing the deputy, and El Moro's incarceration in Yaloquena County jail. Al Rashad sent word for Malik and Akbar to meet with him the next night. Before they arrived at Al Rashad's building, he watched the news of the failed jailbreak attempt and the videotape of the smoldering hulk of the helicopter in a parking lot in Sunshine.

"Stupid Mexicans," he said to the television.

Thirty minutes later, Akbar and Malik walked into Al Rashad's chambers. He told them what happened to El Moro in Mississippi.

~ * ~

Al Rashad learned as much as he could about El Moro's killing of the Yaloquena deputy in the weeks that followed. He instructed his followers to bring him the Jackson and Greenville papers each day, and he pored over the articles and searched the Internet, gathering information and trying to formulate a plan. When he read about the aborted attempt by the U.S. attorney to take over the case and his decision during the hearing to defer to the state's case, he knew what they had to do. He summoned Malik and Akbar once again.

"We must get El Moro into the federal system."

Akbar spoke before Malik had a chance. "What for?"

"The state's murder case against El Moro is air tight. The district attorney is a good lawyer and will convict him of murder. He will get the death penalty in state court for the killing of the popular deputy, and sent to death row at Parchman Farm. There is a real chance he might actually receive a lethal injection after his appeal is complete. At Parchman, he will be kept in isolation twenty-three hours a day."

"What about the other hour?" Malik asked, his eyes wide and dramatic set against his jet black skin.

Al Rashad ignored him.

"In the federal system, fewer than five people have been put to death since 1988 when the government reinstated the death penalty. I have seen the U.S. attorney from Jackson on television and he is weak. He's not a trial attorney like the D.A., but a small man with a high opinion of himself and will likely plead the case down to a lesser offense to get the information El

167

Moro has on the Mexican cartel. El Moro may not be able to provide money to us like he has in the past, but with his intellect and desire he can recruit for us and spread the word of Islam throughout every penitentiary that holds him."

"You want us to kill the district attorney?" Akbar asked.

Malik's eyes grew wider. "Kill the D.A.?"

"No." Al Rashad gave a piece of paper to Akbar then leaned back on the large pillow behind his back. "Those are directions to Sunshine."

"I know where it is," Malik said.

"So do I," Akbar said.

"The date of the trial is written there as well. There will be many days of jury selection beginning that day. I want you two there. I've had a small van confiscated off the streets, and I want you to help prepare it so you can shoot from it without being seen."

"Yes, sir," Akbar said.

"I want you to use your skill with a rifle, with which you killed our brothers in Iraq, and atone to Allah for those murders by killing as many of the white infidel jurors as you can."

"It will be my pleasure, Al Rashad," Akbar said.

"Me, too," Malik said.

"This is not a suicide mission," Al Rashad said. "Use your military knowledge to plan it in great detail. Go down there to scout, pick your vantage point as far away as you can, plan your escape. After you have your plan together, come back to me and let us review it, step by step. We have several weeks to perfect this plan."

Akbar stood and bowed, then left the room. Malik hurried after him, doing a sideways, half-bow on the way out.

~ * ~

Weeks later, after Akbar used the sharpshooting skills he learned from U.S. Army instructors to massacre the innocents on the Yaloquena courthouse steps, he and Malik ditched the mini-van in deep water at the north end of Lake Ferguson in Washington County northwest of Greenville, an oxbow that used to be a bend in the Mississippi River.

Lake Ferguson was less than an hour's drive from the Sunshine courthouse, and the two men knew from their scouting trips to Sunshine they could stay on little-traveled back roads to get there. They torched the interior of the mini-van with two homemade super sized M-80s, each containing two hundred grams of flash powder explosive, enough to scorch the interior. They had searched for a deep-water drop off inside the levee in a remote area, and the north end of Lake Ferguson was perfect. After watching the burned-out mini-van disappear into thirty feet of dark brown water, Akbar and Malik drove away from Lake Ferguson in the Silver 2008 Chevrolet Impala they stashed at the site that morning.

On their third and final trip to Sunshine, Akbar and Malik had arrived two days before jury selection began. They re-checked the courthouse and its environs, and found the perfect spot for the kill shots, a driveway at a vacant house on Cypress Street, across the bayou from the courthouse. Through the mini-van's back flap, beyond the cypress trees in the bayou, Akbar could see everyone on the courthouse steps. In a test run, Malik dropped Akbar at the courthouse and drove the three blocks around the bayou to park in the driveway of the vacant house. Akbar casually tested several vantage points on the steps and concluded that because of the heavy foliage of the cypress trees, had he not been looking for the mini-van, it would not have been noticeable.

Weeks before in Memphis, Akbar and Malik had created the flap in the metal around the mini-van's license plate with a welding torch. The flap was hinged at the bottom, and it lay flat, license plate and all, outside the mini-van when Akbar pushed it out from inside. Akbar tied a thick string to the top so he could pull the flap up and secure it with hasps from within after the shooting.

Malik and Akbar readied the inside of the mini-van by taking out everything behind the two front bucket seats to create a surface on which Akbar could lie. They cushioned the walls, doors, and the entire interior of the mini-van with heavy sound absorbing foam. With the flap down, Akbar had an eight-inch-by-sixteen-inch opening in which to operate. Lying on his stomach with the rifle resting on a small tripod, he could position himself with the barrel of the gun inside the van to limit the possibility of witnesses hearing the shots or seeing the flash when he fired the rifle. Akbar practiced for many hours in the sparsely populated Arkansas Delta, across the river from Memphis.

"Shooting those people on the steps was a lot easier than hitting the targets you set out for me across the river," Akbar remarked to Malik as they headed home to Memphis after murdering the jurors, JPD officer Carl Lippman, and retired wildlife agent Elbert Dowd.

Malik extended his right hand to fist bump Akbar. "You da man," he said. "Way to go."

"No problem."

Chapter Thirty

At six-thirty, David Dunne and Willie Mitchell left the pea-gravel driveway at his house and jogged east at a nine-minute pace.

"This is my usual speed," Willie Mitchell said. "Pretty slow."

"Fine with me. You ready for the hearing tomorrow in Jackson?"

"Ready as I'll ever be."

"What's your gut tell you?"

"I've got the case law on my side and custody of Zegarra. I should win going away, but you never know. Depends on the federal judge and how he jeehaws with the professor. If Judge Stanwyk and Whitman are tight, they might be able to create some trouble for me. Last thing I want is to have to appeal a ruling from the U.S. District Court while Zegarra sits in jail."

"El Moro."

"I'm calling him Zegarra. I don't want to slip up in court. Who else knows about his Muslim connections?"

"Just you. And you've got to keep it to yourself."

"No problem. I'm not sure why you told me."

"Two reasons. First, I know I can trust you. From talking to you, watching you work, I can tell you're an honest man with backbone. You keep your word. Second, right now you're the man in control of El Moro. You're calling the shots over whether he stays here for trial or whether he goes to fed custody. I need you on my side."

"Whitman doesn't know?"

"No. I'm sure he thinks the *El Cártel de Campeche* was involved. Anyway, he's a temp. Next election, if his party loses, he's going back to whatever academic hole he crawled out of. There'll be some other political appointee sitting in his chair."

"Who knows in the FBI?"

"No one at this level. You and I are the only two in Mississippi who know. I want to keep it that way."

"Sheriff Jones is about to pull his hair out."

"I'm sure."

"He's got no leads on the jury killers. State police and their crime lab have come up with nothing."

"My people in D.C. are working it. We haven't been onto El Moro that long. He's just popped up on the radar screen as a spinoff from a black jihadist group we're starting to gather intelligence on in Memphis. We got onto the Memphis cell through some assets inside the federal prison jihadist

170

organizations. There's several groups, kind of loosely connected by ideology, but basically independent."

"Like the Mexican and Aryan prison gangs I see on the History Channel."

"Yeah. But the Muslim organizations in state and federal prisons are all black. Cons in there for years with nothing to do. It's a captive audience, and the black Muslim jihad against the white man is an easy sell to someone who grew up with nothing and who's been put in prison by white cops, white prosecutors, and white judges. We're feeding and housing our next generation of terrorists. They're going to do their best to take down our own country. They'll kill a lot of people in the process."

"Scary shit."

"You don't know how scary. As soon as you get the bastard El Moro convicted and sentenced to death, we can turn loose a bunch of resources on finding out who killed the jurors."

"You're sure El Moro is connected to the black jihadist cell?"

"Look at it like this. We know the drug cartel wants nothing to do with him. Since they bungled the escape they've been hands off."

"You're sure?"

"Positive. And there's only one other criminal enterprise we know he's linked to, the jihadist cell in Memphis. We don't have much in the way of details, but we're working on it. We're almost certain they were involved in the jury murders."

Willie Mitchell noticed Dunne was breathing easily. "Sorry I'm not giving you a better workout."

"No big deal. What is critical is that you use all your skills to convict El Moro in the state system and follow through on the death penalty. I don't want him in the federal system."

"You want him put to death."

"Damn right. I want the son of a bitch dead. There's only one way to deal with these terrorist fuckers, and that's kill them before they kill us. The feds are pussies and will never put him to death. The professor will deal down the murder and drug charges to get information on the Mexican cartel. El Moro will be in prison recruiting more black Muslims to the cause of jihad. It's like throwing Br'er Rabbit in the briar patch. We'll actually be helping the growth of the radical black Muslim cause. In the war on terror, the fed is its own worst enemy."

"I'll do my best."

"That's all I'm asking. And you need to start watching your back more. The black jihadists thought nothing of killing those people on the courthouse steps to help El Moro. They won't blink at doing something to you, too, if they believe you're standing in the way of what they want."

"Which is what?"

"They want him out of jail. But if he has to go to prison, they want him tried in the federal system, where we won't put him to death. I guarantee you they'd love to have him in a federal facility where he'll get to work for the cause."

"Damn," Willie Mitchell said.

"Exactly right," Dunne said.

~ * ~

At ten o'clock sharp the following morning United States District Court Judge Herman Stanwyk entered the federal courtroom in Jackson. Willie Mitchell had appeared before him only twice, once to defend Yaloquena supervisors in a civil suit and next for a hearing on a Parchman prisoner who wanted relief in the federal courts after exhausting his appeals in the state system. Willie Mitchell had convicted the inmate of murder in the Yaloquena courtroom.

Judge Stanwyk was mid-sixties, with a hairline that had receded back to the center of his skull. He wore a gray beard that was still somewhat dark only around his sideburns. He was a thin African-American judge appointed by Bill Clinton in 1995. Willie Mitchell shared the opinion of the Mississippi bar that Judge Stanwyk was an intelligent man and a decent judge who ran his courtroom with authority. He was considered liberal by most Mississippians, but Willie Mitchell had found him to be fair in his two cases before him. In the criminal cases tried before Judge Stanwyk and reported in the Jackson paper, Willie Mitchell thought the judge had handled himself well.

Leopold Whitman and his ever present first assistant, Blake Briggs, were at the U.S. attorney's table. Willie Mitchell and Assistant D.A. Walton Donaldson sat at the defense table with Sheriff Jones. Jake and Kitty occupied the back row with Agent David Dunne.

Media took up just about every other seat in the courtroom.

Judge Stanwyk asked Whitman if he was ready to proceed.

"We are, Your Honor."

"Mr. Banks, will you be representing yourself and the sheriff?"

"Yes, Your Honor."

"Mr. Banks, would you confirm for the court the current location of your defendant Adolfo Zegarra Galván?"

Willie Mitchell said: "Yes, Your Honor. He is in the Yaloquena courthouse jail in the custody of Sheriff Lee Jones." Willie Mitchell gestured toward Lee.

Willie Mitchell sat and watched Judge Stanwyk pick up the record and page through it for a moment.

"I've read your briefs, gentlemen. There's no need for testimony in this matter, is there? Isn't this a question of law? A sticky question of law, I might add."

Willie Mitchell quickly spoke to beat Whitman to the punch. "No testimony is needed, Your Honor. The court is absolutely correct that this is a matter of law, which I submit is well-settled in the state's favor."

Whitman jumped up. "I disagree, Your Honor, on two counts. First, the law is not settled in the state's favor. Second, I feel there is a compelling need for testimony."

"What do you expect to prove through testimony?"

"I have outlined in my brief what I expect to prove about the deplorable, dangerous conditions in the Yaloquena jail and how the antiquated nature of the facility lends itself to escape or to attempts on the life of the defendant."

Willie Mitchell stood. "Your Honor, the state will stipulate that our jail is ancient, but it is clean and does provide adequate safety to the defendant Zegarra, thanks to Sheriff Lee Jones. But, Your Honor, the condition of the Yaloquena jail is irrelevant to this proceeding. It doesn't matter how we're holding the defendant, whether in a penthouse or a pig sty, because it is solely up to Sheriff Jones and it's no business whatsoever of Mr. Whitman's."

Whitman jumped up, red-faced. "See his attitude, Your Honor? He has no respect for my office or this court."

"*Au contraire,* Your Honor. I have the utmost respect for this court. It is true that I have no respect for the U.S. attorney."

"Objection," Whitman said loudly. Blake Briggs lowered his head and used his hand to shield his face from his boss.

Willie Mitchell showed mock surprise. Judge Stanwyk suppressed a chuckle. It was a tell that warmed Willie Mitchell's heart. Judge Stanwyk didn't like the professor either.

"I would like the opportunity to address the objection if the court would direct Mr. Whitman to explain the basis for his objection."

Judge Stanwyk gestured with open palms for both men to sit. "Okay, gentlemen. Let's stay on task here."

Willie Mitchell watched Judge Stanwyk rummage through the record again. Willie Mitchell knew he was stalling, that he sure as hell did not want to hear any irrelevant testimony.

Willie Mitchell took a flier. He stood. "Your Honor, I am set to start jury selection in my capital murder prosecution of

Zegarra on Monday morning, three days from now, and if there is going to be extensive testimony on this jurisdictional issue, I ask this court to continue this matter—"

Whitman jumped up. "A continuance is out of the question."

"Hold on, Mr. Whitman. You gentlemen both take your seats."

Judge Stanwyk turned in his chair to stare at the wall. Willie Mitchell knew that no judge, state or federal, who had served on the bench for a decade or more, would subject himself to the torture of a high-profile, drawn out murder case that would make him work long hours over many weeks, supervising a sequestered jury. Willie Mitchell was confident that Judge Stanwyk, an experienced judge just five years from retirement with an incredibly generous federal pension and benefits, would rather take a beating than hear the Zegarra case. Willie Mitchell glanced at the earnest federal prosecutor who obviously did not understand that. The Professor sat on the edge of his chair, waiting on the judge to rule.

Judge Stanwyk whirled in his chair to face the lawyers.

"Gentlemen, there is no need for testimony on the matter of jurisdiction. It is, as Mr. Banks said earlier in agreement with my assessment, an issue of law. The conditions in the jail, the jeopardy in which Zegarra finds himself in his cell, none of that is relevant."

Willie Mitchell glanced over at Whitman, who was finally starting to get it. His deflation morphed into urgency.

"Your Honor," Whitman said.

"Hold on, Mr. Whitman. Let me finish." Whitman sat down. "I find the jurisdictional issue to be fascinating, and a case of *res nova* for this court. I imagine these sorts of conflicts have generally been worked out informally and amicably between competing agencies so that the case law cited by Mr. Banks, though relevant, I find to be not exactly on point.

"So, I am going to take the jurisdictional issue under advisement and assign my clerk to do further research."

"But Judge Stanwyk, if the court doesn't rule this afternoon, the state will proceed to trial Monday morning and this issue will be moot."

Exactly, dumb ass. That's the point.

"That's fine with me, Judge."

"If you insist on a ruling today, Mr. Whitman, I'm afraid I would have to say I feel the case law cited by Mr. Banks is persuasive, and rule accordingly. If that's what you want me to do."

174

It appeared to Willie Mitchell a light finally came on in Whitman's brain. "No, Your Honor. The court taking it under advisement is fine."

"All right, gentlemen," Judge Stanwyk said with a smile to each. "If there's nothing else, my clerk will notify the parties in due course whether we would like you to submit additional memoranda."

The judge stood and walked out of the courtroom. As soon as the door closed behind him, several television reporters rushed to the courtroom rail and tried to get Willie Mitchell's attention.

Sheriff Jones shook Willie Mitchell's hand. "That's a relief," he said. "Let's get on back to Sunshine."

"You and Walton go on ahead. I'm going to talk to these reporters for a while, then visit with Jake, see what he's up to."

Willie Mitchell signaled Jake to wait around. He noticed Agent Dunne walk out of the courtroom reading something on his phone.

~ * ~

After his press conference and several individual interviews on camera, Willie Mitchell took the elevator down to the main floor. When he walked out, Dunne, Jake, and Kitty were waiting for him. He sensed something was up, and it could not be good.

"What happened?" he asked Dunne.

"In Denver this morning, a sniper in a downtown building fired a number of rounds at people on the street."

"How many killed?"

"No one," Dunne said. "That's the good news."

"What's the bad news?"

"The people he shot at were jurors filing into the courthouse to hear testimony in a case that's been going on for a week."

"Damn," Willie Mitchell said.

"It's all over the news," Jake said. "Fox News and CNN have covered nothing else since they got wind of it. They're interspersing footage from Sunshine."

"He was a bad shot, the sniper," Dunne said. "Hit one juror in the leg. No other juror or bystander was hit."

"Well, it could have been worse," Willie Mitchell said.

"It is," Dunne said. "They dragged the guy off and he was yelling something about dead jurors in Mississippi."

"What?"

"Yeah," Jake said. "He was a copycat. A crummy shot, but he was trying to repeat what happened in Sunshine last week."

Chapter Thirty-One

Willie Mitchell jogged past the courthouse Monday morning on his way home. It was a little before seven, and he planned on being cleaned up and dressed and in his office at seven forty-five. The jurors would start showing up well before nine. Willie Mitchell had asked Judge Williams to enlarge the panel prospects to two hundred and seventy-five, because he knew with the Sunshine jury murders and the copycat in Denver, there would be an unusually high number of no-shows.

He spied four deputies with rifles on the courthouse roof—one deputy for each side of the building. Willie Mitchell ran slowly on the streets around the courthouse to make sure the security precautions he and Sheriff Jones discussed had been implemented. He passed the Fite Oil and Gas bulk plant a block and a half from the courthouse and saw an armed deputy sitting on top of the biggest holding tank in the yard, at least thirty feet in the air. Sheriff Jones said old man Fite was happy to cooperate when Lee explained the strategic importance of the big silver tank.

Willie Mitchell continued running, checking things out. He noticed a state trooper with an automatic rifle on top of one of the buildings next to the bayou. There were deputies and troopers posted at every intersection, manning the checkpoints, stopping drivers at the barricades to make sure they had legitimate business at the courthouse.

He trotted past the white media trucks with large satellites on their roofs. They were parked so closely together he made a mental note to get Lee to make sure no one hid under or between the trucks.

For a late October morning it was exceptionally warm, even by Delta standards. Willie Mitchell's gray T-shirt was soaked. Satisfied that the security perimeter Lee Jones had established was in place and appeared adequate, the D.A. picked up his pace and headed home.

He showered and dressed in his dark blue suit with subtle pin stripes and a red tie, his preferred outfit for opening day of every murder case he tried since his first year in office. He walked downstairs and into the kitchen.

"Don't you look nice," Susan said. She took off her apron and sidled up to him. "You'll win over the female jurors, that's for sure." He kissed her briefly on the lips.

"I've got to go," he said.

"Not before you eat what I fixed you. Just have a seat."

He hung his jacket on the back of the chair and watched Susan take a black-iron skillet out of the oven with brown-topped biscuits bulging up and out over the sides. She put the skillet on a trivet in front of him, then a plate of two eggs, sunny side up, grits with a pat of butter in the center, and three slices of bacon. She opened a fresh jar of fig preserves and spooned some into a small bowl. Finally, she placed his favorite mug in front of him with steam rising from the fresh coffee.

"What a feast," he said.

"Been a long time since I've fixed you a breakfast like this. Picking that jury all day is going to wear you out, so no oatmeal or yogurt this morning. You need something that will stick to your ribs." He raised his mug to toast her and sipped his coffee.

Fifteen minutes later he stopped his Ford F-150 at a checkpoint. He held out his lapel with the royal blue tag for the state policeman to see. The trooper waived him through, giving him a thumbs-up for luck.

Willie Mitchell scanned the parking lot and streets around the courthouse. Everything was still eerily quiet and deserted, no one moving except court personnel beginning to arrive, the media setting up shots with the courthouse in the background, and the deputies and state police working security.

He stopped in the circuit clerk of court's office. Eddie Bordelon, small and bald, scurried behind the counter, his royal-blue tag proclaiming COURT PERSONNEL stuck prominently on his right lapel.

"Morning, Eddie," Willie Mitchell said.

"Hey. Hey," he said, his Acadian Parish lilt still detectable after thirty years living in Sunshine. "Got a little more work to do before I come upstairs."

"Take your time, Eddie. I just wanted to say your idea of the color coded lapel tags was great. Good thinking."

Eddie drew close and whispered. "Mr. Moore didn't think much of it. If you and the sheriff hadn't followed up we wouldn't have them."

"A prophet is without honor in his own land, Eddie. Lee and I appreciate what you do. You have to promise me that you'll never quit this job."

Eddie shrugged. "I've got thirty years in the system, Willie Mitchell. I'm almost working for free now."

"Eddie. You've got to stay. Don't leave me."

"We'll see, Willie Mitchell. I'm getting to the age where these kinds of trials send me over the edge. I didn't sleep last night thinking about all the things I had to do this morning."

"Hang in there. See you upstairs."

Five minutes later the prosecutor sat at his desk reviewing notes on his *voir dire* opening, and the list of prospective jurors for the fourth time. He and Sheriff Jones and Walton had spent many hours huddled in his office, identifying the prospects, discussing what they knew about each potential juror. At times, Lee would know a relative of the prospect, or know people in the vicinity of where he or she lived. Lee made calls to his precinct political captains to find out what kind of juror the person might be, how the prospect felt about law enforcement, whether he or she had ever been in trouble.

He heard a tap on the door. Jimmy Gray entered wearing a charcoal suit, a bright royal-blue tag on his lapel. He saluted. "Your deputy assistant vice-bailiff trainee, reporting for duty, sir."

"Don't show your ass up there. That's all I ask. It's the only way I could guarantee you a seat."

"I'll sit quiet as a mouse against the wall observing you at work. Yaloquena county's trial of the century."

"Pretty big mouse."

"I've dropped some weight since we've been walking."

"How much?"

"Almost a pound. A shade over three-oh-four this morning."

"You still getting weighed at the cotton gin?"

"Watch it, asshole. You know how sensitive I am."

Walton Donaldson and Lee Jones walked in behind Jimmy Gray. Both men wore their blue ID tags. Lee adjusted his beige Stetson and rubbed his hands together.

"We all ready to go?"

Willie Mitchell looked at his watch. "Not yet. Let the courtroom fill up and we'll enter through the side door."

~ * ~

El Moro dressed in his cell that morning in the suit and tie that Jerome King sent. King whispered to him in their last meeting that his appearance before the jurors was important. It did not matter to El Moro how he dressed. He wore the suit because King asked him.

The two deputies who had spent the most time with El Moro in the jail, other than the regular jailer, showed up at his cell. The trim, fit smaller black man they called Sammy Roberts, the one who had served in the military, walked into the cell and put on the leg and wrist cuffs and shackles on El Moro while the fat deputy, the black man they called Big Boy Carter, watched. El Moro tried to meet Big Boy's eyes, but the fat deputy avoided his gaze.

El Moro shuffled out of the cell and into the elevator. One floor below the jail, the elevator stopped. A different deputy held the elevator door open while Sammy Roberts and Big Boy removed the shackles. Jerome King told El Moro to let him know if any of the people there for jury duty saw him shackled or handcuffed. The black lawyer said it would work in their favor if one did.

El Moro walked slowly out of the elevator and into the empty hallway. A deputy sheriff stood at each exit. With Sammy Roberts on his left arm and Big Boy holding his right, El Moro entered the courtroom through the side entrance. The defendant readied himself for the stares of a courtroom full of angry citizens.

He stopped for a moment inside the door. Inside the rail, there were a half-dozen men in suits or uniforms with a blue label on their coats. Outside the rail, sitting in the benches, were about fifteen people, men and women, wearing bright orange tags.

Where are the two hundred jurors lawyer King told me about?

He accompanied the deputies to his seat between Jerome King and the black woman lawyer with the Jewish name, Eleanor Bernstein. He had talked to her on many occasions in the jail. She was always well-dressed and neat, but she was all business. El Moro sensed that she was a cold woman. He heard the other inmates, all black men, at night talking about what they wanted to do to her and how many times. She did not seem like a sexual being to El Moro. She was controlled when she talked to him. He knew from the deputies she was not married. El Moro thought that she might have a girlfriend as a lover, because he could sense that she was not interested in men in a sexual way.

He understood why she was one of his attorneys. The white lawyer from Houston, Mr. Boardman, needed a black face with him at the table in the courtroom. It seemed to El Moro that only a few white people lived in this town of Sunshine, and since the jury would be made up primarily of black men and women, it made sense to have a black lawyer on his side. After Boardman was shot and the woman lawyer was in control for a while, it seemed that she lacked confidence in herself to handle his case.

He was glad that the cartel lawyer had gotten shot and quit. El Moro was through with smuggling drugs and wanted nothing to do with the cartel any more. He knew they might try to kill him for stealing the five million dollars, and he would have to be careful of Mexicans in prison because *El Cártel de Campeche* could get him killed inside for little or nothing. A thousand U.S. dollars would be all it would take.

He was pleased, too, that Jerome King was his new attorney and he had kept the woman lawyer as an assistant. She was smart and knew the law more than King. He was loud, a big personality. No doubt he would be popular with blacks on the jury, but the woman kept him straight on the law.

Al Rashad's hiring of Jerome King pleased El Moro for another reason. It meant Al Rashad valued El Moro and realized what a major contribution he could make to the cause, even if his days of bankrolling the Memphis cell were over. As long as he did not get the death penalty from the hard gringo district attorney, El Moro could add a significant number of recruits to wage war against the United States.

El Moro was surprised at the things Jerome King whispered to him about white people when they met in the jail without the woman attorney. Unlike Ace High Boardman, Jerome King never talked trial strategy or legal things. He wanted to know about El Moro's life and conversion—and about Al Rashad and his plans for jihad. Lawyer Bernstein talked only about legal strategy, never anything personal

At first, El Moro thought Jerome King was a clown, a showman out to make more dollars. Now, the way the lawyer spoke quietly to him about helping the cause of jihad, he wasn't sure what the man's intentions were. It might be a set up. He was an attorney, so El Moro knew in his heart he could not trust Jerome King.

El Moro considered what interesting turns his life had taken since growing up a white outcast in Madero and Tampico, working for Señor Bernal and the cartel for so many years. He thought of his conversion in Cereso Reynosa at the feet of his personal prophet and namesake, and how Allah had delivered Malik to him in prison to lead him to Al Rashad.

Until he had moved to McAllen to live with Dominica Ayala, he had never seen a black person. Now, he was surrounded by *prietos* and had pledged his future to help his *prieto* Muslim brothers wage jihad against whites in the United States.

Allah moves in strange ways.

Eleanor Bernstein tapped his arm, and El Moro stood when Judge Williams walked in the courtroom. He sat down after the black woman judge took her seat. She stared into the gallery at the people wearing the orange tags. El Moro watched her gesture to her small assistant with no hair. He hurried up to the bench and spoke to her in whispers.

"Mr. Banks, are you ready for the state?

180

El Moro watched the district attorney rise. "Yes, Your Honor." He did not look happy.

"Mr. King?"

"Yes, Judge Williams. Ms. Bernstein and I are ready, and the defendant is ready as well." He turned to the few prospective jurors who were seated in the courtroom. "I am not sure what we're going to do, however, Your Honor, because we certainly cannot pick a jury from such a small jury pool."

"The deputy clerk advises that two hundred seventy-five prospective jurors were served their summons to appear." She counted the orange tags. "And from that number we have fifteen jury prospects who have shown up this morning.

"Rather than call the roll, Mr. Bordelon, why don't you take the names of the fifteen prospects then we'll read those names into the record to give credit to the fifteen who are here. We can then assume that the remaining properly served members of the jury pool willfully chose to stay home."

"This is not only happening here," Jerome King said loudly. "There are people not showing up for jury duty all over this country."

"Mr. King," Judge Williams said, "that's enough."

Jerome King sat down. El Moro could tell the woman judge was not pleased with his lawyer.

"All over this country," echoed in El Moro's head.

It has started. We will not stop until there is chaos. A few bullets. A few anonymous deaths. It took so little to weaken their faith in their own systems. In many ways, they are immature, like children. A few more jurors to be killed by Allah's prieto marksmen in cities around the United States, and the gringos cannot have their juries. No juries, no criminal trials, their criminal system stops. Bedlam. Out of the ashes arises a Caliphate in the land of the gringos. Sharia law rules the norteamericanos.

"Your Honor," Willie Mitchell Banks said, "perhaps the court could recess for a few moments and we could meet in chambers."

Jerome King jumped up. "If the court please, I want everything on the record. I don't want to discuss this in secret."

"I tend to agree with Mr. King," Judge Williams said.

"I believe it's time for the district attorney to yield to common sense for a change and allow this case to proceed in the federal system, where the government has the resources to protect not only my client but also the folks who come to serve on the jury."

"There's no motion before this court to that effect, Your Honor."

"Mr. Banks is correct, Mr. King. I don't have the authority to send this case to the federal system. That's not in my power. I am ready to rule, however, on your motion to change venue that I held over until *voir dire*. Based on the apparent knowledge of the county residents about this case, and their obvious fear, I feel that your motion to change venue is valid, and I hereby grant it."

El Moro could not tell whether the D.A. was upset. He could tell from his dealings with the district attorney that he was a forceful man. Persuasive, too. It is a shame, El Moro thought, that he'd had to kill a deputy in this district attorney's county. Eleanor Bernstein told him that if it had happened in any of the surrounding jurisdictions, those district attorneys would have quickly grabbed the U.S. attorney's offer to take over the case. El Moro would have told them what they wanted to know about *El Cártel de Campeche* in exchange for leniency, and he would have been in a federal penitentiary by now, recruiting and converting.

Even so, Allah, in his wisdom, had picked this county, bringing about the death of the jurors and the beginning of chaos and jihad, orchestrated by Al Rashad and others around the United States, all with El Moro's assistance.

"Any thoughts on venue?"

"The state capital, Your Honor," Jerome King said. "It's the most populous county and would give us the widest range of potential jurors."

"Jackson is fine with the state, Your Honor. I've already spoken to the Hinds County district attorney, and they have a jury docket a week from today they will allow us to use. They have a five-million-dollar forfeiture case pending against the defendant in conjunction with the U.S. attorney and they're very interested in this capital murder case getting resolved as soon as possible."

"On your toes, Mr. Banks, as usual."

"I would also ask the court to follow the case to Jackson, to preside over the trial there."

"That is acceptable to the defense, Your Honor."

"I have one more ruling to make, gentlemen, that will impact the state significantly. Mr. Banks, you may not want this judge to follow your case to Jackson after I tell you my ruling on the motion to suppress originally filed by Mr. Boardman on behalf of the defendant, and postponed for determination until the trial."

El Moro sat up straighter.

"After much research and thought, I grant the defense motion to suppress all evidence of the defendant's activity in Jackson the morning of his arrest. The money is out as evidence, the results of the search and forensic analysis of the Nissan Maxima as well. Moreover, Mr. Zegarra has never been convicted of any offense in the United States. Any evidence of Mr. Zegarra's prior conduct relating to the possession or distribution of narcotics is also hereby suppressed."

"Your Honor—" Willie Mitchell said.

"That's my ruling, Mr. Banks. This is a death penalty case, and I find that the prejudicial effect of that evidence far outweighs its probative value with respect to the capital murder charge." She paused. "Now, Mr. Banks, do you still want this court to follow this case?"

Willie Mitchell was grim. "Yes, ma'am."

"Your Honor, next Monday seems like a short time within which to prepare for a trial of this nature."

"You were prepared to start this morning, were you not, Mr. King?"

"Yes, but we'll have to transport all—"

"Jackson is your home, Mr. King. I believe any difficulty occasioned by starting the case in Jackson next Monday is offset by the fact that unlike the jury that is chosen, the district attorney—and me—you will be spending every night of the trial sleeping in your own bed. The motion for speedy trial filed on behalf of your client in the early days of this case puts us on a tight leash, time-wise, and I do not want delay to be grounds for any complaint to the appellate court."

Eleanor Bernstein whispered to El Moro. "This means we are still in the state system."

El Moro nodded.

"What fools," he thought.

Chapter Thirty-Two

Willie Mitchell sat with Susan atop the Mississippi River levee west of Sunshine, watching the current head south. Jimmy Gray owned several thousand acres of wetlands adjoining the river. When Willie Mitchell wanted to relax and put things in perspective, he drove here and sat in the redwood Adirondack chairs on the crude gazebo that Jimmy Gray's caretaker built. Jimmy's man had cut holes in the wide chair arms, primitive drink holders for the comfort of the river watchers.

Willie Mitchell knew he should not have brought the Tuesday morning Jackson paper with him. Bold headlines proclaimed the change of venue ruling moving the proceedings to Jackson. Hyping the trial set to start next Monday in the capital city had officially begun. "State versus Zegarra" would generate front-page stories until and after the verdict, and the testimony would provide a fertile basis for letters to the editor and op-ed pieces. The paper was normally obsessed with two things: the nearly impossible prosecution of fifty-year-old homicides from the dark past of Mississippi's civil rights struggle, and the cost to taxpayers of Jim Bob Bailey's travel around the country on the state airplane. For the publishers, the Zegarra trial was a circulation godsend.

The murder of the jurors in Sunshine had vaulted the case from regional to national prominence. Every time the television news operations reported the developments in the murder case they showed photographs of the victims splayed on the courthouse steps, or the pools of blood after the bodies were removed. They also highlighted every glitch or incident in the selection of juries for trials around the country, stretching to link it to the Yaloquena case.

The Sunshine juror massacre and the Denver copycat sniper had repercussions for jury selection in every state. More and more prospective jurors were staying home in spite of the summons to appear.

The secret that had been buried for decades, that state and federal judges would do little to punish citizens who failed to show, was now coming out into the open. Reporters, anchors, and editorial boards were talking and writing about it. Everyone knew jails and holding facilities were already overcrowded. No state judge who was elected to office would seriously consider incarcerating a taxpayer who ignored an order to appear for jury duty because the taxpayer feared for his or her life. In every state where judges were elected, they depended on the good will of their constituents to be re-elected. Punishing the no-shows around the country after the Sunshine and Denver juror shootings was certain to lose a vote for the judge. Therefore, imposition of a contempt finding, an overnight jail stay, or even a modest fine was out of the question.

"I wish you hadn't brought the paper," Susan said.

"I know, but I didn't get to read it this morning." He paused and pointed to a tug pushing a row of barges up the river. The barges rode low in the water. "Three wide and seven long—that's twenty-one huge barges full to the brim headed upstream against a current that's at least three or four miles an hour. Imagine the horsepower it takes to move all that weight against that current."

"I don't understand how they do it."

"I talked to Ethel's boy, Jessie, the last time he was in town."

"He's the tug pilot?"

"Right. He said the big tugs he operates burn about two hundred and fifty gallons of fuel an hour going upstream, and about twenty-five an hour going down."

He refilled Susan's wine glass and his with a ten-dollar Sonoma Valley Pinot Grigio he had purchased at the Jitney Mart over the weekend.

"I don't want you to come to Jackson for the trial," he said.

"I wasn't planning on it. I'm worried about you being there."

"Don't worry about me. Divorce lawyers are killed and maimed a lot more often than D.A.'s or criminal defense attorneys. The criminals know they're guilty. They don't blame me."

"They've already shown they'll kill innocent people to achieve—whatever."

"They want to disrupt the process. Keep us from trying Zegarra. I've got to say, killing the jurors has sure raised the stakes."

"Maybe you should have let the U.S. attorney have it."

"I couldn't. I'd do the same thing today. It's the principle of the thing. The fed can't swoop down and take over just because they want the case. It's a question of sovereignty. The states have always been in charge of murder prosecutions, except for treason and war crimes, until the last few decades, when the fed has been incrementally getting back into the murder business, mainly for political reasons. Besides, the feds cannot do anything right. I don't care if it's the post office, Fannie Mae, Medicare, or criminal prosecution. If you want something screwed up, get the feds involved."

Susan sipped her wine. Two kayakers heading downstream paddled quickly past them.

"Those guys are brave," he said.

"One is a woman."

They sat in silence for several moments.

"Would you mind grilling marinated chicken breasts for dinner Saturday for Jake and Kitty?"

"Be glad to. I'm not headed to Jackson until Sunday morning."

"What do you think of her?"

Willie Mitchell shrugged. "I don't know. Jake seems to really like her. I haven't really talked to her one on one. She's good looking. Doesn't seem to be all that polished."

"Well, look at how she was raised." She sipped some wine. "I admire her. She's done everything on her own."

"Yes. She's obviously strong-willed. And smart."

Willie Mitchell stood and walked to the edge of the gazebo. Another tug passed, this one headed downstream pushing two dozen barges in front of it, moving many times faster than the earlier barge. He turned to take his seat and stopped. Susan was crying.

"What's wrong?" He sat beside her and patted her arm. "What are you upset about?"

"I don't know. I really don't know."

He sipped his wine and watched the river. "Is it the trial? Is it something I've done?"

"No." She paused. "You're going to think I'm crazy."

"No more than I already do."

She laughed through tears and dabbed her eyes. "I'm such an idiot."

"That is not true. Why would you say something like that? If you keep saying it you'll start believing it. It's destructive."

"I just feel like I don't have control over anything. Even my own life. I just rock along in my own little world, not doing anything of any consequence."

Willie Mitchell said nothing because there was nothing he could say that would make any difference. They had held this discussion many times, and he could never figure out exactly what was making Susan unhappy. Neither could she. After a while, she spoke calmly.

"Sometimes I just need to cry, I guess."

"After the trial is over, let's go spend a week, just you and me, at the little hotel in Cozumel you liked so much."

"The Playa Azul?"

"If it's still there."

"Running away is not the answer. I tried that before."

"But this time you can run away with me."

She took his hand. "I won't leave you behind any more. You're bad when I'm gone."

"Three years is a long time to be good."

"I know. It was my fault."

"I don't believe that. It takes two to tango. I was so downbeat and depressed about everything. I don't blame you for leaving. I know I was as much to blame as you."

"Why don't you retire now? We've got more money than we'll ever spend. You could get more active on the bank board. Jimmy would love that. We could travel. The boys don't need us here all the time. Jake is off the payroll and Scott is on his way."

"Traveling is fun for a little while, but it gets old. And I'm too young to quit and do nothing."

"You can develop a private practice, business-oriented."

He took a sip of his wine and stared into the dark brown water.

"I'll think about it. Did you soak up any answers to the cosmic questions on Mount Shasta, or hanging around the red rocks in Sedona?"

"Those places are truly beautiful and inspiring, but ultimately an expensive waste of time. All the New Age thinking and talking feels good while you're doing it, but it wears off in a hurry when you're back in the real world. Ultimately it doesn't make any sense. The only people who can afford to be New Age are well-off white people with too much time on their hands. If you're worried about where your next rent payment is coming from, you don't have time to think the big thoughts."

"Antidepressants are cheaper."

"They work for you, but not for me."

She jumped when he poked her lightly in the ribs and made a "Zzzzzz" sound like an electric shock. "Maybe shock treatments would jolt some sense into you."

She laughed. "I'm not going to let them shave my head."

"Why not?" He pulled her hair away from her forehead. "You'd be beautiful bald. Like that girl in the *Star Trek* movie." He leaned over and kissed her ear. "Or maybe you need an ear bug like Khan used?"

She pushed him away and laughed, sticking a Kleenex in her ear.

"A wet willie from an old goat does not turn me on."

"How about this from an old goat?" He kissed her deeply.

"That's much better," she said.

He stayed close to her. *"Quien es mas macho? Fernando Lamas o Ricardo Montalban?"*

"Usted," she said with a giggle.

"Sí. That is the correct answer."

~ * ~

Jake sat at the worm-eaten pine table in the kitchen leafing through his boxing magazine that was still delivered to the Sunshine address. Willie Mitchell brought the chicken breasts into the kitchen from the natural gas grill outside and put the plate in the center of the table. Susan put the salad plates around and sat down.

"We're sorry Kitty couldn't come up."

"She said she had a lot of paperwork to catch up on."

Jake cut a piece of the marinated chicken. Saturday night in Sunshine, eating supper with the folks. A trip to the duck camp with Kitty was what he had in mind when they made plans.

Susan took a bite of salad. "Are you two having problems?"

"What makes you say that?"

"I don't know."

Jake could never get anything by his parents. After a while, Jake put his utensils down.

"I got mad at her because she said she hated Mississippi."

"Lots of people do," Willie Mitchell said, "including people who have never set foot in the state or don't know a single person from here."

"What did she say?"

"She said she was putting in for a transfer as soon as she could."

"I guess you're not getting along?" Susan asked.

"I thought we were."

He took a sip of water. Kitty was unlike any girl he dated at Ole Miss or anywhere. The physical attraction he felt was magnetic, powerful. It had been terrific when they first started seeing each other, but now he wanted to spend some time with her when they weren't screwing or jogging. She didn't seem to be interested in getting to know Jake. It was as if he liked her more than she liked him—something Jake had never encountered in a girlfriend.

"When are you going back to Jackson?" Willie Mitchell asked.

"Tomorrow afternoon," Jake said. "I'm going to get in a long run in the morning, and I want to go out to the farm and do some shooting. Target practice."

"I'm leaving first thing in the morning," Willie Mitchell said. "You'll be there for jury selection?"

"Unless the professor tells me I can't. I'm not asking him. I'm just going to show up at trial. I want to be there for the whole thing."

"It's easier to get forgiveness than permission," Susan said.

"If they mess with me I'll take some sick days. You wouldn't believe how many sick days and personal days I get."

Willie Mitchell studied his cell phone. "I need to take this." He got up from the table and walked outside.

"Help keep an eye on Willie Mitchell down there," Susan said.

"I will, but he's not in any danger, Mama. Don't worry about that. Nobody's after him."

~ * ~

Jake sat in the sun on the front steps of the Banks home late Sunday morning. He had showered and dressed after his ten mile run and was reading the Jackson paper's coverage of the Zegarra trial beginning the next day. There were side-by-side photographs and profiles of Willie Mitchell and Jerome King on the inside of the front page, as if the two lawyers were heavyweight contenders vying for a title.

A lot of attention was given to the collision on I-55 of Zegarra's Maxima and the JPD cruiser driven by Hubert Holland. There were a number of images of cops and inmates picking up the hundred dollar bills off the concrete.

James Nixon, the owner of the red Malibu Zegarra hijacked and drove to Yaloquena, was quoted extensively about what he saw that morning. On page three, the paper had two articles about the different Mexican cartels and a history of their drug smuggling. Travis Ware was shown in his official Yaloquena sheriff's office photograph, and in an adjacent picture, his widow, Frances, was shown with her arms around her children outside the rural Baptist church where the visitation and funeral was held.

Two entire pages in the first section were dedicated to the jury murders, including a lengthy article about Carl Lippmann, featuring a photograph of Hubert Holland standing next to Carl's headstone. There were articles on Elbert Dowd and the two prospective jurors who died on the steps and the one that died later in the Yaloquena Hospital emergency room.

Jake lowered the paper.

Look at the devastation Zegarra had brought about. We know for a fact he killed Travis Ware in cold blood. It's not like Lee and Walton arrested the wrong guy. His lawyer Ace High even admitted it in open court the first day of jury selection. But Zegarra gets all these rights, these precious rights, and he's not

189

even a citizen. No telling how many times he crossed the border illegally and delivered carloads of drugs. Or how many people he's killed in his life. The state has to go to all the expense and trouble of giving him a "fair" trial. If things were fair, they'd do it like they did in the westerns. Catch a cattle thief red-handed, string him up, right there. To top it off, in order to avoid "prejudicing" the Zegarra jury, they won't even know about the five million dollars, the drugs, and his history of smuggling. All they'll know is he woke up in a stolen car and killed Travis while he wasn't in his right mind, according to his ex-lawyer Ace High. And now, venue is changed to Jackson, a jurisdiction where the demographics make getting the death penalty a thousand to one shot.

Old Mr. Dowd, the black JPD cop, and those three jurors— they're all dead because of Zegarra. That salient fact will not be discussed at all in the trial in Jackson. It's as if Zegarra murdered Travis in a vacuum. Our system doesn't allow the jury to know critical facts.

Shit.

Everything is upside down or backwards, like Bizarro World in the Superman comics. Why would I spend my whole career in a system that increasingly makes no sense? A system where the defendant gets a lot more consideration than he ever gave the victim? It's like the way we fight in the Middle East. We have arcane rules of engagement that put our troops in danger. Don't fire until fired upon. The terrorists and jihadists don't have any rules. They kill our guys any way they can. They hide among civilians, women and children. They use kids as suicide bombers. We're fighting criminals in this country the same way. We prosecutors follow extensive rules of procedure, protecting the defendant's "rights" at all costs. The hardened defendants follow no rules. It's win at any cost. Use the media, intimidate or kill witnesses, lie and cheat. Accuse the prosecution of hiding evidence. Accuse the cops of planting evidence. Accuse the cops and prosecutors of committing the crime the defendant's charged with. Hire expert witness whores to say anything you pay them to say.

Enough.

Jake tried to shake it off. He had to stop thinking that way or find another line of work.

He dove back into the paper and was deep into dueling op-ed pieces for and against the death penalty when David Dunne drove into the circular pea gravel drive. He jumped out of his vehicle, an older model Ford Expedition, dark blue.

"Where's Willie Mitchell?" he asked.

"Jackson," Jake said. "What's up?"

"You know a quicker way to Memphis than the interstate?"

"Right up Sixty-one. Driven it many a time."

"How fast can you get me there?"

"How fast can I drive?"

Dunne pulled out his FBI identification. "Fast as you want."

"Hour and a half, tops."

"Let's go in your 4Runner. You've got a dark window tint."

"I'll get the keys," Jake said.

An hour later Jake slowed to ninety speeding past Rabbit Island, Goat Island and the huge casino hotels rising out of the cotton fields adjacent to the Mississippi River at Tunica, historically the poorest county in Mississippi. But no longer. Tunica had become home to ten casinos to serve the gambling needs of Memphis and Little Rock citizens who could think of no better way to dispose of their income than driving to Tunica, Mississippi to throw their coins and dollars into slot machines and onto blackjack and craps tables.

Jake pointed to the gambling high rises west of them. "My senior year in college we had some big parties at those casinos."

"I bet. Your pistol loaded?"

"Yep."

"Speed it up."

Jake pushed it back over a hundred ten and darted around the traffic they encountered as they closed in on Memphis. He glanced at Dunne changing the lens on his Nikon and studying a map on his phone.

"When are you going to tell me why we're doing this?"

"You concentrate on your driving. Take the 240 loop north off Sixty-one and head north at the Hollywood Street exit. We'll have some lights and traffic on the surface streets before we get there and I'll tell you then."

Dunne made two quick phone calls and pointed to the Hollywood exit. Jake drove north and stopped at Whitney Avenue, a major intersection. Dunne removed his automatic pistol from the carpeted floor in front of him and moved the slide to confirm the forty-five caliber bullet in the chamber. He checked to make sure his two extra magazines were full.

Jake felt his adrenaline increase. "Where to?"

"We're coming into the southern end of the Frayser district a few blocks up. It's a dangerous neighborhood. I want you to turn left here. We're going to approach Al Rashad's place from the south, but on a smaller street."

"Who is Al Rashad?"

"Wait until we stop."

191

Jake followed Dunne's directions. He pulled over and parked where he told him. The street was in terrible condition, with big chunks of broken asphalt and potholes every few feet. Dunne picked up his binoculars and searched the red brick building a hundred yards away.

"We getting out?"

"Not no, but hell, no. You see that red brick building, looks like an old factory?"

Jake said he did.

"That's the Frayser mosque, home to Calvin Ketchums, aka Hakim Abdullah Al Rashad."

"And?"

"We think he's the one who dispatched the shooters to Sunshine."

"No shit?"

Dunne continued to stare through the binoculars. "That's what my intel people think."

"So it wasn't the cartel?"

"Nope. We never thought it was. They washed their hands of Zegarra after their helicopter rescue through the roof cluster fuck."

"Whitman thinks it was *El Cártel de Campeche*."

"I know. The professor is wrong. On so many levels. I don't want you telling him anything about this. Or your girlfriend."

"Does Daddy know?"

"Yep."

"Who else?"

"Nobody."

"Why are you telling me?"

Dunne laughed. He continued looking at the building through the binoculars. "I wouldn't be if I didn't need you to drive me up here."

"Why not?"

"Because I don't want anyone who works for the federal government to know about this."

"You're a fed."

"I'm different. Shut up a minute."

Jake watched him steady the glasses against the dashboard and concentrate on the front of the building. "Get your gun ready."

Jake reached under the seat and pulled out his forty-caliber automatic. He popped the slide and armed the weapon.

"Start the car and let's move closer."

Jake put the gun between his legs and pulled away from the crumbling curb. He drove toward the mosque for two blocks.

"Pull over."

Jake parked at the curb near the intersection. He was close enough to see the main entrance to the brick mosque; close enough to make out the features of the people coming and going through the door.

Dunne's phone vibrated. He put down the glasses and answered.

"Thanks," he said.

"What now?"

"Just a second."

Dunne pointed to a shiny black Cadillac CTS-V Coupe stopping in front of the mosque.

"Good looking car," Jake said.

"Watch who gets out."

Jerome King stepped from the Cadillac, looked around, and walked into the mosque.

"Son of a bitch," Jake said.

~ * ~

That night in Jackson, Jake and Dunne told Willie Mitchell in his room at the Victorian what they had seen in Memphis.

"So, Al Rashad must be calling the shots for the defense. Maybe Jerome went to pick up additional fee. I know he would not have shown up in Sunshine if he hadn't received a big retainer from someone."

"My intel people tell me they think this the first time he's been to the mosque, as far as they know."

"Are they sure?"

"They can't be. They just started surveillance. King could have been there before we got on to Al Rashad."

"They could have hand-delivered the retainer to King in Mississippi to hire him," Jake said. "He didn't have to go up there."

"Why would he go now?"

"We don't know," Dunne said, "but be careful dealing with King."

"I've known Jerome King a while. All he's about is making money."

"Maybe so," Dunne said. "But I say birds of a feather."

Chapter Thirty-Three

Willie Mitchell walked around downtown Jackson early Monday morning to get some fresh air and clear his mind. When he was in trial, he tried to exercise every day to keep the cobwebs out of his brain and the stress level down. If he went a couple of days without exercise, he felt sluggish and dim witted. It suggested, he thought, an addiction to the endorphins he produced when he exercised. There were worse things to be hooked on.

The Victorian, the recently renovated historic downtown hotel, was within three blocks of the Hinds County Circuit Court building. If the weather permitted, Willie Mitchell planned on walking to court from the hotel. The forecast was clear for the week, but Willie Mitchell was not betting on it, having long since lost faith in the Weather Channel forecasts. Following the advice of the geezers at the downtown Sunshine coffee shop, he now relied only on the local and regional radar.

He passed the oppressive building that housed the federal courts, and the other federal agencies related to law enforcement, including the U.S. attorney's offices. Willie Mitchell supposed that it would have been possible to design and build an uglier building, but he did not see how, without a tremendous effort. It was a gray, dull concrete structure better suited for housing the Politburo or Duma than a United States district court. The circuit court building nearby was less offensive, appeared less like a bunker, but was still ugly, a monument to the design proficiency of a committee staffed by state and local agencies. The Yaloquena courthouse was antiquated, but at least it had style. Its designers created a Georgian structure with large white columns, red brick, and a portico over the main and back entrances.

Adding to the unpleasant ambience in this part of downtown Jackson were the media trucks straddling sidewalks and streets. To Willie Mitchell the trucks were like alien machines from a techno-transformer world. Their white dishes pointed to the heavens for guidance. Black tentacles snaked from under the trucks like roots, seeking sustenance across streets and grassy areas to soak up power from a willing native source.

At eight-fifteen he walked from the Victorian to the court house, at times walking in the street because the media trucks took over the sidewalk. There was a lot of security outside the courthouse, and at least ten deputies were working the main entrance. In a few minutes he was in the half-filled courtroom to join Walton Donaldson at the prosecution table. Walton briefed Willie Mitchell on two of the three legal issues he had researched over the weekend.

When Walton finished, Willie Mitchell turned to glance at the audience, made up primarily of state and national media. The main door opened and Willie Mitchell watched Jerome King walk in with Travis Ware's widow, Frances, on his arm. Her children followed. Eleanor Bernstein and a well-dressed, attractive Asian woman about the same age as Eleanor trailed behind the Wares. Jerome King escorted Frances to the first bench behind the defense table. He displaced several grumbling reporters, shooing them to create a prominent place for the widow and her kids. Eleanor gestured for the Asian woman to sit there as well.

The two defense attorneys walked through the rail and shook hands with Willie Mitchell and Walton, then took their seats at the defense table. Willie Mitchell leaned over to Walton.

"What in the hell is Frances doing with Jerome?"

"I don't know."

"Go find Lee. See if he knows anything."

Walton hustled out the central aisle and into the hallway outside. The Cajun deputy clerk, Eddie Bordelon, walked quickly through the side door and into the courtroom to see if the lawyers were ready. He returned to the judge's chambers, passing two Hinds County deputies escorting El Moro to his chair at the defense table. In less than a minute, Eddie walked into the courtroom in front of Judge Williams, asked everyone to rise, and announced that the circuit court in and for Yaloquena County, sitting today in Hinds County, was in session.

"Good morning, gentlemen," Judge Williams said. "And lady."

The lawyers returned the greeting.

"Before we bring in the first panel of twelve prospective jurors from the jury assembly room downstairs, I've asked the court administrator to give us a report on juror attendance. Mr. Champion?"

A heavy-set black man in his fifties, wearing a navy blue blazer, walked from the back of the courtroom through the rail. He read from a document on a clipboard.

"Judge Williams, we served summons to appear on one hundred seventy-five Hinds County residents, and we have taken the roll downstairs."

"How many prospective jurors for us this morning?"

"Sixty, Your Honor."

195

Willie Mitchell was pleased that slightly over one-third showed up. Jerome King stood to address the court.

"Your Honor, I don't believe we can select a jury of twelve in a death penalty case from only sixty jurors."

"I believe we can, Your Honor. I've selected death qualified jury panels from a smaller number of prospects on at least three occasions."

"I'm with Mr. Banks," she said. "Before I ask Mr. Champion to bring in the first twelve for questioning, are there any motions or other housekeeping matters we need to take care of?"

Neither lawyer brought up anything.

"Very well. Bring in the first twelve, please sir."

Walton returned to the prosecution table. He leaned into Willie Mitchell. "Lee doesn't know why Frances is with King. He said he'd talk to her at the first recess."

Willie Mitchell turned to watch Mr. Champion lead the first twelve prospective jurors down the center aisle to take their seats in the jury box. He checked them out. Eight black, four white. Five men, seven women. Youngest about mid-thirties. Oldest over seventy. He spied Jake in the last row and waved discreetly to him.

"Mr. Banks, are you ready to start?"

Willie Mitchell walked to the podium in front of the jury box.

"First, I'd like to introduce myself." Willie Mitchell went on to give a brief history of the case, and asked if any of the twelve could not consider the imposition of the death penalty under any circumstances."

"Objection, Your Honor."

Willie Mitchell was caught off guard. What possible objection could King have to an innocuous question about the death penalty?

"Mr. King?"

"Judge Williams, I object to the district attorney asking about the death penalty in this case when the widow of the victim," he whirled and pointed to Frances Ware, "has expressly stated she does not want the defendant put to death because she is opposed to the death penalty."

The audience buzzed and Judge Williams banged her gavel.

"Order," she said.

Willie Mitchell glared at King. "Your Honor, that is the most outrageous and inappropriate statement I've ever heard from a defense counsel in all my years of practicing law."

"Approach."

196

Willie Mitchell and Jerome King stood in front of Judge Williams, as close as the bench permitted. She held her hand over the bench microphone.

"Have you lost your mind, Mr. King?"

"No, Your Honor."

"Do you realize what an egregious breach of trial conduct and decorum you just committed?"

He said nothing. Judge Williams turned to Willie Mitchell.

"Any motions, Mr. Banks?"

Willie Mitchell made a tactical decision. If he asked the judge to dismiss the first twelve because they were tainted by Jerome King's outburst, he doubted he could get a jury out of the remaining forty-eight.

"Just a strong caution, Judge Williams."

"Mr. King, we will proceed, but if you attempt anything like that again, you're asking for a mistrial or sanctions. You'll be able to call Mrs. Ware in the sentencing phase and establish her wishes regarding penalty. *Voir dire* is not the time or place, and you know that."

The lawyers went back to their tables. Judge Williams asked the twelve prospects to disregard what King said.

Six of the eight black jurors of the first twelve in the box, and one of the white prospects, said they opposed the death penalty and could not impose it on moral and religious grounds, no matter what circumstances surrounding the death of Travis Ware were proven at the trial.

While Jerome King questioned the seven about their anti-death penalty views, he turned to nod or gesture to Frances Ware in the first row. The implication was obvious, but Willie Mitchell chose not to object because Jerome's reference to Frances Ware's opinion so early in *voir dire* probably irritated the remaining five jury prospects. Willie Mitchell already decided he would not exercise a single peremptory challenge and no challenges for cause unless the jury prospect was insane.

Once he qualified the juror on the death penalty question, he would take them on the jury, no matter what other deficiencies they presented to the prosecution.

Judge Williams thanked and dismissed the seven anti-death penalty prospects, and Willie Mitchell asked the remaining five general questions about their eligibility, then turned the questioning over to Jerome King, who took his time getting to the podium.

"Now, ladies and gentlemen, I have a couple of general questions. Do any of you five citizens think a law enforcement officer is ever justified in violently striking a person who is handcuffed, in custody, and who is fully compliant with the demands of the officer?"

Judge Williams furrowed her brow. Willie Mitchell edged up in his seat, ready to object if King went any further.

"I'll assume by your expressions that you all agree with me that violence against a prisoner is unlawful, and especially, as in this case, where the defendant already has a concussion and head injury."

"I object, Your Honor, and ask to approach."

"What are you talking about, Mr. King?" Judge Williams quietly asked when they stood before her.

"Your Sheriff Jones beat my client when he arrested him."

Judge Williams' eyes grew wide. "Is this true?"

"Lee hit him once, Judge, in the heat of the moment, but the defendant has never given a statement, so the mistreatment is not relevant to this murder case. It can be addressed in another forum, but not this trial."

"It most certainly is relevant," Jerome King said.

"How can it be when it occurred after Travis Ware was killed and the defendant has never given a statement?" Willie Mitchell said. "Judge Williams, testimony or evidence of Lee's conduct toward the defendant is highly prejudicial. I ask the court to admonish Mr. King and instruct him not to mention it again to the jury prospects."

"So ordered. Mr. King, don't refer to it again. If you want to sue Sheriff Jones for battery in a civil suit against him, or ask the attorney general to charge the sheriff with battery, have at it. In light of the fact that there was no admission made by the defendant, you can hardly argue that Sheriff Jones beat a confession out of him. It's irrelevant and excluded from this trial. Take your seats."

The questioning of the five continued past the lunch break and ended at two in the afternoon, when Judge Williams asked the bailiff to remove the five to allow the attorneys to declare their intentions. Willie Mitchell accepted all five of the prospects. As Willie Mitchell expected, Jerome King challenged all five for cause. Judge Williams denied the challenges so the defense lawyer used a peremptory challenge to strike all three of the white jurors.

When Mr. Champion brought in twelve more jury prospects, Judge Williams told him to sequester the two selected from the first twelve, to keep them under guard in a room by themselves. He escorted the two jurors out of the courtroom after he seated the next twelve.

At three-thirty, Willie Mitchell approached the podium and asked the twelve new prospects the same general questions about the death penalty. An hour later, six of the seven black jurors and two of the five white prospects had been questioned enough by Willie Mitchell and Jerome King to establish they could not impose it under any circumstances. The eight were released by the court. The lawyers asked the remaining four prospects questions until five o'clock, when Judge Williams adjourned for the day.

Willie Mitchell spoke to Sheriff Jones and Walton briefly before they drove back to Sunshine for the night. Jake waited in the back of the courtroom and escorted Willie Mitchell out past the security personnel. On the first floor near the metal detectors, they passed Jerome King holding a press conference.

"No telling what he's going to say," Jake said when they were outside. "I can't believe his bringing up Frances Ware's opinion about the death penalty and Lee hitting Zegarra at the scene. Jerome King gets to say whatever outrageous crap pops in his head."

"He's got me over a barrel. He knows I won't move for a mistrial. The greedy bastard can say anything he wants." He paused. "Let's go for a short run or maybe a walk."

"There's a place out at the reservoir."

"Good. I only need about thirty minutes, then we'll get something to eat. You can ask Kitty to join us if you want."

"I don't think so. There's a good sports bar off County Line. We can go there in our running stuff."

~ * ~

The next morning, after Willie Mitchell and Jake cleared security, Eddie Bordelon asked Willie Mitchell to join Judge Williams and Jerome King in chambers. He walked into the judge's office. Jerome King was the only person there.

"Morning, Jerome. Where's the judge?"

"I believe her majesty is taking a royal wee-wee. Her Highness is probably getting ready to chew my scrawny black ass out."

"I saw a little of your act on the local station. I don't guess there's any statement you consider out of bounds."

"Aw, shit, Willie Mitchell. I'm fighting for this guy's life. He's guilty as hell and I've got to throw as much crap against the wall as I can. Maybe some of it will stick. Don't take it personal. You know this case belongs in federal court. Why can't we work out a deal where my guy pleads to capital murder on the state charges and gets life imprisonment, no probation, no parole, and pleads to all the federal crimes, too, and we agree he serves

199

his time in the federal system? You don't want to send this white boy from Mexico to Parchman. He ain't black; he ain't Mexican. He looks and talks white, but he ain't really. He won't belong to any group, and every swinging dick in there will be trying to screw him or kill him."

"If the jury wants to give him life in the pen, so be it. But, I'm not making that deal. I owe it to Travis Ware and all the law enforcement people in the state who lay their lives on the line every day to do all I can to put Zegarra to death. I know you understand that, Jerome."

Jerome jumped up. "I got to take a leak myself. If Zelda comes in before I get back, tell her I'll be just a second." To access the bathroom in the hallway, he walked through the empty anteroom of the judge's temporary office, where a gatekeeper or secretary would normally sit to control access to the judge's inner office.

~ * ~

Alone in the courthouse bathroom near Judge William's temporary office, Jerome King stood at the urinal, taking care of business. He stared at the white tile wall before him.

Goddamn Willie Mitchell's hard fuckin' head.

Jerome could not understand a man like Willie Mitchell. Why would he put himself through the agony of a capital murder trial when nobody would criticize him for bowing to the wishes of the widow on the death penalty issue? It's not like he's going to make any more money whether he tries the case or takes the plea deal.

The stupid mother fucker going to make the same check.

Jerome was a dyed-in-the-wool capitalist. He made all of his decisions based on the almighty dollar. He cared for no one but Jerome King, and there was nothing he really believed in except his own bottom line. He felt no guilt about that whatsoever.

The Great Satan, empire of evil, or infidel mother-fuckin' country, whatever that nappy-headed wild-eyed Charlie Manson-looking crazy nigger Al Rashad in Memphis is callin' the U.S. of A. these days, it's done all right by me. Rashad's cash money is sweet, and I'll take all I can get, but I ain't got to buy in to the shit he's peddlin'. The Mississippi white man legal system has been good to this brother, and if Al Rashad cain't figure out how to get his piece of the pie from the white man, that's his problem. I know killin' the white people ain't gon' make me richer, but if Al Rashad wants to do it, it's a free country. I'll take their cases and their cash, but I ain't drinking that KoolAid. Make mine Cristal or Hennessy.

200

Jerome had made a lot of money in the mass tort litigation cases just for putting his name on the pleadings with big time plaintiff's lawyers from all over the country. He had sat in on some trials in Wilson County, where the population was less than ten thousand, eighty percent African-American. He made opening and closing statements, but the big city lawyers questioned the experts and did all the legal work. Their investigators signed up all the local plaintiffs. In Wilson County, there were more residents who were plaintiffs in the Fen-Phen, asbestos, and tobacco litigation than there were registered voters.

All Jerome had to do was show up on time and talk, and he was good at that. The companies settled for billions, and the lawyers split almost half the money. Jerome got his share.

Tort reform in the legislature slowed down Jerome's mass tort gravy train in Wilson County, but he was making good money advertising for fender bender cases and criminal defense cases, and the occasional bad drug case *du jour*. He had scores of lawyers and paralegals doing the work, and he reported every cent of his income from his profitable, high-profile practice to the IRS.

However, the big cash fees from Al Rashad were tax-free, known only to Jerome and his conscience. Al Rashad told him there would be a need for Jerome's services all over the country when their jihad began wreaking havoc on the legal system in every major state.

Man's religious beliefs don't matter to me. Long as Mr. Green shows up in my pockets.

Jerome washed his hands and hurried back. He stopped in the empty anteroom of Judge Williams' borrowed office suite to check his phone messages. He heard Willie Mitchell and the judge making small talk. Since they could not see him, he listened for a while. Al Rashad told Jerome in Memphis he wanted to know the prosecutor's every move. Jerome was sure he'd be interested in what Willie Mitchell was saying.

~ * ~

Judge Williams and Willie Mitchell chatted while waiting for Lawyer King.

"How do you like The Victorian?"

"It's all right. I slept pretty well. It's quiet. After court adjourned I went for a short run with Jake on the Natchez Trace next to the reservoir and worked up a little bit of a sweat."

"Out there where you can look out over the water?"

201

"Yes. It's nice and peaceful out there. Almost no traffic. I think I'm going to do it every night during the trial to calm my nerves."

"If the entire trial is anything like yesterday, you're going to need something to lower your stress."

Jerome King walked in and sat.

"Speak of the devil," she said.

"Sorry, Your Honor. Nature called."

Willie Mitchell could feel the tension. The judge was not happy.

"Willie Mitchell, did you happen to see Mr. King's press conference and interviews on the news last night?"

Willie Mitchell said, "Just a little."

"I watched one interview on MSNBC, another on CNN. That tough-talking blonde woman with the crime show at night. Mr. King talked about Frances Ware's opposition to the death penalty, and went into great detail about Sheriff Jones hitting the defendant while he was handcuffed at the scene. Then went on and on about why this case ought to be in federal court."

"It's all true," Jerome said. "Every word. You ordered me to avoid those subjects in court, but nothing was said about the press. There's no gag order. And it is undeniable that this case has no business in state court. Look at what happened in Sunshine."

"That's not the point," she said, raising her voice.

"If I misspoke in court yesterday or on television, this court can always grant a mistrial."

"That's what Mr. King wants, Your Honor. He's doing all this deliberately."

"I am vigorously representing my client, is what I'm doing. It's too bad if my zealous defense of Mr. Zegarra interferes with the state's plans to murder him with lethal drugs."

"There's no jury or camera in here, Mr. King. Cut the theatrics. It's lost on me." She paused. "Now, we're going to work long and hard today and continue picking the jury. If you behave, Mr. King, things will move much faster."

"We all know this case belongs in federal court."

"That's your opinion. In the meantime, it's in my court, and I'm in charge. One more outburst in front of jurors about Sheriff Jones or Frances Ware, or federal court and I'm going to hold you in contempt. After this trial is over, we'll have a hearing on the contempt, and you better bring a toothbrush with you."

Her warning did not seem to faze Jerome King. Willie Mitchell walked back into the courtroom. He saw Jake in the back, sitting with Agent Dunne.

They worked through the morning, seating one additional juror. In the afternoon, it seemed to Willie Mitchell that Jerome was dragging his feet, taking longer than necessary to ask his questions, asking for bathroom breaks once in the morning and twice in the afternoon.

Judge Williams kept them working until six-thirty, by which time they had seated a total of six jurors. Willie Mitchell was encouraged because Jerome was out of peremptory challenges. Unless he could manufacture a reason to disqualify a prospect for cause, they should have their twelve jurors by the end of the next day. Willie Mitchell had not challenged a single juror. He waited a few minutes for the courtroom to clear, and walked outside with Jake and Dunne.

"You want to take a quick run with us?" Willie Mitchell asked Dunne. "It's nice this time of evening out by the reservoir."

"Are you doing the jogging trail?"

"No," Jake said. "We're running the Natchez Trace where it parallels the reservoir."

"Like you did last night," Dunne said. "I think I'll pass. Listening to Jerome King all day has worn me out. You guys have fun."

Chapter Thirty-Four

Willie Mitchell got waylaid by reporters outside The Victorian. He was polite and avoided any answer that might be considered controversial. Picking the jury in this case was already extremely difficult, and he dared not add anything to the mix by saying something he shouldn't. He knew he was dull copy compared to Jerome King, but he had to be the adult in the situation. Saying outrageous things in criminal cases was reserved to the defense counsel, and Willie Mitchell was going to follow the protocol.

The fifty minutes he spent accommodating the camera crews and reporters delayed him, and by the time he and Jake parked in the rest area between the jogging trail and the Natchez Trace, it was dark.

They took off slowly on the asphalt road, heading north. They passed a grove of trees and brush between the Trace and the Ross Barnett reservoir, a large body of water that was Jackson's water supply. Willie Mitchell commented on the beauty of the lights reflecting on the water. He and Jake picked up speed. Willie Mitchell's legs were just beginning to warm up when the Chevrolet hit him.

~ * ~

"You see how that mother-fuckin' D.A. flew through the air?" Malik said when he stopped to turn around and go back to let Akbar finish them off. "He just sailed out over them rocks. Like he was flyin'."

"Shut up and get back there," Akbar growled.

Akbar was pissed at Malik. When they got the word from Al Rashad that the D.A. would be a sitting duck on this highway, Akbar wanted to take some time to recon, figure out a way to take him out without being too up close and personal. It was his sniper instinct. Distance provided detachment and cover. The jury murders went without a hitch, just like he planned, because he and the skinny dumb ass driver Malik made three trips to scout the town, the courthouse, and their getaway.

He had found a place across the bayou from the courthouse steps where he could see but not be seen, perfect for long distance killing, far enough away so they were on the road to ditch the mini-van before the people at the courthouse knew what hit them.

Akbar didn't like rushing to go after the District Attorney. They'd left Memphis at noon in the Silver 2008 Impala after Al Rashad got the information on where the D.A. would be jogging after court, but it wasn't enough time for Rashad to check everything out. It was sloppy and dangerous to bust down here and kill the man without making the effort to prepare for any contingency. Then the man and his son didn't show up until after dark, so Akbar couldn't use his sniper rifle.

He tried to make Malik sit tight in the trees next to the water so they could set up to kill them when the two joggers returned to their car, but the hard-headed son of a bitch wouldn't listen. After the runners were a hundred yards north of their car, Malik took out after them.

The Impala hit the D.A. solid. Akbar figured he was most likely already dead. The boy they just clipped, but Akbar saw him fall into the rocks. He was probably hurt pretty badly, and would be easy to finish off.

Akbar got his forty-five automatic ready as Malik, who he figured was the dumbest nigger he had ever been partnered with, finally got back to where they hit them.

"Stop, fool!" Akbar yelled at Malik, who slammed on the brakes. "Wait here and keep the fuckin' car running."

~ * ~

Jake heard Willie Mitchell hit the water, but it was so dark he couldn't see him. Jake thought his left shoulder, where he landed on the rocks, was dislocated. He couldn't move it. Jake stayed down in the rip-rap, and pulled his fanny pack around in front of him. He grabbed the Kel-Tec .380 from the pack. It was small with only a six-round capacity, but it was better than nothing.

Jake heard the Chevrolet engine roaring back toward him. He tried to pull back the slide to chamber a round but his left hand didn't work right. *Nerve damage, maybe.* He forced his uncooperative left hand to grab the slide with more force. A sharp pain shot up his arm, but he got the .380 bullet chambered.

The Impala slid to a stop on the grass between the road and the rocks. In the darkness, Jake squinted to see how many he was up against. He heard the car door slam and saw one figure coming toward him in the dark. Jake took quick aim and pulled the trigger, but nothing happened.

The damned pocket pistol had jammed. Jake began to look for an escape. He turned and dove into the water, trying to stay as shallow as possible, like a racing dive. He knew if he dove too deep and hit the rocks it would probably break his neck. Right when he hit the water he heard a number of large caliber gunshots. Jake swam furiously under water with one arm, hoping to God he hadn't been hit.

~ * ~

Dunne was on the jogging trail that paralleled the Natchez Trace when he heard the Chevrolet slam on its breaks. He jumped off the knobby-tired dirt bike and raced through the oak and sweet gum trees with both guns drawn. In the darkness he saw the outline of a man emerge from the passenger side of the car and move quickly toward the water.

Dunne did not know where Willie Mitchell and Jake were, but he didn't have time to find out, because when he got close enough he saw that the man was moving toward the water, holding a gun.

Dunne opened up with both pistols.

He figured at least four rounds tore through the man's torso. Dunne turned and shot a half-dozen rounds into the Chevrolet. He stuck one of his pistols in his belt and jerked open the car door, ready to fire. The dome light came on. Dunne was relieved to see only one man in the car, a dark, skinny black man in the driver's seat. He had very little face left. Dunne fired another round into the driver's skull just in case, then walked quickly to the other man, crumpled on the ground between the Chevrolet and the rocks. Dunne put his pistol to the man's temple and fired.

"Jake! Willie Mitchell!" Dunne screamed. "It's Dunne."

He heard Jake say, "Out here."

Jake was in the water. Maybe fifty feet, Dunne estimated by the sound of his voice.

"You all right?"

"Yeah. I don't think I'm shot. We were run down by the car."

"Where's Willie Mitchell?"

"I don't know."

"Can you swim to shore?"

"I can make it. Just find Daddy."

~ * ~

Willie Mitchell knew if he passed out he wouldn't make it. Everything around him, the water and the sky, was black. Or so he thought. He wasn't sure his eyes were working all that well.

He had heard the car right before it hit him. He should have been running against traffic, but he liked to stay close to the water, to look out over the reservoir. He and Jake had been moving off the shoulder toward the water when the car hit them. Willie Mitchell wondered how Jake was, hoping the car had not hit Jake as hard as it hit him.

His head throbbed. There was a split second after impact when his head hit something really hard—he remembered that. And his left leg was broken. He could feel it dangling, unresponsive. He hoped it wasn't an open fracture.

Right before he sank below the surface of the inky water he heard a lot of gunfire. It sounded to him as if it was coming from out in the reservoir, but that was crazy. As he drifted down, he knew he had not noticed any boats in the water. He would have seen their running lights for sure. Maybe he was turned around.

When his bare right foot brushed against a slimy log half-buried in the brown ooze underwater, he awoke with a start. "Damn," he thought. "Where am I?"

He tried to breathe and couldn't, and remembered he was in the reservoir. Willie Mitchell knew it was important to breathe, so he paddled somehow until his face broke the surface. He took a deep breath and opened his eyes. Everything was black.

"Willie Mitchell... , " he heard from somewhere. It didn't sound like Jake. Willie Mitchell tried to answer and made a noise. He wasn't sure what the noise was, but it wasn't words, a sentence, or a name. It was just a noise. He meant to say, "Jake."

What the hell was going on?

The last thing he heard before he dipped below the surface again was Susan telling him to get out of the pool, that their food was ready. Jake and Scott were drying off, picking at each other as usual. He was glad the country club finally did the work on the swimming pool, replacing the brick deck with the Cool Crete so the kids didn't have to hop and dance on the hot bricks when they got out. He was looking forward to the hamburger, fries, and a cold beer after he got a quick nap.

~ * ~

Dunne swam as hard as he could to the source of the gurgling sound. He raised up every few strokes but could see nothing in the darkness. He was about to yell out again when his foot struck something below the water. Dunne went under and felt Willie Mitchell's head. He grabbed a handful of hair and pulled him to the surface.

When they burst back through the surface, Dunne could not tell if Willie Mitchell was breathing. He slapped his face twice, then swam toward the rocks, dragging the D.A. behind. "Shit," he said when he realized Willie Mitchell was totally limp, offering no help or resistance.

As soon as Dunne's feet hit the slimy bottom he stood and jerked Willie Mitchell out of the water. Dunne carried him on his shoulder the rest of the way and unloaded the dead weight onto the rocks, careful to cup his hand around the back of Willie Mitchell's head.

"Jake!" he called out. "Over here!"

Dunne could not see him in the darkness, but Jake was already waiting for them on the grass above the rocks. He made his way down to his father's side. Dunne had his ear above Willie Mitchell's mouth. "He's not breathing!"

Dunne pounded Willie Mitchell's chest several times, then started chest compressions. He was about to hit him in the chest again when Willie Mitchell coughed. Water spurted and dribbled out of his nose and mouth. Dunne turned him on his side and hit him in the back.

"Thank God," Jake said.

Dunne lifted Willie Mitchell onto his shoulder and climbed up the rocks. He lay him gently on the grass. Dunne placed his ear on Willie Mitchell's chest.

"His heart's regular." He listened to him breathe. "So's his breathing. I think he'll make it. He's strong."

Willie Mitchell was unconscious.

"How are *you*?" Dunne asked Jake.

"I can't move my left shoulder. Who are these bastards?"

"From Al Rashad's mosque. Ninety-eight percent sure they're the same guys that killed the jurors."

"How did you know to be out here?"

"Some people monitoring Al Rashad. I'll explain later. We got more important things to do now. I felt the back of Willie Mitchell's head when I put him on the rocks. He's got a major head injury. Looks like one broken leg for sure. He might be bleeding internally. We've got to get him to a hospital."

"You have a car?"

"No. I want you to listen to me. What are you willing to do for your father?"

"Anything."

"I'm going to call nine-one-one. They'll have an ambulance here in no time. I want you to monitor his breathing. Make him comfortable. Try to find something soft to put under his head or turn him to the side. If he stops breathing do chest compressions. Keep him alive."

"Where are you going?"

"I'm going to put the two dead fuckers in the trunk of that Chevrolet there, and I'm going to drive it away from here."

"You can't do that. It's a crime scene."

He grabbed Jake by his good arm. "Wrong. It's a battlefield. This is no crime. It's a war. They tried to kill Willie Mitchell. I'm not sure yet they haven't succeeded."

"What do you want me to say?"

"You tell the EMTs that you and Willie Mitchell were hit by a car while jogging and they took off. Hit and run. Tell the police the car hit you from behind and you didn't get a look at it."

Dunne picked up Willie Mitchell and put him across his shoulder.

"We shouldn't move him."

"We have to. Follow me. We're moving you and him about a hundred yards down the road. You tell them that's where it happened. It's too dark to pick up all the brass on the ground, and I don't want the local cops sniffing around here, looking for tire tracks. Tell the cops you're pretty sure the driver never applied his brakes."

Jake followed Dunne, who moved as fast as he could, trying not to jostle Willie Mitchell's head.

"My gun jammed."

"You had a gun?"

"Yeah. A little .380. I kept it in this pack."

"What else you got in there?"

"Small bottle of water. Nothing else."

"Throw that gun into the reservoir. Far as you can. We don't need the added complication. Deep six it just to keep things simple."

Jake stopped and heaved the little automatic as far as he could into the water. "*Owww.* Goddammit. My shoulder."

"Did you have a round in the chamber when you were jogging?"

"No."

"Then you might as well not be carrying. If it's not ready to fire, you can't defend yourself. You've got to get some training."

Dunne found a suitable place and eased Willie Mitchell to the ground. "I'm leaving you now. You know what to do?"

"Got it. You were never here. Hit and run."

"I'll get the ambulance here right away. You watch his breathing."

Dunne stood and started to run back to the Chevrolet.

Jake yelled at him. "Dunne."

"What? I've got to go."

"When will you be back?"

"I'll call you."

Dunne disappeared into the darkness.

~ * ~

Jake started the timer on his running watch when Dunne left. He sat on the ground, close to Willie Mitchell. He did something he hadn't done since he was small—he held his Daddy's hand.

Jake kept his good hand on Willie Mitchell's neck, feeling his blood pulsate through his carotid artery. Jake's left shoulder ached, but he knew he was damned lucky to be alive.

Sitting in the darkness, he began to pray. It had been a while. Jake had stopped going to church when he was an undergraduate, except for holidays when he was home.

Jake tapped the button on the side of his watch and a blue light illuminated the display. He watched the seconds and minutes tick away. What would life be without Willie Mitchell? He wondered if Susan would stay in Sunshine. Probably not. Scott would start looking to Jake for advice he now received from Willie Mitchell.

He shook his head to rid his mind of those thoughts, and felt guilty that he was being so analytical at the thought of his father dying. Maybe it was because he was certain in his gut that Willie Mitchell would not die like this. He was in great condition and perfect health. Willie Mitchell was going to make it.

Jake knew all the damage had been done to his father when the car hit them. He also knew Dunne's showing up rendered irrelevant the fact that Jake's gun jammed. But, the fact remained if Dunne hadn't intervened, he and Willie Mitchell would be dead. Jake's ineptitude under fire underscored the truth of what Dunne told him that day at the courthouse massacre. Jake didn't know what he was doing. He was strong, a good shot, and a decent boxer, but didn't know shit about how to behave in a real confrontation. He swore then and there he would remedy that.

Jake concentrated on his right hand. The pulse seemed to be getting weaker. "This can't be happening," he said.

The pulse stopped.

"Oh my God," Jake said and straddled his father. He began chest compressions like Dunne had. After a minute of compressions, he listened closely for a heartbeat.

There was none.

"You cannot die!" he screamed and pounded Willie Mitchell's chest above the heart, then started the rhythmic compressions again.

"Come on!" he yelled.

He heard Willie Mitchell gasp and quickly felt his neck. The pulse was back. Jake eased up on the compressions. He put his right hand over Willie Mitchell's mouth and nose. He felt his breath, warm and moist, and kept doing the mild compressions.

"All right, God," he said, "if you let Daddy live, I'll—"

What? What could he promise? To live a better life? Help Habitat for Humanity build houses? Jake was not interested in that, and didn't think God would be interested either. God needed nothing from him.

I promise to become like Dunne, do whatever he does. Whatever that means. Whatever that takes.

Willie Mitchell seemed to move under him, but Jake thought it might be his imagination. The carotid pulse was still regular.

In the distance, he heard a faint siren. "You hear that, Daddy?" he said. "Just hang on."

When the siren grew close, Jake ran into the road and flagged them down. He directed them over to Willie Mitchell, and they got to work right away.

Jake told the EMTs about the hit and run driver, exactly like Dunne instructed. He asked them to call JPD and get a cruiser out there so he could show them how it happened. Just like Dunne said.

Chapter Thirty-Five

Susan sat between Scott and Jake on the couch in the St. Christopher's Hospital waiting room. Jake's left arm was in a sling. Jimmy Gray and Sheriff Lee Jones leaned against the wall. Walton Donaldson stood with them.

It was three a.m., five hours after Susan had arrived from Sunshine. Willie Mitchell was in surgery, and there was no word yet.

"They had to have hit y'all on purpose," Scott said. "You said you were moving off the shoulder onto the grass."

"Maybe," Jake said. "Like I said, I don't know who it was or how they were driving, so it's really hard to say."

The double doors to the operating room corridor swung open, and the surgeon walked toward the waiting area. Susan and her sons stood near Jimmy Gray and the others.

"How is he, Dr. Lavin?"

"The good news is, he's going to make it."

Tears streamed from Susan. She hugged both Scott and Jake. Jimmy Gray stepped up.

"What's the bad news, Dr. Lavin?"

Lavin was a small, lean man with white hair and deep wrinkles lining his face. He took Susan's hand. "He's got a lot of injuries, and we only addressed the most life-threatening tonight."

"What kind of injuries?" she asked.

"The two primary emergency procedures we did tonight were a spleen removal and a cranial procedure. The neurosurgeon, Dr. Carson, had to drill a hole through the skull to relieve the pressure on Willie Mitchell's brain. Both surgeries went well. The spleen rupture happened on impact and caused significant bleeding into the peritoneal cavity. The brain injury caused blood to accumulate between the skull and the brain for probably a couple of hours after the injury."

"What else does he have?"

"He's got a closed fracture of the left femur, which we stabilized. If things go all right, I'll have an orthopedist set that in a day or two. He's got a half-dozen fractured ribs, all on the left side. We'll keep those wrapped and that's about all we can do.

"And we think he's got a detached retina. We'll have a specialist look at it tomorrow."

"How serious is that?" Jake asked.

"It has to be surgically repaired when he's up to it."

"Is he still unconscious?" Susan asked.

"He's been that way since he came in. It's the brain's way of coping with the severe injury it suffered."

"Will draining the blood around the brain start the healing?" she asked. "Or will he have to have more surgery?"

"We don't know. We were told he was struck from the back, but his body must have flipped backwards because he suffered a severe coup and contre-coup injury, from striking the metal on the car then the brain striking the other side of the skull. You need to know he had a seizure in the OR right before Dr. Carter operated."

"Oh," Susan said and leaned against Jake. She dabbed her eyes. "Can I see him? I haven't gotten to see him yet."

"He's in the recovery room. I can get the nurse to bring you and your sons back there for just a minute or two. But, you have to leave when she says. He's in a naturally-induced coma and sedated as well, so he will not be responsive."

Susan was distraught. She sobbed and Scott held her. Dr. Lavin patted her shoulder and talked quietly.

"The most dangerous injury he has is the bruising of the brain. He'll recover in due course from everything else, but we won't know for days, maybe a week or longer, the extent of permanent impairment, if any. He's not out of the woods."

"Permanent brain injury?" she asked in tears.

"I only mention it because it's possible. Maybe a seizure disorder, or loss of hearing or sense of smell, for example, is possible. His vision could be impaired. We just don't know. It's too early."

"We'd like to see him now."

"Just family," Dr. Lavin said and walked them to the nurse. "One last thing, Susan. Willie Mitchell has a strong constitution, a heart like a lion. He might totally recover from his brain injury, with no permanent impairment. That is certainly possible. We just don't know yet. I'll see you tomorrow."

The nurse led Susan, Jake, and Scott through the swinging doors. Dr. Lavin waved discreetly to Jimmy, Walton, and Lee Jones.

~ * ~

Judge Williams walked out of her chambers and onto the bench. The packed courtroom was hushed. She turned to the six jurors seated in the jury box.

"Ladies and gentlemen, because of the injuries to Mr. Banks, I am going to release you from your service today. Since this is a capital case, keeping you sequestered while Mr. Banks recovers is simply not fair nor is it a viable option in the eyes of

213

this court. When this case reconvenes in the near future, you will not be asked to return. I thank you for your patience, and apologize to you for any inconvenience your participation these three days might have caused. You may go."

The six jurors filed out of the courtroom.

"Mr. Bordelon, will you ask Mr. Champion to step in to this courtroom, please."

The judge's Cajun minute clerk hurried out the center aisle and returned in less than a minute with the Hinds County court administrator.

"Mr. Champion, please release the remainder of the jury prospects in the jury waiting room downstairs. I will be in touch with you as soon as I know when we will resume so that you can get us another pool. This time, perhaps four hundred."

"Yes, Your Honor." He walked out of court.

"Mr. Donaldson? Mr. King?"

"The state moves to continue this matter until we have some feel for how long Mr. Banks will be in the hospital or otherwise recovering."

"Your Honor," Jerome King said, "at the risk of sounding unfeeling, which I assure the court and Mr. Donaldson I am not, my predecessor, Mr. Boardman, filed a motion for speedy trial. This past Monday was several days beyond the time limit, but I agreed to the start date as a courtesy to the prosecution. I am afraid that I am compelled to oppose any continuance beyond a few days or a week, and insist that my client's rights under the Speedy Trial Act be honored."

Judge Williams stared at Jerome with unbridled disgust.

"Mr. King, I am continuing a determination on your request until next Monday, when I want you, Ms. Bernstein, and Mr. Donaldson back in this courtroom at nine a.m. At that time we will take the matter of resetting State versus Zegarra for trial in light of all the circumstances as they exist then. I don't know about you, Mr. King, but I am going to go home and pray for Mr. Banks' speedy recovery. I hope you can find it somewhere in that heart of yours, if you actually have one, to do the same. Court is hereby adjourned."

She walked quickly out of the courtroom. El Moro stared at Walton while the Hinds County deputies shackled his hands and feet. The look on El Moro's face could only be described as a smirk.

~ * ~

It was a beautiful morning in Jackson. Jerome King stood in front of a small army of reporters, cameras, and microphones.

He was in a jaunty mood, rocking back and forth on his heels as he answered.

"No, I do not think Mr. Banks' accident was related to the jury murders in Sunshine. His son told the police it was a hit and run. I think the most likely explanation is some drunk fool was driving too fast and out of control. That's the typical case around these parts."

An overweight CNN reporter shouted. "Do you think it's fair to insist on going to trial while the Yaloquena district attorney is unable to participate because of his injuries?"

"I'm sorry about what happened to Mr. Banks. He's a very good friend of mine, and I feel deeply for him and his family. And, for those of you who were in the courtroom, for the record, I have already been praying for my friend's recovery. But my primary obligation is to my client. I've taken an oath to zealously guard my client's rights. Mr. Banks has a first assistant, Mr. Walton Donaldson, who is a first-rate attorney and competent to proceed in the absence of Mr. Banks. My client does not deserve the death penalty, and is entitled by law to a speedy trial."

The same reporter followed up. "What about the federal charges?"

"I'm glad you asked that question. My offer to consolidate the federal and state charges still stands. I've been in discussions with U.S. Attorney Leopold Whitman and we are exploring the possibilities. All we need is cooperation from the state and I believe we could reach an accommodation on everything, including an amicable asset forfeiture settlement that would benefit this city. Its part would be about two and a half million dollars. In these hard economic times, I think it's foolish for the state prosecutors to ignore such a solution, a solution that would benefit the state, the city, and federal government.

"Thank you," he said and walked away.

Fifty feet away, Jimmy Gray listened. He watched Jerome King finish his news conference. Jimmy cursed under his breath. "That son of a bitch," he said to Sheriff Jones, next to him.

"Piece of crap," Lee added and turned to Walton. "What are you going to do?"

"You mean besides pray for Willie Mitchell to recover in a hurry?" He paused for a moment. "Hell if I know."

~ * ~

Kitty was glad Jake answered his cell. The way they left things the previous week wasn't how she wanted it. She really liked Jake, maybe loved him, but she wasn't sure if she did, or exactly what that was. Kitty was determined to make her own way in the world. She planned on climbing the ladder in the bureau as high as she could. Getting married and having babies was not in the cards. Jake hadn't mentioned anything like marriage and children, nor had he talked about their future together.

But she could tell from Jake's family situation, the way he was raised, and the whole Delta and Mississippi culture, he was going to want to marry a lady like Susan—and Kitty was not that kind of woman. He was a great lover, funny, and lots of fun. She wanted to hang out with him as much as she could, but she didn't want their relationship to get to the point where she couldn't walk away on short notice to take a better position with the Bureau. Any place in North America or the U.S. territories had to be a better place to live than Jackson, Mississippi.

Jake insisted on driving the 4Runner to St. Christopher's even though his left arm was in a sling. She patted his leg.

"I'm glad Willie Mitchell is through the worst part."

"Good thing he's in great shape. The doctor said he was in remarkably fit condition, and that was what got him through the trauma. He said any other fifty-four year old he knows would have probably died in the reservoir."

"It pays to exercise."

They parked and walked into the hospital to the intensive care ward. Yaloquena deputy Sammy Roberts sat in a chair outside Willie Mitchell's room. He stood, almost at attention, when he saw them approach. Jake shook his hand and introduced him to Kitty.

"Your mother and Scott are in there. The doctor said y'all shouldn't stay long."

"At ease, soldier," Jake said with a smile and poked Sammy in his hard, flat stomach. "We appreciate your help."

"No problem. Sheriff Jones said we'll have someone here around the clock until Mr. Banks gets to come home."

Jake gestured for Kitty to go in first. Susan smiled when she saw them and gave Kitty an extended hug.

"Good to see you, Kitty."

"I'm so sorry all this happened to Willie Mitchell."

"The important thing is he's going to be fine."

"This is my younger brother, Scott," Jake said. Scott walked over and shook hands with Kitty. He smiled weakly, but did not say anything to her. Another handsome Banks man, she thought. But Scott was handsome in a different way. He was not as big or muscular as Jake, who was a clone of Willie Mitchell. Scott was almost pretty, and his coloring and mannerisms reminded Kitty of Susan.

"Scott is a junior at Ole Miss," Jake said and walked to Willie Mitchell's bedside. Kitty watched Jake take his father's hand. She noticed how much alike their hands were. Long fingers, but not delicate. Strong, masculine, well-proportioned hands. Not too hairy; sexy hands, she thought. Kitty glanced at Susan. She admonished herself. In the current situation her private observation about sexy hands was probably not appropriate.

She watched Willie Mitchell as Jake talked quietly to him. His eyes were closed and his head heavily bandaged. His jaw was slack and a tube ran out the corner of his mouth. Oxygen flowed into his nostrils through smaller tubes.

He was totally out and showed no response at all to Jake's words. Kitty noticed Jake's eyes were full of tears. Jake was deeply emotional, a lot more emotional than Kitty. Sometimes she thought it was sweet that he was that way, but usually she equated emotionality with weakness. She was never going to be accused of weakness, and she knew that was why some men thought she was cold. She was tough, that's all.

~ * ~

Jake dropped Kitty off at her apartment. She asked him if he wanted to come up for a while, but he was not in the mood. On the way to his place, he had called Susan to make sure The Victorian gave them no trouble when she asked them for two keys to Willie Mitchell's room, one for her and one for Scott. She said the people at the front desk were quite nice and accommodating. She and Scott would see him tomorrow. He hoped she got some sleep, because she had been up for thirty-eight hours straight.

He parked in front of his apartment and walked toward the metal and concrete steps in the center of the eight-unit building in the middle of the complex of twenty other eight unit buildings. His fellow tenants were primarily young, working folks like him. Most were single, but a few were starting families. Jake had come to know the other residents of his building casually, well enough to say hello and make small talk. He knew no names except for the couple that lived on his floor. Their front door was opposite his. They chatted on the landing on occasion. He was a medical student, and she worked in a bank. All they knew about Jake was that he was an attorney.

The other six units were occupied by people who might possibly be going through something as traumatic as Jake. He

217

would never know. In Sunshine, as soon as someone had trouble of some kind, everyone knew it. Maybe there was a loss of privacy in his small town, but there was also a strong sense of communal suffering and support.

He walked up the four flights to the landing outside his apartment. There was David Dunne, leaning against the brick wall.

Chapter Thirty-Six

Jake handed Dunne a Coors Light long-neck and sat in the stuffed chair next to the sofa. Jake took a sip of his beer. Dunne sat on the sofa with his feet on Jake's battered coffee table that had somehow survived law school.

"How is Willie Mitchell?"

"He's stable. The doc says the bleeding has stopped and his brain isn't swelling any more. He's still unconscious."

"Has he come to since I left you at the reservoir?"

"No. Supposedly that's nature's way of protecting the brain after an injury. Doctor Lavin says it's common after a severe head trauma and not to worry about it. He says his vital signs all look good, and he should come around in a few days."

Both men took a long pull on their Coors.

"He's going to have a long rehab."

"Yeah. He's got to have surgery to fix his broken leg, maybe tomorrow. Sometime down the road he'll have eye surgery to fix the detached retina."

Jake grabbed the remote and ESPN came on. The sportscasters were arguing about the Big Ten football match ups for the weekend. Jake muted the sound.

"He's not going to be able to try El Moro."

"Nah. It could be months before he's up and around. Even if there's no residual brain injury or side effects, he's not going to be himself for a long time."

"What's Walton like?"

"He's sharp. Just three years older than me but he's been trying cases in Yaloquena for about four years now. Daddy knew his folks and recruited him out of Ole Miss law school. He's a good trial lawyer. Honest, straightforward guy."

"Where's he from?"

"Clarksdale."

"Oh, yeah. We blew through it on the way to Memphis."

"At a hundred miles an hour."

"Walton's never handled a capital murder trial, has he?"

"No. But I think he's a better lawyer than Jerome King or Eleanor Bernstein."

"Jerome King is a real showman. You think Walton can keep his cool in court with King the way your father does?"

Jake thought for a minute. "Probably not."

"Are you and Walton pretty good friends?"

"I guess so. He's married and got two kids already, so we don't socialize much. We talk about his cases when I'm in

Yaloquena, and we've been hunting together some. I'd say we're friends. Not really close, but I know him well enough."

The two men were silent for a moment. Jake stared at the ESPN clips of the Michigan running back scoring a touchdown against Ohio State in the Big House at Ann Arbor.

"What are you getting at?" Jake asked.

"I think it's time to cut our losses. I want you to approach Walton about it. See if he's amenable."

"What do you mean?"

"We took out two of Al Rashad's best men. It's going to set him back operationally for a while. I'm thinking it might be best now to go ahead and work something out with Jerome King and coordinate with your little prissy boss. Wrap the state and federal charges at one time and put El Moro away for the rest of his life."

"I thought you wanted him dead. He's going to recruit more jihadists in the penitentiary. That's what you wanted to avoid by staying in the state system."

"You're right. But things have changed now. With Willie Mitchell not trying the case, and the type of jury King is going to get here in his home town, the death penalty is a real long shot now, in my opinion."

Jake thought for a moment. He took a sip of beer.

"You're right. With the kind of jury they were picking this week, I'm not sure even Daddy could have pulled it off. Some of those six jurors he accepted, I don't think he would have ever taken if the jury pool were bigger. With all those people not showing up, there's almost no prosecution-oriented jurors to choose from. They're all scared to come to the courthouse."

"I've got a backup plan to take care of El Moro. If we can get him into the federal system, I can pull a few strings to get him placed where he can't do much harm."

"Keep him in isolation, you mean? Some kind of maximum-security place?

"Well, something like that. I'm working on it now."

"What do you want me to do? Judge Williams ordered the parties back in court on Monday. King is pressing the speedy trial issue. The judge doesn't have a lot of discretion under that statute."

"I know. Why don't you meet with Whitman first thing in the morning and get him on board. He's dying to get El Moro in the federal system to get the cash forfeited and pump him for cartel information. Then talk to Walton about the advantages of taking a deal as long as El Moro gets life imprisonment without parole and goes down on the federal stuff, too. You need to talk to

Sheriff Jones, also. Get him on board. You've got two working days to put the deal together."

"Should I mention that you can work the federal system?"

"No. Keep my name out of it. This is something you've come up with on your own. And don't suggest maximum-security or any kind of restriction on his federal time. I'll be working that through unofficial contacts. I'll be around and you can call me, but this needs to be your idea. You meet with the professor and your Yaloquena people and work out all the details. The bottom line should be he spends the rest of his life incarcerated. Don't worry about anything else."

"Okay. I'll start first thing in the morning."

"And look, when Willie Mitchell regains consciousness and his head starts clearing, he's going to be asking you questions about what happened at the reservoir. He doesn't need to know about me showing up and killing those two knuckleheads. Stick to the story that it was a hit and run, that you never saw who hit you. If he remembers anything that happened after he got hit and flew into the water, just tell him it didn't happen, that he had a massive head injury, and was talking crazy talk, out of his head when you fished him out of the reservoir. I don't want him to know what I did. Only you can know my involvement."

"What did you do with those two fuckers, anyway?"

"I have a cleanup crew I work with. I got them down here pretty quickly, and I laid low for a few hours until I turned the Impala over to them. They took it from there. Believe me, the car and the two bodies in the trunk disappeared without a trace. And when the coast was clear, they cleaned up the scene, picked up and covered up. My men are pros. That shit never happened. The two dead guys never existed."

"I'd like to know more about what you do."

"We can talk about it after this is over."

"I'm going to tell you something, and I don't' want you to laugh at me. When I was with Daddy at the reservoir, waiting for the ambulance, I made a promise to God. Do you believe in God?"

"I do. I talk to Him every day."

"I promised God that if he let Willie Mitchell live and be okay, that I would start doing what you do."

"What exactly do you think I do?"

"You cut through all the legal and political bullshit to kill the bad guys who want to kill innocent people, assholes who think nothing of trying to kill a great man like my Daddy. I want to save people like that JPD cop Carl Lippmann, the old wildlife agent Elbert Dowd, and Willie Mitchell from those bastards, whoever and wherever they are. I want to be a one man justice department."

Dunne put his hand on Jake's good shoulder.

"You've got what it takes. I know that for sure. We can get you trained right, some real-life experience, too. It's not going to be easy, but if you stick with it, and are tough enough, you'll be an unstoppable weapon, on a par with very few men. But, you need to think long and hard about it. It's not the kind of thing you can quit or retire from. It's kind of like in the movie when the beautiful vampire woman scratches her chest with her fingernail, and you suck her blood out of the cut. You're all in, one hundred percent. You're part of the undead from that day forward. No going back. It's a lonely life. Sometimes it's plain miserable. But when I can be around to help people like you and Willie Mitchell at the reservoir, I plan on doing it as long as I can stay alive, as long as the people I'm trying to kill don't take me out." He closed and reopened his fists. "And I need some help. I need someone like you."

~ * ~

Leopold Whitman was so smarmy it almost made Jake sick. He was "thankful" that Willie Mitchell had survived his "incredible ordeal" and "all his thoughts" were with Jake and his family. He urged Jake to "take as much personal time as needed" to get over his shoulder injury and to help his mother and father, "a giant, a legend of the Mississippi bar."

Jake led the professor down the path Dunne suggested, talking about cooperating with the state, coordinating the prosecuting, maybe even a plea on all charges in both jurisdictions, coupled with the forfeiture of half of the five million dollars through the Jackson U.S. attorney's office. It was the sort of coup that could put the professor in line for his dream job, a federal judgeship.

According to the office scuttlebutt, Whitman was always sucking up to Washington, suggesting his own name whenever one of the federal judges relinquished his lifetime sinecure, which they only did if they died. If they merely became senile, they still hung on as long as possible, taking senior status. U.S. District Judge Leopold Whitman—it sounded right to Jake—a position where everyone before him had to bow and scrape, and pay attention to every word the little worm said. Very little work, admiration and respect from the ignorant public, fear and dread in the heart of every lawyer who came before him. Often wrong, but never in doubt.

What more could a man like Leopold Whitman want from life?

Jake emphasized to Whitman how close he was to Walton and Sheriff Jones, and this scenario was what his mother wanted. Actually, Jake had not broached it with her, but he knew in his heart Susan wanted Willie Mitchell as far away from the case as possible.

The professor walked Jake out, saying he'd start the ball rolling by calling Jerome King. He and attorney King had some preliminary discussions, but nothing in great detail. Whitman had wanted to give Willie Mitchell "the full opportunity to put the scoundrel on death row, where he belonged." Now that the situation had been altered by the terrible hit and run, an "unfortunate turn of events," a coordinated plea would probably benefit everyone. It would "add more ammunition to the Justice Department's war on drugs, the bane of our country."

Though he thought about grabbing a quick shower to clean off the crap that Whitman shoveled at him, he went straight to the hospital, where he knew he'd find Susan, Scott, Walton, Sheriff Jones, and Jimmy Gray. They all said the day before they'd be back first thing in the morning. His left shoulder ached as he walked into ICU.

Big Jimmy Gray sat on the couch next to Sheriff Jones. Jake saw a deputy in the chair next to the door to Willie Mitchell's room.

"Where's Walton?"

"He's in the room with Susan and Scott," Jimmy said. "He just got here ten minutes ago."

Jake walked into the room. Willie Mitchell appeared the same as the day before.

"Jake," Walton said.

"I need to see you in the waiting area outside."

"What's going on?" Susan asked.

"Why don't you join us, too, Mother? Scott, would you stay in here and keep an eye on Daddy?"

They joined Lee Jones and Jimmy Gray in the waiting area.

"How is he doing this morning?" Jake asked his mother.

"Good. Doctor Lavin said his vital signs are all in normal range, and there's no bleeding in the brain or from the splenectomy. He said he could take the oxygen off and Willie Mitchell would breathe on his own, but he said he'd give it another day. They're going to set his leg tomorrow morning. The orthopedist wants to get it done before the weekend while they're fully staffed."

"Okay. I'm probably sticking my nose where I shouldn't, but my boss, Mr. Whitman called me in this morning. He said he was sorry about Daddy, but finally got around to his real reason for talking to me. He asked me whether I thought the prosecution would be interested in working a deal with our office to get Zegarra to plead to capital murder without the death penalty, coordinated with guilty pleas on the federal charges. He said they'd want Zegarra in the federal penal system so they could access him for information on the cartel. Jerome King has told Whitman that Zegarra knows everything about *El Cártel de Campeche*, including their routes into the country, distribution hubs, and the names of all the big players. King said earlier Zegarra will take life with no parole on the state charges. The City of Jackson and Whitman are hot to get this done because King says they won't contest the forfeiture and the JPD and Whitman's office will split the five million cash."

When Jake finished no one spoke. Finally, Walton glanced at Sheriff Jones, then Susan. He cleared his throat.

"The way the deck is stacked against us here in jury selection, I gave up on putting the needle to Zegarra after seeing the jurors we seated Monday. Before the case got continued, of the six selected, I didn't think we had but one or two that I thought *might* go with us on the penalty. I don't think even Willie Mitchell could have convinced them. I have to be honest. I can try the case. It's easy to put the evidence on. In my opinion, though, with Judge Williams excluding the evidence in the guilt phase of the crash on I-55, the five million, and Zegarra's history as a drug courier, I feel I have a zero percent chance of getting the death penalty."

"Sheriff?" Jake asked.

"I agree with Walton one hundred percent. If we could have picked a jury in Sunshine, where people knew Travis, we would have had a chance. But not here. Jerome King's billboards are all over this town."

Susan sat up. "If the best we can hope for is a guilty finding with a life sentence and no parole, why would we even take the chance of going to trial? We have nothing to gain and everything to lose." She dabbed her eyes and broke down. "And look what this case has done to Willie Mitchell. And you, Jake, you could have died. And those poor innocent people on the courthouse steps." She sobbed. "My God, what kind of criminals are we dealing with?"

Jake moved next to Susan and put his good arm around her, wincing at the pain that shot through his left shoulder. Susan lay her head against him.

"Walton. Why don't you call Jerome King and Whitman and start making the deal? That okay with everyone?"

"Hell, yes," Jimmy Gray said. "Let's get this done and go home to Sunshine. We need Willie Mitchell home, too, as soon as he's able to leave."

"As soon as I get the general terms worked out, I'll call Judge Williams," Walton said. "She's planning on being here Monday morning. She can accept the guilty plea then."

"Why don't you get everything in writing and get everyone to sign off on it, like we do in federal court?" Jake asked. "I've got a form you can use. I'll go by the office right now and e-mail it to you."

"Good idea," Walton said. "I'll keep everyone in the loop, and see you all back here Monday morning for the plea if everyone agrees."

Jake kissed his mother and started to leave the ICU.

"Wait," she said, and gave him a big hug. "Thank you. Thank you so much. I want to get your daddy home."

Chapter Thirty-Seven

By the end of the work day Friday, everyone, including Zegarra, had signed the plea agreement. Walton had circulated the first draft early that morning, and everyone returned the document with minor recommended changes. Walton amended the first draft to include the changes everyone agreed to and re-circulated it. The document had both the state and federal captions, and was four letter-sized pages long when printed, with a fifth page for the signatures. When everyone was satisfied with the language and terms, Leopold Whitman ordered a U.S. marshal to hand deliver the document to every signatory, wait while it was signed, then proceed to the next office.

Since Walton stayed in Jackson to complete the plea negotiations, delivering the original for signatures was not a difficult task for the marshal. He returned the original to Leopold Whitman with all signatures. The professor faxed or hand-delivered copies to everyone.

Walton sent Judge Williams every draft, and asked Whitman to fax the final signed agreement to the judge's office. Jake did not have to sign the agreement, but Walton kept Jake in the loop with a blind copy e-mail containing every version until the final draft met with his and everyone else's approval.

Jake offered to take Walton out for a drink after the agreement was finalized. Walton begged off, anxious to get home to Sunshine, his wife Gayle, and their twins. He told Jake he'd see him early Monday morning in the Jackson courtroom at Zegarra's plea.

Jake took Susan and Scott to dinner at a Mexican restaurant. Jake told Susan that Kitty had to work late and said she would try to come by the hospital the next day, Saturday, to check on Susan and Willie Mitchell.

During dinner, Susan said the orthopedic surgeon told her and Scott the procedure to set the broken femur that morning went smoothly. It was a clean break, he said, and the surgery and recovery were uneventful.

After Jake dropped Susan and Scott at The Victorian at about nine Friday evening, he decided to go by the hospital to check on Willie Mitchell. Susan said at the restaurant that about three that afternoon, he opened his eyes for a few seconds. She said he did it twice, and she asked the nurse to call the neurosurgeon. The nurse let Susan talk briefly to Dr. Carter, who said opening the eyes was a good sign, and he would check in on Willie Mitchell the next morning, because he was on call all weekend. Dr. Lavin had spoken to Susan and Scott around five and agreed Willie Mitchell's opening his eyes was most certainly encouraging.

Jake spoke to the deputy at the ICU door and walked in. Everything was the same; the tube, the oxygen, the bandaged head. There was one major difference. His left leg rested on top of the sheet, and there were metal rods and bolts sticking out on each side of his thigh. It never ceased to amaze Jake how closely orthopedic surgery resembled carpentry. Jake was pleased that someone thought to put a small cotton sock on Willie Mitchell's toes to keep them warm.

Jake pulled a chair close and sat next to his father. He concentrated on Willie Mitchell's eyes, hoping to see them open. After a while, Jake noticed Willie Mitchell's hand begin to tremble. Jake took his father's hand and felt it shake. Willie Mitchell's eyes were quivering under the lids, like a REM effect. Jake almost called the nurse, but the tremors and quivers stopped. Jake wondered if they might have something to do with the brain healing.

The machines wired to Willie Mitchell began to beep, loud and insistent. In seconds two nurses rushed in the room. The EKG line was flat. His dad's heart had stopped. Jake backed out of the way of the medical personnel, into the corner of the room under the television. He watched them work, helpless.

A male nurse rushed in pushing a cart with defibrillation equipment, just like on *ER* or *House*. A young doctor Jake had never seen before was right behind the nurse. The doctor pulled the paddles off, rubbed them together and placed them on either side of Willie Mitchell's chest. The doc gave the okay to the nurses and the machine went *whump,* and wheezed. The young doc did it again. And again. He waited for about ten seconds, and did it again.

Jake stared at the EKG monitor. Except for the spike when the current shot through Willie Mitchell's heart, it remained flat. The young physician edged past the nurse, shaking his head. He walked over to Jake and said he was sorry, there was nothing else he could do. He walked toward the door. "Nine-fifty-five p.m." the doctor said to the nurses.

"Try one more time," Jake said from the corner.

The young doctor turned. "It's no use."

"Try one more time, dammit."

The doctor cut his eyes to the nurses and shook his head as he walked back to Willie Mitchell's bedside and picked up the paddles.

~ * ~

It was the coolest trip Willie Mitchell had ever taken. He was in a tram, like the ones that move people between terminals at major airports, but smaller. He was alone. He did not know how he got in the tram, or where he was going, but it was way, way cool.

Sometimes the tram went really fast. Lights flashed by on the sides, elongated by the incredible speed he was traveling. He had no control over what the tram did or where it went or how fast. Since he had no control, he just enjoyed the ride. He had no fear. Somehow, he knew instinctively nothing bad was going to happen to him in the tram.

At intervals the tram would slow down and enter a station of sorts. The tram had no doors, and neither did the stations. The tram stopped and Willie Mitchell was in the station, not the tram. It was so bright in the station it hurt his eyes.

The first stop was like the kitchen in his home when he was growing up, before Susan re-did the cabinets and counter tops. Monroe and Katherine Banks were eating breakfast. His mother, as usual, hugged him and gave him a kiss on the cheek. Monroe read the paper and grunted. Even so, Willie Mitchell knew his father was glad to see his only child.

He felt a pull, like the Tilt-A-Whirl he remembered from the county fair every fall, and he was in the tram traveling again. There was music in the tram now: the Beatles, then Crosby, Stills, and Nash, and the Rolling Stones. At the next station he and Susan were dancing to the Bee Gees. In the bright lights and strobes she was so beautiful. He took her in his arms and kissed her.

In the next station Scott was chasing Jake with a nine iron at the Sunshine Country Club. He and Susan followed close behind in a golf cart, laughing themselves silly. He was still giggling when the tram took off. He passed through more stations but didn't linger long in any one. Every person that ever meant anything to Willie Mitchell was in one of the stations, along the way. He loved seeing everyone. He knew they loved him and wanted him to stay, but he had to leave. The tram was inexorable, with a mind of its own.

The tram began to shake so hard that Willie Mitchell thought it would fly into pieces. His eyes and hands were shaking with the tram. He could barely make things out, with the shaking, but he knew Susan was next to him, so he would be all right. So would she. And Jake and Scott, they were there, too. Everything would be all right for them, too. Willie Mitchell could not remember the last time he was so happy. What a great ride.

He kissed Susan and his boys. They evanesced into a station. He was shaking and quivering, alone in the tram. It stopped in the middle of a dark green, winter wheat field, like the kind Big Al Anderson used to grow in his fields right outside Sunshine.

Finally, everything stopped shaking. Thank God. Willie Mitchell was now outside the tram, walking alone. A warm, late fall wind blew the wheat in front of him, this way and that. Behind him he saw the tram in the field. Ahead all he could see was the dark green wheat growing as far as his eyes could see, waving back and forth in the wind. What a beautiful sight.

He continued to walk. In the distance, he saw someone waving. He walked closer, and finally recognized who it was. Beau, wide-load Jimmy Gray's youngest boy, the one whose rifle fell from the fence and fatally shot him in the stomach, was waving Willie Mitchell on. Beau was Scott's best friend. Beau spent the night at Willie Mitchell and Susan's house as much as he did his own. He was part of the Banks family.

Beau appeared to be all right to Willie Mitchell. He guessed Beau hadn't been shot in the stomach after all. Willie Mitchell tousled Beau's hair and they both laughed. Beau took Willie Mitchell's hand and led him on a walk through the wheat. They were almost floating.

Willie Mitchell loved the feel of the warm wind moving over him. It made him happy to be walking in the wheat field with Beau.

It seemed lightning struck them in the field. Willie Mitchell was in the tram again. Outside, Beau waved goodbye.

The tram was heading back. Willie Mitchell was happy....

Chapter Thirty-Eight

"The surgery to set the femur yesterday morning was a success," Dr. Lavin said. "The orthopedist did an excellent job. But the surgery—and this is always a risk with a patient who has suffered so much trauma and broken bones—the surgery apparently dislodged an embolus. It traveled through Willie Mitchell's veins to his lungs, where it created a blockage. I can't tell you if it was a blood clot or a fatty tissue clot. The clot was apparently substantial, and it created so much pressure, that his heart was pumping much harder, trying to push blood through the blockage."

"His heart stopped," Jake said. "The monitors flatlined."

"Yes. But the nursing staff and doctor on duty were able to resuscitate him, shock the heart back into a rhythmic beat. I'm sure Jake has told all of you what occurred."

"Could it happen again?" Susan asked.

Dr. Lavin shrugged. "The truth is, I'm kind of speculating about the probable cause of the heart stopping last night. I had an MRI and a CAT scan done this morning, and neither I nor the radiologists can see any evidence of any other clot anywhere in his body. Nor can we see evidence of the clot we think caused last night's incident. What I've described is the most likely scenario.

"And the good news is now that we're pretty sure his brain and the spleen incision have healed enough that we can start him on some mild blood thinners which will significantly reduce the chance of another embolus forming. Moreover, there's no more surgery we need to do in the short term, so it's unlikely another clot would form and break loose."

"Thank you," Susan said.

"He's not out of the woods yet. We believe he will continue to get better and perhaps regain consciousness shortly. I have to remind you that we have no way to know whether there will be any kind of residual effect, short or long term, from his brain injury. It is possible there will be. We just have to wait and see. The neurologist will be watching him closely as well."

Dr. Lavin left the waiting area. There was a collective exhale from Susan, Jake, Scott, Jimmy Gray and Sheriff Jones.

"Sounds good, Susan," Jimmy Gray said. "I believe the old boy is going to pull through."

"Thank God," Lee Jones said.

"I've got to step outside and call Walton in Sunshine," Jake said. "I promised him I would call as soon as we met with Dr. Lavin."

Jake walked out of ICU and rode the elevator to the first floor. When he was outside his phone rang before he could call Walton.

"Hello," Jake said.

"It's Dunne. How's he doing?"

"Dr. Lavin thinks the danger from blood clots is over, and says Willie Mitchell ought to recover, maybe regain consciousness in a few days. They don't know yet about any permanent brain damage."

"Have you talked to Walton about Monday morning?"

"Not yet. I was about to call him."

"Good. When you talk to him tell him it's important that El Moro plead out in Judge Williams court Monday morning, just like it's set up now. No delays."

"Why?"

"I've got some things working that depend on his pleading Monday."

"Something to do with the federal pen you're pulling strings to get him in?"

"More or less. I'm on a tight schedule, too. There's things that have come up unrelated to this. I need to get out to the West Coast, like yesterday, so things need to be wrapped up here Monday."

"It looks like Daddy's in the clear, so there's no reason to postpone the plea. Walton says we'll probably be through by nine-thirty, and the agreement provides that Zegarra's to be turned over to the custody of the U.S. attorney in Judge Williams' courtroom as soon as the life sentence is imposed. Then he belongs to you feds forever. Are you going to be there Monday morning?"

"Wouldn't miss it. Nine o'clock sharp. You?"

"I'll be there."

"I'm okay with what we've done here. The two assholes that ran into you and Willie Mitchell are dead. And I'm ninety-nine percent sure they're the ones who killed the jurors. They got their death penalty. Eventually El Moro will get what's coming to him. Maybe others, too."

"You mean Al Rashad?"

"Him for one. I'm working up a plan for Mr. Al Rashad. If I have anything to do with it, he's ordered his last killing on behalf of Allah."

"Good."

"What about your promise to the man upstairs?"

"The deal was if Daddy lived, I would join your team."

"I understand the circumstances you were in when you made that promise. If you want some time to think about it before you really commit—"

"No. I want to join more than ever. I'm ready."

"Good. That's what I like to hear."

"So what do I do? Disappear into the night? Never able to contact my mother or Scott again?"

"Nothing so dramatic. I've got a pretty good proposal all worked up for you. But you don't have to do anything right now. You just keep on doing what you're doing. Keep working for Leopold Whitman. I like having you in the Justice Department. I'll contact you when I have everything ready."

"You think months?"

"No. Weeks. Maybe three or four. You're going to have to go through some pretty rigorous training. That will take some time."

"I'm up for that. I'm going to start getting into better shape. Five miles every morning. Seven days a week. I'm going to step up my boxing and my strength training."

"You speak any languages?"

"My Spanish is pretty good. I know a little French."

"Good. No one can know about this. You can never tell your family. Not even Willie Mitchell."

"What about Whitman?"

"If everything goes like I plan, you're going to still be an assistant United States attorney. Whitman will be told at the right time that the Justice Department has a new assignment for you, and you'll be transferred. By the way, don't even think of telling Kitty."

"I won't. Not a chance."

"And you might not see her for a while after we get started."

"No sweat. That was in the cards anyway."

"Oh, yeah?"

"Yeah. Kind of a strange chick."

"What other kind is there?"

"They're not all crazy."

"Whatever you say. After all this is over, I'll be in touch with you, Jake. You can take that to the bank. See you in the courtroom on Monday."

Chapter Thirty-Nine

Monday morning El Moro shuffled into the Jackson courtroom in his ankle shackles. He stopped walking when the Hinds County deputies on either side tugged on his arm just inside the courtroom door. Sheriff Lee Jones walked toward him. He knew the hot-headed *prieto* sheriff would not hit him in front of all these people.

El Moro winked at the sheriff when he told the local deputies to remove his shackles. *"Gracias, jefe,"* El Moro said directly to Lee Jones.

"Shut up, you bastard."

The woman judge was not on her elevated bench. Neither was her little bald assistant with the South Louisiana accent. El Moro had encountered many Cajuns when he was running drugs through the Louisiana marshes, and he had no bad feelings about them as a people.

The assistant to the district attorney, the young man who was there the day he was arrested at the red Malibu on the side of the road, made eye contact briefly with El Moro. He should be happy about this agreement, El Moro thought. He will not have to try the case and can go home today. Maybe he is angry about the injury to his boss.

It was true that El Moro had benefited from the injury to Willie Mitchell Banks. He looked forward to life in whatever federal penitentiary they sent him to. There would be no women for a while, but El Moro was confident that Al Rashad would arrange for conjugal visits after time passed and the interest in El Moro was no longer so intense.

Regardless of the accounts he had seen on the TV in the Hinds County lockup, where the reporters said it was a hit and run driver, probably intoxicated, El Moro knew it was the hand of Allah, working through his efficient servant, Al Rashad. The loud-mouthed *prieto* lawyer would not admit it, but El Moro could tell by the way Jerome King told him about it. Al Rashad had arranged it. Since there was no arrest of anyone reported on the television or in the Jackson paper, Al Rashad's people must have gotten away clean.

El Moro admired Al Rashad's ability to plan and carry out projects. He was two for two in El Moro's eyes. The dead jurors and the hospitalized district attorney were proof of Al Rashad's skill as a general in Allah's army.

After growing up on the streets and in the slums of Madero and Tampico, federal prison would be a cakewalk. El Moro would become a man of importance, spreading the word of

Allah, recruiting new jihadists to their worthy cause. Today was the beginning of a new and exciting chapter in his life, and El Moro was ready to get started. Allah had led him through mysterious passages in his days on earth, and El Moro knew, down deep, that he would not spend the rest of his life in prison. Allah would see to that.

With their numbers rising as his recruits returned to civilian life from the prison, it was only a matter of time until the doors of the prisons were blown open to release all inmates to join in the holy war against the Christian empire of the U.S.

Behind the assistant district attorney on the front row were the district attorney's son and the woman FBI agent who was always with him. El Moro avoided eye contact with the young man, because he knew he was angry and wanted to kill him. El Moro did not blame him. He would kill the people who murdered his sweet mother if he ever found out who was responsible. The D.A. had seemed to be a good man, and was certainly a formidable attorney. But in war, El Moro reasoned, good people on both sides get hurt. The young Banks should be grateful that his father managed to live.

Also on the front row was *El Gordo*, El Moro's nickname for the district attorney's fat *amigo*, the one who was working in the courtroom in Yaloquena before the jurors were killed. The fat man wanted to kill El Moro, too. He could tell from the look in his eye. Prison was not going to satisfy *El Gordo*.

El Moro sat next to Jerome King. The chair occupied by Eleanor Bernstein was empty. El Moro searched the room for the lawyer's Asian girlfriend, but she was not in the courtroom either.

"Where is Ms. Bernstein?" El Moro whispered.

"She said she was too upset about the injury to Mr. Banks and asked if I could handle the pleas without her this morning."

El Moro wondered if Ms. Bernstein suspected that the hit and run was no accident. He put her out of his mind. After all, he would never see her again.

Across the courtroom, seated against the wall inside the rail was the U.S. attorney with the closely trimmed beard, Leopold Whitman. With him were many *federals* with short hair and grim faces. Seated at the end was *El Asesino,* what he called the *federal* who spent so much time with the district attorney in Sunshine, the one with the hard eyes. El Moro made eye contact with him for a while, but finally turned away.

Asesino is one federal I want no part of.

El Moro stood when the woman judge entered the courtroom following her little Cajun assistant who told everyone to rise. She got right to business.

"All right, gentlemen, let's get this done. I want to get back to Yaloquena County by noon."

El Moro and Jerome King walked between the tables, stepped up on the riser, and stood before the judge.

"Mr. Zegarra, I have before me an original document signed by all parties, including you." She held up page five of the plea agreement so he could see the signatures. "Is this your signature?"

"Yes, Your Honor."

"Has anyone forced you to take this plea?"

"No, Your Honor."

"Has anyone made you any promises of any kind, concerning prison sentences or anything else, other than what is contained in this plea agreement that you admit you signed."

"No, ma'am."

"Are you pleading guilty today because you are in fact guilty?"

"Yes."

"Did you shoot and kill Deputy Sheriff Travis Ware?"

"Yes, Your Honor."

"Do you understand that after you withdraw your not guilty plea previously entered, and enter your guilty plea this morning to the charge of capital murder, that I will sentence you to life without parole?"

"Yes."

El Moro whispered to Jerome King.

"Mr. Zegarra wants to make sure his life term will be spent in the federal penitentiary system."

"Yes. It's all spelled out in this written agreement, Mr. Zegarra."

El Moro tuned out. He had heard enough. The judge continued to ask questions and he answered as directed for another ten minutes. It was all a big waste of time. He had already agreed to everything, so why all the talking?

"I find that you have knowingly and voluntarily entered your guilty plea to capital murder in accordance with this written plea agreement, the original of which is now part of the permanent record of this proceeding, and I hereby sentence you to life in prison, without probation or parole, said sentence to be carried out in the custody of the United States of America, and I hereby release you from the custody of the State of

Mississippi and County of Yaloquena, and transfer you into the custody and control of the United States attorney.

"Mr. Whitman?"

Leopold Whitman stuck out his chest and strode toward the bench.

"Yes, Your Honor."

"The prisoner is now in your custody."

"Thank you, Your Honor. For the record, I will now transport the prisoner to federal court where U.S. District Judge Herman Stanwyk awaits us, and where the defendant will enter his plea to the federal charges and the forfeiture claims of the City of Jackson and the U.S. Government as set forth in the joint state and federal plea agreement, to which I am a signatory, Your Honor, on behalf of the Justice Department of the United States."

Whitman gestured to the federal agents, all of whom, including Dunne, walked over and surrounded El Moro as soon as he stepped down from the riser. Two agents placed El Moro in shackles. El Moro watched them work. One had a shaved head, and the other a short buzz cut. They were efficient with the equipment.

Judge Williams banged her gavel and said in a loud voice: "Court is hereby adjourned." She walked out of court past El Moro without so much as looking at him.

It didn't bother El Moro. She had no business being in a position of authority. The Quran was clear about the status of women.

The federal agents and Leopold Whitman began walking El Moro out of the courtroom. He turned to see Jerome King give him a thumbs up and say loudly that he would see Zegarra at the federal courthouse in a few minutes.

The agents led him out the side door. The phalanx approached the intersection where the small hallway fed into the main corridor outside the courtroom. El Moro noticed that U.S. Attorney Whitman moved the agent on his left arm out of the way so that Whitman was now side by side with his prized defendant. When they turned into the main corridor, El Moro understood why.

At least a dozen video camera crews lined either side of the long corridor, together with at least thirty reporters. El Moro felt Whitman grab his left elbow. El Moro noted the look of pride and accomplishment on the little man's face as the video lights and still cameras flashed, illuminating the corridor in white light.

The two agents leading the way gestured for the media people to back up closer to the wall so they could pass. Some of them did, but others didn't. El Moro flinched when a reporter sidestepped the *federals* and jammed a microphone in front of him.

El Moro was pushed from behind and felt a pinch in the back of his left upper arm. He turned and glared at *El Asesino*, the agent El Moro wanted most to avoid. *Asesino* had pushed the offending reporter back against the wall and fallen forward, displacing Whitman in the process. *Asesino* had apparently grabbed El Moro's arm to keep from falling. El Moro was angry that *Asesino* had been allowed to touch him.

"Let's go," El Moro barked to Whitman, who regained his position on El Moro's left flank. *El Asesino* returned to his position behind them.

El Moro, Whitman, and the federal agents were the only persons in the elevator. There was dead silence all the way to the basement. El Moro looked at the floor.

When the door opened, the agents surrounded El Moro and escorted him a short distance, then through a door to a large room with a concrete floor and an automatic steel door to the outside, large enough to accommodate a big vehicle. El Moro knew the room well. It was a room for the secure pick up and delivery of prisoners, the same room into which he was driven by the Hinds County deputies every morning; the same room from which he left the courthouse at the end of every day. "Sally port," was the term he heard the deputies use.

Today the room was different. There were news camera crews inside the sally port with them. El Moro thought it had to be a breach of security protocol to allow cameras inside, but it was clear that the U.S. attorney was not interested in the protocols at the state courthouse. He made sure he was next to El Moro at all times in the sally port as the camera crews recorded the scene.

El Moro saw Whitman gesture to the crews to determine if the crews had taped enough for their broadcasts. "Yes, sir," they said.

"All right, men," Whitman said. "Let's load up."

As El Moro walked toward the transport van for the short hop to the federal court, his knees buckled and his legs gave way. He felt strange. It was not an illness. He could tell it was something more severe. El Moro pivoted to search for *El Asesino*. The other federal agents were all there, but *Asesino* was not in the sally port.

El Moro grabbed Whitman on his way to the floor and pulled the U.S. attorney down on top of him. The little man's beard scratched El Moro's face.

The last thing El Moro saw was the CNN camera crew turn its light on to tape his death. Fox News had done the same thing, but El Moro could not see the Fox people because Whitman was on top of him blocking his view. But by now El Moro's eyes had rolled back so far in his head that only the whites were showing. He foamed at the mouth as well, but was unaware because the nerves in his brain had ceased to function.

In a matter of seconds, so had El Moro's black heart.

Chapter Forty

Later the same day, Kitty walked through the Sunset Grill and slid into the booth across the table from Jake. The waitress appeared and Kitty ordered a Michelob Ultra. Jake took a sip of his Coors Light draft in a frosted mug.

"What's the latest on Zegarra?" Jake asked.

"I've been in the office all afternoon," Kitty said. "You wouldn't believe how many agents are here in Jackson. They're from all over. My boss George Milton said Mr. Whitman got on the phone to Washington and they flew in an FBI forensic team from Quantico. They're checking the sally port for evidence and as much videotape as they can round up of Zegarra in the courthouse. They've sent some people to the jail to see if there are any remnants of what he had for dinner last night and breakfast this morning."

"They still think it's poison?" Jake asked.

"It's definitely some kind of exotic poison. The forensic team has run preliminary tests on Zegarra's body fluids and tissue and ruled out the typical poisons they usually see."

"I saw the video of Zegarra falling down in the sally port and pulling Whitman down on top of him." He leaned closer to Kitty. "That little prick got just what he deserved for trying to get himself all over the U.S. on cable and network news. He wanted to be seen as the one bringing down the big cartel guy. It turned out Zegarra brought Whitman down, right on top of him, and threw up on him before Whitman could get clear."

"It had to be embarrassing."

"Sweet was what it was."

"Have you talked to Dunne since this morning?" Kitty asked.

"No," Jake said. "I saw him in the courtroom with the security detail and that's the last I've seen or heard of him."

"Nobody has seen him," she said.

"Well, he's got a separate agenda from the rest of you FBI agents," Jake said. "He told me he reports only to the director."

"I spoke to a friend of mine last week. She's a clerk at Quantico, a real super-techie type. I asked her to see what she could find on Dunne in the bureau's data bases."

"Why did you do that?"

"I don't know. I was just curious, I guess. We've been around him all this time and I've never had the first conversation with him about the bureau. No war stories, nothing."

"He told us from the get-go that he wasn't a regular FBI agent, that he didn't work through normal agency channels."

239

"I know that. My techie friend says there is no FBI agent by the name of David Dunne, either now or in bureau's history."

Jake shrugged.

"What do you think of that? You think I ought to talk to George Milton and get him to make some official inquiries?"

"I think if you want a future in the FBI, you need to mind your own business. Dunne's credentials were real. You saw them. If he had wanted you and me to know details about who he reported to he'd have told us. He might have told Daddy for all we know. You could get in some trouble snooping after Dunne. Isn't it a violation of FBI rules for that clerk to do a computer search like that for you?"

"I'm not sure."

"I'll bet you a dollar to a dime it is and you just broke some regulation, maybe committed a crime. If I were you, I would shut up. Let Whitman or Milton check him out if they see a need to, but Kitty Douglas ought to play dumb about it."

He patted her hand on the table as the waitress set the Ultra in front of her. "That's free legal advice from your attorney."

Chapter Forty-One

It was dark by the time Jerome King pulled into his driveway. It had been a long, miserable day. The death of Zegarra in the sally port was one thing, but the feds keeping Jerome King the rest of the day for questioning was altogether uncalled for. He didn't know who got to Zegarra and really didn't care much. Jerome had been paid in full for his services. The fact that somebody knocked off Zegarra and he couldn't make it to federal court to plead in front of Judge Stanwyk wasn't Jerome's fault. He was not rebating any part of the fee, no matter what Al Rashad said.

Jerome punched the button again for the garage door to open. It did not work. "Damn," he said and depressed the button again. Nothing. It had happened before. He turned off the engine and stepped out of the sporty black Cadillac. Jerome whistled as he walked to the front door, wondering which one of Miss Sophie's new girls he was going to ask to join him for an evening of fun and relaxation. The thought put a spring in his step, and he unlocked the front door and walked in, continuing to whistle Otis Redding's *Sittin' on the Dock of the Bay,* one of his all-time favorites. Jerome thought it was a major shame that Otis drowned when his plane crashed into the freezing water of Lake Mendota after a show in Madison, Wisconsin. That had been many years ago, but it was still a tragedy. Jerome locked the front door behind him.

You can't be too careful these days.

He removed his tie and walked into the kitchen to mix himself a Bacardi and Coke to take the edge off. "Aahhh," he said after taking a big sip. Jerome opened a kitchen drawer and removed the phone book. He admired his wall-to-wall photograph on the back cover for a moment. Jerome opened the back cover and searched for Miss Sophie's private number. He dialed.

"Fuck," he said. "Busy."

Jerome sipped his Bacardi as he sauntered into the den. He sat in his easy chair and grabbed the remote. He turned on the fifty-two inch Sony Bravia to catch the local news on HD. Make sure they quoted him right. When the television lit up the room, Jerome almost had a heart attack.

"Hello, Jerome," David Dunne said. He sat on the sofa across the room. His blue steel forty-five automatic was pointed between the eyes of the eminent personal injury and criminal defense attorney.

Jerome grabbed his heart and closed his eyes. After a moment, he exhaled loudly.

"You almost gave me the big one," Jerome said. "Now put that gun down and tell me what the hell you are doing in my house. And this better be good, because I am just about to call the chief of police."

"Go ahead and call him."

Jerome stood up from his chair and pointed his finger at Dunne.

"If you don't put that gun down, I'm going to have your ass so far under the jail you're going to wish you had never met me."

"Sit down or I'll shoot you in the foot."

Jerome sensed tough talk was not going to work on Dunne. He sat down. "Can I have a sip of my drink?"

"Absolutely. Have several."

Jerome figured it was time to turn on the charm. "Mr. Dunne, I know you're upset about the injury to Willie Mitchell, but think of all the years you have in, years of good service to this country. It looks like he's going to make it after all, so you don't want to do something foolish and throw your career away. Let's just forget about this visit. Keep it between you and me."

"You can put your mind at rest. I'm not jeopardizing my career."

"What is it you want? I'll help any way I can. I don't know much about Zegarra."

"I just want to talk to you for a while. Like it says on your billboards: 'Talk to the King. Give Him a Ring.' If you and I come to an understanding that satisfies us both, I'll leave you in peace."

"All right. What can I do for the FBI?"

"Who paid you to represent Zegarra?"

"You know that falls within the attorney-client privilege."

"Let's try it this way. Tell me why Al Rashad hired you."

Jerome tried to remain cool. This was not a good question to start with. He had to dodge it. Dunne might be recording him.

"I don't know anyone by that name. And, I can't discuss my dealings with anyone that hires me. You know that."

Dunne threw a photograph across the room like a frisbee. It struck Jerome in the leg and fell onto the carpet in front of the easy chair.

"Pick it up."

Jerome picked up the photo. He recognized himself next to his Cadillac in front of Al Rashad's mosque. "This is obviously me. I'm there in Memphis to see an individual named Calvin Ketchums."

"It's a mosque."

"What?"

"The building's a mosque. Run by an imam named Hakim Abdullah Al Rashad."

"The man I know in that building in Memphis is Calvin Ketchums. I don't know anyone by the name of Al Rashad."

"How much cash did he pay you?"

"You know I can't divulge that information."

Dunne left the sofa and put his automatic against Jerome's temple. In his left hand he had a roll of duct tape.

"You see that wooden armchair over there, Jerome?"

Jerome knew he was in serious trouble. Better do as the man says. He walked slowly to the chair.

"Pick it up and put it in the center of this room."

Jerome picked up the chair. It was solid oak and heavy. Jerome felt a twinge in his lower back. He grimaced. Dunne moved closer to him and kept the pistol aimed between Jerome's eyes.

"Don't hurt yourself. Put it down right here."

Jerome placed the chair on the carpet in the center of the room.

"Now sit down."

Dunne reached over and picked up the Bacardi and Coke and gave it to Jerome. "Go ahead and finish your drink."

Jerome gave Dunne the empty glass.

"Are you going to hurt me?"

"I just want some information, and I'll leave you in peace. If you don't tell me the truth, I might have to make you uncomfortable."

"How much did Al Rashad pay you?"

Jerome said nothing. Dunne kept his eyes and the gun on Jerome, and pulled the end of the duct tape off the roll with his teeth. He gave the roll to Jerome.

"I want you to tape your right arm to the arm of the chair."

Jerome took the duct tape and stuck the end to this right sleeve and made one circle under the arm and over his sleeve.

"Again."

Jerome wrapped it a second time.

"Again."

They continued until Jerome had circled his right arm seven times.

"Now bite off the tape and put your left arm on the left chair arm."

Jerome bent over to tear the tape with his teeth. When the tape ripped he continued the roll's momentum upward and hit Dunne's automatic as hard as he could with the heavy roll of tape. Jerome was sorely disappointed to see Dunne still had a firm grip on the big automatic. Dunne chuckled and popped Jerome on the back of the head with the pistol.

"Ow, shit," Jerome said. "That hurt."

"Quit clowning around."

Dunne slammed Jerome's left arm to the chair, stuck his gun in his waist behind his back, and deftly wrapped the duct tape around Jerome's left arm. Dunne added more tape to Jerome's right arm, too. When he finished, Jerome tried but could not move either arm.

"Do you want money? I have money in a safe in my bedroom."

"I've already got that." Dunne stood in front of Jerome. "Now, Mr. King, this is taking too long. I have a scheduling problem. I've got to leave your fair city tonight and I am running out of time here. I'm going to ask you some more questions, and if you don't answer me truthfully, I'm going to have to hurt you a little."

"How much did Al Rashad pay you?"

"Seventy-five thousand. Most of it is in the safe back there."

"Was. Now it's in that black duffel bag over there on the floor. Along with some other fabulous bling you kept in that crappy little safe."

Jerome began to sweat.

"How much additional did he pay you to tell him that Willie Mitchell would be jogging at the reservoir Tuesday night?"

"I never did such a thing."

Dunne took his time screwing a silencer on the end of the gun. When he finished, he shot Jerome in the left knee.

"Jesus!" Jerome yelled.

Dunne stuffed a towel in Jerome's mouth. He waited until Jerome stopped screaming. He pulled out the towel.

"You can't shoot me. Don't you know who I am? I've got friends all over Washington, D.C. and when they get through with you—"

Dunne jammed the towel back in his mouth.

"I've got the phone records where you called Al Rashad Tuesday morning at ten-thirty, the same time as the first bathroom break you took that morning. Now tell me the truth." Dunne pulled the towel out.

"Okay. Okay. He asked me to let him know everything the D.A. did. I didn't know he was going to have him run over.

Honest to God. I'm just doing what my client asks. They pay me and I do their bidding. It's that simple. I'm the attorney for the mosque."

"Now, Jerome. I know a fellow who was listening when Al Rashad took the call from you Tuesday morning. He told me exactly what was said. And this man I believe. Every word he says. Unlike you."

Sweat poured from Jerome's face.

"I know for a fact that you were in on the plan to kill Willie Mitchell. I believe that you might have been involved in the juror deaths, too, even though Ace High was representing Zegarra then. But I have no proof. I was late getting to the party. Therefore, no punishment for you on the juror deaths."

Jerome was relieved.

"Thank God. Thank God. I had nothing to do with that. I swear. And I don't care about these people's politics, Agent Dunne. Or their religion. I'm not one of them. I'm an attorney. I have a duty to represent unpopular clients. You know that. That's all I was doing. It was just money to me. A man's got to make a living."

"I'm sorry to be rude, but I have to be on my way."

Dunne picked up his duffel bag and stood in front of Jerome.

"Let me tell you a simple rule that I've started following in my work. I think you'll find it logical and refreshingly straightforward. There's none of that splitting hairs you lawyers do."

"What is it? I can follow it from now on. I promise."

"He who helps a terrorist, is a terrorist."

"I didn't know. I swear I really didn't know. I was just doing my best to representing my clients."

"Well, like I say, it's a hard and fast rule. And these days, I have to adhere strictly to it." He backed off a couple of paces. "I wish I had some discretion in the matter. However, Mr. King, I do not. You get a pass on the jurors. This is for what you did to Willie Mitchell."

Dunne shot Jerome twice between the eyes. The bullets blew the back of his head off and emptied it of blood and brain matter. Dunne stood over Jerome and peered into his hollow skull.

"I told you I'd leave you in peace."

Chapter Forty-Two

Early Tuesday morning Jake was running hard, putting in his five miles. He ran the course in Jackson he had laid out and clocked when he first moved to town.

The sun pushed just above the horizon and it was warming up. Jake sweated, but it felt good. He kept upping his pace.

Jake pushed it even harder on the straightaway that ended at the turnaround point, half-way through the run. He turned to head back to the starting line and saw a dark blue government vehicle coming toward him, slowing down. It was the only car on the road.

Jake stopped. Kitty was alone.

"Listen to this," Kitty said. "Jerome King was found dead early this morning by his housekeeper. Shot in the head."

"You're kidding," Jake said.

"JPD says it looks like a home invasion. The front door was kicked in, splintered. The maid said he kept a lot of cash and jewelry in a wall safe in his bedroom and they cleaned it out."

Jake said nothing.

"Just wanted you to know," Kitty said. "Can I call you later?"

"Sure. I'm going by the hospital to check on Daddy. Let's get together tonight. If you want to."

"I'd like that very much. I think we need to talk."

Kitty drove off. Jake continued running, just a shade under full speed. His legs began to hurt, then his chest. He ran faster, now at full speed. There was a lot of pain, but he ignored it.

He finished the run and grabbed his phone out of the 4Runner. He checked for messages while he cooled down. There were two texts, one from UNKNOWN, and one from Scott.

Jake read the first one: "Al R. in the wind. Call u later."

"Dammit."

He read Scott's: "Daddy opened eyes. Recognized us. Get here asap."

"Thank you, God," Jake said and pointed to the sky. He hustled to the 4Runner and took off for the hospital.

As he neared St. Christopher's, he thought about David Dunne. He could hardly wait for him to call.